W9-BZD-069

THE SALVATION CYCLE

BOOK ONE

NIGHT RENDER

JODI MEADOWS

HOLIDAY HOUSE NEW YORK

HOLIDAY HOUSE is registered in the U.S. Patent and Trademark Office.
Printed and bound in November 2021 at Maple Press, York, PA, USA.
www.holidayhouse.com
First Edition
1 3 5 7 9 10 8 6 4 2

Library of Congress Cataloging-in-Publication Data

Names: Meadows, Jodi, author.
Title: Nightrender / Jodi Meadows.
Description: First edition. | New York : Holiday House, [2022] | Audience: Ages 14 Up. | Audience: Grades 10-12. | Summary: The three kingdoms of Salvation have been at war so long that they have forgotten to watch an even bigger threat: the Malstop and the incursion from the demon plane which it contains; but as Princess Johanne of Embria contemplates her upcoming marriage to Prince Rune of Caberwill which will unite two of the kingdoms (if she does not kill him) the Malstop is weakening—and Nightrender, the only warrior who can save the world, sleeps in her castle, waiting for someone to summon her.
Identifiers: LCCN 2021036182 | ISBN 9780823448685 (hardcover)
Subjects: LCSH: Imaginary wars and battles—Juvenile fiction. | Heroes—Juvenile fiction. | Demonology—Juvenile fiction. | Princesses—Juvenile fiction. | Princes—Juvenile fiction. | Adventure stories. | CYAC: Fantasy. | LCGFT: Action and adventure fiction.
Classification: LCC PZ7.M5073 Ni 2022 | DDC 813.6 [Fic]—dc23
LC record available at https://lccn.loc.gov/2021036182

For Lauren,
the ambitious.

PROLOGUE

This is the world:

A continent called Salvation, three kingdoms, and a war so old that no one has any idea what it's about. They fight, they retreat, they scheme, and—most important—they forget what should never be forgotten.

Rather, they try. It's impossible to *truly* forget the Malice, because in the center of Salvation—at the meeting point of all three kingdoms—is a magical barrier that hums and shimmers. It's called the Malstop, and it's the only thing standing between the three kingdoms and the darkness seeping from the Rupture.

In four hundred years, nothing has breached the Malstop. Even the scars from the last Incursion have grown commonplace to the people of all three kingdoms. They just deal with the reality they've been given. Avoid malsites, like season traps or gravitational voids. Make sure to bring extra provisions if traveling through the ever-burning forests. Wear obsidian, if possible.

It's understandable, this wanting to forget. People must adapt, or they'd live in constant terror of the next Incursion. Nothing would get done: no farming or blacksmithing or baking, no ruling or taxing or building, no mining or milling or making babies. Life *must* move on, and by now, the people of Salvation are experts at that.

Still, adapting is one thing. Forgetting is another.

Since they're all so busy fighting, forgetting the things they should have made a special point to remember, they've neglected to prepare for the inevitable:

Another Incursion.

It always happens eventually, and with four hundred years since the last one, some might say it's overdue.

This is the world—the continent, the kingdoms, the war—but soon none of it will matter, because the Malstop is weakening, and everything trapped inside will come spilling out, and the only one who could defend this mess of surviving and forgetting and fighting—

Well, she is still sleeping.

The island of Winterfast lies just northeast of Salvation. No one goes there. It's all iced-over rock where nothing grows, and the only building is a wind-pitted tower that could collapse any day.

Ages ago, the tower was a work of art, a monument built to honor the people's champion. The exterior walls were solid limestone, with bands of marble and granite and sandstone ringing the structure at regular intervals. A plating of pure gold covered the southern face of the tower, stretching into the shape of wings splayed wide. When sunlight caught the tower, the wings shone.

But after four centuries of neglect, faint movements in the island have shifted the stonework, first casting off the gold, then loosening the bands so that they slipped and cracked. Chunks litter the ground beside the tower's base, but no one comes to steal the precious material. Even if it wasn't covered in snow most of the year, they don't dare tread too close to the sleeper inside the tower.

Nightrender.

She is a legend, a being of both light and dark, built for the single purpose of defending Salvation against the rancor.

That's what lies behind the Malstop. Rancor. Demonic creatures that warp everything they touch. Nightmares incarnate, which have nearly brought Salvation to its knees too many times to number.

Only Nightrender can defeat them, and for countless centuries, the people of the three kingdoms worshipped her as a sort of demigod. They built her tower, made offerings, and ensured she wanted for nothing. (Not that she ever desired wealth or land or possessions, but she could have had everything.) In paintings—those that weren't destroyed after the Red Dawn—she is tall and fierce, with great feathered wings and a sword made of pure night, terrible and wonderful to behold.

No one paints her anymore.

Here, in this tower, she looks like a girl sleeping under a canopy of cobwebs, perfectly still, barely breathing, and ice to the touch. (But no one in their right mind would risk touching her, sleeping or otherwise.) With the storm raging outside and piling snow as high as her window, Nightrender dreams.

Behind her closed eyelids, she sees the Malstop. From a distance, it's an enormous dome, tall enough to get lost in the clouds, but up close, it is a straight and impassable wall that stops the Malice from expanding. Hence the name.

The truth is that the Malstop is neither a dome nor a wall; it's a sphere, extending down through the layers of the earth until it plunges into magma. This does the Malstop no harm; if anything, the fire strengthens its magic.

It's all crackling energy, piercing mountains and valleys, rivers and canyons. There are even remnants of a town sliced in half, and a cemetery where—during one Incursion—the dead got up and left. No one's buried there now.

In her dream, Nightrender slips through the Malstop.

She enters a nightmare reality that doesn't observe the same sort of rules as everywhere else. Oh, the topography is expected—hills where hills should be, streams where streams should be—but after millennia of corruption, there have been some . . . changes.

They are not easy to look at.

But Nightrender has seen it before, and she doesn't allow it to bother her. After all, she's been inside the Malice more times than anyone—physically, not just in dreams—and this time is no more difficult than the last.

Except.

Except now there's something different, something that makes her startle straight out of the dream and push against the boundaries of consciousness. She struggles to wake and fulfill her duty, but she has not been summoned, and until the people desire her help, she's trapped here, sleeping.

Small, short gasps escape her lips, the only signs of life she's shown in the last four hundred years. Then, she exhales, long and steady, a puff of breath billowing in the cold air above her, and she is asleep again.

They have not summoned her.

But they should. The people living near the Malstop should pay attention to its shivers and its thin spots, and to their own ominous dreams. The rulers should look up from their squabbles long enough to notice it's time to stockpile food and water and bring their citizens into the dubious safety of walled cities. And someone—anyone—should wake her.

Because deep inside the Malice, beyond the mutilated mountains and sludgy rivers and strange slips of time, the rancor have raised what some might call a castle, built from millions upon millions of human bones.

As with most castles, this one has a throne room. Two thrones sit in the center of an octagonal space, though only one is occupied. The other is empty. Waiting.

This is the source of Nightrender's anxiety, her desperation to wake. Rancor do not construct castles, nor do they build thrones. Which means that something has changed in them.

The figure on the throne.

That is the threat.

She knows this immediately but cannot act. If no one summons her, it won't be long before the Malstop fails.

Then this will be the world:

1.
Hanne

Before this, Hanne had lots of practical ideas about marriage.

From childhood, she'd prepared herself to be matched off to the wealthiest, most powerful person with political leverage. She'd been satisfied imagining a loveless marriage; only in stories did princesses get to fall in love with handsome knights or clever farm girls. And there was no forgetting that talk with her mother—the one when she was thirteen—that encouraged her to make heirs, then make *arrangements.* That was, arrangements to engage with parties other than her spouse, if she liked.

It was how most political matches worked.

But even by Hanne's rather businesslike ideas of marriage, her situation was unusual.

Crown Princess Johanne Fortuin of Embria to Wed
Crown Prince Rune Highcrown of Caberwill.

That was the headline of every paper from Solcast, Embria, to Brink, Caberwill—and likely every paper in Ivasland, too. A royal wedding. Two enemy kingdoms, united by mutual contempt for the third.

Not included in the papers or gossip? Her plans for *after* the wedding. First, Hanne would conquer Ivasland with the might of her two armies. Then she'd eliminate her husband and his entire family. Finally, she'd rule everything.

Unconventional as it might be, this was a war-ending plan, which all of Salvation desperately needed.

True, the three kingdoms were not currently engaged in active, formal war, but this nervous pause they found themselves in would last only so long. Eventually, the ceasefires would end, the trading would stop, and the slaughter would resume. It always did.

So Hanne's chief ambition was peace. If such a thing were possible, she would achieve it. That her plan would lead to Embria's victory—and Hanne's elevation to Queen of Everything—was a happy by-product.

"At least he's nice to look at." Nadine—Hanne's favorite cousin and lady-in-waiting, and the only person in the whole world Hanne actually *wanted* to spend time with—peered from the window of their stuffy carriage. They were alone in here, but surrounded outside by a whole company of nobles, diplomats, and soldiers, all traveling to Brink for the wedding.

Hanne had liked the idea of a journey, at least until she'd realized she'd be stuck in the carriage for the duration. She wanted the breeze, the exercise, but her parents wouldn't permit it. They insisted that she sit in her airless cage while other people enjoyed themselves.

"We still think he's handsome, right?" Nadine glanced at Hanne from the corner of her eye, then looked back out the window where they had a fine view of Rune Highcrown. "He does have that going for him, if nothing else."

Nadine, sweet Nadine, always tried so hard to see the bright side of any situation.

But for Hanne, the only bright side was the end result, and she would endure whatever misery was required in order to reach her goals.

"He has a stupid name," she said shortly.

Even so, that didn't stop her from admiring his tall form, his riding posture impeccable on the back of his raven-coated stallion. He rode slightly ahead of them, so she couldn't see his strong jaw, or the stubble he'd been growing since they'd left Solcast, but she'd had time to fix it in her mind. Every evening, when their caravan stopped for the night, she and he were given "alone time," during which they'd take a turn about the clearing (or a turn about the lakeshore, or a turn about the edges of an ever-burning forest) to get to know each other better, while Nadine and a few other ladies-in-waiting followed at a respectable distance.

"He can't help his name," Nadine pointed out. Between the two of them, she was definitely the nicer person, which meant that Hanne had to look out for Nadine, because if experience was anything to go by, regular people took advantage of nice people. Hanne hated regular people.

"Nor his looks," Hanne said. "Don't credit him for one attribute he has no control over and make excuses for another."

Nadine rolled her eyes, something she'd never have done if Hanne's other ladies-in-waiting had been here; but when it was just the two of them, they were at ease. Nadine tried to show Hanne every silver lining in existence, while Hanne did her best to teach Nadine how to guard herself from the aforementioned regular people. "He could refuse to comb his hair or take care of his skin. He could slouch or chew with his mouth open. Fortunately for you, he has enough vanity and manners to make looking at him pleasant."

"At least until I have to kill him." Hanne touched the dagger she kept in a boot sheath.

"At least until you have to kill him," Nadine agreed. "But try not to hold his silly name against him. His ancestors are to blame."

That was true. Once, the people of all three kingdoms shared a common naming system: first name–last name, all taken from the invaders and refugees who'd landed on the shores of Salvation ages ago. Things blended, as they do, but when the three kingdoms decided they hated one another and split apart, the people of Ivasland began going by the towns where they lived, and the people of Caberwill decided to name themselves after virtues, compositions, and other absurd things.

Highcrown. Ridiculous.

Of course, Hanne's last name was Fortuin, which was only better because she had decided it was.

Still, there was something about Rune Highcrown that she liked, despite herself. Perhaps it was his determination to protect his kingdom, or the fact that he'd been willing to come to Embria—enemy territory—to negotiate the marriage contract himself. No proxies for this prince. She wouldn't soon forget how he'd looked striding into the throne room that first day, clad in the subtle blacks and grays popular in Caberwill, his dark hair arranged into immaculate disarray. When he'd presented himself to the entire Embrian court, he'd spoken with an air of confidence that demanded respect.

Her people could have killed him then and there—and he must have known that—but the situation with Ivasland was too dire. If Ivasland had indeed broken the Winterfast Accords, as was now whispered everywhere, that demanded a swift and unflinching response: marriage.

It was amazing Embria's spies had discovered the plot, actually. Thanks to rigorous security measures—frequent random inspections, the constant presence of soldiers, and an impressive indoctrination campaign that encouraged unquestioning loyalty in Ivasland youth—it was notoriously difficult to place spies in Ivasland's courts, university, or Grand Temple. But it *was* possible. And occasionally, Embria could find someone to turn—someone tired of being poor or ignored. It was from one such Ivaslander, an old man seeking wealth and power for his grandchildren, that this ultimate betrayal had been discovered.

None of the kingdoms—*none* of them—had broken the Winterfast Accords in thousands of years. It was the sole agreement between them. Using malice—dark magic from beyond the Malstop—in the war . . . It was unthinkable. Reckless. Evil. It was the only thing the kingdoms were not willing to do to one another—or to themselves, because the end result would be mutually assured destruction.

Unfortunately, the details were unclear: the old man's confession had been smeared and ripped by the time it reached the Embrian spymistress, and the dove carrying it had died right there on the windowsill. The turncoat quickly disappeared, of course, and whatever information he'd possessed had died with him. So the exact nature of Ivasland's plan to harness malice was unknown—but a threat to the Winterfast Accords left two options.

The first was sanctions. Tariffs. Every penalty the Winterfast Accords suggested. Ivasland's economy wouldn't recover for a hundred years or more.

But such action would be enough to trigger another round of outright warfare, so a second option had to be considered—something less formal but more profound.

After days of prayer and conversation with Tuluna—Tuluna the Tenacious, Hanne's patron Numen—it was Hanne who'd proposed the, ah, proposal to Rune, and the king and queen of Embria (Hanne's parents) had promptly taken over everything, as they always did.

Of course, the upcoming nuptials made Ivasland even more nervous about its richer and more powerful enemies, and *they* were likely scrambling to find a way to stop the wedding. . . .

Hanne wasn't worried. Tuluna had chosen her to win this war.

"It's your turn." Nadine motioned to the marble board between them, which held a stack of facedown cards and two stone figures. The rose quartz was carved into the shape of a galloping horse (Nadine's) while the onyx was a prowling cat (Hanne's), and they were neck and neck to the finish line. Nadine might be the nicest human to ever grace the planet, but she was a mean competitor when it came to Mora's Gambit. She never let anyone win, not even her future monarch.

Hanne drew a card. Queen. With a smile, she moved her figure along the board.

Just as she was about to claim the space before the finish line, the carriage hit a bump and the onyx cat went flying toward the glass window.

The cat stayed pressed against the vertical pane, blithely ignoring the law of gravity. Unease stirred in Hanne's chest, but she forced it down and reached for the figure. Strange things happened sometimes. That was all.

But as Hanne's fingertips grazed the figurine, the cat swiped at her with little onyx claws.

Hanne jerked back. The carriage jumped again. The cat figure fell to the floor.

Nadine's voice was tremulous. "Did it just . . ."

"No." Hanne inspected her fingers. There was a small cut, but it had probably come from one of the playing cards, or perhaps from the note she'd written this morning, reminding Devon Bearhaste of his deadline. "We're just anxious for the wedding. We imagined it."

Nadine looked as though she wanted to argue that two people did not typically imagine the same thing, but she kept her mouth shut while Hanne retrieved the onyx cat.

Cautiously, Hanne touched the cat to the glass again, to see if it would hold, but it dropped back into her palm.

Yes, it had been her imagination. Nadine's, too.

Hanne returned the figure to the board, then rested her fingers against the obsidian pendant at her throat. Nadine mirrored her movement, perhaps unconsciously, because her gaze was fixed on the window glass, and Hanne imagined she could see a prayer flying from Nadine's heart straight to the Bright Land where the Numina resided. Obsidian and unanswered prayers: that was all most people had in these bleak times.

Hanne was not most people. But she kept Tuluna to herself.

"I am glad that we are so well armored." Nadine's fingers grazed the black stones of her rings and bracelets, which shone darkly against her fair skin and emerald-green traveling dress. Like everyone in Embria—everyone who mattered, anyway—Hanne and Nadine wore vivid colors to allow the wealth of their obsidian to stand out. That was one of the things that made Caberwilline fashion so bizarre. Why hide obsidian with all those dark colors?

Obsidian was the most valuable resource in all three kingdoms, as it was said to repel the rancor. Not that anyone had seen such creatures in four hundred years, but malsites still existed and there were always rumors. People believed in rancor, even if they weren't under constant threat. No matter how poor a family, they'd spend their last pennies buying pouches of crushed obsidian to divide among the children, although most of it was likely regular glass dyed black. If there was any true obsidian in there, it wouldn't be enough to repel even the weakest of rancor.

"Nothing can hurt us." Hanne touched the carrying case at her side, her family's dearest heirloom within.

It was a crown of solid obsidian. Heavy. Black. Beautiful. This ancient piece had been passed down through Hanne's family since they'd come to power four hundred years ago. (It had belonged to the previous royal family before then—the Aska family—but none of the Fortuins ever thought of them anymore.) Though invaluable, it was far from fashionable; the crown bore a series of jagged spikes, not graceful points, and the band had little padding to ease the weight.

Normally, Hanne wore a softer, gentler (though still studded with obsidian) crown when she traveled or conducted state business, but this was a unique circumstance. She'd worn the obsidian crown almost every day since the Caberwilline delegation arrived, as a show of her power and wealth.

She cleared her throat and returned her attention to the game. "It's your turn."

"I was going to call your bluff." Nadine's eyes dropped to the stack of cards. "But I'm not sure I want to play anymore."

"Nadine, please." (Nadine had gently suggested that Hanne start saying please more, and Hanne was making her best effort.) "If you quit now, I'll think it's because I'm winning."

"You're barely winning."

"I'll win on this next round."

"Only if you draw a one." Her tone was uncharacteristically tart.

Hanne gave her a pointed look. "Are you still worried about the engagement?"

"What if he isn't kind to you? What if he parades mistresses around court just to weaken your position?" Nadine bit her lip. "What if he hurts you somehow?"

"Weren't you defending his honor not five minutes ago?"

"Only his name. And his looks. But those aren't *him*."

Hanne shook her head. "I've told you a thousand times: I know what kind of man Rune is. Our spies have been reporting his movements for years—*doubly* so since he became the heir. He was under observation every second in Solcast. Caberwillines are not complicated creatures. Our new allies have very little capacity for deception."

The word *allies* tasted strange on her tongue. Allies were relatives or noble families who had the same goals. Allies were not either of the other kingdoms. The only word for them was *enemies*.

But this alliance was only temporary. Once Ivasland and Caberwill were crushed, she could turn her gaze homeward and set things right there—starting by elevating Nadine. She'd been so unfortunate to be born into the nonroyal side of the family, with little in the way of power or inheritance, but Hanne trusted her cousin's counsel more than anyone else's. Nadine was always measured and thoughtful and, most important, loyal. No one else in Hanne's life—not a soul—had ever given her what Nadine offered freely.

Nadine laced her fingers, then unlaced them. "I know all of that. I just . . . You deserve so much better than him. You deserve happiness."

"And through this marriage, I will achieve it." Hanne touched Nadine's arm. "As will you, I hope."

"What of Lord Bearhaste?" Nadine asked. "Can we trust him?"

"We don't trust *people*—only their greed." The words came out harsher than Hanne had intended. She softened her tone. "Our spies have confirmed three times over that Lord Bearhaste has effectively defected. He wants more than Caberwill has to offer, as do others. Even now, on this journey, he is gathering support for my rule. By the time we are ready to move, the Caberwilline nobility will welcome me with open arms."

"Open arms leave the heart exposed." Nadine pulled a card from the deck. She moved her pink horse to the square in front of Hanne's, crossing the finish line.

Hanne scowled at the board. "You're bluffing."

Nadine revealed the card, which showed a bright, indistinct light and the letter *N* in the corners. Numen. It outranked the king and queen cards by one point. "Burn it. How do you always do that?"

Nadine flashed a crooked smile, the genuine sort, not the kind brought out for court and parties. "Perhaps I will feel more comfortable with the arrangement once Lord Bearhaste delivers the names."

"That will be today, if he keeps his end of the bargain. And tomorrow evening, when we arrive in Brink, you can begin charming everyone on the list. You'll tell them what a good queen I will be one day, how much they will prosper under my rule. Once I have support from enough nobles, generals, and merchants, I will be able to deliver Caberwill from their current brutish leaders."

Nadine looked dubious. "You'll have to conquer Ivasland first. And conceive an heir. Only then will Caberwill have no choice but to accept you."

"Yes, well." Conquering Ivasland would be easy. As for the heir part—she would do what was necessary. For Embria. For peace.

"This isn't my favorite plan."

"I know."

"You're the one taking all the risks."

They both left a space for the unspoken end of that sentence: Hanne's parents were taking no risks. If this went awry, they could blame her for everything and use one of their hundred contingency plans to put an end to Ivasland's aggression.

"Tell me you're still in," Hanne whispered. "I cannot do this without you."

"Of course I am." Nadine leaned forward, worry written across her face. "It was never really a question, was it?"

Hanne wouldn't admit aloud that it *had* been a question—that she needed confirmation every time, because her only true fear was that Nadine would one day realize Hanne did not deserve such devotion, and then Hanne would be alone.

For now, Hanne put on a grin and took her cousin's hands. "You and me, Nadine. It's going to be us at the top of the world."

"Or we'll bring it down to meet us."

Lunch was a typical Embrian affair, as not even traveling across the continent could prevent Hanne's people from enjoying a meal.

Tables were unloaded and set out, delicate linen cloths draped over the polished bloodwood. Some poor Embrian seamstress had embroidered both families' crests onto one such cloth—a dragon claw clutching a crown for Caberwill, and a stooping eagle for Embria—their outer circles linked together. The seamstress had probably choked on bile with every stitch, but it made a clear statement and Caberwillines loved clarity.

When everyone was seated (aside from guards, servants, grooms, and anyone else who wasn't sufficiently titled to earn a place at a table), the meal arrived. The first course was a fine soup, spiced with ginger and a few other ingredients meant to aid digestion and sharpen hunger, so that more of the main courses could be consumed without that uncomfortable feeling of fullness. Then came smoked pheasant, stuffed with spices and vegetables; dishes of fruit and cream; and, finally, pastries drizzled with honey and soft, sweet cheese.

"Everything is delicious." Rune sat at the high table beside Hanne, eating with as much poise as any Embrian noble. Nadine had a point about the prince's manners: they could be *far* worse.

"It is," Hanne agreed.

"How your chefs manage to prepare such a divine meal while riding in wagons," Lord Bearhaste said from the far side of Rune, "I will never know."

"The royal chefs are the best in Embria." Lady Sabine tapped her napkin to the corners of her mouth. "They have every incentive to make the best of the situation." The elderly Embrian lady traded knowing glances with Hanne. Two years ago, a chef had complained he couldn't possibly work with his current set of knives. Queen Katarina had ordered an inspection. It turned out the blades *were* brittle and unbalanced; one had broken while the royal disciplinarians pressed it against the chef's smallest finger. It ended up shattering the bone rather than cleanly removing the fingertip, to which Katarina had replied, "This will not do at all."

New knives had been purchased and the chef had no more reasons to complain.

"Indeed." Hanne bit into the soft, flaky pastry while conversation moved on around her.

The tension between the two parties remained heavy, but a few lords and ladies were doing their best to get along—or at least give the appearance of getting along. At the next table over, Lea, Maris, and Cecelia—the other three ladies-in-waiting Hanne had brought with her from Embria—were all deep in conversation with Caberwilline nobility, discussing the weather, books they had read, and what they would wear to the week of parties planned to accompany the wedding.

Hanne shot each of her ladies a small, approving nod, and then turned to Rune. "I'm eager to see Honor's Keep tomorrow. It's hard to believe we're nearly there."

On the opposite side of the crown prince, Lord Bearhaste stiffened. The message had been received. He was expected to deliver the names of her prospective supporters *before* arrival.

Have faith, my chosen.

The voice was cool and sweet in the back of Hanne's mind, like frozen cream. It was Tuluna's voice, and every time the Numen spoke to Hanne, a sense of pride washed through her. Numina did not speak to people anymore—they hadn't for thousands of years. But Tuluna had chosen *her* to end this war. Tuluna had chosen *her* to speak with. Not even the most devout grand priest could say the same.

You have done well to set our plan into motion. Soon, all of Salvation will bow to you—will tremble before you.

A small shiver of excitement worked through Hanne.

"The castle is a sight to behold." Rune set his fork beside his plate and looked at her, his handsome face tense with thought. Hanne hoped he didn't hurt himself too much; she still needed him to make an heir. "Though not conventionally beautiful in the way you're used to," he went on. "Solspire is quite remarkable in that regard."

Hanne and Lady Sabine traded another knowing look.

Gaudy, Rune meant. *Garish*. Those were the words he'd used in a note written to his parents, sent from his room in Solspire. Hanne's people had intercepted the dove, copied the note, and resealed it so cleanly that the Highcrowns would never know the difference.

"But I hope that you find a certain charm in Honor's Keep," Rune continued. "We like to think it's impressive, especially when seen from a distance."

Presumably it was most impressive from a distance because there was no hiding its flaws up close. "I'm sure it's wonderful." Hanne had endured many hardships in her life. Honor's Keep would be nothing compared to the trials of her childhood.

Finally, the plates were cleared away and people began to drift back into groups of their own countrymen. Hanne looked up just in time to see Devon Bearhaste vanish into the woods.

Good. He meant to keep his word.

She stood and crooked her finger for Nadine. "Accompany me on a walk, cousin," she said when Nadine hurried forward.

"I'd be honored to join you as well, Your Highness." As much as Hanne hated to admit it, Rune had a warm way of speaking, the kind of tone that threatened to disarm her with its sincerity. She wouldn't buy it, though. It would take only one mistake—one inkling that she had anything planned—and she and Nadine were dead. (Probably everyone else, too, but they were less important to Hanne.)

"It's so kind of you to offer, but we won't be long. We only need to stretch our legs." She gazed up at him, disarming him in turn: round blue eyes, upturned nose, and pink lips tipped into a sweet smile.

He took in the sight of her. It was the one thing they'd appreciated about each other right off, the pleasing nature of their faces. "Shall I send Captain Oliver after you?" he asked, speaking of her personal guard from Embria.

"That won't be necessary. I'm certain the forest around the Brink Way is quite safe, and we shall keep very near." She smiled again, and if there was any suspicion in him, it didn't show.

"Of course," he said. "I'll await your return."

And that was it. Hanne and Nadine swept off into the Deepway Woods, which bordered the road.

They walked in easy quiet for a few minutes, listening to birdsong, feeling the heat of late summer push between the broad leaves, watching rabbits and other small prey dart away from them. There wasn't much of a path here, just a narrow deer trail, but Hanne liked finding her way through the brush: minding where to step, avoiding getting her dress torn, and keeping track of what direction they were actually going in. It was a lovely day, now that they weren't trapped in the carriage.

A cardinal flew across the path before them.

A second later, an identical cardinal flew across the path in an identical way.

Shivers forced themselves up Hanne's spine. "Did it—"

The cardinal dove again. Then again. Above, clouds began to darken the sky, and a sour smell flooded the woods.

"Yes, it did." Nadine's voice trembled.

Birdsong ceased as a *crack* sounded farther up the path.

Nadine's eyes were wide with fear. "Hanne, we should go."

The cut on Hanne's fingertip—the one from the onyx cat—began to throb. "Not until we have those names. Bearhaste is waiting for us out here. We're risking everything—"

Ahead, a man screamed. Birds fled overhead, and before Hanne thought better of it, she was running toward the noise.

"Hanne, wait!"

But Hanne was ducking, darting between the trees, only stopping once she came to a small clearing. Sweat crawled down the back of her neck as she scanned the space.

There. A depression in the grass.

Her hand did not tremble as she bent and drew her dagger from her boot sheath. Somewhere in her wake, she could hear Nadine following, and she knew she should feel guilty for leaving her cousin behind, but Lord Bearhaste's information was vital.

She crept toward the flattened grass, the source of the putrid odor, but as soon as she heard the low drone of flies clouding over the shape, she knew it was too late.

It was Lord Bearhaste. Dead. No, not just dead, but mutilated, his body torn open and strewn about in pieces, like a toy with all the stuffing ripped out. Blood stained the grass around him, and mold grew on his withering skin—what remained of it.

She should be sick, and indeed, the smell alone tested her gag reflex, but Hanne knelt, trying not to touch the sprouting mold as she used her dagger to move the man's coat toward her. Perhaps he'd written down the names.

"Hanne, what are you doing?" Nadine's voice came from the edge of the clearing. "What is that?"

"Stay back," Hanne warned, still maneuvering the torn jacket. At last, a pocket. "Don't come any closer." Nadine, sweet Nadine, did not need to see this mess. But what had done it? He'd screamed only minutes before. How had all of *this* happened? The mold, the rot, the flies?

What if the same thing happened to them?

Paper crinkled in the dead man's pocket. Hanne's knuckles went white around the dagger hilt as she stabbed the cloth and dragged it closer, pulling the bisected ribcage nearer. The turncoat may be dead, but if his work remained, she could use it.

"Hanne?" Fear filled Nadine's voice.

"I'll be right there." Hanne shook her head, trying to dislodge the flies that settled on her face. If the man's scream had carried to the road—and that seemed possible—then dozens of soldiers would be pouring into the woods, from her side and Rune's. She couldn't afford to be found over the body. She had only moments.

Hanne worked the dagger tip into the weathered fold of the pocket, stuck the paper, and—twisting her wrist—at last slid it free.

"All right." She glanced at the paper long enough to confirm it held names, then stood and backed away quickly from the body, the blood, and the buzz of flies. Her skin itched with the memory of their tiny legs crawling across her face. "I'm coming, Nadine. Just stay there."

But Nadine gave a startled cry, and Hanne spun just in time to see a gray figure darting between the trees, heading straight for her cousin.

It was humanoid, emaciated and hunched, with a barrel chest, too-long limbs, and awful spikes protruding from its back and shoulders. And the way it *moved*—somehow fluid and stuttering all at once, as if the world flickered in and out of existence around it. A howl poured out of the creature, entirely inhuman. All predator.

Hanne stumbled, certain her eyes were seeing this wrong. But the creature was closing in on Nadine, so Hanne scooped up a rock from the ground. "Nadine, run! Get help!" Then, with all her might, she hurled the stone at the beast.

The rancor—for it could only be a rancor, she was certain—twisted toward Hanne, opening its stretched-wide mouth to reveal two rows of barbed teeth. It lunged.

She ran.

She didn't care where, as long as she led it away from Nadine. Somewhere in the distance, her cousin cried for help.

Branches lashed against Hanne's chest and face as the rancor closed in. If her obsidian rings and bracelets were doing anything to repel this creature, it wasn't obvious. The beast was so close.

Breath heaving, blood dripping down her face, Hanne threw herself deeper into the forest. Her vision tunneled, dim around the edges, so she saw only the trees and brush and trail directly in front of her, although she imagined she caught the outline of the rancor to her right—no, to her left.

It was everywhere. If it caught her, it would kill her. It would do to her what it had done to Devon Bearhaste.

She ran faster.

Hanne didn't realize, because fear had her in its grip, but even when she ducked left or right, weaving what she thought was a random path through the woods, she was moving in one very clear direction. The rancor was *herding* her.

It was that fear, that narrow focus on surviving, that caused her to miss the ribbons tied around the trees—a warning yellow—with small bells fastened at the ends. They were on every tree, in fact, making a ring of bright, noisy caution around a specific place in the forest.

But Hanne didn't see the ribbons, because her vision had grayed out.

And she didn't hear the bells because she was out of breath; blood roared through her ears.

And then, a mere ten strides after she'd crossed the ribbon boundary, she crossed another barrier.

This one she felt. She met a pressure, a faint resistance, but she didn't have time to stop herself.

Alarm flared up in her mind and panic spiked in her chest. But she was already through, and too late, the fact caught up with her.

A malsite.

The rancor had driven her into a malsite.

Immediately, Hanne turned and tried to run back the way she'd come, but the pressure from this side was too great. She couldn't push through. The second boundary—invisible, silent—was firmer than stone.

She was trapped in a pocket of malice, a rancor nearby, with only a few pieces of jewelry and a dagger to defend herself.

With a dark clarity, she understood this:

She, Johanne Fortuin, crown princess of Embria, was about to die.

2.
Rune

At the first scream, everyone scrambled for their weapons.

By the second scream, Rune and his personal guards were entering the Deepway Woods.

And with the third scream—high, feminine, moving closer—a young lady came crashing through the brush, twigs and leaves in her loose hair, tears streaming down her face. The sleeves and skirt of her dress were shredded, trailing after her like emerald smoke.

Rune caught her just as she tripped over an exposed root. She flailed in his arms, then pushed away from him only to trip over the same root again. She landed on the ground in a heap of torn silk.

"Lady Nadine?" Rune sheathed his sword and knelt in front of the girl, raising her face. She was, indeed, Princess Johanne's cousin and closest friend. They were hardly ever apart. "What has happened?"

Her breath came in short, panicked gasps, and her eyes were glazed and unfocused. If she saw him, if she recognized him, she didn't show it.

"She's in shock." Rune glanced up at the guards. "Where is Captain Oliver?"

"Here, Your Highness." The Embrian man stepped forward.

"Please escort Lady Nadine back to the caravan. The rest of us will search for Princess Johanne." Captain Oliver wasn't Rune's guard to order about, but the moment called for action, for someone to be in charge.

Captain Oliver bent beside Lady Nadine. "My lady."

"Lord Bearhaste was out here, too," said Daniel, one of Rune's guards. "Perhaps he's seen Princess Johanne."

"All right. Let's get moving. Whatever frightened Lady Nadine is likely still out there." Rune started to stand, but Lady Nadine's hand darted out and wrapped around his wrist.

Her eyes were wide and terrified but intensely focused. "It was a monster. A monster went after her." With her sweat-dampened hair hanging in tendrils, jeweled pins trembling with her every shuddering breath, Lady Nadine looked like a madwoman.

"A monster?" One of the men snorted. "She's hysterical, Your Highness. She probably saw a deer and fled for her life."

"Embrians." Lieutenant Swifthand laughed. "Oh, I bet it was a squirrel."

"How terrifying," said the first, pretending to shiver.

Captain Oliver stood, his hand flying to his sword. "How dare you? How *dare* you?"

"Stop." All at once, Rune became aware of the silence around them, of the reek of ammonia and rotting flesh, of the clouds blanketing the sky as if the world were trying to smother these woods. Unease wormed into his stomach. "We must take her seriously. Captain Oliver, get her back to the caravan. The rest of you—you will cease your mocking."

"I'm going with you." Lady Nadine's grip around Rune's wrist tightened; her knuckles went bone white as her fingernails dug into his skin. "You need every man at your side, and I can show you where—" She twisted around and vomited suddenly onto the side of the tree.

When she was finished, Rune gave her his water canteen so that she could rinse her mouth. She drank, swigged, spat, and offered it back, but he shook his head. "Please keep it."

Lady Nadine climbed to her feet and pinned a curl back into place, as though buckling armor. "We must go immediately. I can show you where we saw the creature, and I can point out the direction Hanne started running."

Rune bit the inside of his cheek. Bringing this traumatized girl along was a terrible idea, but she might be helpful, now that she could speak. And presuming they found Princess Johanne in one piece, she would be furious to learn he'd ordered her dearest lady-in-waiting about as if she were his to command—he'd learned that much about his betrothed's temperament.

Finally, he drew his sword and nodded. "Show us the way. But if something happens, hide, or run back to the carriages. I won't have your princess thinking I put you in undue peril. Captain Oliver, you will mind her?"

"Of course."

"I'll be fine," Lady Nadine said. "It's Hanne we need to worry about.

Now please, *hurry*." With surprising strength for someone who'd just lost every bit of her extravagant lunch, she turned and started marching back the way she'd come. Rune hastened after her, with the guards close behind.

Burn it all, he thought as they followed a deer trail through the woods. He'd been *so* careful to choose the safest route, to send scouts ahead to secure the road, and to bring more soldiers than anyone thought was necessary. And now everything was at risk—this entire alliance—because he hadn't insisted on sending a whole company of guards with the princess on a simple walk.

"It's probably nothing," Lieutenant Swifthand grumbled under his breath.

"Well, we did hear screaming."

"But you know Embrians," Swifthand muttered. "It's a trap, most like. The princess is spinning a scheme of some kind, and the prince is falling for it."

Rune clenched his jaw. After Opi had died, the royal guards all looked at Rune differently. And since the engagement, this sort of talk had only gotten worse. Many of these men had reached their positions by fighting in the war against Embria, and they felt this marriage was a betrayal. They didn't understand the depth of the threat to the Winterfast Accords. All they saw was Rune saying yes to a beautiful princess from an enemy kingdom—a kingdom they had devoted their lives to hating.

A few had asked to be reassigned, but even those who'd stayed on had strong opinions—opinions they usually remembered to keep to themselves.

Rune scanned the forest for any signs of the princess—a flash of blond hair, a scrap of sapphire fabric from her dress—but he found only the same eerie silence, as though a huge predator had come this way.

He picked up his pace, keeping his expression hard. Later, he decided, he would have words with his guards, and remind them that they could do their jobs with the level of professionalism their positions demanded—or they could be dismissed without honor.

For now, he clenched his jaw, keeping pace with Lady Nadine as she led the group into a small clearing, where the foul odor slammed into them, half knocking them back. A few guards coughed and cursed, turning away to try to catch their breaths.

Rune pressed his arm over his lower face, but there was no blocking out the overwhelming stench of rot. He blinked away tears as he took in the sight before him: a brown-black circle—not perfectly round, but reaching out and growing before their eyes—surrounded something dark and moldering in the center. A mass of buzzing flies haloed above the dark shape.

"What *is* that?" one of the guards gasped.

"It's a body," said another. "I can see clothes."

But whose body? Rune couldn't force himself to ask. Not yet. This alliance relied on his marriage to Princess Johanne, and if that was her . . . There was no hope for Salvation.

"It's changed," Lady Nadine whispered. The clearing was absolutely silent, save the drone of flies. "This is where we saw the monster. Hanne was over there"—she pointed at the thing in the center—"and I was standing here. The monster came for me, but Hanne threw a rock at it and led it away. She saved me. She saved my life."

Then the body in the center of the clearing *wasn't* Princess Johanne's. *Thank Nanror*, Rune thought. But Nanror was the Numen of Mercy, and clearly there was no mercy here—not for the corpse in the clearing and not for Princess Johanne, who was still missing. With a monster. He stepped closer to Lady Nadine as a tremor racked through her, but she didn't fall. "Which way?"

She pointed west. "I think. I'm not sure. Everything happened so fast."

"What kind of creature was it?" asked John Taylor. He was Rune's primary guard, and living proof that some people from Caberwill had straightforward names. "A wolf? A bear?"

"No." Lady Nadine wrapped her arms around herself. "No, it was a monster. I've never seen anything like it before."

Suspicion worked through Rune, but he wouldn't name it. Not without evidence.

"All right, spread out. Search for anything unusual. *More* unusual, that is. And one of you"—Rune nodded toward Swifthand—"take a look at that mess. See if you can identify the body."

The man cringed, but he stepped onto the brown expanse. The grass crunched under his boots like broken glass.

Rune turned to Lady Nadine. "Are you sure you wouldn't prefer to go back to your carriage?"

Lady Nadine shook her head so hard that some of the pins slid farther down her curls. "I won't abandon Hanne again."

"You didn't abandon her. You ran for help. You did exactly as she ordered." Rune walked around the edge of the withering grass, moving in the direction Lady Nadine had indicated earlier. "But I meant what I said: If something happens, you must hide or run to the caravan. Your captain Oliver will ensure it."

"I will not hesitate," confirmed the captain.

She gave a tight-jawed nod, showing more bravery than half Rune's men. Yet they mocked her, even though *she* was the only one who knew what everyone was up against. *She* was the only one who had faced the monster.

He stuffed down that uncomfortable feeling of respect for an Embrian. It wasn't bad, he supposed, to *not* hate one of his new allies, but he was already in a tenuous position with his own people. No need to make it worse.

Ahead of them, a folded paper rested against the base of a maple tree, its corner rasping against the bark. Rune started for it, but Lady Nadine darted forward and snapped it up.

"This is mine." She quickly stuffed it into her pouch. "I must have dropped it when I ran."

Rune started to ask her what it was, but a sapphire thread snagged on a leaf caught his eye. Then, other signs of Princess Johanne's passage presented themselves: trampled grass, broken twigs—even a strand of golden hair, glimmering in a shaft of sunlight. The clouds, which had come on so quickly, were breaking up now.

He signaled his men. "John, take the lead." John was the best tracker in the company. "Swifthand, could you identify the body?"

The lieutenant's face was green with the need to be sick, but he nodded. "I believe it was Devon Bearhaste, Your Highness."

Lady Nadine gave a small *meep* of horror.

How strange to think of the man being dead. They'd *just* been sitting beside each other at lunch. They'd made polite conversation, traded pleasantries. "Are you certain?"

"Reasonably," the lieutenant said. "I won't describe it, for the lady's sake—"

"Thank you." Rune wasn't sure he wanted to know, either.

"But the Bearhaste crest was on the jacket. I don't know how he"—Swifthand swallowed hard—"got like that so quickly, but . . ."

A few of the men shifted uncomfortably.

"All right." Rune nodded toward John. "Let's find the princess. Keep a wary eye out for the creature." But with the sunlight returning and the birdsong beginning again, it seemed the immediate danger had passed—at least for them.

It wasn't long before they began to uncover what had happened to Princess Johanne.

"She must have been in a blind panic," muttered John, following her trail. "She zigzags a little, probably moving toward the clearest route, but every time she started to turn toward the road again, she cut north for no reason."

A sense of terrible foreboding stalked Rune as the group followed after John. He'd heard the grim stories—the ones his parents and the other Caberwilline nobility dismissed as paranoid rumors and fearmongering—but to potentially be caught up in one of them . . . It was a different thing entirely. It was far more frightening than exciting.

"Halt!" John called ahead. "Everyone stay where you are."

The party halted.

John turned to Rune and jerked his head. "Your Highness."

Rune approached cautiously. He and John weren't close anymore—not after the incident with Rune's brother—but he'd always trusted the man's instincts.

Immediately, Rune saw what had John so concerned.

Yellow.

Ribbons fluttered in the breeze, the tiny bells clinking every time a gust came through. The yellow silk was picked at and faded in some places, but still bright enough for anyone to notice. And if they somehow didn't, there were those bells, crafted from a lightweight metal developed solely for this purpose. Bells attached to these yellow ribbons were the only ones in the world to use this particular alloy and make this particular tone, because they needed to be recognizable to anyone from any kingdom.

Lady Nadine pushed her way between the guards. "What—Oh."

On the other side of the ribbon-bound trees, there was only a faint shimmer in the air, a suggestion that something wasn't right. It could have been heat ripples. It could have been his eyes watering. It could have been any perfectly natural thing—if not for the yellow line.

Then: "*Hanne!*"

Lady Nadine surged toward the malsite in a flurry of emerald silk, but a guard—Daniel—grabbed her just as she reached the line of ribbons. She struggled, yelling raggedly for Princess Johanne. Manicured fingernails scraped across the guard's cheek, but he ignored it as he hauled the lady-in-waiting away from the yellow line. Other men-at-arms moved to block her way if she somehow escaped and tried again. Still, Lady Nadine fought and strained, an anguished shriek tearing from her throat.

"Lady Nadine." Rune clenched his jaw as he stepped forward, empathy welling up inside. He knew that panic, that sense of utter dread; he knew every horrible thought the lady-in-waiting must be having. If Princess Johanne had been too frightened to notice the warning . . . "My lady, please. Throwing yourself into a malsite won't help. If you cannot control yourself, Captain Oliver will remove you to your carriage."

Slowly, Lady Nadine came back to her senses, but her whole body began to tremble, both with the realization of what she'd almost done and with the truth about her cousin. "Oh Ulsisi," she groaned, and her knees buckled. If the Numen of Pain and Sorrow heard her cry, they didn't move to help.

Daniel did, though. He held her upright, gentle in spite of the fact that they were enemies. "I'll stay with her," he said. "Captain Oliver and I will make sure she doesn't . . ." He glanced at the malsite.

"Good." Rune nodded, then lifted his voice. "Everyone else, search the perimeter. Double up, in case the creature is still nearby. Look for footprints, broken plants—anything that might indicate the princess went around the malsite—but *do not cross the yellow line*."

The law was the same in all three kingdoms: malsite warnings should be posted ten paces outside the actual site, but it wasn't always ten paces *exactly*. It was difficult, and dangerous, to measure for and place these warnings. Not to mention that Rune's stride was longer than, say, Nadine's, so ten paces was different for each of them. And anyway, most of the lines had been made four hundred years ago, after the last Incursion, and no one had ever volunteered to remeasure the distance from the yellow lines to the malsites.

These malsites were the scars of that event, that last Incursion: any time the Malstop flickered, globules of darkness spewed across the world. As malice had the self-attracting properties of quicksilver, it gathered, built upon itself, and formed malsites. They all should have been cleared away—they always had been after *other* Incursions—but the Red Dawn . . . So much pain had come from that.

Rune joined the search around the yellow line, but without much hope. The only trail they saw went straight into the malsite.

Nevertheless, they scoured the area, calling the princess's name as the sun drifted westward and evening began to close in. No one went past the yellow line, but when Rune came back around after his latest circuit, he found Lady Nadine slumped on an exposed root, her hands covering her face as she sobbed. Daniel and Captain Oliver stood over her uncertainly.

Rune knelt in front of the young lady, waving the guards to join the search.

"I'm sorry," Rune said, and it was the truth. Lady Nadine clearly loved Princess Johanne. She admired the princess in the same way Rune had admired his brother, all warmth and respect and willingness to follow him anywhere.

Although the girls weren't sisters by blood, he imagined them growing up similarly to Opi and him: sharing studies, training, and trouble; trading gossip and tips for surviving in court; fighting about things that didn't matter.

Red rimmed Lady Nadine's eyes as she gazed beyond the yellow line. "What kind of malsite do you think it is?"

"It's difficult to be sure," Rune said. There were two main classifications of malsites: bipermeable and unipermeable, which was a technical way of saying a person might pass in and out of one kind, but the other kind . . . once a body was in, they could never leave. This was the latter sort. If Princess Johanne had gone in, she would never come out. It was a terrible trap for anyone.

But that wasn't the question Lady Nadine had asked. She wanted to know the subclassification—what kind of horror lurked within this bubble of malice.

Some were obvious, like those where gravity ceased to be relevant, or where breathable air had been sucked out and destroyed as the malsite formed. A person could look at those and see what was wrong. But others—no one knew. When people went in, they were never seen again. There were no stories, no theories, no reasons to hope.

There was just nothing.

"I can't tell," Rune murmured. "I am sorry."

Lady Nadine dropped her head into her arms to muffle an anguished cry, and Rune's heart broke.

"How could this happen?" Lady Nadine sobbed. "What will we do?"

Rune stood and offered her a hand. "My lady, please allow me to return you to your carriage."

Sniffing, she took his hand and let him draw her to her feet. He gave her a moment to compose herself, and then called for the others to give up the search.

"I'm sorry," he said, gazing toward the malsite. How terrible that it looked perfectly normal, just like the forest surrounding it. An illusion; a lie. "I'm afraid Princess Johanne is beyond our reach. Our best course of action is to return to the rest of the group for the night. We can send another search team out in the morning, but . . ." He didn't finish the sentence. He shouldn't have started it. Princes—especially crown princes—ought to know what to say to raise morale, but how could he even suggest that anything good might follow this?

The moment they'd crossed the border between Embria and Caberwill, responsibility for the delegation had shifted from the Embrian commander to him. Rune Highcrown. Royal bungler.

Years ago, the safety of his brother—Opus Highcrown IV—had been entrusted to him. Rune had trained all his life for that duty, to be his brother's guard, his second, but when it mattered most, he hadn't been fast enough. His failure had robbed the kingdom of their most-loved prince, and a man who would have made an unforgettable king.

And now he hadn't been smart enough to protect Princess Johanne.

Only this time, the cost of his failure was so much higher. The alliance. The dream of peace. And the chance to address the *true* danger to humanity—the Incursions.

The burden had already been so heavy. From the moment his parents had informed him of the prospective alliance and the role he would play, he'd been terrified he would find a way to mess it up. But he'd endured the negotiations without incident—even secured a few items they'd wanted but been ready to concede if necessary. By the time they were ready to leave, he'd started to believe all of this would work out just the way he'd hoped.

And now his fiancée was trapped in a malsite, as good as dead.

Worse still, he feared he knew the identity of this creature Lady Nadine had seen. She wouldn't name it; she was still too wrung out and terrified. But what other creature would shepherd a girl into a malsite? What other creature could destroy a man so thoroughly that a seasoned warrior refused to speak of it? What other creature might be described as a monster?

A rancor. It had to be.

But Rune kept that word to himself, for Lady Nadine's sake.

As everyone prepared to leave, Lady Nadine felt through the pouch she wore and removed a clean handkerchief. Carefully, she placed it on the ground, then unclasped her pendant, tugged off her black rings, and fumbled with the catch of her bracelets. It was a fortune in obsidian.

"My lady?" Captain Oliver asked.

Lady Nadine didn't bother to answer. Instead, with only a moment's hesitation, she secured everything inside the fabric and fastened it using the clip on her own brooch.

"Who has the best arm?" She spoke softly, but looked around the group with a fierceness that rivaled Princess Johanne's.

Swifthand stepped forward, and the rest nodded agreement. With great solemnity, he took the bundle. "Are you certain, my lady?" He wasn't mocking her anymore.

She gave a firm nod, then handed the lieutenant Rune's canteen; water sloshed inside, but there was precious little. "I would do anything for Hanne."

Everyone watched as Lieutenant Swifthand hurled the obsidian-laden package across the yellow line, then the canteen. They sailed through the evening gloom, seemed to catch along that faint shimmer, and then vanished.

They waited a moment, to see if anything would happen, but then it was full dark and they needed to leave. They needed to collect Lord Bearhaste's body—what was left of it—and get to Brink as quickly as possible. Perhaps they could find some way to rescue the alliance, if not the princess.

"Do you think it will make a difference?" one of the men asked, not quite low enough to escape Rune's notice.

"I don't know," said another. "It's probably too late."

Rune hushed them, but privately, he agreed. A rancor had escaped the Malice; it was too late for all of them.

Still, in the morning, he sent John and a few other guards back to the malsite, bearing packs stuffed with food, water, and other supplies.

Just in case.

3.
Hanne

Hanne spent her first day in the malsite searching for a way out.

She ran her hands along the pellicle—the membrane-like barrier of the malsite—pushing and prodding, trying to find any weakness in the dark magic that had trapped her. It was *so* frustrating, because she could see clear to the other side. There were the trees she'd stumbled through, the yellow ribbons she'd overlooked in her terror. There was the cloudy sky, like lace through the green forest canopy.

She just . . . couldn't get there.

The malsite was roughly circular, with a diameter of a hundred paces. It might have been an impressive size from the outside, had she noticed the yellow line and gone around it. Inside, however . . . Inside was a completely different story.

There were only trees here. Brush. The thinnest trickle of a stream, which somehow passed through the pellicle. When she tried to follow the water out, she couldn't; she just jammed her fingers. She wasn't the only one who had attempted to escape that way, either; when she felt around in the mud, the bones of tiny fish pricked her fingertips. They were piled up at the edge of the membrane. She dug a little deeper, hoping to open enough space for more water to come through to her, even though it was probably filthy and filled with diseases, and she had no way to boil it—but she got nowhere.

Still, she had to do *something*. Sitting and waiting for rescue was not in her nature.

She studied the space again, committing every tree and every bush to memory. If she was forced to stay here overnight, she needed to know her way around.

But surely the others would come for her before dark. She was the crown princess of Embria. She was arguably one of the most important people in all of Salvation—and she was imperative to this alliance. There couldn't be a wedding without her. Someone would come. Nadine would come. Nadine would *insist*.

But as full night descended, a new fear tightened around her heart. What if Nadine hadn't been able reach the caravan? What if the rancor had gone after her, once it had Hanne trapped?

Hanne went cold with the thought, images of her broken cousin flashing through her mind.

No. No, she couldn't think like that. Instead, she bit her cheeks, letting pain distract her. Her cousin was *fine*. She had to be. (But what if she was trapped in another malsite—)

Hanne sat with a grunt, pressing her back against a tree with a gentle curve in its trunk. Here, she could see most of the malsite, and she was sheltered from a rear attack.

She still hadn't seen the rancor. She hadn't seen anything but the fish bones.

It was too dark to search for insects or worms, but surely they lived in here. Such things were not her specialty, but didn't soil need them to support plants? What about birds or rodents? She hadn't noticed any earlier, but she hadn't exactly been listening for squeaks or rustles. Where *was* the other life in this malsite?

She listened. And all at once, she became aware of the silence.

Oh, there were noises in the malsite: wind breathing through the trees, the faint trickle of water, her own thundering heartbeat. But the silence was real, like a layer of death under everything else. It was like a ringing in her ears, if the ringing were the absence of sound. An opposite. It was negative noise, ceaseless and maddening.

Hanne ground her knuckles against her ears, trying to drive it away. But the silence had already lodged itself inside her; there was no way to be rid of it.

Sleep would not come. With thirst and hunger gnawing at her—and the terrible sense of absolute separation from the real world—all she could do was remember Solspire and wish she'd never left.

Tonight, there would be a banquet. There were always banquets. If she'd been at home, Hanne would have sat at her mother's side, both of them undeniably beautiful and regal, clothed in the finest silks and crystal beads, both wearing obsidian-dotted crowns. Together, under the light of a hundred diamond chandeliers, they would study the lesser nobles and decide who to elevate and who to destroy. They would feast on braised veal, roasted vegetables, and dainty cakes with frosting piled up like snowdrifts. They would be powerful, alluring, and when the night was over, they would retire to the royal apartments.

Hanne's personal suite had a dozen large rooms, filled with all the things a princess needed to be happy. Right now, more than anything, she wished for her bedroom, where she had a giant mattress stuffed with the fattest of down feathers and blankets softer than clouds. Stretched out in her own bed, Hanne always felt like she was floating in a warm bubble of wealth.

Her stomach growled, waking her. Lunch had been hours ago, and this tree was nowhere near as comfortable as her bed. She could endure without the bed, though. She'd slept alone outdoors before—it was part of the rigorous training her parents had put her through—but never in a malsite. Never even near one. Except . . .

She clutched the obsidian pendant that rested against her breastbone. Why hadn't it protected her?

Or—there was a chilling thought—what if it *had*? What if the only reason she wasn't a pile of rot like Lord Bearhaste was because she'd been better protected?

She pressed herself deeper into the curve of the tree and said a prayer to Sardin, the Numen of Luck, that she would survive this ordeal, and then—because one could never be too careful—Sylo, the Numen of Trees. Since a tree was currently her only protection, it seemed prudent.

Just as she was readying a prayer to the Numen of this particular tree—likely one of the Unknown Numina, their name forgotten to time—a shimmer caught her eye.

Daylight. She could see *daylight* past the screen of trees.

It was nighttime around her. How could it be daytime beyond the malsite's barrier?

Cautiously, she climbed to her feet. The air felt cool, like night. Everything seemed real enough. But as she crept to the edge of the pellicle, careful not to trip over anything in this strange darkness, she studied—for the first time—the movement of things outside.

She'd seen the ribbons earlier, of course, once she'd calmed down and regained her sense of self. But she hadn't noticed how they'd moved. They'd been up, caught in a breeze, but they hadn't drifted or danced. They hadn't lowered or lifted. They just hung there. Suspended. Absolutely still.

No, not *absolutely* still.

When she waited, watching the yellow ribbons long enough, she saw the movement she expected—just so much slower than it should have been.

Then she started seeing other things, too: birds barely fluttering their wings, a leaf falling in slow-motion, and a deer mid-leap as it fled the path she'd taken to get here.

Heart pounding wildly in her throat, Hanne searched the area for the rancor. It was impossible to decide which she preferred: seeing it out there, watching as it slowly lurched toward her, or not seeing it at all. Because if it wasn't out there, then where was it?

"Help me, Tuluna," Hanne prayed, but the patron Numen of Embria remained silent. "How can I follow your path if I'm trapped here? Am I not your chosen one?"

Still, nothing.

Tuluna had not always been with Hanne, but nine years ago, the Numen had selected her to become their voice, their cure for all of humanity's darkest impulses.

Hanne closed her eyes and thought of that first conversation, seeking comfort in memory.

> ***I can help.*** Those were the first words, sweet and cool, a soothing balm after the pain Hanne endured when her parents had taken her . . . away.
>
> "Who are you?" Hanne whispered, young enough to be intrigued by a voice in her head, but old enough to be cautious, too.
>
> ***Who do you think I am?***

Hanne considered that question for a while. Lying in bed, her whole body hurting, she didn't have much else to do. Finally, she said, "I don't know. You haven't given me enough information."

The presence laughed a little. Not *at* her, like grown-ups might have, but in simple acknowledgment that she was correct. ***I will tell you about myself. Then, you can make an educated guess.***

"Very well," Hanne agreed.

I want to unite the world under a single flag, they said. ***Yet I am trapped, unable to do this on my own. I cannot reach Salvation in the way I require. Therefore, I seek a partner. A sword. A queen.***

Hanne's breath had caught. *She* was going to be queen one day.

It is ambitious, I know. But ambition drives me.

"You can't get to Salvation," Hanne murmured, her mind racing.

No.

"You aren't human."

Again, the presence laughed. Gently. ***No. I am not.***

"Are you going to hurt me?"

I won't lie to you, Hanne. If you agree to be my partner, there will be trials. Sometimes they will be painful. But I will not hurt you. I need you. I care about you. You are precious to me, my tenacious little princess.

Tenacious. Ambitious. "Are you Tuluna?"

You are such a clever girl. It sounded as though they were smiling.

Hanne's heart swelled. People had always needed her, and they complimented her whenever compliments suited them. But no one, especially not her parents, had ever said so clearly that they cared for her. She had never been precious to anyone, aside from Nadine. "Very well, Tuluna. I will help you, and you will help me. I will be your partner."

From that moment, the patron Numen of Embria had been with Hanne, guiding her, teaching her, training her. Tuluna hadn't lied—it *was* painful to be their chosen sometimes—but the knowledge that she would stop the fighting and become queen of all of Salvation one day . . . that kept her going.

But now Tuluna wasn't answering. Perhaps they *couldn't* answer.

Perhaps the malice blocked Hanne's prayers or Tuluna's voice. Did the rancor know that? Did the rancor know that *she* was Tuluna's sword? That must have been why it chased her in here—to thwart Tuluna's plans to end the war.

For an hour, Hanne scanned the trail she'd made, finding no sign of the rancor. But a bird had started to take flight, and the leaf had gotten caught in a shaft of light, and the deer was on all four hooves again, its body coiled to make another jump.

Hanne's mind reeled. Her instincts told her that everything outside the malsite was broken, and that was why it all moved so slowly, but the logical part of herself knew the truth. It was the inside of the malsite that was broken. Where she was.

Here, everything moved quickly. Too quickly.

Hanne was trapped in a time slip, which meant she could be long dead by the time anyone found her.

The second day—well, the second day inside her small prison; it was still yesterday outside—she studied the malsite again, anxiously searching for anything that might be useful.

Already, she was dehydrated. Hungry. Her thoughts felt floaty, and she struggled to focus on the tasks she'd set before her. Her head throbbed at her temples.

First, she needed a way to collect water. This morning, she'd licked dew off the wide leaves of some of the trees, but it wasn't enough. A little more water had collected where she'd dug by the stream, but she wasn't ready to risk that yet. It was shallow and slow, and too many dead bugs floated there. Anyway, it went directly through the pellicle. Who could tell what that did to water?

So she focused on finding a piece of curved bark, then lined it with thick, shiny leaves until it resembled a saucer. She would angle other leaves so that their dew dripped into it.

But even if it worked, tomorrow morning was a long way off.

Her next task was food. She foraged a few berries, carefully testing them for poison by rubbing them on her wrist and waiting, rubbing them on her lips and waiting, touching one to her tongue and waiting. It was torturous—all that waiting when her stomach was hollow with hunger—but when she had no reactions, she put a berry in her mouth and ate it.

More waiting. After a small eternity, when she wasn't dead, she deemed the berries safe and ate two handfuls. It didn't occur to her until after they were all gone that they might be tainted with malice.

Well, she'd find out.

That evening, the forest outside the malsite came alive with people. A search party, *finally*.

Caberwilline guards arrived first, and beyond them, through the veil of trees and forest undergrowth, she caught the bright emerald of Nadine's dress.

Hanne's heart lifted as pieces of her cousin slowly came into view: a hand, a lock of hair, a worried expression on her dirt-streaked face. Nadine was alive and safe, and she'd brought help.

"Nadine!" Hanne's voice sounded froggy with thirst and hunger, but even so, the sight of her cousin gave her a burst of energy. "Nadine, I'm in here!" She pounded on the pellicle with all her might, creating a racket loud enough to wake the dead. When her arm began to ache, she stopped and stared out, waiting. They'd see her soon. They had to.

Slowly, they discovered the ribbons and bells. Half an hour later, Nadine hurled herself at the malsite, her face contorted with horror.

But that was good. That meant Nadine saw her. Adrenaline spiked through Hanne as she beat against the pellicle until her knuckles bled, screaming so loudly her voice cracked. "Nadine! Nadine, help me! Get me out!" Hanne's heart thrummed painfully fast as the scene unfolded outside.

A guard caught Nadine. She scratched him. He dragged her away, toward Captain Oliver. Rune stepped in.

It was all achingly slow, giving Hanne enough time to take in every detail of her cousin's face—and of the wretched expression that must have been a mirror of her own.

"Nadine?" Hanne's spirit sank deep, deep into the earth as Captain Oliver and the other guard sat with Nadine while the rest moved to search around the malsite. They never crossed the yellow line, not once, and though they looked directly into the malsite, their eyes never focused on Hanne herself.

They couldn't see her.

Hanne's knees buckled, but she pulled herself up and refused to give into the fear coiling in her gut. She beat against the pellicle, calling Nadine again and again. For hours, while the search party crept around the malsite, she screamed and cried, and nothing changed.

Finally, she had to acknowledge the truth: if they couldn't see her or hear her, and if they wouldn't cross the yellow line, then there was no way they were going to rescue her.

She was alone.

The third morning—her time, not theirs—the search party was readying to leave. They'd clearly accepted that she was beyond their reach.

Even Nadine.

Quietly, with her face turned away, Hanne cried.

She'd drunk the morning dew, though it did nothing to sate her thirst, and eaten another handful of berries, but there was so little inside her that she could hardly move.

And even more painful than the hollow ache in her belly was the absence of something greater: hope.

Hours later, a bundle came flying through the barrier and clapped her on the head.

She glanced over her shoulder to find a man with his arm outstretched, as though he'd just hurled something, and Nadine with her hands clasped to her chest. She wasn't wearing her obsidian pendant.

Hastily, Hanne unwrapped the bundle and found all her cousin's jewelry.

The agony inside her heart eased—just a little. Nadine hadn't given up, not really. Hanne should have known better. They were best of friends, after all, and they looked out for each other even when no one else would. Nadine was her rock. When the court had mocked Hanne for being an ugly child, Nadine had protected her. When Hanne's parents had violently forged her into their perfect daughter, Nadine had soothed her. And now, when Hanne was trapped in a malsite . . . Nadine still believed in her.

"I know you will never abandon me, cousin."

Hanne leaned her forehead on the pellicle and watched as another object slowly sailed through the air. A canteen. Thirst soared up inside Hanne, and she scrambled for the canteen when it arrived, only to find that it was less than half full and the rim stank of bile. Even so, she poured a small amount of water into her mouth and held it there, savoring the sensation of liquid against her parched and swollen tongue. As the water slid down into her stomach, she capped the canteen and put it beside the pile of Nadine's obsidian.

"At least I'll be well-accessorized when I die," she rasped, then laughed a little, then bent over herself and tried not to cry. She couldn't afford to lose the water. "Tuluna, please." Because *please* always worked on Nadine.

But the patron Numen of Embria did not answer, and outside the malsite, the prince and guards led Nadine away.

Two days later, several heavy packs came flying into the malsite.

Hanne didn't register them at first; her mind was elsewhere, her eyes seeing the glittering towers of Solspire. Ever since she'd been a little girl, she had admired the way sunlight caught the facets of diamonds and sapphires and rubies, making the palace sparkle like a dream. And as she'd gotten older, she'd appreciated how that same sunlight could pierce the eyes and blind a person—usually a peasant looking above their station.

She could see it so clearly though: individual gemstones refracting light, the wide avenue leading up to the palace on its hill, and the hundreds of soldiers standing statue-still at every entrance and on every corner. In her mind, she meandered through the grand courtyards and carefully curated gardens, which were filled with glory-lilies, oleander, and nightshade—along with a few less-poisonous species of plants, for variety.

In real life, Hanne rarely had the opportunity to wander the gardens or explore the labyrinthine halls of the palace—her schedule kept her occupied every waking moment—but now, as hunger and thirst rolled through her shuddering body, she retreated into memories of home. She knew, perhaps, more than she'd thought about the closed-up passages of Solspire, and the off-limits towers where previous Fortuin queens had locked away their rivals or political enemies. Once, when Hanne had been eleven or twelve years old, she'd been sparring with an instructor in the Ember Corner Courtyard, only for their lesson to be interrupted by the disgraced countess of Silver Valley. For a week and a half, she'd been kept in one of those towers, and just as Hanne was about to win the match against her instructor, the countess's body landed with a loud, messy *thump*.

Thumps. Right. There had been several thumps nearby. Hanne's eyes fluttered open and she twisted around until she spied a leather pack, filled to bursting. Beyond it, there was another. And another.

She was almost too exhausted to go to them, but she summoned all her strength and crawled. Halfway there, her arms gave out and she had to rest, but she forced her eyes to stay open and on the bags. Once she caught her breath, she pushed herself up and clawed her way to the closest pack.

It was filled with food. The second held a dozen canteens of water. The third had blankets, a silver bowl, a packet of matches, and several other things she didn't care about as urgently as she cared about the water.

Though she was desperately thirsty, she drank a few sips at a time, letting the water settle in her stomach before she took more. After an hour, when her head felt clearer, she drank again.

Then, when she decided she was going to live out the next few days after all, she started to sort through her supplies.

Two and a half weeks later she was still trapped in the malsite, but she had a fire she never let burn out, stream water always boiling in the silver bowl, and bags of carefully rationed food.

She still couldn't escape, but it was only a matter of time before Nadine and Rune returned with a way to set her free. He needed this alliance. He needed *her*.

She would escape this place.

But the moment she allowed herself to believe that, something else came into the malsite.

Flint-gray skin, too-long limbs, a thousand teeth, jerking movements: the rancor pressed itself through the pellicle and clambered toward her.

4.
RUNE

Rune was trapped. He'd finally reached Honor's Keep, only to receive an urgent summons from the Crown Council the moment he'd climbed off his horse. There'd been no time to wash up and change, and now, stinking of sweat and failure, he stood before the ten most powerful people in Caberwill as he finished relaying the previous day's events.

"I interviewed Lady Nadine carefully on the way here." Rune did his best to keep his voice even, but he'd always felt small in this grand room. The ancient tapestries, the portraits of Crown Councils past, the massive oak table hewn from a single tree: it was all designed to intimidate. "The details of her story never changed, and she was genuinely terrified for the princess. She even threw her obsidian jewelry into the malsite."

Several councilors touched their own obsidian rings and pendants, while King Opus III nodded slowly.

"The Embrians are waiting in the courtyard, complaining about the delay," Rune finished. "I assured them that they'd be roomed and cared for as soon as possible."

"Thank you, my son." King Opus sat up straight in his chair, the wood creaking under his weight. He was a huge man, with wide shoulders, a strong jaw, and a deep growl of a voice. Opus, like his father before him, was the result of generations of careful breeding, matching couples not only for political expediency but for the offspring they might produce as well. The larger the better. Temperament and cleverness were also considerations, of course, but if there was a message their ancestors had wanted to send to their enemies, it was one of strength and bravery. "So we are certain that this was not an Embrian plot to dissolve the alliance."

"I'm certain," Rune said, wishing an extra chair had been brought in for him, even if there wasn't a place at the table. His mother and father sat at opposite ends, while the eight councilors were evenly spaced between them, four on either side. Everyone wore a frown. "I'm as certain as I can be, anyway."

"They are Embrians, after all." Duchess Charity Wintersoft looked up from her notes and shot Rune a narrow-eyed glance. "Just because we don't understand how imprisoning their princess in a malsite benefits them doesn't mean it wasn't their plan all along. They are conniving."

Noir Shadowsong leaned on her elbows. "I don't see how the loss of the princess—"

"Are you an Embrian?" Charity snapped.

Noir scowled. "Obviously not."

"Then of course you don't see. How could we, good Caberwilline people, understand what depths Queen Katarina and King Markus would plumb in order to achieve some advantage? This alliance was their idea, after all."

Noir stayed quiet. She was the industrial chancellor, one of three councilors who'd been elected to their positions by their constituency rather than appointed by the crown, but Charity looked down on anyone who wasn't nobility, even if they were very good at their jobs.

"I agree with Noir." Rupert Flight, an earl from the eastern coast, leveled his glare on Charity. "Notwithstanding, the threat to the Winterfast Accords remains."

Several councilors nodded.

"But with regards to Embria, the questions we should be asking are about Devon Bearhaste and his part in all this." Rupert turned his gaze on Rune. He was a plain-looking man, totally unmemorable even to people who thought they were good at faces, so he wore a pin—a winged lion—to make it easier for others to recognize him. "You say Lord Bearhaste had been taking a walk as well? And he was dead by the time you reached him?"

Rune nodded. "Not just dead—decomposing. Lieutenant Swifthand can tell you more. He saw the body up close."

Rupert made a note of that. "Did anyone else take a walk?"

"Not that I recall." Rune wanted to shift his weight, but forced himself to remain still. His father was watching.

The earl narrowed his eyes. "My friends have told me that in Solcast, Bearhaste penned several letters they could not intercept."

"A traitor," Opus muttered. "Rupert, get me everything about

Devon Bearhaste, his family, and all associates. I want them thoroughly investigated."

"It will be done, Your Majesty." The earl—the information chancellor—made another note.

Swan Brightvale, the merchant chancellor—another commoner—spoke next. "That does leave the question of what to do with our visitors." Her dark eyes were steady as she gazed around the chamber. "Will we honor the agreement to give the nobility rooms in the castle? Or should I have space made for them at the inns in Brink?"

Everyone looked toward the grand general, a man called Tide Emberwish. He was a hero of the three-kingdoms war, and no one—not even Charity—disputed his place on the Crown Council, lowborn though he was.

The old man pursed his mouth, thinking. Then: "They should stay in the castle. I want them where we can keep an eye on them. If you agree, Your Majesties."

King Opus looked across the table to meet Queen Grace's eyes. When she nodded, he said, "We'll keep the nobility and their trains in the east wing, as planned. Allow them to move throughout the castle, but make sure they are always watched. I want to know who they visit, what they talk about, and even what they eat for breakfast."

The grand general nodded. "And their soldiers?"

"The barracks we cleared out for them will suffice."

"What of the alliance?" asked Dayle Larksong, a pale man with ashy skin and tired eyes. Rune had always liked him, even before he'd become the grand priest; he was one of the few people who still possessed books about certain forbidden subjects.

"Indeed," said Rupert. "Without the princess, how can the alliance move forward? No doubt Queen Katarina and King Markus will blame us for Princess Johanne's predicament."

Predicament. Was that what they were going to call this?

"Yes," murmured the grand general. "We must prepare for the worst. I would suggest a preemptive strike against Embria, before word of the princess's disappearance reaches them."

"Embria will know soon enough," Rupert said. "They may know now.

Since no effort was made to hide the incident, everyone in the Embrian delegation has the same information we have heard. I can intercept letters and other correspondence, but that will be effective for only a short time. After all, the Embrian monarchs will expect their people to return in a month. And they will expect news of the wedding. Which is, apparently, off for the time being."

Behind his back, Rune curled his hands into fists. Perhaps he should have sworn his guards to secrecy, but what of Captain Oliver? What of Lady Nadine? Neither were under his authority, and keeping Lady Nadine with Caberwilline soldiers would have been indecent. No, she (and the captain) had ridden to Brink with the Embrian delegation, where her own people could comfort her.

It was impossible to keep this a secret, and everyone here should know it. A *princess* was missing. It wouldn't be long until all of Salvation knew.

"So the wedding is off," mused Charity, "and we are to make a preemptive strike against Embria. I do not like this plan."

"We don't have other options," said the grand general. "It is the princess's own fault that she is trapped in the malsite, but Queen Katarina and King Markus will not see it that way. They will see negligence on the part of Caberwill as a whole."

On the part of Rune, he meant, but he would not say that aloud.

"Why is attack our only option?" Rune stepped forward, keeping his fists behind his back. "I promised the Embrian delegation we would do everything in our power to rescue Princess Johanne from the malsite. Surely there is a way. Perhaps if we approached Markus and Katarina with a list of our efforts, they would join us in putting every resource to the task of ensuring the alliance will continue as we planned."

"You speak as though they are a reasonable people," said the grand general. "But there is nothing reasonable about them. It was before you were born, but I'm certain you have studied the Battle at Dead Water Hill, in which a ceasefire was to be discussed—but the Embrian military ambushed General Ring and killed every Caberwilline soldier escorting him. Or the massacre at Brightfell Mine only five years ago. They didn't like the quality of iron they had purchased and sent a squad of men to kill our miners. Remember?"

Rune remembered. Embria was notorious for responding forcefully. Violently.

"No matter what facts we offer," the grand general went on, "they will twist these events and motivations into something sinister, and they will respond in a way that only they could view as proportional. They will set fire to our farms. They will dump poison into the Bluestone River. They will murder our people until they reach you, my prince, and then they will throw you in a malsite, too. An heir for an heir. We cannot permit that."

A chill worked up Rune's spine, visions of Tide's dark prophecy playing out in the back of his mind. He'd spent enough time with the Embrian monarchs that he couldn't fully disagree. The queen had been, to put it bluntly, terrifying. She was as beautiful as Princess Johanne, but a thousand times more severe. When she'd looked at him, he had the distinct impression that she was imagining what his innards would look like spilled on the floor.

"Perhaps there is another option," Rupert said, breaking Rune's morbid reverie. "Princess Johanne was an only child, so there is no substitute of equal rank, but Lady Nadine is her cousin. She may not be royalty, but she is as close of a relation as we could ask for, and beloved to the princess."

Rune's eyebrows shot up. Marry Lady Nadine instead? "You think Embria would accept a different marriage?"

"A new contract would need to be drafted." Rupert gave a piercing smile. "But wouldn't that be preferable to all-out war? We should do everything possible to maintain our current tenuous peace with Embria. Especially given the gravity of the situation in Ivasland."

"Hmm." King Opus leaned back in his chair, lacing his hands together. "Continue that line of thought."

"A lady-in-waiting is no princess, of course," Rupert went on. "We'd need to make concessions, but perhaps we could arrange something that would be agreeable to both Caberwill and Embria, especially if we can remind them that the threat to the Winterfast Accords looms even larger. Perhaps there is even a way to shift the blame for Princess Johanne's disappearance to Ivasland."

"Think on it," the king instructed. Then he turned back to the grand general. "Tide, you look concerned."

Grand General Emberwish nodded slowly. "Avoiding war would be preferable, of course."

"Of course," people all around the council chamber murmured.

"I'm sure Lady Nadine is a fine young woman." Tide leaned back, too, mirroring the king's posture. "However, if we approach King Markus and Queen Katarina with Lady Nadine as a potential substitute, we will lose our chance of making a preemptive strike. They will know that Princess Johanne is gone, putting the power of war or peace into *their* hands."

"That is a good point." Queen Grace's pewter eyes were hard as she gazed over the room. "I do not like giving Katarina and Markus the upper hand."

"The real threat comes from the south," Rupert pressed. "We should take the risk and offer peace."

"They will reject it," Charity said. "Yes, peace is the more desirable outcome, of course, but as the grand general said, these are not reasonable people. If we try to contract Lady Nadine instead, they will likely attack us first."

Rune's fingernails dug into his palms. Apparently, everyone had accepted that Princess Johanne was lost. No one was willing to even entertain the idea of a rescue. Not that *he* knew how, but once, hundreds of years ago, there *had* been someone who could destroy malsites.

Rupert's expression did not change. "I could speak with the Embrian delegation, get a sense of their receptiveness. We will be monitoring their communications to Solcast, so there will be little opportunity for any of them to warn the Embrian royalty, regarding Lady Nadine, before we're ready."

King Opus and Queen Grace met each other's eyes again, and finally the king said, "If I believed Katarina and Markus would be willing to accept a substitute bride, then I would encourage you to try. But Tide is right: they are not reasonable people, and I'm loathe to give them an advantage."

"Sire—"

"I've made my decision, Rupert. We can vote on it, if you insist, but I don't think it'll be necessary." The king pressed his hands flat on the table and looked around. No one spoke. Then Opus turned to the grand general. "Tide, ready our troops to march on Embria. The war will continue."

"Yes, Your Majesty."

No, this couldn't be it. This wasn't nearly the type of reaction needed to protect the kingdom. The Crown Council couldn't just leave Princess Johanne to rot in that malsite, not if there was a way to rescue her! And—to make matters worse—they'd completely ignored the thing that had driven her in there.

"And what of the creature Lady Nadine described?" Rune asked loudly, before the council could be dismissed. "She called it a monster. It could still be out there."

Queen Grace smiled pityingly. "The poor girl's probably never seen a wolf before. Or a bear."

"I agree with Her Majesty," said Charity, which wasn't a surprise. She always agreed with Her Majesty. "Wildcats roam that part of the Deepway this time of year. That's likely what she saw."

"Lady Nadine described a different sort of creature—" Rune started, but the king shook his head, halting the words.

"No, the princess fled a wildcat," Opus said. "There is nothing else to discuss on that front."

Rune gritted his teeth. He knew he shouldn't say it—there'd been enough fights over the years—but he was so burning exhausted and *done* being used as a political game piece. "It was a rancor, I'm sure of it."

The council chamber went absolutely silent.

King Opus let out a long sigh, while Queen Grace closed her eyes as though resorting to prayer.

"Please say that again, Your Highness." Grand Priest Larksong's hands flitted to the tiny bottle of crushed obsidian around his neck.

"I believe the creature that killed Devon Bearhaste, that hunted Princess Johanne, and that Lady Nadine described, was a rancor. The lady-in-waiting is hardly a fool. She knows what is natural and what is not." Rune clenched his jaw. He shouldn't be so eager to defend Embrians. "The rot surrounding Lord Bearhaste's body was *certainly* not natural, nor was the advanced state of decay. And John Taylor—the best tracker in my personal guard—said it appeared as though the princess had been forced in the direction of the malsite, even when there'd been a clearer path toward the road. No wildcat could have done that."

"A wolf pack, perhaps," suggested Swan Brightvale.

Rune just shook his head. "Wolves are clever enough not to drive their prey into a malsite, where it would be lost to them."

Swan frowned, but didn't challenge him again.

"Enough." Opus's expression clearly communicated his desire to talk about anything else, but Rune wouldn't have it.

"Father, I would love to put an end to our discussions of another Incursion." A headache pulsed behind Rune's eyes. "But every week I receive letters from commoners describing strange anomalies. The threads of the world are weakening. I *smelled* the stink of malice. And the creature Lady Nadine described fits the old depictions of rancor."

The grand priest's fingers tightened around his bottle of obsidian. "I should like to speak to this Lady Nadine."

Opus—and everyone else—ignored him. Instead, the king sat up straight, his commanding presence even more imposing than before, his glare fixed on Rune. "We do not need to worry about another Incursion. Stop listening to the paranoid masses. I've heard no trustworthy reports of malice or rancor or any other abnormalities whatsoever. People are safe, and you must stop encouraging their fears."

None of that was exactly true. Opus Highcrown had *discouraged* people's "fears" by royal decree, forbidding all public talk of Incursions, malice, and rancor. Rune was one of the few men of rank whose ears were open to the people, and they knew it. They sent letters, yes, describing shadows that began to speak, moments of uneven time, a day without full gravity—evidence of malice working on the foundations of the world as the Malstop weakened. But they came to him, too, petitioning him for help when their fields turned to glass or their houses to salt, and when he progressed through Caberwill, he met with them from horseback, listening—always listening.

A prince should care for his people. He should protect them, comfort them, feel for their terror. And he did. For two years now it had been clear that an Incursion was coming. If only he could get the council—or his parents—to burning *open their eyes*.

"There are many who worry that we are ill-prepared for the next Incursion," Grand Priest Larksong tried again. "A princess trapped in a malsite will not help matters. Perhaps we could take small measures to assure the people that we have everything under control. If we could find the creature that chased her, prove it was nothing but a wildcat—"

"No." Opus stood, and everyone hurried to rise. "This meeting is over. You have your orders. Put the Embrians where we can watch them. Ensure their communications are monitored. Prepare the army to march on Embria. I will leave nothing to chance. You are all dismissed. Except"—the king turned on Rune—"you."

As the Crown Council filed out of the room, Rune held his ground, bracing for a storm he could not avoid. For a moment, he wasn't the heir. He was merely their second, less-favored son—the one who'd failed the whole family, the one who'd had to step into his better brother's shoes. They'd never quite fit, and his parents knew it.

As the chamber doors clicked shut, Opus rounded on him. "Why? Why are you like this?"

There was no way out of this fight, so Rune hardened himself. "Someone has to care about the next Incursion," he said, his voice tense. "Someone has to try to prevent the world from falling to darkness."

Grace snorted. "You think we don't care? You think you, little more than a child, have superior insight into the next Incursion because you've read a few letters from peasants?"

"I think a rancor chased Princess Johanne into a malsite." Rune swallowed hard. "I don't care who I marry. Princess Johanne, Lady Nadine, or some cousin of theirs I've never heard of. I'll do what's right for Caberwill. But I cannot ignore the terrible things I've witnessed with my own eyes simply because you tell me I must."

"Son." Opus bared his teeth as he glared down at Rune. "We have been the reigning monarchs for longer than you've been alive. We've heard all the same stories you're hearing. The common people have been blaming bad harvests and bad luck on the malice as far back as anyone can remember. But that's all it is. Superstition and misplaced anxiety."

"The Malstop is working, Rune. We have nothing to fear from the rancor or anything else within." Grace took a long breath, as though clearing her head. "Please stop obsessing over things you cannot affect. Put that effort into your studies and relationships. You will be king one day. You'll need the Crown Council behind you."

The king nodded. "Son, you did well in your report today. You were clear and even-tempered. Everyone was impressed."

Oh, how Rune had always longed to hear such praise, to feel as though he'd done something deserving of his father's admiration. This, however, would not be that moment.

"But," Opus went on, "you ruined it with your outburst. Rancor? Rescue? You must learn when to stop."

"How can I stop when there's more to be done?" Rune swallowed hard, because he knew what was needed—and what his parents would never allow. "We can save the princess. We don't need to prepare for another two-fronted war. There is already someone who can destroy the malsites and ensure the Incursion goes no farther than this one rancor."

Opus's face paled, while Grace took a step back. Both of them seemed to stop breathing for a moment.

Then: "No." The king's voice trembled. "No, that is not an option."

"It's been four hundred years," Rune pressed. "We need her."

"No," the queen echoed quickly. "You must accept that Johanne Fortuin is lost to us, that the alliance is lost."

"This isn't about just the alliance. There's a rancor somewhere in Caberwill. This is bigger—"

"No, it isn't. Put an end to these fantasies. We won't entertain them any longer." The king's frozen stare left no room for argument. "Whether or not you were born to this position, you are now the crown prince. Try to behave like it."

After his parents left the council chamber, Rune stayed where he was, face burning with shame and heart burning with anger. His father's words echoed in his head, over and over, reminding him once again that he was a poor substitute for the true crown prince. The dead crown prince.

Rune did his best, of course. But he studied, trained, attended meetings, worked on this alliance, and strove for a better future only because preserving the line of succession demanded that *someone* fill the position of heir—and he had been the spare.

But that didn't mean everyone liked the situation. Some had tried to fight it.

After Opi had been killed, some members of the Crown Council—Rune never found out who—had wanted Princess Sanctuary or Princess Unity named heir, out of the belief that Rune was partially responsible for Opi's death. But the law of primogeniture was absolute.

Still, there were many people in Honor's Keep who believed Rune wasn't worthy of the title. Well, they were not alone.

"Your Highness?" The voice came from the doorway, and Rune looked up to see the grand priest standing there. "Forgive me for interrupting your thoughts."

"It's fine," Rune said stiffly. "But if you're hoping for a meeting with Lady Nadine, you'll need to request it from whomever Grand General Emberwish puts over the east wing."

Grand Priest Larksong shook his head. "No. I mean, I *would* like to speak with her, but I couldn't help but overhear you and your parents arguing."

A smile twitched at the corner of Rune's mouth. "Well, that's what happens when you lurk outside the door after you've been dismissed."

"Indeed." Dayle touched his bottle of obsidian again, his (very noticeable) nervous habit. "I think you're right to want to save the princess."

Of course he was. And of course Dayle would think so, too. He was committed to peace, and he believed that the Numen he served—and all Numina—would return to this world someday and put an end to the constant warring. But people had to want it, he always said, and they had to be ready for it.

Rune wasn't so sure he believed in that particular prophecy, but he and the grand priest had other shared interests.

"And," Dayle went on, "I think you're right about the one who can help us."

Rune's breath caught, and longing twisted inside his chest. "And have you come to make a case for summoning her? Knowing that my parents have already forbidden this course of action, and that disobeying their wishes could have serious consequences beyond simply angering them?"

"I serve Elmali, first and foremost," said the grand priest calmly. "They, and the other Numina, gave us a single weapon with which to battle the forces of darkness. If we do not use her as they intended—to cut down the malsites, to end the coming Incursion—then we won't have to worry about the alliance or the war for much longer. Darkness will sweep across the land and put an end to all of us, as it has done to the rest of the world. You say it is coming, and I agree. I have had the same letters, heard the same fears. The people who come to the temple for help—they do not mince words."

Hadn't Rune been making this very argument to his parents just minutes before? But they had reasons to be concerned—even he had to admit that. The danger of actually doing this was so high. "I know," he said. "I know that we need her, but if she brings disaster, then I'll be the one at fault. I'll carry the burden of whatever happens to my family. My sisters. They're so young."

Dayle nodded slowly. "Decisions like this are different when they rest solely on your shoulders—when there's no one else to bear the weight of failure or success. But one day, you will be king, and decisions will be yours alone."

Rune closed his eyes. "Her arrival would put the world into a fresh state of panic."

"Perhaps the world needs to panic," said the grand priest. "Perhaps if people see their crown prince summoning someone so dangerous, so feared, they will begin to understand the gravity of our true situation. You would not make such a dire move unless there was no choice. There is a *rancor* in the Deepway Woods. Numina know what more chaos it will cause. It's already put our alliance in peril."

"Yes," Rune agreed.

"She wasn't always such a terrible figure," Dayle went on. "You know what she was like before the Red Dawn. She was our hero—our savior. I believe she could be again. It is what she was made for."

Rune turned his gaze out the window and pressed his fist to his chest, where his heart was tight with wanting. For years, he'd listened to every whispered story, read every tale of her valor. Secretly, of course, because so many books had been burned four hundred years ago. And even more secretly, he'd imagined escaping the confines of this castle and his complicated role here. He'd imagined fighting at her side, engaging in uncomplicated heroism, battling evil, finding friendship with someone so *good*, so *worthy*.

The Nightrender. She who banished death and darkness. The champion of dawn.

But her story had such a terrible, violent end. And that was the only thing people remembered about her now.

"It was divine judgment," Dayle murmured. "She is a divine creature. If she—" He couldn't seem to form the words. "There must have been a reason."

Rune had told himself the same thing a hundred times. The Red Dawn had happened four hundred years ago. What did he—or anyone—*really* know about what happened then?

It was a risk, though. Waking her. Inviting her into the castle. The Nightrender was dangerous, everyone knew, and if she was still angry . . . Rune could hardly bear to think about what would happen to his family.

But his people complained about the Malstop constantly—and now a crown princess was caught in a malsite. Even on the way here, things hadn't been *right*. He'd noticed little loops of time, snow that fell even though it was summer, and a whole flock of geese flying backward. Everyone had pretended to ignore these things, as though acknowledging them would make the threat real.

The threat was real whether or not they acknowledged it.

His parents refused to stop these travesties, and no one else *could*.

Perhaps—

Perhaps the council had been right to want one of his sisters instead of him. Perhaps he *wasn't* worthy of the crown. But that was because he'd never done anything to *become* worthy. That needed to change.

His kingdom was counting on him.

The entire world, in fact.

He had to take the risks others could not. He must be the kind of prince who earned his crown.

"All right." Rune turned away from the window. "I'll do it."

The moment he left the council chambers, Rune—still covered in road grime—went to the Forsaken Tower.

He went immediately, because he didn't want to think too much. He might talk himself out of it. He might consider again how dangerous this was.

There existed only three keys to the Forsaken Tower: the heir's, the queen's, and the king's. Rune fingered the key where it hung—as always—around his neck. The hall at the tower's base was deserted—few people ventured to this corner of the castle anymore—so there was no one to witness as he fitted his key into the lock and turned.

A heavy *thunk* sounded as the tumblers lurched into place. Hinges squealed as the door swung open. His footfalls echoed on the dust-covered stairs as he started his way up to the top of the tower.

He should have brought a light globe. The lancet windows had been boarded closed ages ago, so only splinters of daylight pierced the gloom, forcing him to go slowly up the narrow, twisting stairs. Finally, he came to the top, where another door waited. He fumbled for the lock, turned his key again, and then emerged into a dim, musty room.

It was here, hidden behind shattered furniture and giant cobwebs, that the Caberwill shrine had been abandoned after the Red Dawn.

When Rune had come here before—only once, with his parents when he'd become crown prince and inherited Opi's key—it was over quickly, and he hadn't been given a proper chance to look. But he'd never forgotten that little spark of mystery and wonder, and sometimes he dreamed of climbing the tower stairs again. (At other times, somewhat shamefully, he'd dreamed that he'd traveled to Winterfast Island to awaken her, that he'd become her second in battle, worthwhile, selfless, more like his brother.)

It was a thrilling yet terrifying fantasy, one he'd often turned over in his mind in the moments before he fell asleep, polishing every detail into perfection.

Of course, he hadn't had time for that lately. He'd grown out of it, and if anyone asked, he was completely over his fascination with the Nightrender.

Now, his heart pounded, and with no one here to draw away his attention, he gazed at the simple stone altar, filthy with dust and grunge, and even droppings. There was a relief of her on the front, just a faint suggestion of a body and upraised wings, but it was obscured by dirt and the bone-white scrape of rock, as though someone had tried to scratch away her image.

Ire stirred in his chest, seeing the Nightrender's shrine in such a state.

He knew the history—of course he did—but she'd protected the people of Salvation for thousands of years. This was disrespect of the highest order.

It didn't feel right to summon her like this, when she'd been neglected for so long. Quickly, he tried to brush off the grime, but it had sunk into the pores of the stone and would not be removed without more effort than he could give right now.

A thin, warning voice sounded in the back of his head, but he crushed it. This moment required action.

"Perhaps it won't even work," he whispered.

But perhaps it would.

And if he was being honest, he wanted this. He knew he shouldn't, but he did. Every piece of him wanted to see her, just once, and to deny that feeling would be to deny destiny.

This was destiny.

Rune's whole body was lightning as he knelt before the shrine and pressed his palms to either side of the relief. Even scratched out and hard to see, she was magnificent.

"Give me strength," he prayed to Elmali. The patron Numen of Caberwill had never helped him before, but praying—in this moment of all moments—couldn't hurt. "Bless me with courage and wisdom."

Then he spoke the simple and forbidden words: "Nightrender, I summon you."

Dark light erupted from the shrine, flooding across his hands and arms and face and chest. It grew, stealing his breath until the blast overwhelmed him, and he fell backward, unconscious.

5.
Nightrender

For the first time in four hundred years, Nightrender opened her eyes.

Cool darkness shrouded her room, but daylight speared the crumbling shutters. She could feel the sun slipping lower in the sky, feel the drifts of snow that rippled up against the base of the tower. There was the sound of the surf far below. Otherwise, her world was dim and quiet and strange.

And wrong.

When she sat up and peered through the gloom, it was only to discover the battle against entropy had been ceded long ago. Dust and snow covered the floor, while cobwebs crackled with a fresh coat of ice. Where she'd lain on the bed was a negative space: dirt and mildew and rot stained the sheets around her with darkness.

It didn't even stink anymore; the odor of abandonment had expired a hundred years past.

A moment of discomfort pulsed through her. One beat. Two.

Usually when she awakened, there were caretakers with offerings of fresh food and clothes in the latest fashions. Not that she cared for the latest fashions, but she had always done her best to put the humans at ease—a challenge with her wire-thin frame, sword-sharp gaze, and midnight-dark wings that stretched twice as wide as she was tall. More than once, she'd been told that humans found her unsettling to look at, even when they *wanted* to look. Even her soul shard had been taken aback a few times.

Nightrender pressed her hand against her heart, yearning for a connection lost hundreds and thousands of years ago, so many times, and suddenly she was steeply aware of how alone she was.

No humans, no food, no clothes. All the gowns and trousers and fine silk shirts left in the wardrobe had crumbled away. As she drifted through the empty rooms and corridors of Winterfast Tower, as softly as a breeze, she stretched her senses wide. There were no sounds, save the rising wail of wind outside and the occasional scuff of her footfalls where the stones had shifted over the centuries.

Her passage disturbed only the dust and snow collecting in the halls and the heavy air that hadn't been breathed in hundreds of years. It tasted like death where it touched the back of her tongue.

Nightrender moved down the grand spiral stairs, past the library of decomposing stories and the armory of rusted memories. There was something disconcerting about walking through a home that had somehow become a mausoleum.

They're probably all dead.

The thought crept in, prickling against her mind before she could stop it.

All the humans? All the kingdoms? All the world?

What if there's nothing left for you to protect? What if you're completely alone in the universe?

For a heartbeat, the sense that they had all left her was utterly complete and—she gripped the splintering stair rail—terrifying.

But then the sensation vanished, and her customary calm confidence came rushing back.

Someone had summoned her, or she would not have awakened. If they were all dead, all the millions of humans who lived on Salvation, then she would have slept through to the end of time.

Millennia of memories stretched behind her; Nightrender could easily imagine sleeping for the rest of eternity, her tower crumbling in, her body covered in debris and earth and water and the weight of both forever and never.

She resisted the temptation to indulge in melancholy any further. No one was going to appear to dress her, to inform her of the happenings in the human kingdoms, to prepare her for battle against the rancor. No one would tell her that her Dawnbreakers had been chosen, that her armies were raised and waiting at the Soul Gate. No, it was only her now, but their absence didn't absolve her of her duties.

With great ceremony, as though she'd been attended by dozens of caretakers, Nightrender ascended to the top of the tower once more, where her chambers waited in snowy silence. Only the windows admitted light, but even that was waning as the day began to pinch off at the horizon, casting a golden shadow across the land.

She donned her armor, a heavy black material that mortals mistook for leather but was much more than that. This armor had seen countless battles, mending itself when torn, cleaning itself when filthy. The numinous fabric slid smoothly over her skin, fitting itself to the lines of her muscles. Her boots and gauntlets came next, as old and powerful as the rest.

Then, she gathered up her sword and slung the baldric over her body, the straps and buckles making an *X* over her chest. Briefly, she touched the sword hilt over the back of her shoulder—Beloved had not abandoned her, at least—and then stepped out onto the balcony, tall and black-winged and dressed only in her ancient armor. Wind caught her hair, promising freedom.

As stars pierced the darkness, a great spiral of light above, Nightrender stretched out her arms to the world beyond Winterfast. This should have been a holy moment, when she took on her duties, but if there was no one here to chant the ancient litanies, she would do it herself.

Glory to the dawn. Glory to the night. Glory to the Numina of the dark and the light.

These were her creators, the beings of the Bright Land. They were strangers to her, as the aperture between their realm and the laic plane had closed eons ago, but never had she failed to honor them for her life. Their names puffed white on the cold air, catching on snow and stars and the shivering lonesomeness.

Eluve

Nanror

Valsumu

Vaath

Sylo

Monga

Elmali

Tuluna

Ersi Ulsisi

Syra

Vesa Sardin

Yzi

Name after name spun into the sky, hundreds of them, as none were unknown to her. And when she finished, she threw herself over the edge of the balcony. Wings caught crisp night air and carried her upward.

Nightrender flew a circuit around the tower, noting the places where stone had fallen and snow had drifted as high as the upper windows, and all the other signs that she had lost favor with mortals.

And yet, she would save them.

She stretched her black wings wide and soared over the narrow sea that separated her island from the mainland, following the pull of the summoning to the ancient city of Brink.

Always, every awakening, she could feel her way to where she'd been summoned, and though she showed no favoritism between the three kingdoms, her first destination was always to those who'd sought her aid. Usually, it was the kingdom in most need of her help, the kingdom that most desperately wanted her protection.

Although . . . perhaps not anymore.

How unsettling, this uncertainty. What had she done to offend them? She had been sleeping.

Nightrender veered upward, flying vertically as she reached steep cliffs looming over the thrashing waves. From there, long northern plains stretched out, unfurling under a perfect night sky.

It was late summer on the mainland, and the air smelled of green plants and distant lightning storms. She had always liked summer.

For hours, she flew for Brink, passing over forests and roads and towns. So much had changed during her sleep: the roads had grown wider and more worn, and lights glowed in golden knots where new towns had cropped up along the banks of rivers and lakes. Even so, a sense of familiarity and homecoming strengthened her, and every wingbeat brought her closer to destiny.

It was not quite dawn when she reached Brink.

The city stood midway up a mountain, between two steep cliffs: one above and one below. Only a few roads led up to the main gates, all switchbacks with stretches under waterfalls and over rivers. Mountains extended along either side of the city, their jagged peaks black against the plum-colored sky.

Brink was a defensible city, many of its buildings carved straight out of the mountain's warm gray stone. Even the castle—Honor's Keep, they called it—was built into the mountainside. Towers rose over the main keep: the observatory, the ruler's walk, others. The Grand Temple stood directly beside the castle, also hewn of stone. This view always made Nightrender imagine that they were natural pieces of the mountain, exposed by the relentless winds. Even the walkways that connected different floors and towers of the buildings were cut from the stone, like shelves.

It was not a sparkling city built from wealth, but Nightrender had always found Brink beautiful, all strength and stubborn endurance. And far below it, where the land leveled off and people could live away from the bustle, farms spread out as far as the eye could see. They sent half of their yields up a series of lifts inside the mountain: some filling tables, but most filling caches reserved for Incursions.

At least, they *should* have been doing that.

Because the Malstop was visible from here, south and west of the city, and even from this distance it was clear that the barrier was weakening. Huge sections were translucent and dull—a sign of danger that anyone should be able to read. An Incursion was imminent. All it would take was a rancor pushing against one of those veil-thin spaces and chaos would spill across Salvation.

What had humans done *this* time? The Malstop hadn't looked so faded in a thousand years.

With a heavy sigh, Nightrender took to the balcony that led into her tower. (Caberwillines, believing she had a special fondness for towers, had built this one onto Honor's Keep just for her.) In the past, gardens had been planted up here, lilies and roses and other decorative flowers, which, admittedly, she enjoyed looking at. And for her arrival, the kingdom's best chefs would offer their latest delicacies, in case the flight from Winterfast taxed her. It never did, but she always ate and admired the display; it set humans at ease.

But now the balcony was bare, the boxes of plants so long ago removed that there weren't even marks along the weathered stone. Time had erased all traces of their adulation.

Unease worked through her. *Someone* had summoned her. But where were they?

Nightrender crossed the balcony and tried the door. Locked.

Alarm tightened in her chest as she pushed the lock through the wood, ripping out the bolt. It thunked on the other side of the door, and she kicked it away when she strode into her room.

But it wasn't her room.

It occupied the same space as the place where she used to arrive to be fed and greeted, but gone were the grand pieces of furniture, the heavy tapestries depicting her victories, the gold candelabras, and the shining displays of weaponry. Instead, the room was dark and empty, and her shrine—the one they used to summon her—had been defaced and shrouded with dust.

Before it, a young man lay sprawled out on his back.

Dead? No. She could hear his heartbeat, a steady *thump-thump* in his chest.

Summoning was said to be overwhelming—the shrines were Relics, after all, powerful artifacts built by the Numina themselves—but typically there were people here to help and revive the summoner. She'd never seen a summoner abandoned on the floor like this.

Nightrender stepped around him, the sense of wrongness blooming blacker as she opened the inner door and gazed down into the darkness of the stairwell. Her eyes adjusted instantly, and she saw the thick layer of dust coating each step, broken only by a single set of boot prints.

Voices floated from farther below, servants moving through the castle as they prepared breakfast for the nobility. None of them were nearby or coming into her tower. No one even spoke of her. It was all *porridge* and *princesses* and *wars*, the same things mortals always talked about.

At once, Nightrender understood the truth: she had been summoned in secret.

Never, not in the hundreds of times she'd been called, had it been done with such furtiveness. Like rousing her was something shameful. Her lip curled as she turned back to the unconscious figure by her shrine.

"Wake up," she commanded.

The young man did not wake.

Nightrender walked over to him and knelt, her wings fanning out. He was tall and broad of shoulder, and his clothes were fine: well-tailored leathers and silks, all in the typical Caberwilline grays and blacks. After all these centuries, the cut of the cloth had evolved into something sharper, but the color preferences remained. In spite of his clear status and wealth, he was covered in dried sweat and muck. He had prepared *nothing* for her summoning, not even himself.

"Wake up," she repeated, and raised two fingers with which to send a small spark of numinous power into him.

But she didn't have to, because his breathing changed, and his eyes—deep brown and framed with long black lashes—opened to find hers. His gaze was warm and gentle. Kind.

His lips moved as he started to speak, and a faint jolt of recognition ran through Nightrender. Feathers rustled, and morning sunlight hit the far wall, illuminating Nightrender and her summoner.

But the moment shattered as suddenly as it had come together. His eyes widened as he seemed to notice her sword and wings, and then he went very, very still. Even his breath seemed tied up in his chest as he registered who she was. *What* she was.

Nightrender stood and stepped away in one motion, tucking in her wings. "You summoned me." The words came out shorter than she'd intended.

He scrambled to his feet, boots crunching broken pieces of wood and stone. "Please—" But he bit off whatever he was going to say after that.

She waited.

"I did. Yes." His eyes darted to the shrine, the door, and back to her. "I summoned you."

"It wasn't a question."

"Oh." He looked her over again, as though making sure he saw what he thought he saw, but he didn't bow or genuflect, like people used to. "Are you going to hurt me?"

Hurt him? Mortals were paranoid about all the wrong things. "I came to prevent an Incursion."

Her summoner's shoulders dropped just a fraction. "And the king and queen? The princesses? Do you intend to hurt them?"

"No."

He gave a little half laugh, the sort people did out of nervousness or anxious relief. "Good," he said. "That's good."

"You know the royal family personally." That was the only reason she could imagine he'd wanted to ensure their safety immediately after his own.

He nodded warily.

"Inform them of my arrival. Have my Dawnbreakers prepared. Unless there is an urgent need on Salvation, I will march into the Malice without delay." Her wings flexed, as though they, too, were anxious to fly into battle.

Her summoner paled, his eyes straying to the stairwell door like he couldn't wait to escape. "I—I'm sorry, Nightrender. There are no Dawnbreakers."

She just looked at him. "Explain."

"No one has held Dawnbreaker trials in centuries."

No Dawnbreaker trials? Those were meant to be held every decade, so that at the first hint of an Incursion, her elite guard could be ready to follow her into battle. Without them, she was alone.

"Trials must be held immediately," she said. "Inform your monarchs. Wait"—because she'd just remembered monarchs did not like to be ordered about by their subordinates—"I will inform them. Tell me their names."

He looked uncertain, but he said, "The king is Opus Highcrown the Third, and the queen is Grace Highcrown."

Nightrender scowled. The ruling family of Caberwill had been named Skyreach during the last three Incursions, and while she didn't care who ruled what kingdom—the squabbles of mortals were nothing to her—the change troubled her. Like she should have known about it.

It didn't matter. Nightrender served humanity, not dynasties.

"Tell me your name," she said.

"Rune," he said softly. "And yours?"

"You may call me Nightrender."

"No, I meant—" He drew a deep breath, suffocating an edge of frustration in his tone. "Is Nightrender your name?"

"No."

"Oh. All right." The tension wound up in his shoulders again.

It was a kind gesture, wanting to call her by her name. People had done that before, and it was always a little . . . sad. They wanted to humanize her, to make her more like them. She wasn't, though. She was different. Apart.

The only person she had ever given her name to was her soul shard, and when she and they were reunited, they wouldn't need to ask her name. They would know it. Remember it.

"You summoned me in secret," Nightrender said. "I do not like that."

He flinched, as though she'd hit him—or hurt his feelings. "Things have changed, Nightrender. If you'll allow me to explain—"

"No," she said, even though she did want answers. Those could be had later, *after* she'd met with the king and queen, *after* the Dawnbreaker trials had resumed, and *after* they'd all formed a strategy to end the Incursion. Her personal curiosity and irritation could wait. "Collect the court for me. I will go to my gallery in the throne room, unless it, too, has been turned into a slack heap."

"I'll have everything ready for you," he said, then glanced around the room and seemed to realize that he had already failed in that task. "I'm sorry about all of this. I should have—"

"You have your instructions, summoner."

Another flinch, and his breaths came short and fast. He was terrified. Of *her*. But then he turned and went to the door, leaving without another word.

Nightrender listened to the sound of his retreating footfalls for a moment, and when it didn't seem he would turn back, she relaxed her shoulders and wings and let her gaze fall on the shaft of morning light that streamed through the balcony door.

She had so many questions. Mainly, why did they fear her? She had always desired a healthy respect from mortals—some distance was best for both her and them—but she had never *hurt* them. She had never—

An image spiked through her: blood seeping from the walls of Honor's Keep, screams muffled in the distance of time.

It vanished in an instant.

Her knees buckled, but she squeezed her eyes shut, slowly breathing around the horror of that violent illusion. It wasn't real. It was the wisp of a nightmare, a fragment of her long dreaming, and that was all. Nothing like that had ever happened in Honor's Keep—not while she'd been awake.

She shoved the image aside, burying it along with her questions, with that sense of wrongness that had been tugging at her since she'd awakened. She had a duty to fulfill.

After all, she was humanity's sole weapon against the darkness.

She could not be broken.

6.

Rune

It was done. Whether she was truly here to help, Rune would soon find out.

As he made his way through the royal wing, the pounding of his heart began to ease and the rushing in his head began to subside. She'd *said* that she didn't intend to hurt anyone. He would have to trust that for now.

Perhaps Dayle had been correct and the Red Dawn had been divine judgment. The Nightrender hadn't said anything about what happened four hundred years ago, and if she wasn't going to bring it up, then neither was Rune.

Anyway, he was already going to be in enough trouble when the Nightrender stood before his parents in the throne room. There would be no hiding his insubordination then. So much for that fantasy of presenting a newly rescued Princess Johanne to the court, before anyone ever realized the Nightrender was here.

Burn it. He hadn't expected her to demand to see Opus and Grace. Perhaps if he'd been able to speak in complete sentences, he could have explained the situation to her. But every moment he'd spent in that room had been so charged, so uncertain, so terrifying.

Well, ultimately, they wanted the same thing: to end the Incursion. And if they could do that—as well as rescue Princess Johanne—perhaps the king and queen would forgive him and come to understand that war did not have to be the only solution to their problems.

Finally, he reached his door to find John Taylor standing at attention.

"Your Highness?" John's throat worked. "I thought you were inside."

For a moment, Rune felt sorry for the man. The guard, or any number of maids, should have noticed Rune wasn't in his chambers. He hadn't planned to get knocked out by that overwhelming light and sleep on the floor until morning. If anyone had come looking for him, if they'd charged into the tower—that could have gone poorly.

"It's all right," Rune told John, even though it wasn't all right that his personal guard hadn't known he was missing. "I need you to send a message to my parents. The Nightrender is here. She wants to see them."

John's hand went to his sword. "The Nightrender? For your parents?"

"Yes." Rune glanced toward the Forsaken Tower. "She's here to save Princess Johanne."

"She said that?" John's breath hitched; he was being too familiar. "Your Highness."

"She will save the Embrian crown princess," Rune said. "And she will fix the Malstop."

John looked uncertain. "I don't see how we can possibly believe her."

"I'm alive, aren't I?" But Rune understood John's fear, because again he was thinking of the way the Nightrender had loomed over him when he'd awakened. She'd been so beautiful, but so strange and formidable. He'd wanted to reach up and touch her—until suddenly he'd realized who he was staring at, and his whole body had gone cold. If he hadn't opened his eyes when he did . . . "Send the message to my parents. Alert the palace guard. And tell the staff to have all her spaces cleaned. The gallery. The tower. Whatever else used to be hers. We should make her feel welcome." It was too late for that, really, but perhaps she could forgive them if she saw they were trying.

The guard saluted and—once Rune opened his door and started inside—went to send the messages.

An hour later, Rune was washed and wearing fresh clothes as he strode toward the throne room, John following behind him. A nervous energy filled the castle hallways, but he couldn't tell if it was because people knew the Nightrender was here, or if it was simply because Princess Johanne was still missing and the threat of war loomed heavier than ever.

He could fix this. He would persuade the Nightrender to help him free Princess Johanne before marching on the Malstop (although she didn't seem very persuadable . . .), and then they'd all three put an end to the wars and the Incursions. Then, when he became king, he would be a *worthy* king—someone who'd earned his place, someone who had proved he could protect his people, rather than simply inheriting the crown.

Anticipation made Rune's heart thrum as he stepped into the throne room.

The space had always been intimidating, with its high ceiling and marble pillars, its black-and-gold banners hung from the four in-use galleries, its stained-glass windows that held images of kings and queens past. Sometimes, Rune felt those ancient monarchs could see through the glass eyes. He felt as though they watched him, judged him, and found him undeserving of the crown he would one day wear.

But today, those eyes looked down on a crowded chamber. There had to be five hundred people here, stuffed into every corner they could find. The galleries—all except the Nightrender's gallery—were packed with the noble houses who'd let those spaces from the crown, while the main floor held merchants and upper-class families who typically didn't come to court. All the window seats—meant for those who had trouble standing for long periods of time—were full, and there was even a section close to the western wall where the Embrians had gathered. Lady Nadine was among them, standing with Princess Johanne's other ladies-in-waiting; all of them had haunted, red-rimmed eyes.

Rune made his way up the center aisle, ignoring the probing looks and accusing stares. Members of the Crown Council were scattered about, too, also watching him. There was Rupert Flight, murmuring instructions to one of the spies in his employ, while Dayle Larksong gazed up at the Black Gallery, his small jar of obsidian clutched in his wrinkled hand. As Rune passed by, the grand priest met his eyes, then nodded slightly.

People had gathered here awfully fast, summoned by the crown, and it was hard to blame them for their interest. No one had seen the Nightrender in four hundred years. No one had *wanted* to see her.

Five tall thrones stood on the far side of the chamber, one for each living member of the royal family. Opus and Grace sat in the middle, on the highest thrones, while Unity and Sanctuary sat to the queen's left. Rune's throne waited beside his father's. They were stone, hewn from the mountainside, same as the castle, and while the back was draped with runners that bore the family crest, the seats themselves had no cushion. Ruling a kingdom should not be comfortable.

As Rune approached, King Opus shot him a dark look. "You will answer for this," Opus murmured. "You've put us all in mortal danger. What of your sisters?"

Rune's heart kicked, but he clenched his jaw and ordered himself not to respond. He'd done the only practical thing. Of course, his father probably thought engaging in an unwinnable war at the cost of thousands of lives was far more practical than asking the Nightrender to free Princess Johanne. It was all a matter of perspective, perhaps.

Above the wide-open double doors, the Black Gallery waited in darkness. Once, that space had been called the Nightrender's Step, and she must be there now; it was where she said she would go. No one ventured up there anymore, so unless the castle staff had been unusually fast, the space was probably filthy with dust and mold and echoes of everything that happened four centuries ago.

Shame made Rune's face hot. He should have sent a team to scrub it spotless *before* he went up to the shrine.

"She'll kill us all," muttered Queen Grace.

Rune looked sidelong at his mother, but stopped before snapping back. Beyond her, Sanctuary and Unity—one dark haired and one light—sat stiffly on their thrones, their frightened faces soft with adolescence. For them, Rune kept his mouth shut.

They were so painfully obedient when the king and queen were present. As for when they were alone . . . Rune didn't know. He'd forged a bond with his brother, and the girls had created their own. It did not include him. When Opi died, Rune couldn't have imagined connecting with anyone else—not even his grieving little sisters. And now, now that he wanted that, it seemed too late to act.

There was no space for Rune in his sisters' lives.

A few minutes later, the shuffle of footfalls and the buzz of conversation quieted, and the royal guards placed a rope barrier outside the double doors to prevent anyone else from entering. (Often, they'd close the doors all the way, but given the heat of so many bodies packed in on a summer morning . . . And just as likely, no one wanted to be trapped, in case the Nightrender was still upset.)

A mousy man in castle livery stepped in front of the door and unfurled an ancient scroll, coughing at the dust that puffed off the tattered parchment. Rune could only imagine the hasty research the servants must have done this morning, diving into the Grand Temple library to find the centuries-old protocol for introducing the Nightrender.

The Champion of the Three Kingdoms. The Sword of the Numina. The Hero Eternal. The—

Well, he didn't want to tempt her by even thinking it.

He gazed up at the Black Gallery again, searching for her shape among the shadows, but she was hidden, out of sight until she wanted to be seen.

Beneath the balcony, the herald cleared his throat. "It is Caberwill's greatest honor to welcome our beloved Nightrender. Please rise."

Most people were already on their feet, but the royal family all pulled themselves up from their thrones, as well as a few elderly noblemen who'd been sitting by the tall windows.

"Hands to your hearts."

Rune pressed his palms, one over the other, to his chest. He breathed in, watching the darkness above, waiting for her to show herself.

"We honor you, Nightrender, and your service to our people. We honor your past, your present, and your future. May you watch over us always." The herald's voice caught on those words, and flashes of discomfort spread through the room. "As before," continued the herald, somehow keeping his voice from cracking again, "we have need of your service. Please grace us with your presence."

The court looked up at the Black Gallery, keeping their hands pressed against their hearts as protocol dictated, but their faces held different stories—fear, shock, disgust, anger at whoever had summoned this creature. But Rune didn't see that. He saw only the Nightrender stepping onto the balcony rail.

It was different from earlier, when he'd seen her in the gloom of the Forsaken Tower. Then, he'd been frightened, foggy headed, unable to truly comprehend the sight of her. But now, his eyes were open.

The Nightrender was exquisite, with long, dark hair, wild from the wind, and feathered wings like the blackest obsidian. Her face, pale from so long sleeping, held a proud and unknowable expression as she surveyed the people below. Though physically younger than he'd expected, the weight of millennia shone in her eyes; she was ancient but eternally youthful. Even her attire was centuries old, thick leather cut in an unfamiliar style, and boots that climbed up to her knees. A baldric made an *X* across her chest, and the black hilt of a sword showed above her right shoulder. Her sigil gleamed darkly against her breast: a golden light streaking across a shadowed moon.

Night-black eyes swept across the room, evaluating everyone as she stepped down off the balcony. Her wings flared to slow her descent, and courtiers rushed away as quickly as they could. Then, without regard for anyone, she strode through the aisle between the nobles, merchants, and favored families, toward the king and queen and princesses.

And Rune.

Her stride had purpose, with no wasted movements. Her arms stayed by her sides, her wings were lifted just so, and her gaze focused straight ahead.

She stopped three paces before the thrones—a full two closer than anyone else dared—and pressed her own hands against her heart. She did not bow or kneel or prostrate herself in any way. She remained upright, as an equal. "Your Majesties. I have urgent warnings."

Sitting once more, the king and queen assessed her, not quite masking their coldness or their fear. "I'm afraid there has been a mistake, Nightrender," said Queen Grace. "Though we are grateful for your attentiveness, your presence here is unnecessary."

Whispers hissed through the chamber.

"What? Didn't they summon her?"

"What bravery, telling the Nightrender she's not needed!"

"That doesn't mean it's wise. Don't you recall your lessons?"

The Nightrender's expression gave nothing away, no surprise at the queen's refusal, no reaction to the gossip scuttling around the room. Only Echo, the royal secretary, hurried to mark down every word from every person; her pen scratched on paper, even louder than the whispers.

"I must disagree," said the Nightrender, lowering her hands to her sides. "I have seen the Malstop, and it is weakening. An Incursion is imminent. Surely your audiences must be filled with the worries of villagers from the southwest. Every town within a day's walk of the Malstop will be seeing signs."

King Opus forced a smile, one that nobody, not even the Nightrender, could perceive as genuine. "Happily, the Malstop is as secure as it has ever been. The nearby villages have reported nothing unusual, and my own patrols bring only good news."

That was true, but only because the king had decided not to hear the bad news.

"Then your patrols lie," said the Nightrender. "The rancor press ever closer to your people, King Highcrown. Soon, the Malice will spill free across your land."

All through the chamber, there was a short, indrawn breath of shock.

"Further, I awakened in response to a summoning." The Nightrender took a step closer to the king and queen, and everyone tensed.

"We did not summon you." Queen Grace smiled, somewhat more naturally than her husband had managed, but even so, it was a far cry from warm.

"Then you are fools."

Stunned silence met the Nightrender's declaration, and everyone—absolutely everyone—wondered if she would murder them all where they stood.

"She's right." Rune lurched to his feet, drawing the stares to himself. "The Malstop *is* failing. Just look at it."

"Sit down." Opus's voice tightened. "Have some pride."

"We must pay heed to what is right in front of our faces." Rune was already an embarrassment to his family. He might as well fully commit. "We are running out of time to prevent the next Incursion. For too long, our policy has been to ignore problems—to deny they exist, to turn away those who raise the alarm. But that will no longer suffice. The Malice has already stolen our best hope for peace. What more will this court let it steal from future generations? *If* there are future generations."

A rumbling emanated from the audience, and Opus had risen to his feet. The king grabbed Rune's arm. "You will stop."

"There are more wars than our wars!" Rune pressed on. "There is the war between life and death. A rancor is running free somewhere in Deepway Woods, the Malstop is thinning, and we are wasting time. We *must* push back the Malice. That is why I summoned the Nightrender.

That is why I will be the first to enter the trials to join her Dawnbreakers—"

"We have not held Dawnbreaker trials in four centuries," interrupted the queen, also rising, "and we won't begin now. Court is dismissed. This audience is finished."

Everyone turned to the Nightrender, who had hardly moved during the exchange between Rune and his parents. Her sword remained sheathed, her wings tucked neatly behind her, but her face—she wore an expression of undisguised disgust.

"Mortals," she said. Then, without waiting to be expelled, she simply turned and walked away. Down the aisle. Out the doors. There, she paused and said over her shoulder, "I came here as a courtesy, not to ask permission." She knocked the rope barrier aside and vanished down the hall.

At her exit, the throne room went graveyard silent, everyone looking at one another for some sort of answer.

"She didn't mention the Red Dawn," a woman whispered. *"Do you think she's forgiven us?"*

"Why should she forgive us? We did nothing to her. She should wonder if we've forgiven her."

"Does she even see a difference between humans? We probably all look the same to her."

"Could what she said be true? About the Malstop?"

"Rune." Opus's voice was soft, meant only for the royal family. "This was burning dangerous."

"I'm not the one who told the Nightrender she wasn't needed." Rune closed his eyes a moment, gathering courage. Then, before he could think better of it, he pushed away from his throne, following the path down the aisle the Nightrender had taken. The crowd parted around him—the halfwit prince who'd summoned the Nightrender.

"Now what are you doing?" Opus's question carried over the hum of the audience.

Rune didn't look back as he strode out of the throne room. "I'm going to join her."

7.
Nightrender

Nightrender hadn't made it halfway out of the castle before clipped footfalls sounded right behind her. The steps were fast, determined, and considering the hostile reception in the throne room, it seemed possible that someone—an unwise someone—intended to attack her.

They would fail, of course. She was Nightrender and they were but mortal. She spun, drawing Beloved in the same motion.

The sword gleamed darkly. Obsidian. Perfect blackness. It was a Relic, created by the Numina eons ago, before their plane became inaccessible from this one. The blade was cut from a single piece of volcanic glass, its leather hilt wrapped in fine gold wire and topped with a flawless diamond on the pommel. Ancient, numinous magic reinforced the weapon, giving it the strength and flexibility to endure battle after battle.

At its tip, the young man went perfectly still. He was her summoner, the one who'd spoken out in support of her—and who'd been sitting beside the king and queen.

"Rune." She tilted her head. "Your surname is Highcrown."

A flush crept up his throat and cheeks, but he nodded. "I should have told you."

"You did say you know the royal family personally." Nightrender sheathed her sword, and it was subtle, but his shoulders dropped and his breath lengthened.

He was still frightened of her.

They'd *all* been frightened of her.

But why? She searched her memories for answers and found only a gaping hole, its edges crumbling away every time she prodded.

Typically, Nightrender did not allow herself to worry. Worry (mostly for mortals) might crush her if she let it. But now, here in this hall, summoned in secret, reviled by the court, completely alone in her duty, and unable to remember all of her past—the worry built like a shadow in the back of her mind.

"Tell me why you've followed me," Nightrender said. "Tell me why you summoned me, when no one else here would have."

Prince Rune stepped forward, cautiously at first, and then—as though satisfied she wasn't going to draw her sword again—more confidently until he stood just a breath away. "I need your help. The three kingdoms need your help."

Nightrender said nothing, because he clearly wanted praise for being smart enough to summon her, and she wasn't in the habit of rewarding people simply because they possessed basic survival instincts. She already rewarded them with their lives, saving them from the rancor every couple hundred years.

"My parents may not admit it," Prince Rune went on, "because they've closed their eyes to the truth. They won't allow anyone to even speak of another Incursion."

"I heard," Nightrender said.

Rune cringed. "I apologize for them. They were unacceptably rude to you."

Nightrender hadn't been aware there was an *acceptable* level of rudeness.

"But you're the only one who can stop this war with Embria."

"I do not choose sides in your battles." Nightrender didn't raise her voice or tilt it toward an emotion. It was unnecessary. Regardless, he flinched.

"That's not it," he insisted. "I'm not asking you to take a side. I'm asking you to save a life—no, many lives. My fiancée—"

"I don't save fiancées, either." *This* was why he'd summoned her? *This* was why he'd acted in secret? No wonder he hadn't been able to communicate clearly when she'd awakened him in the tower. His request was absurd. "My duties are simple: I fight the rancor so you don't have to. I prevent the Malice from growing. I fight real war so that you can all wage your petty battles in peace. Summoning me for any other purpose is punishable by death." She'd never needed to enforce that rule before, at least not that she could recall. Her memory was perfect—or rather, it had been until now.

Prince Rune seemed taken aback. "They're not petty to us," he said softly. And then, with more strength: "You owe us."

Nightrender bristled. "I owe you nothing." She had served the three kingdoms for thousands of years, and while they probably believed they gave her everything in return, they refused to give her the one thing she truly wanted: an end.

An end to their constant warring, to the rising rancor, to the *need* for her to keep coming back to solve the same problems over again. There was no hardship they endured that they had not caused themselves. She was so tired of it.

Nightrender started to turn away, but when the prince spoke again, his voice was dark. "You don't know what I'm talking about, do you?"

She stared at him. Did he know? Could he tell that she'd lost memories?

"What I mean to say," he said, a little more cautiously, "is that the three kingdoms have a chance for peace."

"You said the Malice stole that opportunity." She studied him again, searching for the truth. "Tell me what you want."

"My fiancée, Crown Princess Johanne Fortuin of Embria, is trapped in a malsite."

Two facts struck her. First, a Caberwilline prince was engaged to an Embrian princess. Those two kingdoms had been trying to slaughter each other for as long as there'd been kingdoms, but now they were talking *marriage*?

That was, they would be, if the princess wasn't trapped in a malsite.

Which brought her to the second, more alarming fact: people were getting trapped in malsites.

But she always cleared those spots before she went to sleep. Always. She would never be so careless—

But she couldn't *remember* cleansing them last time. So there was *another* hole in her memory. The thought sent a bolt of unease through her.

Perhaps there'd been an Incursion while she'd slept. "Tell me how long the malsites have been here."

The prince's tone went somber. "Four hundred years."

Nightrender drew in a breath. She hadn't missed an Incursion. She'd just . . . neglected her duty. Somehow. The unease deepened.

"They're all over the three kingdoms," Prince Rune said. "Like scars. We've adapted to live around them."

That must be why the people hated her. They'd been living in constant terror for four hundred years.

But that didn't make sense either. Surely she wouldn't have just *gone back to sleep* while people suffered and malice poisoned Salvation. And even if she had been so careless, mortals should have summoned her again to remove the malsites. They'd had four hundred years to do it.

"I see," said Nightrender. But she didn't. She didn't understand this at all. Nothing was as it had been before.

"It's your job to cleanse the malsites, isn't it?" Prince Rune glanced over his shoulder as voices rose in the throne room. When he looked at her again, worry filled his dark eyes. "We could start with the one where Princess Johanne is trapped. If she's still alive"—he swallowed hard—"then the alliance can move forward. We could end these *petty* wars."

Sarcasm. Mortals wielded it like a weapon.

Still, if it were possible to end their wars, if peace fell over Salvation, then the Malice might stop growing and she could have the end she craved.

"Tell me of this alliance."

As the noise in the throne room crescendoed, Prince Rune motioned for her to walk with him. "About three months ago, Embria sent dozens of doves, each with a piece of a letter. It took us days to put it together. I suppose they reasoned a messenger—a person—would have been killed before the letter reached us. But at last, we realized it proposed an alliance by marriage, because Ivasland intended to break the Winterfast Accords."

Nightrender's fists clenched.

The Winterfast Accords were the only thing all three kingdoms agreed upon: no one, no matter what, would use malice in their endless war. To do so would damn the entire continent, because uncontained malice spread, infecting everything in its path. Malice *destroyed*.

"If I can't rescue Princess Johanne," Prince Rune was saying, "then

Caberwill is going to attack Embria, and neither kingdom will be able to stop Ivasland."

"Caberwill has no cause to attack Embria."

"It would be a *preemptive* attack," the prince explained as they turned a corner. "Get them before they get us. Considering their princess was lost here, in the Deepway . . ."

That was such a mortal attitude—"*Get them before they get us*"—but they had been living with this hatred and distrust for thousands of years. Perhaps they couldn't help it anymore.

More pressing was the trouble with Ivasland. If Embria and Caberwill were embroiled in their own battle, Ivasland would be left unchecked.

If one kingdom finally conquers the others, suggested some dark part of her, ***then they'll stop trying to involve you in their every little dispute.***

Nightrender shook that feeling away. She was a neutral party, so she would not advance one kingdom's victory over the others. Still, she could not allow the use of malice on the battlefield. They had put her in an awkward position.

"What do you think?" Prince Rune asked. "Will you help me?"

"My focus should be on gathering Dawnbreakers and marching through the Soul Gate." Nightrender strode more quickly down the hall.

Prince Rune walked beside her, keeping up easily. "Is the Malstop going to collapse tomorrow? Or the day after?"

"No." She could feel the barrier from here—sense the thin spots, the soft places under constant attack from the inside—and it wasn't in danger of *imminent* collapse. But soon. Very soon. "The Malstop is weak, fracturing under the constant pressure of evil. I must destroy the rancor inside the Malice to ease the strain on the Malstop."

"Can't you stop the rancor from coming here?" he asked. "To this world, I mean."

"The Rupture sits within the Malice, but it isn't a door that can be opened or closed on a whim. One day, the Dark Shard and the laic plane will move out of phase. The gateway will close, preventing rancor from venturing here, but I don't know when that day will be. Until then, my excursions into the Malice are this: fighting rancor and lowering the pressure of evil inside. The Malstop will repair itself in time, but only if it isn't under constant attack."

"That doesn't seem like a very efficient system."

"Some battles are fought solely for the sake of resisting. Of enduring. Of surviving."

He glanced back the way they'd come, frowning. "I suppose."

"If I could prevent rancor from traveling through the Rupture, I would. As it is, I must always hope that someone summons me at the first sign of weakness in the Malstop, before rancor escape their prison."

The prince's jaw clenched. "I fear one already has. I believe that is what chased Princess Johanne into the malsite. Her lady-in-waiting described a monster."

As he repeated the descriptions—the barrel chest, the spines, the mushroom-gray flesh—a tightness grew around Nightrender's heart. "Indeed, it was a rancor. Princess Johanne has likely perished."

"I can't believe that," he said. "Not without seeing for myself. If we leave now, we can make it to the malsite by dusk."

Nightrender turned away and stepped into the stairwell that led to the shrine room.

"Help me rescue Princess Johanne, and my parents will have no choice but to listen to you! We can hold Dawnbreaker trials. You'll have everything you need to stop the Incursion. Armies. Obsidian. Anything."

That was a tempting offer, but could he deliver?

She reached the top of the stairs and stepped into the room. Some of the surfaces had been dusted, a few pieces of rotting wood removed. Light shone through the window and open balcony door, and a single potted morning glory sat beside the rail outside.

"Sorry it's not cleaner yet." Prince Rune walked in behind her. He seemed more at ease, now that they'd been talking. Perhaps she could win back the rest, eventually: the respect, the trust, the armies she needed. "Everything will be in order when we return. Well, it will be comfortable, at least. A place you can rest."

"I haven't agreed to go with you."

He flashed a tentative smile. "I think you will."

Nightrender studied him for a long moment, the soft brown of his eyes, the straight line of his nose, the strong set of his jaw. He was muscular—most Caberwilline princes and princesses were—and had the posture to go with years of martial training, but there was a gentleness to him, too, the sort of hopeful warmth that wasn't encouraged here.

"What do you think?" he asked.

She stepped deeper into the room and paused, head cocked, listening. Chewing. "I hear termites."

"Um." The prince glanced around, clearly confused. "I'll make sure the staff is aware."

"Tell me why they're not here now."

"The staff?"

She gave a single nod. "Clearly they began efforts to restore this place but left without finishing. I want to know why they're not here now."

He glanced out the balcony door, toward the morning glory. "They're afraid of you. Everyone is."

"Because I failed in my duty before. Because I did not cleanse the land of malsites."

He drew in a sharp breath. His brow knitted. But then, he nodded. "Yes. That has something to do with it."

That explanation didn't quite make sense, but mortals could be irrational. And since they had not summoned her in four hundred years, they could have forgotten that she was here to serve them. She was their sword against the dark.

"You summoned me in spite of the fear," Nightrender observed.

"My need was greater than my fear." He turned toward the shrine, still filthy with cobwebs and embedded dust. "I acted impulsively, but I would do it again."

If their anger at her—their fear—was because she had neglected to cleanse the malsites before, perhaps her fulfilling that duty now would appease them.

It wasn't choosing a side in the war, she reasoned. If, by saving his princess (assuming she was even alive), she helped an alliance, that would mean she had furthered a hope of peace. And it would mean, more simply, that she cleansed a malsite. She would cleanse them from Embria and Ivasland, too. All of Salvation would benefit from her awakening.

She would do this. And then she would uncover the truth about Ivasland. And then she would march into the Malice, having attended to the kingdoms equally and—hopefully—proven that they could trust her again. If she did everything right, perhaps they would send their warriors along with her and begin training Dawnbreakers again.

"Very well, Prince Rune." Nightrender drew herself straight, burying every single worry and fear—so foreign to her—beneath the armor of her duty. "Gather what supplies you need. For now, you will be my Dawnbreaker, and I will rescue your princess."

8.
Hanne

It was impossible to say what saved her.

The obsidian? Her resourcefulness?

The rancor's good mood?

Regardless, the rancor had not immediately killed Hanne, for which she was enormously grateful. Instead, it perched on a thick tree branch and peered down at her, its eyes glowing a sickly yellow.

In the morning light, its mushroom-colored skin gleamed damp, wet with dew or sweat or something even more vile. Though it had no nose—just raw, open holes in the middle of its face—it sniffed the air in her direction. Its mouth gaped and two tongues flickered out, as though it were tasting Hanne's terror.

At first, she did nothing but tremble on the ground, waiting to be devoured or violently melted into black sludge like Lord Bearhaste. But after an hour, when the creature made no move against her, she chanced a sip of water. It helped clear her head. And then she darted for her pile of obsidian jewelry. Most of it was already on her person, but she'd been sleeping with the remaining pieces around her like some sort of mystical barrier. More than anything in the world, in that moment, she wished for her crown. The jagged tines of obsidian could be broken off and made into daggers, and she could attack the thing.

At least, she wanted to imagine it was possible.

Doing nothing became too much, and finally, after another hour, she began to move about her prison, forging and gathering water, all her senses alert to the threat lurking above. Though the rancor did nothing but watch her, every move she made crackled with caution. Anytime she had to step closer to the creature, she shook, and she charted the quickest route back to her tiny wall of obsidian.

Adrenaline kept her awake the rest of the day and all through the night. She was hyper aware of its presence. Of the thousand questions straining her mind—why was it watching her, could *it* get out of the malsite?—the most important one was this: *Was it going to kill her?*

By the next morning, the answer seemed to be no.

The rancor hadn't shifted from its place. In the stillness of the forest, she could hear its breath rasping in and out, hear lines of saliva as they dripped and hissed against the leaves, its spit acid.

Then, as the sun worked its way toward noon (inside the time slip, not outside), the rancor spoke.

That voice.

It was the crunch of a cockroach carapace underfoot. The keen of a dying creature. The sense of standing over a vast, black emptiness. Overwhelming and uncompromising madness.

Hanne slapped her hands over her ears and shrieked. Tears squeezed from her eyes, and her head felt as though it would explode.

The rancor closed its mouth and the pain stopped.

Hanne doubled over, her breath coming in quick, frantic gasps as she struggled to reorient herself in the world. "What do you want?" she choked, even though she didn't want it to speak again. "Why did you trap me?"

She supposed she couldn't be sure this was the same rancor as before, but sightings were rare. Rare as in nonexistent for hundreds of years. Surely she wasn't unlucky enough to meet *two* rancor in her lifetime.

The maddening cacophony of its voice struck again, this time with the black buzzing of a swarm of cicadas, the scrape of claws on iron.

Hanne cried out and pressed her palms against her ears, but it wasn't enough. Another sound came through as well, almost like words. Almost: *"Do you want to live?"* But she couldn't be sure. And when she pulled her hands away from her head, blood dotted her skin.

She sank down into her bedroll and tried not to sob, but never had she been forced to endure this level of fear for so long. Never had she felt so much like prey.

Tuluna, she prayed, *tell me how to survive this.*

But if the patron Numen of Embria was listening, they didn't respond. They hadn't said anything to her since she'd been trapped in the malsite.

Now is when I need you, she tried, but only silence answered.

For several tense minutes, nothing happened between Hanne and the rancor. Then the creature opened its mouth again and made the maddening noise, but now it was . . . not more bearable, because her ears rang and bled, but more understandable. Now, she clearly heard words.

"Do you want to live?" it asked.

The question hit her in the gut. Of course. Of course she wanted to live. Who wouldn't, especially when the alternative was being mauled to death by a rancor? What was more, she needed to get to Brink, where Nadine was likely imprisoned. If Hanne didn't survive this, what would happen to her cousin? Rune might not harm her, but Queen Grace and King Opus had dark reputations. Even if she were traded back to Embria, there were Hanne's own parents, who had never liked Nadine. . . .

The rancor stared at her, unblinking, and suddenly Hanne remembered the Winterfast Accords, the alliance, and the peace she intended to build. Salvation was eating itself alive, but Hanne could bring an end to the warring—if she lived.

"Answer," the creature demanded.

Hanne pushed aside a whisper of concern. The cost of *yes* was a worry for tomorrow; the cost of *no* was immediate death.

With a shuddering breath, and blood dripping down her jaw, Hanne nodded.

"Then listen," it said, "to everything I have to say."

Limbs shaking, mind rebelling from this idea of *conversation* with a rancor, Hanne climbed to her feet and made herself as strong and steely as possible. "I'm listening."

"Your enemies seek to destroy you."

Every word the rancor spoke was torture. It must have been fully aware; that was the only reason Hanne could think of as to why it was telling her things she already knew.

"Your enemies in the south are creating a device that captures malice. Transports it."

Hanne's breath caught. This was it: Ivasland's betrayal of the Winterfast Accords. No kingdom, not in all of recorded history, had dared use malice against another. It was simply inconceivable. But not to

Ivasland, apparently. Queen Abagail and King Baldric had no shame, no morals or decency.

"The machine is not yet complete. At the current pace, it will be finished by the autumn equinox."

Then there was still time to stop it—if only she could get to Brink, marry Rune, and lead her armies south.

Slowly, as though making an effort to avoid startling her, the rancor shifted its weight. The tree groaned. "You will help Ivasland finish the machine."

"What? No!" She must have heard it wrong. She intended to *prevent* Ivasland from using malice against Embria. There was no way she would *help* them achieve their goals.

"You said you want to live." The rancor's tongues flickered out. "You will do as I say."

Hanne shuddered, but kept her gaze pinned on the creature. "I won't *help* my enemies break the Winterfast Accords."

"Your treaty was breached years ago. Centuries ago." The too-wide mouth curved up into a terrible grin, and the air around it seemed to stutter. "You will do as I say."

It was a bad idea to argue with a rancor, she knew that, but no one ordered Johanne Fortuin about. No one. (Aside from the king and queen of Embria, but that was different.)

"Kill me if you wish," Hanne said, "but I will not do your bidding."

The rancor's jaw unhinged, giving Hanne a view of row after row of teeth. Drool slid out of its mouth, ropes of it dripping onto the tree branch and blackening the bark.

Bile rolled in Hanne's stomach.

"It doesn't matter what you do to me." Her voice shook, but she said the words, and she meant them. "I will never help my enemies destroy my kingdom."

The space between them flickered, and before Hanne could so much as summon a scream, the rancor stood over her.

Hanne held her breath, heart pounding, torn between running and freezing. But she couldn't outrun the rancor, and anyway, she was trapped in the malsite; there was nowhere to run. So she stayed as still as she could, like a rabbit hoping to avoid a hawk's talons. The rancor's breath was hot and sharp, cutting through her lungs as she took in a shallow gasp of air.

Slowly, the rancor reached forward and stretched its clawed hand across Hanne's face. She squeezed her eyes shut; a whimper escaped her throat, and she hated herself for it. She had to look. She had to face it. But when she opened her eyes—she wasn't in the malsite anymore.

An unending black expanse stretched all around her, like a sky that had swallowed every one of its stars. Now all that remained was . . . emptiness, an endless swath of hunger and darkness.

No sound carried. No scent caught her nose. She was alone, but for the yawning black sky.

Shuddering, she sank to the slick, glasslike surface where she'd appeared. It was such a small space, with jagged edges that would surely cut her if she touched them. Her head throbbed with the breadth of all this nothing around her.

A *crack* shattered the silence, and ruddy light exploded across the sky. Below her, to her sides: there were other shards, larger than hers, and these were not empty. Hanne was too far to see details, but as her watering gaze swept across the bloody expanse, she caught the suggestion of towers and bridges that spanned the empty space between shards. She saw movement, *things* flickering from place to place.

Thunk. Her shard jolted, sending her sprawling, sliding toward the edge. She scrambled to hold on, but the surface was too slick; she couldn't slow herself. Soon she'd reach the lip.

Before she could so much as scream, Hanne slipped off the side, the shard's dagger-like edges slicing her body.

She fell.

And fell.

And stopped.

Breath whooshed out of her. When she finally managed to open her eyes again, she was in the malsite, the rancor drawing back. Within a heartbeat, it was up in the tree again—away from her obsidian—and glaring at her with those yellow eyes.

"What was that?" Hanne rasped. Her legs were so weak. She wanted to drop to the ground and catch her breath, but not with the rancor watching.

"The Dark Shard." The rancor shifted, not quite hiding the way its skin had turned red and mottled where it had been close to the obsidian. "Now," it said, "I will tell you how to complete the malice device. You will go to Ivasland and offer to help. I will tell you *exactly* what to do, and you will do it."

"Why did you show me the Dark Shard?"

Its nose holes flared. "I want you to know that I can put you there. Forever."

Hanne's heart thundered in her ears as two paths stretched out before her: obey the rancor's commands and live, or resist it and be trapped—either here or in the Dark Shard—for the rest of her short life.

"Do you want to live?" the rancor asked.

She hardly had to think about it. She just said the first word that came to her mind: "Yes."

The rancor talked for the rest of the day.

Hanne could only look at it for seconds at a time. Otherwise, she started to get lost in the way its mouth stretched too wide, or the way the air around it rippled with heat or slips of angry time. If she looked at it for too long, she knew she would lose her mind. It was hard enough *listening* to the thing.

But listen she did, and look when necessary, because her choices were few.

Obey and live.

Defy and die.

And Johanne Fortuin needed to live. A single mal-device could not tip the scales of fate—but the combined might of Embria and Caberwill *would*.

Only she could unite the kingdoms.

When night fell, the rancor said, "Do you understand everything I've told you?"

Hanne had remained on her feet for the duration of the rancor's lecture. Yes, *lecture* was probably the best word for it. It hadn't asked if she needed clarification, or given her space to ask questions. It had merely paused its address long enough, now and again, to give her head a few needed moments of respite, and then it continued. And through the pain, Hanne had listened to every word because her life depended on it.

Did she understand everything it had told her?

She looked up at the creature, which had not moved since it had shoved that vision of the Dark Shard into her mind. Its obsidian-induced wounds were healing, and it remained a nightmare against her eyes, a violence that followed her even when she blinked. So many teeth. Such jagged claws. It stared hungrily down, all predator.

Blood crusted down the sides of her face, clumped in her blond hair, and stained her filthy blue dress like rust. Her ears rang and her head throbbed, but the rancor didn't care about any of that. Only:

"Yes." She made her voice as strong as it could be, given the circumstances. "I will go to Ivasland and do everything I can to help them finish the mal-device using the information you've given me."

"I will know if you fail," the rancor said. "You will not like the consequences."

Again, Hanne's thoughts flashed back to the Dark Shard and the overpowering sense of terror she'd felt—not just for her life, but for whatever was left of her soul. "I will not fail."

EXCERPT FROM NADINE HOLT'S DIARY, DECIPHERED FROM EMBRIAN MICRO-CODE

Hanne would warn me against writing anything that might be discovered, even though I'll only use the royal micro-code, but I'm in Brink without her, and I cannot confide in the other ladies-in-waiting—not without them losing hope of her return. I must pour out my feelings somewhere, as the others pour out their feelings on me.

I have been very lonely here. As Hanne's primary lady-in-waiting, I inhabit the suite she and I would have shared until her wedding, while Lea, Maris, and Cecelia reside in the suite next door. I almost asked to be placed with them, but such a request would have reflected poorly on me—and therefore Hanne. So I stay here, surrounded by all of Hanne's belongings, everything she would have needed for her wedding.

Fortunately, the other ladies and I have been given leave to move between suites, and I went to them this morning to break our fasts. We should have spoken of important matters, but instead, our meal was quiet. Subdued.

No one knows how to feel or how to behave without Hanne here to guide them. In her absence, they've begun looking to me. What do I think? What do I suggest?

It's because I know Hanne best. It's because Hanne shared her plans with me.

So, even though it pains me to do anything but kneel by my fire and pray for Hanne's safe release, I will do what I know she would want: move forward with our plans. I have the list of names taken from Devon Bearhaste, Caberwilline people willing to work on Hanne's behalf. It may be difficult to fully persuade them to her side when she isn't here, but perhaps they can be won by promises of her favor when she returns to us.

Because she must *return. She must. Hanne is the strongest of us, the most tenacious.*

Even Prince Rune believes there is a chance, for he summoned the Nightrender.

I saw her this morning. Just as the other ladies and I were finishing breakfast, word went out and we all hurried into the throne room, where the Nightrender intended to present herself to the king and queen of Caberwill.

The Nightrender is a frightening creature, almost as terrible to behold as the monster I saw in the woods. She has pale porcelain skin, cobalt veins, and coal-black hair and wings. That sword was strapped to her back, and several times this morning I thought she might use it against us.

She restrained herself, however, even when Queen Grace told her that she was not needed and tried to send her away. It makes me wonder if Queen Grace and King Opus really want the alliance. Does it benefit them if Hanne is dead? That is something I must keep in mind as the other ladies and I work on Hanne's behalf.

I know the Caberwilline monarchs don't care about Hanne herself. They've never met her.

Most people don't understand her. They fear her. They obey her. But few make the effort required to see who she truly is.

Hanne has always been a tool for her parents to use. They sharpened her so much that I was afraid she would break, but she never did. In spite of all the ways they molded her into the daughter they wanted, she resolutely refused to become them. She desires peace.

That is why I will move forward with her plans. I miss her so much, but whatever she is doing now, I know that she wants me to move toward her goals. So this afternoon, I will put all my feelings aside, and I will begin doing Hanne's work.

9.
Rune

It seemed impossible that something had actually gone his way.

The Nightrender—the actual Nightrender—had heard his case and agreed to help. It was almost too good to be true. She hadn't even tried to kill him.

Optimism was something of a foreign feeling to Rune, but as he left the Nightrender's tower and went to his quarters to grab his pack, there was a strange lightness in his step. He would—rather, the Nightrender would—rescue Princess Johanne, and the war against Embria would be called off, and the war against Ivasland would be called on. Together, they would ensure the Winterfast Accords were secure, and then they would destroy the malsites and—perhaps—the entire Malice.

It was a perfect plan.

He smiled as he strode into his apartments. Then the smile fell.

His parents were waiting in the parlor.

Of course. He should have expected them.

The strange lift in his chest evaporated as he took in their postures: his father, sitting at the table, head resting on his fist; and his mother, standing behind the king, her hands clasped behind her back. The weight of paternal disappointment hung heavy over the room.

Rune considered running back out the door, embarking on his mission with the Nightrender without his personal provisions, but his father's glare pinned him in place.

"What," said the queen, "were you thinking? How could you invite that—that thing into our castle?"

Opus cleared his throat, straightening as he said, "My love, we've talked about this. She's a person, too, and she has very good hearing, according to the legends."

She has extremely *good hearing, if she can hear termites chewing*, Rune thought.

Grace drew in a long breath. "Very well. Person." Then she turned on Rune again. "You invited that *person* into our castle against our wishes. You put everyone in immense danger. Your sisters could have been—"

Rune shut the hall door. He would have to face his parents sooner or later, and, when it came to them, nothing had ever been gained by procrastinating. "I summoned the Nightrender because it was the necessary thing to do."

The king rose to his feet, and the queen moved to his side. With the bookcases in the background, the hand-polished bloodwood paneling on the lower third of every wall, and the diamonds affixed to sconces, the pair would have looked very regal. The crown prince's chambers—Rune's chambers now—were quite grand.

It was their unfettered anger that wrecked the scene. "We should have spoken about it first—as a *family*," the queen seethed.

"I tried. You dismissed me out of hand, because you would prefer to go to war against Embria."

"We would *prefer* you to marry Lady Nadine."

"You rejected that option because you believe that Embria will not see her as an acceptable substitute for Princess Johanne. And I agree: there can be no peace without the princess."

"And so we must have war," the king pronounced, the queen nodding solemnly. "Not by preference, but by necessity."

Rune clenched his jaw.

"Now, as for the Nightrender. You've put all our lives at risk, and there will be consequences for your actions. Do not think you can get away with this reckless behavior."

Rune had never gotten away with any sort of behavior—reckless or otherwise—in his life. This moment was no different. "A war against Embria is just as reckless, Father. It puts the entire kingdom at risk."

"How dare you—" Grace started.

Rune didn't let her finish. "The Nightrender has agreed to help me rescue Princess Johanne."

That quieted both of them.

"I talked to her," Rune said. "I told her what is at stake. She's agreed to help."

"What of the Red Da—"

"Not an issue."

Opus glanced at Grace. "She swears she is not going to—"

"No," Rune said. "She will do her duty, and that's all."

"I don't trust her." Grace lifted her chin. "She's deceived Caberwillines before. She may change her mind."

Rune had no evidence that the Nightrender *wouldn't* change her mind and revisit the events of four hundred years ago, but having spent time with her, he felt certain of her intentions. Something deep within him *knew* that she was here only to fight the rancor, not to harm mortals. But he kept that to himself; his intuition would make no difference to his parents' opinions. Instead, he said, "We'll leave for the malsite immediately, and return tomorrow with Princess Johanne."

"Oh no." Grace stepped toward him, her eyes narrowed. "You will not be going anywhere with the Nightrender. Send one of your guards, if you must. Or Grand General Emberwish will assign someone."

"It's too late. I've already given my word, and she's named me her Dawnbreaker."

"No," Grace breathed. "No, you cannot be a Dawnbreaker. Royalty does not enter the contest."

"Perhaps not historically." Rune lifted his chin. "But these are unprecedented times. There were no trials."

"That's not the point," Opus said. "Becoming a Dawnbreaker during an Incursion is a death sentence."

Red flared in the corners of Rune's vision. "I thought we weren't having an Incursion."

"We are not," Opus said sternly. "But the Nightrender is here, and she'll expect you to follow her into the Malice, where there *are* rancor and other terrors. You will surely die in there. Then what of our line? What of Caberwill?"

"You don't know that I'll die," Rune shot back. "I've been training since I was a small child, and under your direction. If you don't think I'm good enough—"

"No one is good enough to survive the Malice." Grace's jaw was tight, but slowly, deliberately, she let go of the tension and spoke more evenly. "But even if you were to survive an expedition into the Malice, you'd still be bound as a Dawnbreaker for the next ten years. We need an heir, not a hero."

He'd had his chance to be a hero, after all, and failed when it counted the most.

Rune pushed away the pain of missing his brother, tucked it back into the corner of his heart it always occupied. "It doesn't have to be an entire decade," he said. "The Nightrender said *for now* I would be her Dawnbreaker. She knows the traditions better than any of us; I've passed no tests, completed no trials. This is a temporary honor. She'll release me when we've accomplished our goals—and probably ask for the regular trials to renew, so that we're never in this position again. But someone needs to join her, to show her that we are still good people, and no one else volunteered."

"That's not fair," Grace said. "You did this behind our backs. You made the decision and forced the rest of us to scramble in your wake. Is that the kind of king you will be?"

Rune's chest went tight with the pain of those words, with the unspoken reminder that he hadn't been meant to be king. He'd been the spare. The shield who protected the heir.

They said they didn't blame him, that the fault resided with Ivasland and its assassin, but Rune knew the truth: they saw him as a sorry replacement for his brother, and if someone had to die between him and Opi—well, Opus Highcrown IV should have lived.

That preference was a secret, shameful thing, he knew. They never spoke of it aloud, most likely never even allowed the feelings to fully form. But Rune could see it in their eyes when they looked at him, hear it in their voices when they spoke of his future, and sense it in the air around them like waves of grief that would never recede.

He often felt he should have grown a callus over his heart to protect it from that sting, but it hurt every time. Rune, too, had lost the person he loved most in the world.

"I want to be a king worthy of the crown." He pushed past his parents and went into his bedroom, where he grabbed his run-pack, the one he always kept fat with fresh supplies whenever he traveled. It was the only thing he required for this journey.

Rune slung it over his shoulder and started for the door, but his parents both stood in the way, immovable this time.

"There is no Incursion." In spite of Opus's firm words, the anger seemed to have drained from him. "However, as you noted, we are missing a princess, and wars *are* costly endeavors. You are convinced the Nightrender will do as she promised? She will rescue Johanne Fortuin?"

"That seems to be her goal," Rune agreed.

"Having the Nightrender on our side could help us win—"

"She will not fight our wars," Rune said. "She is not ours to command."

Opus looked as though he wanted to argue that point—she'd come *here*, to Honor's Keep, and she owed Caberwill for the atrocities of four hundred years ago, but all he said was, "Very well. I abhor what you've done, but it *is* done, and there's nothing I can do to change that, is there?"

Finally, they were understanding. Perhaps Rune was getting through to them after all.

"Try to rescue the princess," Grace said. "If nothing else, perhaps your new friend will allow us to proceed with the alliance. And should a few malsites be destroyed along the way, I would not object."

Rune nodded.

"You are responsible for her, though," Grace went on, holding his gaze. "Whatever actions she takes are yours to answer for. And once Princess Johanne is recovered and the malsites cleared, *you* will be the one to put the Nightrender back to sleep."

Rune drew in a sharp breath. "She will want to go into the Malice, Mother. She believes there is an Incursion, and she will expect me to help her end it."

Grace smiled coldly. "Then you will need to convince her of the truth."

Rune swallowed hard. He wanted to push, but arguing with his parents never got him anywhere. No, he needed to get the princess first, and then—when his parents saw that he had accomplished this goal—he could persuade them to let the Nightrender stop the Incursion. He just needed to work them one step at a time.

Anyway, did they really think that he could force the Nightrender to sleep if she wasn't ready?

"Succeed. Succeed in rescuing the princess," said the king, "and you will avert this war, just as you wanted."

Anxiety deepened in Rune's chest. "There's a chance I will fail," he admitted. "I don't know what kind of malsite it is." Or if the rancor had killed her and left her body inside the malsite, just to torment them.

The king nodded slowly. "Do not fail, my son. We may have gotten our way with the Crown Council before, when you were elevated to heir, but they blame you for losing Princess Johanne. If you can get her back, if you can preserve this treaty, you will have proven yourself suited for kingship. But if you can't . . ."

Oh.

Rune swallowed back a knot of unease, then nodded. "I understand."

A moment later, after the king and queen had left, Rune found himself staring at the closed door that led to the room Princess Johanne would occupy once they were married.

She had to be alive. She *had* to be.

10.
NIGHTRENDER

"Are you ready?" Prince Rune emerged from the stables, a pair of charcoal-gray geldings following on leads. One horse was so dark he was nearly black.

Nightrender didn't deign to answer. She swung herself onto the darker horse and motioned for the prince to hurry.

"Why do you—" But Prince Rune's mouth snapped shut. He nodded, then he clipped his pack to the other gelding's saddle.

Well, if he'd had a preference, he should have spoken up.

"We can take the mountain roads down." Prince Rune mounted the lighter horse. "Rather than the main road through the city."

She cocked her head and frowned. "You're embarrassed to be seen with me."

"No!" He cleared his throat. "I mean, of course not. But if people see you, they'll worry about what that means."

"They should. The Malstop is weakening and your king and queen have no plans to stop the Incursion. If not for the princess's disappearance, even you would have chosen to do nothing." She squeezed her horse's sides and directed him toward the main avenue. "Let them see me." She didn't bother to look over her shoulder. "Let them know there is danger, but that I am here to protect them."

Prince Rune didn't move.

"You have to squeeze your horse's flanks," she provided. "Otherwise he will stay put."

"I know how to ride. But I—" He glanced over his shoulder just as a half dozen guards emerged from the stables, all astride horses of their own. "I may be your Dawnbreaker," he said resignedly, "but I'm still the crown prince and these people follow me everywhere."

She looked at the six of them in turn, and they looked back at her, not quite disguising their trepidation. "It is entirely possible you will all die today. If you do not wish to risk that, then leave now."

"That's a horrible speech," Prince Rune muttered.

But they deserved the warning. Too many men had followed her into battle and died. She could not let this moment be an exception just because they were not *her* men.

None of the guards moved, and one said, "We are sworn to accompany His Highness in every situation. There isn't one of us who would forsake his duties."

The other five nodded, although a couple of them frowned in a way that indicated they weren't pleased about following the prince into *this* particular situation.

"This is Lieutenant Swifthand," Prince Rune said, indicating a tall, broad man, his skin tanned and reddened from time in the sun—the one who'd spoken before. "He's the commander for today. Usually it would be John Taylor, but he'll have to meet us later."

Nightrender wouldn't turn down more help. She'd been denied her proper Dawnbreakers, so these men would have to do. Even though they probably *would* die, should they encounter that rancor.

"John is in trouble," Prince Rune said quietly, as he nudged his horse toward hers. "He failed to notice that I wasn't in my rooms last night. Once he's back with me, I'll never get rid of him."

Why should he confide in her? That was curious.

In silence, they left the small but green castle grounds. Dour statues watched them pass until they rode through the outer gate. Then, the residents of Brink emerged from their houses to stare.

"That's the Nightrender!" a young woman whispered.

"How do you know?" asked a man.

"She has wings, you dolt. And that sword!" The young woman shuddered.

And so the whispers went, some filled with disbelief, while others commented on her armor or weaponry, and a few on her looks. Most wondered what her presence meant.

"Will the rancor attack?" a child asked, her face half hidden behind a halo of black curls. She clutched a small glass bottle of obsidian dust, which was tied on a yellow ribbon around her neck.

"No," said her mother. "Certainly not."

"Then why is the Nightrender here? The Red Dawn—" The rest was hastily cut off. The mother pressed her hand over her daughter's mouth as, at the same moment, she looked up and caught Nightrender's gaze.

The mother said nothing else—just took her child and left.

Nightrender faced forward again.

They hate you, murmured the voice. ***They'd rather die than allow you to help them.***

She pushed the dark whisper aside. Perhaps they hated her now, but they would be grateful when she cleared away the malsites and they could move freely about their world again. Everything would go back to normal . . . she hoped.

"Does it bother you?" Prince Rune asked quietly.

She wasn't supposed to lie. The Numina generally didn't approve of falsehoods, and since she was closer to them than most, she should be first to follow their commands. Instead of admitting the truth, she just set her jaw and gazed straight ahead; she would not show her discomfort.

Traffic on the Brink Way moved aside as they headed down the street toward the lower parts of the city—the poorer sections. Various odors rose up: tanning and dyeing, slaughtering and smoking, and plenty of other things people preferred to keep out of the way. All down the road, people stopped what they were doing to get a look at the pair riding by: Crown Prince Rune Highcrown and Nightrender.

It was well into the afternoon when they finished navigating all the switchbacks and the road widened on the foothills. Green and shimmering summer heat spread before them, deceptively peaceful as far as they could see.

But she could feel the Malstop to the southwest, crackling against the dark energies contained within. And when she looked, there was the thinning dome rising into the blue infinity, surrounded by two dozen long-abandoned guard towers.

They really had given up trying to protect themselves in any meaningful way.

Nightrender glanced at the prince. "I believe we have sufficiently shown off for your people. If you'd like, I could fly ahead—"

"No," he said. "We stay together."

She shrugged. "It's your marriage. If she ever finds out she could have been set free an hour earlier, you're the one who will have to explain it."

He gave her a look that suggested he was well aware of how terrible this marriage would be. Then, they urged their mounts into a long, easy gallop. The horses were more than happy to oblige; sweat formed on their necks and flanks.

Once, a thousand years ago, her soul shard had bred horses for the Embrian monarchy; Nightrender had loved riding ever since. Though it wasn't freedom in the same way as flying, there was a deep connection to the earth as the horse's hooves thumped the ground—one-two-three-four—and then an incredible moment of lift when every part of the horse hung in the air. It amazed her how a creature big enough to carry a human could not only walk on those spindle-fine legs, but run—almost fly.

They ran for a league or so before the horses huffed and slowed to a trot, and then walked for a stretch.

"Tell me what happened during the last Incursion." Nightrender hadn't minded the quiet between them—she was a solitary creature, generally—but mortals often felt more at ease if they were engaged in conversation. Besides, she needed answers, and they were several horse lengths ahead of the guards. They could speak in relative privacy.

Prince Rune gave her a sideways glance. "Surely you remember better than I could tell you."

"I want to hear what you believe happened." It wasn't a lie, not exactly.

"All right." He glanced over his shoulders—at the guards following—then pulled his horse alongside hers. "Before I begin, though, I have to say that I don't think you'll like the story people have been telling."

"I will not punish you for being the messenger, Prince Rune. You may speak freely."

He flashed a tight smile, but didn't quite look convinced. "I don't know everything. Most of the details are lost because the people in a position to know them died."

This definitely didn't begin like a story she was going to enjoy.

"There were signs of an Incursion, and so you were summoned. You were sent to a place called Sunview."

"I remember Sunview." Nightrender's heart twisted painfully. Sunview hadn't been an important town. There'd been no mine attached, no industry beyond a few farms, a granary, and a blacksmith and cobbler. It hadn't even been close to a main road. No, Sunview had just been a peaceful little town, filled with peaceful people.

Its most notable feature was that it happened to be close to the Malstop.

Nightrender had seen a lot of death over the millennia, but that scene had been uniquely terrible. By the time she'd been summoned and sent to Sunview, it was too late, and her attending Dawnbreakers—warriors who'd bloodied their swords in countless battles—had wept at the sight. The entire town had been drenched in malice, rancor stalking in the shadows. Houses had become gaping skulls, while streets peeled themselves out of the dirt and wrapped themselves around people, squeezing like pythons. It was all blood and pulverized bone, with no one to save, nor remains to be burned.

She'd hunted the rancor and killed them, but not before they mauled three of her Dawnbreakers to death. She'd barely learned the men's names, but felt each death as deeply as though she'd known them a hundred years. It was always that way between her and her warriors.

Then, heart heavy, she'd doused the entire town of Sunview in kindlewater and hurled in a torch. The fire had blazed for a day and a half, burning up every trace of the horror.

All this, she kept to herself. People didn't generally want to hear about the messy parts of being their champion. They wanted her to be the righteous fury of the Numina's holy light made flesh. They wanted their victory *clean*. No dead children to burn; no towns turned to ash; no one to mourn.

"Right," said the prince, still blissfully under the illusion that she was untouched by human loss. "Those were only the first of the rancor to escape. There was a thin spot in the Malstop no one had noticed, and rancor had been slamming themselves against it until they got free. After a half dozen more attacks, you told the people of all three kingdoms to withdraw into their cities. Not everyone obeyed. Thousands of lives were lost when people refused to evacuate—"

Nightrender shook her head. "Not all were given the means to evacuate. The rulers of the time hadn't prepared for such an invasion, and I cannot be everywhere at once. The rancor were too numerous by then." That was why they were to summon her at the *first* sighting. At the first *hint*.

Waiting meant death.

Prince Rune paused to consider that—the idea that monarchs and nobles wouldn't have ensured everyone's survival—and a frown turned down his mouth. "All right. Well, everything escalated from there. You tried to save as many as you could, but it was never going to be enough. Not with the Malstop flickering and malsites popping up across the kingdoms. So you took the Dawnbreakers through the Soul Gate."

She could almost remember that. It was her normal procedure, when there was no more she could do from the outside. But the details were fuzzy, blending with expeditions into the Malice before that. Her memories spanned thousands of years, like stars on the dark scroll of her mind. For most people, it would have been easy to mix the different timelines, but she'd never had trouble before this.

"Tell me what happened then," she whispered.

"Some of your warriors started coming back through the Soul Gate. Most of them were near death—horribly wounded. They said you had sent them back, because whatever you found in the Malice was more terrible than you'd anticipated."

Nightrender frowned. More terrible than rancor? But what . . .

A face tore through her memory, horrible and twisted, with a thousand too many teeth and alabaster flesh—

Then the memory was gone, flashed out like a dead star.

But it had been there. Just a moment ago. She remembered remembering, and now it was nowhere to be found, not in any corner of her mind. Memories didn't just vanish like that. They couldn't.

"Nightrender?" Prince Rune's voice came from just up ahead. "Are you all right?"

She'd stopped moving.

Her grip was too tight around the soft leather reins, and her horse's head was pulled tall, as though he sensed the wrongness, too.

"Are you all right?" Prince Rune asked again.

"I forgot something." Hollowness yawned through her.

He frowned, like he thought she meant something had slipped her mind or she'd left something important in the castle and needed to fly back to get it, but when she didn't say anything else, his eyes hardened as he glanced beyond her—toward the guards—and then looked back at her. His voice was soft, so that no one would overhear. "Something is wrong with your memory, isn't it? That's why you wanted me to tell you what happened."

She couldn't deny it.

And she should probably tell *someone* that she wasn't completely well. The prince was her summoner, her sole Dawnbreaker. She had no one else.

"I'm struggling to remember the last time I was here," she admitted, her voice equally quiet. "There are pinholes in my memory. I remember lifetimes before this, billions of moments both large and small, but as for the events of my previous awakening: I have almost nothing."

It was a dangerous thing, her losing her memory like this. If she couldn't draw upon her centuries of knowledge and experience, then what hope did she have of protecting humanity from this impending Incursion?

"A minute ago," Prince Rune said, "when you forgot something. It just happened, didn't it? Just then."

She pressed her mouth into a line, unwilling to say more, even to her Dawnbreaker. If anyone—even Prince Rune—knew too much of this, future generations might refuse to summon her, believing she'd been incapacitated.

They might be right.

The gaps in her memory were growing.

"Tell me what happened inside the Malice—what kind of trouble I faced."

If Prince Rune knew she was dodging his question, he didn't confront her. He just nudged his horse and they started west again. "The stories all say that you came back from the Malice and you were furious. But then"—he looked ahead, hard determination on his face—"then you returned to Winterfast Island and went back to sleep."

"Without clearing the malsites." It wasn't a question. Obviously she hadn't cleared them. No, it was a statement of disbelief.

The prince nodded, still avoiding looking at her, and she had the strongest feeling that he was . . . not lying, but omitting something of significance—something he now knew she couldn't remember.

"You're right," she said. "I don't like those answers."

They ran the horses a few more times hoping to reach the malsite before sunset, but either they'd left too late or the prince was terrible at distances, because it was dark when they arrived on the stretch of road where the caravan had stopped for lunch the other day.

It was a stretch of road like any other, completely unremarkable except for the broken brush and trampled grass where the prince and his guards had gone into the forest.

"It's too dark for the horses." Prince Rune dropped to his feet. His guards followed suit. "We should leave them here."

Nightrender brushed some of the sweat off her mount and guided him toward a stream that ran alongside the road. "I'll return soon," she promised, only to realize that Prince Rune was watching her with a faint smile.

He ducked his face and fished through one of his packs. "I like horses, too." Then he produced a small metal tube and shook it until it emitted a buttery-gold light from one end.

"Tell me what that is."

"It's a lightrod. Ivasland alchemy." He twisted one end and slid out a long, fully enclosed glass vial. Glowing liquid sloshed inside. "When the chemicals mix, they make light for about an hour. Then they separate and you have to shake it again. They come in all sorts of shapes, mostly globes, but these are good for keeping the glare out of your eyes." When he slid the vial back into the tube and replaced the cap, the light formed a sharp beam ahead of him. "The metal tube has mirrors inside, to focus the light."

He offered the lightrod to her, but she waved it away.

"I can see in the dark."

"Oh." He hefted his pack onto his shoulders. "Of course you can. Well, for those of us who aren't part cat, the chemical lights are helpful. Safer than torches." Indeed, his guards all pulled lightrods out of their packs as well.

"I don't like this," muttered one of the guards.

"You're not supposed to," snapped Lieutenant Swifthand. "Now quiet."

They headed into the woods, Prince Rune leading the way as he offered a more detailed description of the events leading to the princess's disappearance. The guards added quick comments occasionally, such as, "Lady Nadine was behaving strangely, even for an Embrian," and "Lord Bearhaste had gone into the forest before the princess and her lady," and "It was the most disgusting thing I'd ever seen."

Nightrender scanned the dark woods ahead. Starlight limned the edges of tree trunks, leaves, and the black-winged birds that observed their passage.

"Show me where Lord Bearhaste died."

The prince and his lieutenant led her and the rest of the company to a clearing thick with the stench of rot. A swath of blackness covered the ground, crawling up the bordering trees and suffocating brush. "Lord Bearhaste was there," Lieutenant Swifthand said. "In the center. I can still see the mold growing from his mouth and nose when I close my eyes."

The body had been removed, but Nightrender could hear faint squishing and slurping where some of the unfortunate lord had been too . . . soft to be recovered. "It's just worms and maggots now."

Prince Rune grimaced. "You don't have to tell me those things."

"I thought you'd be interested."

He shook his head. "Do you want to see the malsite?"

Nightrender closed her eyes and stretched her senses. This close, she could feel the small pocket of malice, like a bubble of *wrongness* against the edges of her mind. And splitting off it, a trickle of death and decay. It was leaking. "I can sense it," she said. "I will lead."

Prince Rune and his guards fell into step behind her as she moved through the woods. The glow of the lightrods flickered over leaves and branches.

"I would like a map of the malsites." Nightrender glanced over her shoulder, finding the prince's face tight with concentration. His free hand rested on his sword.

"There are several such maps, although they don't all agree. When we get back to Brink, I'll show you the best one."

She nodded her thanks. She'd be far more efficient in clearing malsites if she had a general idea of where to go. Then she stopped. Small metallic clanks drifted on the wind, ominous and otherworldly.

"Bells," she murmured.

"The yellow line." Prince Rune motioned her forward. "It's how we mark the malsites."

It was disturbing, the way he said that, like this was just another fact of the world. He might as well have showed her a loaf of bread and explained that they eat things like this to stay alive.

An uncomfortable feeling twisted inside her gut. Guilt, perhaps. She'd never left a task undone for so long. She could have prevented all this.

If only she'd cleared the malsites.

If only she'd done her duty.

The yellow line was nothing more than ribbons tied around trees, small bells fastened at the ends; it would not *prevent* someone from wandering through. "You should have strung a tough rope from tree to tree." She said. "Or built an even stronger barrier."

Prince Rune looked at her, his expression unreadable. "They did that centuries ago, but animals were caught on the ropes and ripped them down. Now, after hundreds of years, even forest creatures know not to go beyond these ribbons. As for a barrier—that would be admitting defeat. It would be admitting these places would always be dangerous to us."

"They would," Nightrender said. "Malice doesn't go away on its own. It takes effort, the right skills, the ability to cut through the pellicle—and none of you have that."

Prince Rune just looked at her, said nothing, and then shone his light beyond the yellow line. The glow stopped ten paces away, as though it hit a wall. "The princess was trapped in there."

Nightrender could feel where the pellicle cut through the regular world, holding back the poisoned space inside. It was a slippy-smooth bubble, and when she adjusted her eyes to look at the pellicle itself, rather than the world around it, she could just perceive the oil-slick sheen of malice.

"This isn't a scar," she muttered, wrinkling her nose as the stink of rotting flesh rose up from the soil. Decay, ozone, and ammonia, perhaps. "It's a septic wound." And even after she drained the infection, it would take a long time to finish healing. "I'm surprised you haven't noticed strange occurrences around it."

"Like what?"

"Nightmares made manifest. Corpses walking. Gravity behaving strangely. Anything. Bearhaste's black rot was likely caused by the rancor Lady Nadine saw, but this"—she gestured before her—"certainly made it worse."

Prince Rune's eyes were watering with the stench as he stepped up to the yellow line and stopped. "It didn't smell so bad before. Can you destroy it?"

"I live to destroy it." She drew her sword and marched forward, and then she *swung*.

Beloved touched the pellicle, and she breathed in anticipation of the rush of energy.

Instead, cold and blinding pain struck her mind, fracturing across her body so sharply she almost dropped her sword.

"Nightrender?"

Sparks cleared from her vision. She'd stepped backward, and she was gasping, but the pain had subsided.

"Nightrender?" Prince Rune didn't move from the yellow line. Behind him, his guards looked uncertain. "Is something wrong?"

Yes, something was wrong. Fulfilling her duty was supposed to feel *good* and *right*, not induce agony.

Perhaps it was a fluke. Gingerly, she hefted Beloved once more and pressed the sword point against the pellicle. It bent inward, rippling like a bubble, but even as the tip of her blade pierced the malsite, the same icy pain ripped from the back of her head and scattered across her body.

She recoiled, her heart pounding, her breath catching, but this time she was prepared for the feeling and she recovered before betraying her weakness any further.

"Nightrender, can you—"

"Yes." The word came out harsher than she intended. "It's fine. Just old and strong."

That had to be it: the malsite had been festering here for four hundred years, and she'd never cleansed something so deeply rooted. It was just another reason to be annoyed at the humans—fixing this Incursion was going to be painful because of their slowness—but at least she was prepared now, and she would warn them not to let malice sit this long ever again.

You don't have to clean it, murmured the darkest of her thoughts. ***They did this to themselves.***

She shook it away. She *did* have to clean the malice. It was her duty.

"All right," Prince Rune said. "If you're sure."

Again, she lifted her blade, braced herself, and swung. Obsidian hit resistance, ice-cold agony burned through Nightrender's head, and the razor edge of Beloved sliced through the wall of the dark little world she'd come to destroy. Pieces of the pellicle unraveled, shredded into iridescent ribbons. Light shone out, like illumination falling from a cracked-open door.

Nightrender breathed through the stabbing agony and swung again, and another section of the pellicle broke down.

More light.

She kept cutting, and the malsite rippled and fluttered and collapsed on itself as the entirety of its structure came undone.

Perhaps if the site hadn't been so old and steeped in dark energies—

If the pain hadn't been close to overwhelming—

If she'd been paying attention—

Freed from the pellicle, malice spilled outward, faster than she'd anticipated. Roots tore through the ground, growing at an impossible rate, and wrapped around her ankles, trying to drag her to the earth. A nearby vine gripped her sword arm and *pulled*. Trees bent toward her, their branches reaching to form a cage.

She flared her wings, the black-glass edges of feathers cutting clean through the angry vegetation. Within seconds, she was free, but now more malice-infected plants were growing at this accelerated rate.

Shouts erupted behind her, and Nightrender spun around just in time to see vines close over her mortal companions. She roared and ran for the prince, whose eyes were wide above the ivy curling around his throat. He clawed at it, but couldn't get a grip. Nightrender ripped away the vine, and he gasped for breath as she sliced and chopped at the foliage ensnaring him.

"How is this possible?" he rasped, cutting at plants with his sword.

That was the least important question of the moment.

Green rushed around them, and the guards' shouts rose louder.

Nightrender spread her wings again, slicing apart a fresh volley of roots and vines. Ice stabbed all through her mind, but she would give this pain no ground. She had work to do. "Help your guards. Get to safety. I will finish this."

Prince Rune hurried to his guards, and Nightrender turned and arced her sword into the air, cutting short another barrage of plantlife. This was worse than she'd anticipated. Far worse. But this ground—these plants—had been soaking in malice for four hundred years, and now they sensed a threat. Now they sensed *her*.

Nightrender pushed through the shreds of the pellicle, into the strange afternoon light that existed within. She paused only to drive her sword deep into the roots of afflicted plants, letting the holy fire of the Numina pour through her and into the earth. She destroyed evil with her hands and wings and heart.

But for every bit of malice she felled, a new stab of pain cut through her, frigid reflection of her own fury.

She wouldn't stop, though. She couldn't.

In her wake, she left dozens of trees and bushes turning black from the inside out. The odor of burning wood joined the other stenches; behind her, the mortals gagged against the assault of toxic air.

Inside the malsite, where the sun had fallen behind the trees, Nightrender plunged her sword into every plant she found, heedless of her own agony. The leaves of picked-clean berry bushes shriveled like broken fingers. Tree trunks sloughed sideways and ash fell from above like a deadly snow. Every time something came for her, she stabbed or sliced, letting her wings do their share of the work as well. The body of the malsite fell in pieces around her.

She was relentless, because this was the only mercy left for this patch of land. In a thousand years it might heal, but until then, the only way to save it was to cauterize the wound.

Even when sweat poured down her body, mixing with the falling ash. Even when the ground bubbled and slurped beneath her feet. Even when the rancid stench of malice coated the back of her throat, thicker with every breath, she pushed herself harder.

"Nightrender!" shouted the prince. "I don't see—"

She turned to find him standing on the burned ground just inside the malsite opening; his jaw was slack and his eyes wide, and there was a sick tint to his face. He was staring at his guards.

All six of them.

Dead.

Their bodies were already blackening, rotting and sprouting mold, but it didn't quite disguise the claw marks crisscrossing their armor, the blood coursing from deep gashes.

She hadn't even heard them die.

The sun fell below the horizon—sending them into the second dusk for today.

Time. This malsite affected time.

"Nightrender," Prince Rune breathed. His eyes shifted from his guards to something else.

It was tall and gaunt, its parchment-pale skin scaled and coated with a film of acidic sweat that made the whole creature glow under the scattered lightrods.

It looked at Nightrender, a terrible grin stretching its face, barbed teeth like wet spikes.

The whole forest seemed to take a breath.

Then the plants stopped fighting. The air went still. And she understood what the prince had wanted to tell her before:

He didn't see Princess Johanne.

The malsite was empty, except for him and her—and the rancor, which lifted its arms high above its head. With one clap of its clawed hands, the malsite snapped back into shape, circular, taut, and closed.

They were trapped.

11.
Rune

His guards were dead. Princess Johanne was dead. And it seemed more likely than not that he was next. Victims of a rancor, all.

He hadn't been prepared for the horror of the beast. Just the sight of it challenged his mind, his assumptions about reality: the disproportionately long limbs with too many joints, the spines along its back and shoulders, the way the whole world seemed to shift in and out of existence around it.

The first glance made his eyes unfocus. The second made him retch.

And this, he was certain, was what Princess Johanne had died feeling—what Swifthand and the others had died feeling. Shock and fear and horror beyond measure, because nothing like this should exist. But the evidence was right in front of his eyes, undeniable.

Unlike Rune, the Nightrender didn't waste time realigning with reality. The moment the rancor closed the malsite, she lunged and thrust her sword deep into its body—but the creature flickered and the blade cut nothing.

That was when Rune came back to himself. He'd failed with Opi and Princess Johanne, but his kingdom still waited beyond this space, fragile and falling apart.

When the beast reappeared, it was mere paces in front of Rune, facing away. Rune seized his opportunity, stepping into an attack, swinging his sword in a long, silver arc that cut through the air so quickly it whistled. But then, the rancor spun. Faced him. Its mouth split into a wide, dreadful grin of sharp teeth and yellow saliva.

It was too late for Rune to pull his attack; without a care for its own flesh, the rancor batted the blade to the ground. Tarry blood oozed from its clawed hand, hissing where it touched the grass.

And Rune was disarmed.

But he'd served as a distraction. The Nightrender stepped in, thrusting her obsidian sword into the creature. Lightning sparked through the rancor's body. A dark and dangerous smile formed on her lips as the creature shrieked, convulsing as electricity poured through it.

For a moment, Rune thought it was over. Then, the rancor ripped itself off the Nightrender's sword with a terrible slurp and jolt of energy.

Rune staggered back in shock. How was it still alive?

The rancor surged toward him, claws slashing like daggers, but the Nightrender blocked and shoved the thing away.

Her shoulders were set, her face a grim mask of determination. She stabbed and sliced, on the offensive now that the rancor was weakened, and she was magnificent. She pursued the creature around trees and brush, sword snapping through the air like thunder; it must have weighed three times his, but she wielded it as an artist might a paintbrush.

And every time her weapon struck flesh, numinous fire shot through the dark blade, lighting the malsite with a holy glow.

Incredible, he thought. *I am witnessing absolute greatness.*

What a remarkable sensation.

He steeled himself to rejoin the fight, to make his moment in history alongside the champion of the three kingdoms, and dove for his sword.

But their advantage ended before either he or the Nightrender could make full use of it.

The earth shattered in an eruption of dirt and leaves and unidentifiable bone fragments, cutting a long gash into the ground. A terrible, acrid heat belched up through the malsite, along with a deep crimson light. It was a vein of the earth's hot blood, running far below.

Rune gripped the tree he'd braced himself against, legs still limp after the ground's betrayal, and scanned for his sword. But it was lost.

And maybe it didn't matter.

The fissure sliced fully across the malsite, cutting him off from the Nightrender and the rancor. He couldn't jump over it. He couldn't fight. He couldn't help.

Heat pumped from the fissure, making sweat dampen Rune's clothes as the battle intensified. Both the rancor and Nightrender fought with a supernatural fury, the speed of their strikes too dizzying to follow.

Then, the rancor leaped atop the Nightrender and thumped her to the ground. Its claws tore at her throat as it let loose an awful, mind-scouring noise.

The sound caught in Rune's ears, buzzing like a thousand wasps. He retched as his whole self struggled to make sense of it.

Now the rancor wasn't just clawing at the Nightrender's throat but was biting it, tearing into it with long, jagged teeth, and no matter how she fought, it kept its jaws clamped tight.

Terror kicked through Rune. He scrambled to find his sword, sweeping away chunks of rock and bone and plant matter. It had to be here somewhere. It had to.

Then, he looked over the edge of the fissure.

Dry, ancient heat roiled up, sapping the moisture from his skin and eyes and mouth. A vein of molten rock crept far below, the kind of blood only the deepest parts of the world could bear. Rune started to pull back, but then he saw it: his sword had been lodged between two huge rocks, and the metal glimmered in the glow of magma, losing integrity with every blast of heat.

A drum crashed inside Rune's chest. The Nightrender had forced the rancor off her, but her wounds bled freely as she lunged and blocked, defending only. Fear choked Rune. What if she couldn't do it? What if—

Rune didn't waste time. He turned and shimmied into the fissure, scraping the toes of his boots along the crumbling walls. It was loose, all shaken-apart stone that scattered where he searched for a toehold. Everything he tried broke apart and fell into the inferno below.

Perhaps this had been a bad idea.

At once, the rock in his grip collapsed—and he slid down the side of the fissure faster than he could think.

Panic seized him. Hands and feet scrambled for purchase. Nothing was enough. Every time he dug his fingers against the rock, it crumbled and he slid farther, but he bit off any scream; if the Nightrender noticed his fall, if she were distracted for even an instant, she could lose the fight.

With a brutal jerk to his shoulders, he caught himself at last.

He'd dropped several body lengths below where he thought his sword was, and the swelling heat surrounded him completely. Sweat dried as it formed. His skin started to crack before his eyes. If he'd fallen any farther, he'd be dead.

His limbs shook with stress and strain as he clung to the side of the fissure, cooking in his own skin, breathing in the malodor. His heart kicked harder. He would *still* be dead if he didn't climb up.

Rune fought the urge to scramble, to flail blindly, as he had on the way down. No, he needed to think. To plan. To test each grip before he released the previous.

And what if there were no handholds?

He looked away from that thought.

Carefully, he took a slow, small breath in—just enough to clear his head without sending him into a coughing fit from the dry miasma—and he felt the cliff face above him for something to hold onto.

Nothing.

He tried again, digging his fingers deep into the dirt. His grip slipped, making rocks and pebbles spray across his face, landing in his eyes and mouth. But after sweeping away the loose material, his fingers finally struck solid stone.

Thank Sardin, he thought. The Numen of Luck.

Another rush of noxious heat plumed past him as he pulled himself up with the first handhold. Every muscle protested, but he couldn't quit now.

Slowly, methodically, Rune found the next handhold and the next. It took a million years, but at last he came level with his fallen sword. He shifted closer to it, until it was within reach, and then braced himself on the wall.

Above, obsidian clashed against claws, and the rancor howled. Was that a good sign? It was impossible to tell.

Rune grasped his sword—then recoiled, almost throwing himself down the fissure again. The hilt was too hot to touch. Of course. It had been down here baking even longer than he had.

Redness welled up on his palm, and it wouldn't be long before blisters formed. He used his teeth to pull his sleeve over his hand. It wasn't nearly enough protection. As he took the sword again, heat radiated through the linen, and he suppressed a small cry of agony as he slid the blade into its sheath. Then, balancing his weight against that of the hot sword, he climbed the rest of the way up.

The sounds of battle grew, all rancorous shrieking and thumps and angry grunts.

A quick glance revealed a terrifying scene: two figures in the center of an ashy, flattened world. It looked like there had been an explosion, the blast wave felling every tree, uprooting every bush, and charring everything else. The pellicle had contained the damage, but if this didn't end soon, the outside world—the forest, the roads, the farms—would feel the effects.

He had no choice. He needed to help. Or—at least—be a useful distraction.

He didn't think. He didn't worry. He just acted.

Rune threw himself across the fissure, grasping wildly for the opposite ledge. Fingertips scraped stone, peeling skin and ripping back nails from their beds, but he clutched the ledge, dragged himself the rest of the way in, and—in the same motion—hauled himself up to level ground.

There was no time to celebrate, no time even to breathe. Rune staggered toward the battle, reaching for his sword.

Black blood poured down the rancor's body, seeping from dozens of wounds. Its stamina was flagging, but it lunged and slashed without care for its own safety. Burned skin flaked off its body, littering the ground.

But the Nightrender wasn't winning; she breathed heavily as she defended the rancor's wild attacks, and her expression was the same as she'd worn earlier—before they'd arrived at the malsite, when she said she'd forgotten something.

Was she forgetting how to *fight*?

Rune's sword was cool enough to hold now, but to the burned and blistering skin of his palm the hilt was pure fire. Still, he drew the blade from its sheath and let out a fierce cry, throwing himself into the battle.

His sword was steel, not obsidian, but even so, the blade sliced into the rancor's flesh; it was already so weak.

Weak for a rancor, at least. Not a human. It was like cutting into a tanned hide.

"You fool!" The Nightrender shoved Rune aside, but the rancor was just as fast: it grabbed his arm and dragged him close, and the proximity was overwhelming. The sword slipped from Rune's grasp.

Hot, rank breath washed over his face, stinging with droplets of acid. Eyes like malevolent stars searched him, weighing, as they pulled him in with a terrible gravity. The rancor bent everything, time and space and sanity.

The rancor made a noise, almost like words. "Ah, the puppet prince. Such a sad thing you are. But my king could make you great."

Rune reeled with the shattered-glass horror of its voice, his mind darkening with tendrils of madness.

Then, the Nightrender drove her blade through the beast's eye and out the back of its bony skull.

Numinous light erupted from its remaining eye, its mouth, its nose holes, and the slits where its ears should have been. Some of the spikes on its shoulders and back began to split open with the blinding illumination.

Rune stared. "What—"

The Nightrender whipped him away, her arms squeezing him tight as she threw them toward the ground. Her wings surrounded them in darkness. "Put your head down!" she shouted in his ear, just as an immense crash rocked the malsite.

Chunks of burned flesh and black slush hurtled through the air. The debris hit the pellicle and slid downward, utterly revolting.

When the Nightrender released him, Rune was shaking, just a breath away from dropping his face into the dirt. But a rotting shade of black spread through the ground, giving him just enough energy to lurch away.

"Tell me how you feel." The Nightrender gave her wings a sharp jerk—rancor gunk flew off the black feathers—before folding them behind her once more. Dried blood coated her skin and armor, and she was a mess of sweat and scratches. Even so, he'd never seen anyone so dangerously beautiful. "Prince Rune. Tell me how badly you're hurt."

He was staring at her, he knew, but she'd just saved his life when he'd meant to save hers—and there was something significant about the way he'd felt when she touched him.

Or perhaps not. Perhaps the rancor encounter had rattled his mind into nothingness.

"I'm fine." A lie. She'd know it, too, he was certain, because his guards were dead just over there and the princess was nowhere to be found.

"That was unwise—attacking the rancor like you did."

"I was trying to help."

Her wings opened wide as she strode toward him, and though they were of similar heights, he suddenly felt small. "I am the Sword of the Numina, the Hero Eternal. I alone stand between you and infinite darkness. *I* do not need to be rescued."

He swallowed hard.

"Now"—she bent to take his fallen sword, then tossed it to him—"this is yours."

Reflexively, Rune caught the hilt. His burned hand throbbed, but he didn't drop his weapon again. He sheathed it, fighting to control his expression against the pain. "Thank you."

She flicked her own sword clean and marched across the wasteland of the malsite. Within minutes, she'd cut away the pellicle for good. Rune couldn't see it, but he could feel the entire thing ribboning and rippling to the earth. A change in the air pressure. A knot of tension evaporating. The false afternoon fading into night.

He didn't miss the way the work seemed to cause her pain.

"What about that?" He nodded toward the fissure, which belched hot gas and spurts of molten rock.

She regarded it with a frown. "It'll have to stay, for now. We'll just have to hope nothing worse comes out of it."

"Worse?"

"There are other planes. Surely everyone still knows this. It's possible that there are other gateways buried below the crust of the earth." Her black gaze shifted to his. "You should have stayed on the far side. I was able to save you from the rancor. I would not have been able to rescue you from the fissure; there was no time."

He didn't particularly want to talk about his poor decision-making skills anymore. He'd done his best.

"What was that rancor?" he asked. "Some kind of prince or general?"

The Nightrender cocked her head.

"It just seemed very strong. From what I've read, it always sounds like the fights are over quickly. But this . . ." He clamped his mouth shut. It was probably a bad idea to suggest she'd been struggling.

She gave him a long look, a tired expression that reminded him just how old she was, how she'd been doing this for thousands of years. "The battle for your souls has never been easy."

He lowered his eyes.

"There are princes and kings and generals," the Nightrender said after a moment. "Rancor have hierarchies, just as you do, but the positions are won by conquest and slaughter, not inherited by blood. I have not been to the Dark Shard, but my impression is that it is ruled by a thousand different kings. The rancor that come through the Rupture might be sent by a superior, but . . ."

"The superiors themselves don't usually come here?" Rune guessed.

She shook her head. "Kings are trapped in the Dark Shard unless summoned by name, and such a summoning would take an incredible amount of power. Besides, they have their own endless wars to keep them engaged."

"Then what did it mean when it talked about its king?" *My king could make you great.* Rune suppressed a shudder.

The Nightrender opened her mouth like she knew the answer to that, but nothing came out. She took a deep breath and then said, "I used to know. I'm certain I knew before, but that memory is gone."

Rune's heart twisted. It was hard to see someone as strong as the Nightrender made vulnerable by something so insidious and invisible. "If you need help," he said cautiously, "you can tell me anything you want to remember, and I'll remember it for you. I will not forget. I will never forget anything you tell me, I swear it."

She gave him a tired, curious look, like she didn't believe him. Then, at last she said, "I dreamed of a castle. Bones and death. A terrible choice." She swallowed hard. "I can't recall anything else about it. Just a castle in the center of the Malice."

The Nightrender could dream. "Do you think the castle had something to do with a rancor king?"

"I don't know." Irritation filled her tone. "I don't remember anything else. I just"—she swallowed hard—"thought I would tell you in case I forget."

"Oh." Guilt bubbled in his chest. "What about your wounds?" Rune asked. "Do they hurt?"

"I will recover." She motioned for him to join her by the edge of the ex-malsite. "More quickly than you will. Show me your hands."

He held up his palms; blisters already covered the burned one, and both were crusted with blood and dirt.

"You need to treat those," she said. "Before the wounds become infected. Go to that stream. I must check the perimeter to be certain no malice remains."

When she was gone, Rune spent a moment staring at the half-decayed bodies of his guards. He wished they hadn't come. He wished he'd borne this risk alone. He wished he had commanded them to remain in Brink.

But he hadn't, and now he would have to arrange for recovery of their bodies. He'd have to notify their families, first with letters, later with a personal visit—if they would have him.

Heart heavy, he picked his way through the flattened trees and over the clean line where the pellicle used to stand. One side: a lush summer forest. The other: remnants of a nightmare made reality. Then, he lowered himself to the ground—well away from the ex-malsite and the shredded corpses of his men—and thrust his hands into the fast-moving stream, letting cold water wash the grit from his burns. It stung, but he didn't care. This whole thing had been for nothing.

The princess hadn't been here.

But the rancor had.

There was only one way that math worked: the rancor had killed Princess Johanne, and the alliance was lost forever. Rune had failed.

12.
Hanne

She was out. That was all that mattered.

Such was Hanne's mantra as she stumbled through the Deepway Woods, and when she staggered down the empty road, and when she slouched across someone's farm. Though it must have been very early morning—and she'd been moving for hours already—everything was still and quiet, as though she were a ghost no one could see.

As she moved down the path between the fields, rich and green with corn and wheat, the potential for danger stood dark at every turn. Whenever she closed her eyes, even to blink, she feared she'd open them to see the rancor standing directly before her. Hanne's heart was a hummingbird's wings.

A rickety granary loomed against the starry sky. She hurried inside, but not to rest; there was no time. Instead, she stole a sack of grain, a rake, and the farmer's only horse. She needed it more than he did. After all, even though this family was clearly poor (and now relieved of their only animal), *they* had not been trapped in a malsite for the last three or four—or maybe more?—weeks. So Hanne's need was greater.

She considered leaving a piece of jewelry in its place, so that she could tell herself that she was buying the horse, but unfortunately she had nothing of low value—even Nadine's rings were worth more than the entire farm—which meant that anything she left was of considerably more worth than the near-motionless nag. It wouldn't be a fair trade.

With those thoughts churning through her mind, Hanne climbed onto the horse, which came alive at her touch, and didn't pause one moment more to reflect upon her options. The rancor's instructions had been clear. She kicked the horse and left the farm as fast as possible.

She was out.

That was all that mattered.

Somewhere along the Brink Way, she dropped the stolen rake. It wouldn't actually be a useful weapon if she was accosted on the road, and its bulk only slowed her pace. If the rancor changed its mind about sending her out of the time slip, nothing would save her.

The violence of the rancor's voice; the agonized hiss of withering grass as acid dripped from its mushroom skin: those were the memories she dragged along behind her as she fled for her very life.

And after those came the actual moment of her escape, even more terrifying. The rancor had lumbered in her direction—and she'd feared it would send her back to the Dark Shard—but then it veered around her, a rancid smell in its wake. It stopped at the edge of the malsite, peeled the pellicle open, as though splitting the skin of a peach, and pulled back a flap big enough for her to fit through.

But that slit in the malsite was somehow even more appalling than the smooth, unbreakable wall had been, because where the two realities collided, a mossy, oil-slick shimmer coated the air. It got in her lungs, sticking to all the tissue-thin layers of those delicate organs, so that when she inhaled and exhaled, there was an audible slurp.

Nevertheless, she'd thrown herself out of the malsite without a second thought, because it seemed entirely possible the *rancor* would have second thoughts.

Now, she urged the horse faster, desperate to put as much distance between herself and the malsite as possible. If she could have flown to the other side of the world, it still wouldn't be far enough. (Everyone knew the other side of the world was covered in darkness and would never be habitable again, but that was beside the point.)

Hooves thumped against the packed dirt road. Sweat soaked both Hanne and her stolen horse. But she would not—could not—slow. Even when she felt lightheaded. Even when the horse heaved long, tormented breaths. She would not let either of them stop.

"Faster," she urged.

Scholars gave lectures on the speed of light, demonstrating how instantly a candle's glow reached the far side of the room, while a person would need several seconds to walk there. They said nothing was faster than light, but Hanne knew better: darkness flew on the swiftest wings of all.

"Faster," she begged, but there was no outrunning fear. It kept pace no matter where she went.

Still, she had survived this. She had endured the sort of trauma that few could imagine. Yes, she would always be afraid, but from this new height of terror, she could see that everything else was small. Because she knew this darkness so intimately, nothing else was worthy of her fear.

"I am not afraid," she whispered.

But she was.

Hours later, the horse stumbled.

She pulled up his hooves to check for rocks, and then felt along the knobby legs in search of cuts or knots. Nothing. He was just exhausted, and she understood that feeling well enough. She could barely keep on her own feet.

Somehow she guided him toward a slow but deep stream, its water like glass ripples in the moonlight, and both of them drank until their bellies could hold no more. For weeks she'd been rationing water, too scared to drink more than a sip or three. Splashing water on her face, letting it dribble down her chin as she gulped greedily: it felt wildly indulgent.

When the horse lowered himself to the bank and slept, Hanne went with him, leaning against his sweaty flank as she drifted toward the nightmares clawing through her mind. Only as her eyes fell closed did she finally register the fact that the sky was still dark, studded with a spiral of stars and a halo of moonlight, even though she'd been riding for hours. It sent a small jolt of concern through her, a warning that something was wrong, but then sleep took her, blanketing those concerns in cool fog.

Dreams came swiftly, all jagged with the horror of the Dark Shard. Wrongness vibrated through her bones, rattling her thoughts and breaths and the whole world around her. While she slept, the grass beneath her turned brown and brittle.

It was dark again—or perhaps still?—when she awakened, and she did not linger beyond another delirious gulp of water. Then she mounted her horse and they were running.

Always running.

She rode along the Brink Way for a time, but soon came to a crossroad: the Brink Way continued east, toward the Caberwilline capital, Nadine, and an army; another king's road ran from north to south toward Ivasland, slipping between the mountains and curving around the dark glow of the Malstop. A tall signpost listed the major towns she would travel through in either direction.

Near the signpost stood a small shrine to Vunimmi, the Numen of Crossroads. Trinkets, candle stubs, and low-value coins littered the surface, all offerings to Vunimmi in hopes of safe passage and good weather regardless of the path taken.

The only Numen Hanne worshipped was Tuluna, but this seemed like a good opportunity to gain favor with another. She nudged her horse toward the shrine and sprinkled a small amount of grain across the stone. She didn't notice the way it slowed when it left her fingers; she was too exhausted, too torn.

"Which way should I go, Tuluna?" she whispered. Now that she was out of the malsite, surely the Numen would speak to her again.

But there was only silence in the back of her mind.

She would have to decide for herself.

East meant the path she'd intended to take before all this started. South meant the path the rancor had directed.

Uncertainty swallowed her whole. What the rancor had demanded of her was abhorrent. Treasonous, even for a princess. But it had promised to send her to the Dark Shard if she didn't obey.

Surely Tuluna would protect her. After all, it was Tuluna's influence that had sent her into the arms of Rune Highcrown to begin with.

Pulse throbbing with trepidation, Hanne remounted and turned east, toward her destiny.

A stink rose up, sharp with ozone and the sticky sweetness of death. From the corner of her eye, she caught a pale shape looming near the signpost, one long and many-jointed arm pointing southward.

It was here. The rancor.

Hanne screamed and jerked the reins, causing the poor nag to rear up, but when she looked again, the area around the signpost was empty and the air smelled only of wildflowers and horse sweat.

The rancor wasn't here. Or wasn't here *anymore*. It was impossible to tell.

It didn't matter. Before she could reconsider her actions, Hanne steered the horse south. She'd been foolish to hope the rancor wouldn't know of her disobedience. It *would* know.

She kicked the gelding into a gallop, heading south and around the Malstop. Never before had she been so aware of the great dome, but now its presence was a constant blot on her mind, refusing to be ignored as it shimmered with arcane energy.

And now that she knew what sorts of terrors lurked within . . .

If she could have made a wider berth around the Malstop, she would have, but speed was more important than her comfort. The faster she reached Ivasland and did as the rancor had bidden, the faster she could return to her real life.

All of this would be over someday, just a story she and Nadine revisited when they were old and far away from all this horror.

She hoped. (Of course, she knew better than to believe.)

After that first time, she barely stopped to sleep, pausing only when the horse flagged, because the danger of losing her stolen mount was too great. She let him rest when necessary, and tried to rest herself, but it was impossible to feel safe.

Because the rancor might come after her.

Because what she was about to do was ludicrous.

Because, impossibly, it was still dark.

It had been dark this entire time. When she'd rested before, she hadn't slept through an entire day. No, the sky was just dark all the time now. Forever, perhaps. She'd escaped the malsite only to find the world had completely broken in her absence.

Was it an Incursion?

If so, had Nadine even made it to Brink?

Hanne pushed the horse even faster.

13.
Nightrender

You almost lost that fight, whispered the dark voice. ***You almost lost your prince. Then what would you have done? Gone back to sleep? Let darkness spill over Salvation?***

Nightrender did her best to ignore the voice, but it was right. Prince Rune had been right. The rancor *had* been harder to kill, but not because it was a prince or a general. No, it had been a normal rancor, and she was simply broken.

The malsite's age might be to blame for the difficulty in destroying it, but this rancor was just like any other, and she should not have experienced that blinding, debilitating pain while fighting it.

Worse, it had spoken of a king, which meant . . . What?

If only she could remember.

If only.

Nightrender stopped walking.

Somewhere in the distance, a bird chirruped—one cautious high-pitched trill. Another answered. Wildlife began to stir. She could feel eyes on her, finches and sparrows, squirrels and possums. Slowly, life crept back into this section of the forest, watching her from the safety of the trees, as Nightrender stood before the fissure, that gash carved into the world. The red-orange glow and terrible reek rose up around her.

How long before you lose everything?

Nightrender closed her eyes as her thoughts flashed back to that heart-stopping moment when Prince Rune had disappeared into the fissure, how quickly he'd been gone.

Then, there'd been an explosion of energy that knocked down everything inside the malsite. The rancor. Trees. Even her.

It had *come* from her.

It would have been a stomach drop for a human, or a primal scream of complete and utter devastation. But for her, it had been a real, physical blast of emotion—one that tore plants from their roots and threatened to rip holes in the sky.

The rancor had recovered first, then attacked, and she'd had no opportunity to consider what she'd done, or why. But now she surveyed the damage soberly. In all her time, there'd only been one soul she'd have destroyed the world in order to save.

One soul; many people.

She couldn't always know her soul shard immediately. Humans were deeply complex creatures, and even if the soul was the same, the body and heart and mind were different. The *person* was different.

Was Prince Rune's soul a shard of hers? It might explain the flash of recognition when they'd first met in the tower, or her terror when he'd fallen, or the surge of relief when he'd climbed up.

Royalty made for especially inconvenient soul shards, even if there was a lot to appreciate about this prince (besides the fact that he was the one person alive who seemed to like her). He genuinely cared about his kingdom, and he'd put himself in danger because he'd thought she needed help. (Perhaps she had.) He was a good person. A kind person.

She could deal with the inconvenience for someone like Rune Highcrown.

No, in truth, it was his role as Dawnbreaker that would wreck things. If he was also her soul shard—he could *not* be her Dawnbreaker, because Dawnbreakers died.

She couldn't protect him *and* ask him to ride into battle. She would have to forgive his oath, and that was just as likely to hurt him as any physical assault.

But perhaps he wasn't her soul shard. Perhaps her reaction to his fall had been simple fear of losing another person.

She pulled her wings tight around her and lifted her eyes to the stars. *Please*, she prayed to all the Numina, though she wasn't quite sure what she was asking for.

They're not listening anyway. The voice coiled around her heart and squeezed. ***They've never listened.***

Everything was so *wrong* this time.

Nightrender knelt at the fissure, working through the names and faces her soul shard had worn throughout history. There'd been the horse breeder, who'd given Nightrender a new appreciation for equines. There'd been a miner, who'd kept a small shrine to the Numen of Silver in his home. And there'd been a musician, with instruments tucked away in her apartment; Nightrender had gone to her first performance and—

And what?

A star flashed out in Nightrender's mind: the performance. She could remember going into the music hall, but then there was nothing.

"No." Nightrender pressed her fingertips into the blackened, burned earth, but even as she struggled to hold on to these moments, these precious pieces of her history, another went, and then another, all swept away by the monster stealing her memories.

Nightrender choked out a sob, clutching the earth with bent fingers, but it, too, crumbled in her grasp. Nothing stayed.

A little time later, she and Prince Rune made camp along the Brink Way, where all the horses were still tethered.

"I'm sorry," she said.

"Why?"

"For the loss of your guards. And the princess. I know what the alliance meant to you."

He gave her a look that said she couldn't possibly understand, but then dropped his gaze. "I'm just so tired of losing people," he said, very softly.

So was she.

She pulled a medical kit from one of the saddlebags, peeled off her gauntlets, then rinsed her hands with the help of a waterskin. For a moment, they both watched the blood and dirt and sweat fall away. "It wasn't your fault." She dried her hands on a clean rag.

"It feels like my fault."

She opened the medical kit. "Give me your hands. The burned one first."

He held out his blistered hand, palm up. It looked wretched, like half-cooked meat, but he hid whatever pain it caused behind a clenched jaw and stoic expression.

Nightrender dabbed a generous amount of silver ointment onto the worst of the burns. The prince gasped, but didn't jerk away.

"Tell me if this hurts," she said.

"It doesn't matter if it hurts." His voice was tight.

She worked quickly, thoroughly. "Tell me what you'll do now. Dawnbreaker trials, perhaps. An army to follow me into the Malice."

Prince Rune sighed into the darkness. "I will try. But when the Crown Council learns that Princess Johanne is dead, they will likely attempt to replace me with one of my sisters," he confided. "I will not be forgiven for failing yet again."

"Failing again," she murmured, rinsing the rest of the ointment off her own hands. Her body would heal itself.

"In Caberwill, spares are protectors for the crown prince. It was also that way before, right? With the Skyreach monarchy?"

She nodded. At least she could remember that much. For now.

"I am not the eldest. My brother was meant to be king, and I trained as his protector. But when Ivasland sent an assassin, I failed. His entire guard failed, truly, but his life was my responsibility above anyone else's. My brother had gone to pray, as he always did. And as his protector, I always went with him, even though—"

A beat of silence pulsed between them.

"You don't believe," she supplied, removing a bandage from the medical kit.

"I do believe." His eyes met hers. "I have always believed in the Numina. How could I not? We have the Malstop and malsites—all this evidence of evil. There must be good, too. But I also believed the Numina didn't care about me. My problems. My desires."

Nightrender loosely fastened the bandage around his burned hand.

"One day, I told Opi—Opus IV, that is—to go to the family's private chapel without me, and that I'd meet him after. I didn't have a reason for missing the service. I just didn't want to go. So I skipped it. He went. I spent the hour in bed reading, and took my time getting there.

"My brother was just leaving the chapel when I arrived. There were no other guards, since I was supposed to be there. But I was still down the hall when I saw the shadow move, and then the knife . . ." He started to clench his fist but cringed and rested his hand on his knee, palm up. "I couldn't get to him in time. The assassin slit my brother's throat in front of me, and there was nothing I could do to save him."

Nightrender swallowed hard. "And now all your grief is tainted with guilt." She knew how that felt.

"Yes." The word came out rough. Raw.

She opened the ointment again and began working on his other hand, though it was far less damaged than the first. "It isn't true—that the Numina don't care. They do."

His eyes flicked to meet hers in the darkness.

"Thousands and thousands of years ago, the Numina and rancor waged great and devastating battles across the laic plane. Mortals died in innumerable masses, felled by the armies of the Dark Shard. Then, the worst happened: the aperture between the numinous and laic planes began to close. The Numina here would be cut off from their home unless they retreated from the war."

Prince Rune didn't say anything, but a heavy, waiting silence pulsed between them.

"Rather than leaving this world to perish, they spent their last hours on the laic plane pushing the rancor back toward the Rupture. Many were slaughtered, but they succeeded in building the Malstop—and me." She didn't speak of her own creation often—it was so personal—but humans used to know this basic history. They had, collectively, forgotten it over the millennia. She hadn't even realized.

"Then they left," Prince Rune said quietly. "Once the Malstop went up, and you were"—he frowned over the word—"built, the Numina left. How could they abandon us if they truly cared?"

It wasn't as simple as that. The Numina had left a number of artifacts, Relics like her sword and armor, the summoning shrines, and others, all meant to help defend the world. Once, she had believed a few Numina had stayed, either because they could not bear to leave or because the gateway had closed without them, but she'd never seen any real evidence of that. She couldn't even remember why she'd thought it so.

She gazed at Prince Rune, who wore a frustrated expression. "Imagine the choice: you could give people you loved a chance at survival, and then return home; or you could stay and fight, uncertain of the outcome, knowing only that you would never again go home."

"I would stay and fight."

"Tell me the truth," she pressed.

"I am. I would stay and fight, no matter the cost."

Humans said that, but they so rarely meant it. This was the difference between what they wanted to be, and what they truly were. She did not blame them.

"The Numina chose to go home," she said. "Having given humanity its best chance of survival, they returned to a place of unparalleled light and beauty, where the air smells of honey and pain is a distant thing."

His voice went soft, almost wistful. "Have you been there?"

Nightrender's shoulders dropped. "No. I had no opportunity before the gateway closed, but the knowledge of it was worked into me." When she had been new, she'd believed the Numina had not taken her to their plane because they didn't want her to miss what she could not have. Now, she knew better: she had never been meant to go to a place of perfect peace, because she was a creature of endless war.

"If they loved us," Prince Rune whispered, "if they loved *you*, they would have stayed."

He said it with such conviction, and she was in no mood for argument, so she finished bandaging his hand and shut the medical kit with a snap.

The lightrods had all faded by now, so Nightrender pulled out a blanket and offered it to the prince. "Get some rest."

14.
Hanne

Her fear had been misplaced. The world was no more broken than usual; it was Hanne who had changed, moving at higher speeds than everything else.

As early morning crept upon the world and people began to slip out of their houses, they saw only a dark blur in the corner of their eyes—a smear of brown horse and blue dress, like a giant's thumb had smudged the world.

When they saw Princess Johanne Fortuin ride by, they merely believed themselves imagining things.

Those who lived near the Malstop were used to *something* playing tricks on their eyes.

But Hanne didn't know that—couldn't know that—thanks to her terrified focus on *getting away*. In spite of all the evidence, she had no idea that she was still existing in a different time from the rest of the world.

Eventually, as she raced past towering statues of Caberwill's oldest heroes, through timber-framed towns, across covered bridges, dawn broke. For everyone else in the world, it was a normal sunrise, but for Hanne, it lasted hours.

One at a time, the stars winked out of the dark sky, so slowly Hanne would have had time to count them if she'd wanted. Blackness eased into velvet blue, hints of rose and coral breathing across the horizon, catching on woolen clouds. At the same time, morning birds began to sing the glory of the coming light. Hanne didn't recognize it at first because it was such a strange sound, like her ears ringing with long, low tones, but some short trill—which still took several minutes—caught in her mind and she knew: the birds were welcoming dawn. Very slowly.

No. She was just very fast.

She didn't want to think about what that meant, so she didn't.

As light poured into the deep pass carved between two mountains, Hanne rode faster, always pushing her mount to his limit, only focusing on the progress she'd made. When she burst out of the pass, through to the southern side of Caberwill, dawn stretched long and gold across the plains, making fields of wheat and hay glow like coins.

It was still early morning when Hanne reached the border crossing.

On the other side of a low stone wall, which ran all the way from the Malstop to the sea, lay Ivasland.

The wall wasn't much to look at, just some ancient rocks piled up in a somewhat straight line, and people probably hopped over it all the time. Legend claimed there was magic in the old stone, but depending on who told the story, it was either numinous magic to divide the three kingdoms, or malicious magic that bled out from the Rupture. Hanne didn't believe either story, as the borders were as porous as lace, and the only things that prevented people from crossing where they shouldn't were the well-armed patrols.

This crossing was, as expected, fully staffed with guards and clerks and customs authorities on both sides of the wall. They looked like they were in the process of admitting a group through the wide gates. Everyone wore tight expressions, too aware of the tension between the kingdoms and how it could shift into all-out war at any moment.

But the truth was that even countries on the brink of bloodshed needed things from each other, so as Hanne slipped her stolen mount between the slowly moving people, she caught sight of crops, chemical light in various shapes and sizes, and raw materials inside carts and wagons.

When she went through the gate, she paused before exiting the other side. Outside of the Malice, this border crossing was one of three truly neutral places in all Salvation. (That, and the Nightrender's island of Winterfast, but Hanne almost never thought about the Nightrender.) She gazed around at the people of her two enemy kingdoms, taking in the way their clothes caught in the breeze and their expressions shifted in the smallest, most minute ways. Even their voices were slow, deeper and more muddied than normal.

She knew she should move, because even though she was faster than they were, staying in one spot for too long was dangerous. She couldn't be caught. Not here. Not when the rancor's spiny words were still sharp in her mind and the stench of ozone wafted through the air.

But these were the first people she'd seen in weeks—her time—and she hadn't realized quite how much she'd missed faces. The last she'd seen had been Nadine's, Rune's, and a few soldiers'. She'd almost died a thousand times since then. That sort of thing brought perspective.

None of these people had particularly special faces: they were plain, damp with sweat, and lined with worry, but Hanne took in the sight of them anyway. Humans. Real humans.

A man looked at her.

Her heart jumped from shock as a cacophony of a few dozen voices rose to their regular pitches. Someone stepped straight into her horse. A woman shouted. And hot, flesh-melting agony flared from Hanne's bones, radiating through her skin until she thought she might explode.

But as a handful of strangers turned to look at her, everything stopped. The pain. The others' movement. Hanne was fast again, although bent over and gagging on the remnants of that blinding pain.

She peeled herself up and looked around to see what had changed. The first man who'd spotted her—his eyes were wide and round, utterly terrified. Others were pointing. One was starting to push his way through the crowd, away from her.

They were frightened of a girl suddenly appearing in their midst.

They had no idea what true darkness looked like.

Fighting panic, Hanne kicked her nervously dancing horse and sped across the border as quickly as possible, a billowing cloud of dust in her wake.

There was no more ignoring it. Somehow, Hanne had taken some of the malsite's slippery time with her. Perhaps it had come from the berries she'd eaten or the water she'd drunk, or perhaps she'd absorbed it from the very air. But either way, it was running out.

15.
NIGHTRENDER

As dawn purpled the sky, Nightrender and Prince Rune rose to find a man standing over the tightly wrapped remains of the fallen guards. Nightrender had moved them last night, while the prince had pretended to sleep.

"John!" Prince Rune staggered toward the guard, and the two spoke, looking at the bodies every few moments.

Nightrender gave them some privacy, taking the time to load the bodies onto the horses. Then, in contemplative quiet, they all rode back to Brink, the horses tied together in a silent chain. They went up the back paths to the castle, avoiding the city proper so as not to alarm anyone with their bleak cargo.

Nevertheless, their arrival was noted. Sentries ran ahead, and by the time they reached the stables and gave the horses to the grooms, the king and queen of Caberwill were waiting, a small troop of well-dressed mortals clustered around them. Several of the faces were familiar from the throne room, but now they didn't bother to hide their fear and disgust of her.

Well, she was still covered in rancor blood and gore. People had never enjoyed seeing her like this, even when they'd liked her. Plus, she was bringing the bodies of six people she had not been able to protect.

"The Crown Council," Prince Rune provided quietly. He stood at her side, tension knotting his shoulders and fists. "About half of them. Rupert Flight is the one with the winged lion pin and the forgettable face; he's the information chancellor, the master of spies. Charity Wintersoft—she's the well-dressed one who looks down on everybody. Stella Asheater, the grand physician, and Dayle Larksong, the grand priest. I'm fairly certain the whole council hates both of us right now."

"I'm not here to make friends."

"Good job so far."

"Thank you."

The king and queen stepped forward into a banner of light falling from between castle parapets. Queen Grace crooked her forefinger, and—with a resigned sigh—Prince Rune straightened his back and strode toward his parents. As he moved, he became a different man, his posture terribly stiff, braced against attacks.

The group regarded him as one might a slug, certain it had a purpose in this world, but not sure why it had to be *here*. "No princess," observed the king unnecessarily, but people sometimes said things for dramatic effect. The councilors glanced at one another and murmured.

Prince Rune was ready, though. "Unfortunately, the princess was killed shortly before our arrival. If only we hadn't wasted so much time bickering about how to proceed."

"Is she among these bodies you've returned with?" Queen Grace asked.

A breath of unease filled the stable yard.

"Regrettably," the prince said pointedly, "there was no body to recover. Only the rancor. It killed my guards—all except John, who reached us this morning."

Gasps rose up. "You saw it?" Grand Priest Larksong asked.

"Lady Nadine wasn't simply hysterical?" Flight murmured.

They all set their eyes on Nightrender.

"Did you kill it?" asked the queen. That was the first important question they'd asked.

"Yes."

A collective sigh rippled through the stable yard.

"You have our thanks," said the queen. "The rancor you killed might have been a real threat to the security of Caberwill. It seems it was a fearsome foe."

Everyone's eyes returned to the bodies.

"They died protecting the crown prince," Nightrender said. Because people needed that kind of reassurance, that death had purpose, that it had been faced with courage. It brought them comfort.

"Indeed," Queen Grace murmured. Then, with more force: "We're grateful for your swift action and invite you to remain in Honor's Keep. Your old quarters are being restored, and the servants assigned will see that a bath is drawn within the hour."

This wasn't the normal level of gratitude Nightrender received, but it was certainly more than she'd expected from the Highcrowns, given the cold reception yesterday. "Thank you," she said. She really was quite ready for a bath.

They're only doing this to keep you from the other kingdoms.

"We hope that you'll use your time here to clear the malsites plaguing the kingdom," the queen went on. "I'm sure Rune has explained that we have suffered with them for four hundred years."

They didn't care yesterday, whispered the voice. ***They aren't suffering as much as they claim. They are accustomed to their malice.***

It was difficult to disagree with that assessment, but then she'd known the Highcrowns for only a day. That was hardly enough time to pass judgment.

"Of course I will remove malsites. I must cleanse one each from Embria and Ivasland, and then I will return to Caberwill to take down another." She couldn't show favoritism.

The king and queen frowned, but neither of them argued; that fear still lurked behind their eyes. After a moment, King Opus said, "I see. Regardless, we are all relieved the Incursion was dealt with swiftly."

"It's hardly been *dealt* with, Father." Rune fumbled with his pack, but even with his bandaged hands he managed to unlatch the flap and draw out a canvas sack. He hurled it at the group's feet and the contents spilled over the flagstones, dark and stinking of ammonia and rot.

At first, it looked like nothing, just globs of black slime and white gristle, but the foul smell (and small splash) made everyone jump back.

Nightrender curled her lip. Prince Rune had gone off on his own earlier, but she'd understood that he wanted to relieve himself in private. Now she realized he'd been gathering pieces of the rancor instead. She hoped he hadn't *touched* any of it.

"That was uncalled for," muttered a sharp-faced woman from the cluster of nobles.

The king turned to a secretary, who was already poised with a pen and paper. "Make a note for us to discuss my son's behavior at this afternoon's council meeting."

"A meeting?" Prince Rune stalked forward, fury spinning around him.

"A *meeting*? Our problems are bigger than whatever you all think of me. First, the Incursion is happening *now*. Forces inside the Malice won't stop with one rancor. There will be more. Hundreds of thousands more, and they will overwhelm every kingdom, including Caberwill."

Someone in the back of the group laughed faintly—the nervous sort that indicated they didn't want to believe the truth, but they did. A little.

"And second," Prince Rune went on, "when our people find out that their fears were warranted, they will blame you. This Incursion began in *our* kingdom. Under *your* watch. Father. Mother. *You* are the rulers who repeatedly refused to hear the truth from your own people." His breath heaved with anger, and his fists would have curled if not for the bandages.

So he wasn't a perfect ally, what with the secrets he was keeping from her, but at least he seemed to care about the impending darkness.

"And what would you propose we do?" asked the king, his tone impassive. "We're already fighting a war on two fronts. You'd have us add a third?"

"The third has always been there." Nightrender stepped forward, causing a significant number of councilors to step backward. "You decided long ago to ignore the signs because you'd rather fight one another than face the true enemy. What stirs inside the Malice is larger and more deadly than you could ever imagine. The fate of humanity rests in your hands, yet you sow discord rather than take up arms against the rancor. With your wars, you enable darkness."

King Opus glared at her for a long moment, then turned back to Prince Rune as though she hadn't spoken. "You were to return with Princess Johanne, and, once our malsites were cleared away, you were to send the Nightrender back to Winterfast Island to sleep. You were to make her see that we have no Incursion."

"I never agreed to that—"

A flash of red crossed Nightrender's vision. Prince Rune had made different bargains with both of them.

"You swore to petition your parents for Dawnbreaker trials," she growled, advancing on him. "You said I'd have everything I needed to stop the Incursion. Armies. Obsidian. *Anything*. Tell me you will not go back on your word."

"I'm not. I just— Well, Princess Johanne wasn't there." Prince Rune was starting to sweat. "As the crown prince, I have to think about what that means for my kingdom, and unfortunately, it greatly limits our options. But I intend to end the conflict with Embria swiftly, any way I must—whether through negotiating an alternative bride or a prompt end to any resistance. We can't linger on this fight, I know that. Once it's over, you and I will end the Incursion. I swear to you."

"The Incursion will not wait," Nightrender said. "It is already here."

Where did he think they would find the time to fight a *whole war*? Did he expect she'd simply pluck a spare year or two from the air?

"What do you want from me?" Prince Rune held up his bandaged hands. "I'm doing my best."

"It is not enough," Nightrender said. "I need Dawnbreakers. *Real* Dawnbreakers. Hold the trials immediately and get me an army I can actually use."

The prince's expression tightened, as though she'd struck him. Then, his eyes hardened. "Holding trials is not my decision, as I told you. I'm not king. You need my parents for that."

Nightrender glanced at the king and queen. They did not look as though they intended to hold Dawnbreaker trials. Not now. Not ever.

"You yourself said that our wars fuel the Malice," Prince Rune said. "Let me end the wars. Then we can figure out how to end the Incursions."

"That isn't how this works. You've been filling your cup with poison every day of your life, and now you say you'll quit—after you drink an entire barrel. You cannot cure poison with more poison. You will die."

"Was becoming your Dawnbreaker any safer?"

"You're a prince. You shouldn't be my Dawnbreaker."

"Finally," King Opus muttered. "She says something that makes sense."

"You may have the privilege of ignoring our political problems," Prince Rune pressed, "but I don't. I have to look at the world head-on, without blinking. Embria *will* want an answer for the death of their crown princess. Perhaps you can afford not to take sides, but I don't have that luxury. I must address this."

"Your hands are not as tied as you believe they are. There is a choice, and the best one is to stop the Incursion. Fight *with* me."

Prince Rune breathed out through his teeth. "I promised to help you," he said stiffly. "And I will."

"Your promises are now meaningless to me, Rune Highcrown." Her wings flared wide. Perhaps she was being too hard on him, but this was all so frustrating. He was the only Dawnbreaker she had, and he shouldn't be one at all—royals had other loyalties. (Also, he was, quite possibly, her soul shard.) And now he intended to go off to war and leave her with *nothing*? The Incursion wouldn't wait for him—or the world—to be ready to fight it. "I joined you in your quest to rescue your princess. I cut away your malsite. I have fulfilled my end of our bargain, but you seem to have forgotten that you agreed to help me."

The prince hissed. "*I* have forgotten nothing. I am simply asking you to wait. Do you not understand my position?"

Her jaw clenched, and her eyes narrowed. Her wings stretched until they were fully extended. Several people in the crowd stepped away, but Nightrender ignored them.

"Go on, then," Prince Rune taunted. "Fly off, if you have no respect for our *petty* problems. Abandon your only friend in this whole burning world."

"We are not friends."

Again, he flinched as though struck, and she knew with certainty now that she was pushing too hard, but it was too late. Prince Rune took an angry step toward her, keeping his voice a low growl. "I summoned you," he said. "I trusted you. I believed in you when no one else did. You may not like me, but I am the only one here who doesn't want you to go back to Winterfast and sleep for the next thousand years."

"Boy, be silent—" King Opus started, but Nightrender didn't give him a chance to finish.

"You may trust me," she said, "but I cannot trust you. Not when you are hiding things from me."

Prince Rune let out a long, bitter laugh. "Do you want to know what you can't remember? Do you want to know why everyone fears you?"

She glanced around the middle ward, catching the shock and terror on people's faces—not just the council, but the watchmen on the top of the curtain wall, the grooms from the stables, the people peering out the keep windows. "We will not speak of this now."

"We have to speak of it sometime. Why not now?" Prince Rune was shaking with anger. "So here it is: four hundred years ago, when you came back from the Malice, you turned on us."

Nightrender went still, as though ice encrusted her body. All around the middle ward, people gave horrified gasps as they covered their mouths with their hands.

"You *murdered* us."

She couldn't feel her hands. Her wings. She couldn't feel anything except this reflexive refusal of his accusation. It couldn't be true. "No." Her denial was a mere whisper, a breath—a plea. "I wouldn't."

"You did." Prince Rune spoke coolly, levelly, as though he knew exactly how much the words cut her. He met her eyes and said, "You slaughtered every royal from every kingdom. You're as much of a monster as the things you kill."

16.
Rune

She'd hurt him, so he'd hurt her back. He hadn't even stopped to consider the wisdom of it. But as soon as the words were out, he knew he'd made a mistake.

He'd just told the Nightrender the truth about the Red Dawn.

A beat passed between them—Rune's heart pounding, the Nightrender's expression one of absolute horror—and then she spun, drawing her sword in the same motion, and before he had time to wonder if she meant to massacre another royal family, she flew up and away, skimming past an open window on the third floor. A girl watching from there ducked back inside.

The middle ward was absolutely silent, save the wind, the horse's gentle snorts, and the hum of the city on the mountain below.

Then, softly: "What has happened?" Grace turned her gaze from the sky to Rune. "What have you done?"

"Could she not remember what she did?" Charity's voice was quiet, but filled with unease. "Is the royal family in danger now? What of the girls? Sanctuary and Unity. We must hide them, Your Majesty!"

"The Red Dawn was divine judgment." Dayle spoke calmly. "The princesses have done nothing—"

"If the Red Dawn was divine judgment," Rupert murmured, softly enough that the gathered crowd in the ward could not hear, "then what, exactly, was being judged? Look at our current situation. Our fair rulers weren't going to summon the Nightrender at all. They tried to send her away. They kept secrets from her. And, dare I say it"—Rupert looked directly at Rune—"hurt her feelings."

Rune swallowed around a knot in his throat. The torment in her eyes still pierced him. He had lashed out with the most cutting thing he could think of, the one thing he knew would wound her.

Regret lanced through him. He didn't usually think of himself as a cruel person, but he had the capacity for it, same as anyone, and not to mention he'd seen a *rancor* the day before, he hadn't slept, and his burned hand sent a shock of pain through him every time he so much as twitched his fingers. The combination slowed his mind, making him speak without thinking. And he'd turned his unkindness on the Nightrender. . . .

"If she had intended to bring harm to the Highcrowns," Dayle tried again, "then she would have."

"It doesn't matter." Opus's face was red with anger, his eyes dark and his jaw clenched tight. "We are now in more danger than ever, because *this child* could not control his temper. Who's to say whether the Nightrender will fulfill her duty and destroy the world's malsites—or whether she will go to one of our enemies and warn them of our plans? Unfortunately, I cannot imagine that the *crown prince* was exactly careful when it came to sharing information with the Nightrender."

Shame burned up Rune's throat and cheeks. Was it too late to return to the ex-malsite and throw himself back into the fissure?

He hadn't been careful. He knew that now. He'd been reckless from the beginning, acting on impulse because he was hungry for action and desperate to see this Incursion ended.

And now all his problems remained, complicated by the fact that everyone who could help him was angry with him.

If only Princess Johanne had been alive. Her presence would have solved so many of his problems: the imminent war with Embria, his parents' reluctance to hold Dawnbreaker trials, the general fear of the Nightrender herself. If they'd been able to return to Brink with the missing princess (and perhaps the majority of Rune's guards) alive and well, the Crown Council and the rest of the Caberwilline court would surely have viewed the Nightrender differently.

But no. He'd been too late to save anyone.

He was always too late.

Around him, the Crown Council and his parents were still buzzing, working themselves up into a froth.

"This won't end here," Charity said. "I move to hold a council meeting right away."

"I second," said Rupert. "We need to get this situation with the Nightrender under control."

"Absolutely." Charity linked her arm with Rupert's, and Rune's heart sank to all-new lows. This was well and truly out of his control. Those two never agreed.

"I'll tend to the prince's wounds first, if that's all right." Grand Physician Asheater glanced at the king and queen, and when they nodded she stepped around the splash of melted rancor. "Please come with me to the infirmary." The grand physician's tone was kind, but that didn't mean anything. Her tone was always kind. There was a look in her eyes that clearly signaled her anger. His failure meant her department would be forced to work even harder, what with war being deadly by nature.

Dayle shot Rune a sympathetic glance. He would defend Rune, no doubt, but as for what good it would do . . .

"Once you're finished in the infirmary," Queen Grace whispered stiffly, catching Rune's arm as he passed, "go to your rooms and wait for us. We will come visit you when a decision has been reached."

Rune's heart pounded in his throat. "What decision is that?"

"Whether or not you have any place in this kingdom's future."

17.
Hanne

Several times as she raced along the highway, Hanne lost her speed.

The horse would stumble. Bone-searing pain would tear through her body. She screamed with the agony of slowness until the spell passed and she could move quickly again. People noticed her, like the first time, but she'd always speed up again before they could ask questions.

Until she didn't.

The fifth or sixth time it happened, Hanne slowed and stayed slow, and then the pain grew so intense that she had to climb off the horse and vomit into the grass. A woman driving a cart along the road stopped and gave her a sip of water. When she noticed the blood crusted on Hanne's face, her torn dress, and her emaciated figure, she insisted on giving her a ride into the city.

Hanne sat in the back of the cart, stuffed between two canvas-covered crates. The horse plodded along beside them, tethered by his reins looped and knotted around one of the wooden slats.

The cart was marginally more comfortable than riding the stolen horse, mostly because it didn't rub the saddle sores that had developed on her thighs.

"How did this happen to you?" asked the woman. Martina, she'd said her name was. She couldn't have been much older than Hanne, but there was a startling weariness to her eyes. What had this woman been through? Yes, she lived in a kingdom with a terrible climate and low crop yields, and she drove a cart filled with—Hanne peeked under the tarp concealing Martina's wares—turnips, but it wasn't as though she'd been trapped in a malsite. It was *her* kingdom that was trying to inflict malice on Embria and Caberwill, in fact.

Hanne coughed weakly. "I'm on my way to see the king and queen. How far is Athelney?"

Martina looked at Hanne pityingly. "Not far, dear. We'll be there in less than an hour."

Hanne couldn't believe her fortune.

"Why do you need to see them?" Martina asked.

Well, that was rather rude. It wasn't any of her business. "I've never spoken with them before," Hanne said, as though admitting something very personal and embarrassing, and definitely not like she was avoiding the question.

"Oh." The woman smiled a little. "It's very easy to speak with them. They hear every case from every subject."

That was the rumor, but it was hard to believe it was true. Hanne had lived her entire life around the rulers of Embria—they were her parents, after all—and the last thing they had time to do was hear the petty grievances of the peasants at all hours. Perhaps if the Ivaslander monarchs spent more time ruling, their kingdom wouldn't be in such a sorry state.

Hanne couldn't wait to tell Nadine about this.

"What should I expect when I meet them?" Hanne asked.

"Ah. Well, it's simple enough. Once morning verses are finished, you'll go in with anyone else from your town—they divide you into groups by region—and then tell them what's on your mind."

That didn't seem like a very good system, and it didn't really answer Hanne's question. And morning verses? Hanne had heard that Ivasland required its people to recite various pledges of commitment to the kingdom, but every morning? And how did they know if a person skipped?

But asking any of her questions—about practices *everyone* was supposed to know—might seem suspicious.

They rode the rest of the way in quiet. It was strange now, being at normal speed. She'd almost gotten used to the slowed-down sounds, the long sunrise, the eternal night. . . .

She shook those feelings away. The speed had come from the malsite, and the malsite was evil.

Hanne was *not* evil.

She wasn't *good*, she understood that much, but *Nadine* was good, and Nadine wouldn't be able to love someone who was evil.

I'm coming, Nadine, Hanne thought. *Just as soon as I know the rancor won't kill me.*

After an hour, the city came into view.

It wasn't anything like she'd expected. Granted, she didn't have much in the way of experience with capital cities—only Solcast, which was a glittering gem, refined over generations of Fortuin rule and evolving fashion—but knowing that Ivasland was poverty-stricken, she'd anticipated a run-down version of home.

Not . . . dust.

The dust was everywhere, covering the small, withered gardens, the people begging for scraps on the side of the road, and the pathetic wooden buildings that lined the main avenue. At first glance, she didn't see one single statue of a revered war hero—or a journalist, physician, or lecturer, which was more likely here.

Then the stench caught up with her. Like dead animal plus dust plus brackish water. Having been in close proximity to a rancor recently, it wasn't the *worst* odor Hanne could think of, but nevertheless, she wrinkled her nose.

"I know," said Martina. "With the drought, the city's stopped cleaning the streets. Perhaps if Embria had permitted us to dig those canals all those years ago . . . But, well, we couldn't afford their water anyway. And a little dust isn't a *terrible* price to pay for independence, is it?"

Everything would be better once Hanne ruled all three kingdoms.

She would bring a peace Salvation had never known. It was ambitious, but the world would change for nothing less.

As they entered the city center, the woman offered Hanne a hopeful smile. "Do you think you can make it from here? I'd take you the rest of the way, but I'm afraid I'm behind on my delivery."

As though there might be some sort of turnip emergency. The horror.

Hanne forced herself to appear thoughtful, yet worried—but not *too* worried. She didn't actually want Martina coming with her. "I think I'll be fine," she murmured. "Thank you for all your help, but I'm afraid I don't have anything to repay your generosity . . ." She glanced at the stolen horse, reluctance in her eyes. "He's all I have, now that Mama and Papa are gone, but I could give him to you—"

"No, no!" Martina waved that idea away. "I wouldn't dream of accepting anything. We were heading the same direction anyway. And really, I'm just glad to be able to do something for a fellow young lady. We have to stick together."

A small chill worked through Hanne as she picked herself up out of the cart. "Thank you," she said again, surprised to find that she actually meant it this time. It was strange, meeting someone from Ivasland who might actually be a good person. (But how good? Surely she wouldn't have offered a ride if she'd known Hanne was a water-withholding Embrian—particularly an Embrian *princess*.)

Unsettled, she buried the feeling. Then—for better or worse—she went to help Ivasland break the Winterfast Accords.

After roaming Athelney—learning the layout of the city, watching the people go about their business, and working herself up to follow the rancor's instructions—Hanne headed away from the barn where she'd stashed her horse, away from the chicken coop where she'd stashed her dagger and her black glass worth more than the entire kingdom of Ivasland. It seemed unwise to leave such a fortune—in wealth and protection—in a stranger's outbuilding, but she couldn't waltz in to the Ivaslander court with all that obsidian on her.

Ivasland—continually defying expectations—didn't have a castle. They had a large building, which was kept in good repair, at least, but it just *looked* . . . Well, it wasn't a castle. A bland stone facade, a handful of practical columns, and tan-curtained windows to block out the heat: this was where the king and queen of Ivasland ruled.

Hanne was almost embarrassed for them.

Figuring out what to do next was easy. A line of petitioners twisted out the low gate, everyone shifting anxiously from side to side. Hanne took her place at the back of the line and waited, even though everything inside her screamed to push to the front; she was royalty, after all. *Real* royalty.

But announcing herself here wasn't part of the plan, so she waited as people shuffled forward, and then, at the gates, a female guard looked through her bag and patted her torn dress, searching for weapons.

Hanne pulled herself tall, as though she didn't mind being stripped of her dignity in front of everyone.

The guard nodded at her partner. Safe.

"Name?" the second guard asked.

Hanne bit back her real name and position. Yes, it would grant her an *immediate* audience with the king and queen. And then it would grant her an audience with the gallows or some other death machine. She'd heard reports of how . . . creative Ivasland could be when it came to executions.

No, she had to follow the rancor's instructions *exactly*. "Hildy Boone," she said, using the name the rancor had given her.

"You're from Boone?" He squinted at her face. "Are you sure?"

"Of course!" She put on her most haughty tone. "I know where I live. Do you know where *you* live?"

He scowled. "Where's your identification?"

She stretched out what was left of her skirts. "Sir, I was robbed. Is that not obvious?"

His scowl deepened, but he motioned her through. "Fine. Go stand with the other Boone folk."

Once through the gate, Hanne found signs for all the notable Ivasland towns and their surrounding villages, and once she joined "the other Boone folk," she understood the guard's skepticism. They were, for the most part, dark-haired with soft facial features. With her (admittedly filthy) blond locks and angled cheeks, she looked nothing like them.

Nevertheless, she stood under the Boone sign and waited, both utterly infuriated to be made to endure *patience*, and also frighteningly adept at such a task now. Surviving the malsite had made her harder. Smarter. Stronger.

Better than all these peasants.

The others were summoned first, and hours passed in agonizing slowness as groups from Burke and Haist and Cole went inside, but at last her false name was called and she was escorted inside.

Yet again, Ivasland failed to meet even the lowest of her expectations. The throne room was all wrong.

Certainly, it had a pair of chairs at the far end, but they weren't *thrones*, not by her definition of the word, nor was there a proper court, or banners, or anything that would have signaled a royal presence. A rank odor soured the room—not just Hanne's current personal stench, but a more permanent stink that had long ago soaked into the walls and furniture. Had they ceased cleaning the royal estate, too?

Still, it wasn't anywhere as bad as the reek of the malsite and rancor, so Hanne schooled away a look of disgust and ignored it. She had perspective now.

Sitting on the—*ahem*—thrones: the king and queen of Ivasland. Both were skinny and short, in the sort of way that indicated they'd lived hungry lives, but they sat straight and watched her with keen eyes. They were younger than she'd expected, perhaps only five or six years her senior, but the difficulty of ruling Ivasland had marked them. And, rather than robes or gown, as befitting of monarchs, they wore matching tunics and trousers, dyed blue and yellow, with small gold pins on their collars to denote their ranks.

A shudder of loathing rolled through Hanne's entire body.

This was their fault—all of it. They'd decided to break the Winterfast Accords.

That, of course, necessitated Embria and Caberwill forming an alliance, which meant she'd been traveling to Brink and thus been caught in the malsite. The blame for *everything* fell squarely on their shoulders.

"Come forward," said the king.

Hanne did, but only because she didn't want to yell to be heard.

King Baldric consulted his notes, offered by a haggard secretary, and frowned. "This says you're from Boone, but you didn't come with the petitioners earlier. And you look nothing like them."

"I am Hildy Boone," Hanne maintained. "I moved to Boone when I was young."

"And that's why you don't sound like you're from Boone either?" the queen asked, one eyebrow raised.

Burn it. Hanne was trying to soften her consonants the way she'd heard while waiting in line, but clearly she was failing. Well, hopefully the story about moving to Boone would hold up until she finished with everything the rancor wanted. Then she'd get out as quickly as possible—on to Brink and marrying Rune Highcrown.

"You don't have to believe I am who I say I am," Hanne said, giving up the pretense of her accent. It was too thin, and she didn't have time to waste. The rancor would know if she quit, and it would come after her. Or it might go after *Nadine*, and that was one thing Hanne could not allow. "But you should believe that I came here to help you."

"What do you mean?" Abagail tilted her head. "How do you intend to help us?"

Resolved to see this through—for Nadine, if nothing else—Hanne drew herself up to her full height, as though she were in her own palace in Solcast, and smiled grimly. "Your malice device."

Tension spiked between the king and queen as they exchanged alarmed glances.

"I have no idea what you're talking about," Baldric said stiffly. "We uphold the Winterfast Accords."

Hanne allowed herself a small smile. It wasn't a shock that the general public of Ivasland didn't know about the mal-device. If they had, Embria would have learned *how* exactly Ivasland was breaching the Winterfast Accords, after the death of their informant. But this . . . this revealed that even the guards and trusted servants didn't know. The Ivaslander monarchs were still putting on a show in their throne room.

And that gave her the advantage.

"I know all about the mal-device," Hanne said, not bothering to keep her voice soft. "I know that the machine draws in malice through a negative-pressure suction. I know that your problem is containing malice for longer than a few minutes, but once you've succeeded there, you'll be able to capture malice from your own malsites and place it in strategically useful locations in Embria and Caberwill. Farms. Mines. Castles. Any idea what I'm talking about now?"

The secretary's mouth dropped open, and some of the guards turned to stare at the king and queen.

Hanne smiled to herself. She loved being right—and in control.

"Guards!" Baldric shouted, and all the men-at-arms stood at attention.

"Will you have them arrest me?" Hanne let her body relax. Yes, she was dirty, hungry, and surrounded by enemies, but she had all the leverage she needed here. "Do you think it would make you look more or less innocent of my allegations? What kind of kingdom is this? Arresting people who speak out in dissent of breaking treaties." Hanne shook her head sadly, even though her parents in Embria would absolutely have had someone like her arrested. But she was gambling on what she knew about Ivasland and its public facade of fairness.

Baldric's face was red as he growled, "Give us the room. I would not have my people listen to such blatant lies."

Immediately, a handful of worried guards exited. The secretary's pen hovered over parchment, and he looked around, unsure if he should go, too. But when Abagail dismissed him again, more forcefully, he followed the guards out the door.

Hanne loved winning.

Of course, she'd just angered the most important people in Ivasland—the people she needed to persuade to let her help finish the mal-device if she didn't want to get eaten by the rancor. But she could do this, she was certain now. She was Johanne Fortuin and she'd never faced a truly insurmountable obstacle—at least when it came to humans.

Finally, it was just Hanne and the two Ivaslander monarchs. So vulnerable. How easy it would be to kill them right here. Even without her dagger, which was hidden with the obsidian, she could end the Ivasland monarchy using her own two hands. She could save Embria—and Caberwill, since it would soon be hers—from this long, unsustainable war. She could put the entire continent out of its misery in mere minutes.

But while that would be temporarily satisfying, there'd be no time for *Hanne* to enjoy the victory. Guards would be on her the moment one of the monarchs screamed. She'd be executed. And murdering these two wouldn't solve the problem of the mal-device, or even of the Ivasland state, not really. Someone—someone *not* the king and queen—was working on the machine, after all. Other people did know of its existence. And if they learned Hanne's identity, they'd be even more inclined to use it against Embria.

Not to mention the rancor had specifically forbade her from killing them.

"All right," said Abagail. "You have our attention."

"Good." Hanne squared her shoulders. "As I said, I am here to help you with the device." Even if she couldn't rid the world of these two, she would make the best of the situation. Control it. Guide it. The rancor had instructed her only to help Ivasland finish the mal-device. It hadn't said she couldn't try to destroy the kingdom from within.

Tuluna the Tenacious was Hanne's teacher. For years, the patron Numen of Embria had whispered advice and plans into her mind, training her how to handle every situation imaginable. With such preparation, Hanne could turn any situation to her advantage.

"Why?" Baldric asked.

"How do you even know about it?" The disdain in Abagail's tone was a knife, but she was far from an expert at wielding scorn. Hanne, however, had studied the art of contempt since the moment she'd left her mother's body, and the best way to rile someone like Abagail was to stay silent. The queen went on: "Are you a spy?"

"No." Embria did have one spy here, but they hadn't heard from the man in a fortnight. (A normal fortnight. It was, of course, longer for Hanne herself.) "As for why: Does it matter? I can help you."

"It matters if you expect us to trust you with our most valuable project."

Hanne's smile returned. Easy, like lighting bugs on fire. They didn't even know what was happening to them.

"Well, clearly you have a leak somewhere. I wouldn't have found out about the device otherwise, would I?" Hanne settled into herself. At last, she was returning to her true identity, engaged in the sort of verbal combat she excelled at. None of this surviving on dirty stream water and eating berries.

She'd been made for more than enduring; she'd been made to conquer.

"Tell us where you've heard these rumors," Baldric said.

Hanne glided closer, as though she were a swan in a swamp. "I heard about the device from someone who *wants* it to be completed. I cannot compromise that source."

"Hmm." Abagail narrowed her eyes.

"Here's the truth." Hanne looked at her enemies face on. "I'm not from Ivasland, but Embria. I know you know that."

"It's obvious," said Abagail.

"Anyone can tell," said Baldric.

Hanne nodded. Now they were more at ease. Now they'd seen through her charade and thought they had the advantage. "I grew up in Solcast," she went on, "but I'm a pariah among my people. I wanted to learn about science and math—about mechanics. I had ideas for improving grain production, but even at the university I was told to keep those thoughts to myself. Such improvements would work, but the Fortuin family isn't happy unless their people are pushed to the absolute limit. Much easier to keep them in line that way. They are brutality itself, those Fortuins."

Abagail's expression was hard. "I find your story difficult to believe."

Hanne gasped in perfectly manufactured outrage. "What? You find it hard to believe that I don't want to be worked to the bone every day when there's a better way? That I want more food for my neighbors?"

"Tell the truth," Abagail said softly. "How did a young girl like you learn of our little project?"

"Everyone in Embria knows that something is happening here." Hanne made her voice gentler. "That's why the princess was sent off to marry Rune Highcrown. I'm sure you're aware."

"Of course." Baldric's face contorted with anger. "They mean to crush us, but it won't be long before they destroy each other."

Hanne nodded knowingly. "The alliance will only last so long, but I think it will last long enough for real harm to befall Ivasland—unless your machine is finished quickly. That's why I'm here."

"Because you, an Embrian, don't want Ivasland brought to its knees?"

With a long sigh, Hanne approached Abagail and Baldric. "No. I don't want Ivasland to fall. As I said, there are aspects of your kingdom that I respect—more than respect. I *admire* the education you guarantee to all your people. I admire your efforts to treat people equally, regardless of birth. And I admire that you don't forbid ingenuity simply because you like to make people work harder than necessary."

"True enough," Baldric said cautiously. "But is that sufficient reason to betray your homeland?"

"It is. It's why I'm here to help you. I want Ivasland—and its culture and ideals—to have a fighting chance against the combined regression of Embria and Caberwill. I want knowledge to be the light in this world."

The monarchs glanced at each other, uncertainty clear on their faces. "How can we trust that you won't sabotage the machine and delay our schedule?"

Hanne tilted her head, not bothering to hide her exasperated look. "It won't be just me and your machine, will it? I'll be observed, certainly. Unless you don't trust those who work on the project."

It was so easy to plant the seeds of mistrust and watch them grow. First in the guards and the secretary. Now in the monarchs themselves.

Again, the king and queen looked at each other. A hard quiet wove through the room.

Now she had to soften it.

"Think about it," Hanne said. "Not only could you win your war against

Embria and Caberwill, you could capture malice inside malsites and take it to the Malstop—put it back where it belongs. You could throw it into the ocean, even. Clean up the land and make it safe for your people to travel and work. You can have war *and* you can have peace."

It was a nice thought, Hanne reasoned. Every monarch—all across Salvation—talked about peace as though it were a possibility, but they never meant what they said. The war-hungry Caberwillines didn't actually want it, and Hanne's power-mad parents couldn't truly conceive of such a thing. And the Ivaslanders . . . Well, they were breaking the ancient Winterfast Accords, and that said enough about their views. (True, Hanne was helping them do it, but she was being coerced.)

None of the three kingdoms deserved peace, but Hanne would bring it to them anyway.

Abagail's shoulders curled in, as though the weight of constant war decided to make itself known again. Of all the kingdoms, the war had affected Ivasland the most. They had few natural resources and the climate was not kind to them: crops struggled in the oppressive heat, rain mostly refused to fall, and when it *did* turn wet, towns were washed away by huge storms.

Ivasland needed peace. They were desperate for it. They would die without it.

"Are you certain you know how to finish the device?" Baldric asked. He managed to keep the despair out of his tone, but Hanne had seen the condition of his kingdom, even the state of his throne room: filthy, dusty, dry; an endless parade of petitioners; and beggars on every thoroughfare. He wasn't fooling anyone, least of all her.

Briefly, Hanne closed her eyes and recalled the rancor's voice, the terrible way it spoke, the threat of the Dark Shard if she didn't succeed. Every word it had uttered was etched into her mind, carved with the hot knife of pain.

"I'm certain," she whispered.

"Very well." Abagail stood up. "Finish the device, and we will grant you asylum here in Ivasland. You'll be entitled to a proper education, just like everyone else. But know this: if you fail, or we discover you've lied to us, you will be immediately executed."

18.
Rune

Just as Rune started to fall asleep, his mind conjured up pallid gray flesh and the reek of ozone and rot. Heat rushed through his bandaged hands. Jagged teeth closed around his throat, piercing soft skin. He was going to die. He was going to bleed out. He was going to become a decaying black mess on his own bed.

He jerked awake, gasping, his heart racing as he scanned the darkness of his room for the rancor.

But it wasn't there, just like it hadn't been the last seven times he'd startled away from sleep, not having rested at all.

Rune groaned, just to hear his own voice and prove to himself that he was alive. The *rancor* was dead. He'd seen the Nightrender kill it. But the beast lived on in his mind, and he couldn't stop seeing the way it had *looked* at him before it died. He couldn't forget the cacophony of its voice as it had said, *Such a sad thing you are. But my king could make you great.*

Bile rushed up his throat as he lurched out of bed and stomped around his room. It was a real noise. An intentional noise.

But even as he fumbled his way through shaking a light globe—difficult with the bandages around his hands—he couldn't help but think of those blood-soaked words the rancor had uttered.

The vein of magma where he had nearly died.

The plants surging up to strangle him.

The guards' bodies strewn across the ground.

Everything about the malsite had been too much. He'd spent the night after staring at the forest-dappled sky and trying to comprehend what had happened to him, how his world had become completely different from how it had been that morning.

One sleepless night hadn't been enough to make sense of his new world. Apparently he needed at least two.

"Perhaps tomorrow night, I'll simply pass out from exhaustion," he muttered to the globe of light, still cupped in his hands. The burns throbbed. Earlier, the grand physician applied a pain-numbing salve to the burns and scrapes before wrapping his hands in bandages. It had given him a few hours of relief, but now it was starting to wear off.

Ah, the puppet prince.

Rune shuddered and—a moment later—realized he was checking under his bed, like a child afraid of an imaginary monster.

But this monster was real.

And *dead*, he reminded himself.

But what of the rancor king it had spoken of? He was still alive, still sending his army through the Rupture, still planning to send them into Salvation.

A loud bang sounded against Rune's door, making him jump. The light globe nearly fell from his hands, but when the bang came again, he realized it was only someone knocking. He breathed out long and slow, hoping his heart would lower from his throat and back into his chest where it belonged.

As Rune started for the suite door, he remembered that it was after midnight. Only bad news came this late.

Perhaps it was an assassin—a polite assassin who knocked first.

The door opened before he could get to it, and—dashing his hopes for a polite assassin—his parents walked in. Both were still wearing the same clothes from earlier, which meant they'd been with the Crown Council since Rune had blabbed the Nightrender's secrets—both the secrets he was keeping *for* her and the secrets he was keeping *from* her.

He'd done his best to avoid thinking about that, how he'd estranged the single best hope for Caberwill. She'd trusted him, and then he'd ruined it all in a fit of fury. The only other time he'd felt this bad about something . . . Well, he would always be paying that price, every time someone called him crown prince.

Guilt drove its claws deeper into Rune's heart as he took in his parents' tired expressions, the slowness with which they moved, and the weariness of their postures.

"Rune," Opus said softly, and it occurred to Rune that they weren't exactly angry—not like they had been earlier, or any of the other times Rune had disappointed them. No, they just looked wrung out, as though the meeting had cost them years, not hours.

None of this—the council running late, his parents too tired to yell—was a good sign.

He wished again for that assassin.

"What's the news?" Rune sat at the table, motioning with his bandaged hands for them to sit as well.

They did not sit.

"The council meeting was, as I'm sure you've guessed"—Opus rubbed his temples—"quite heated."

"No one came to actual blows," Grace said. "But I think I would have preferred that to the verbal sniping."

Burn everything. Rune was *so* tired. He wished he'd asked the grand physician for a sedative so he could have avoided this conversation until morning. "Well, skip to the end, I suppose."

"The council has many grievances, all compelling. We went in circles for a long time. There are those on the council, first, who are unhappy that you failed to follow through on your apparent promise to the Nightrender. 'He swore to join her in battle against the malice' was the exact phrase. There is fear that this will fatally offend her."

"They *wanted* me to help her against the Incursion?" Rune scowled. "That doesn't sound like the council."

"It was Charity." Opus crossed his arms. "She, in particular, thought you should have immediately gone through the Soul Gate with the Nightrender."

Ah, well, that made more sense. Charity was still hoping either Sanctuary or Unity would become crown princess—and that *she* could be a regent, should something terrible befall the king or queen (a real possibility, with more war brewing). It was true that Charity spent an inordinate amount of time visiting Rune's sisters and bringing them little gifts. Everyone knew she wanted the girls to trust her, even love her, and there'd been plenty of efforts to limit her time with them, but as a fixture on the Crown Council, it was hard to tell her that she could *not* visit the royal family.

"Other members of the council were upset that you'd summoned the

Nightrender to begin with. As you no doubt knew they would be. A bigger decision you could not have made alone."

Rune nodded.

"And as for Princess Johanne . . ."

Rune tilted his head.

"They are furious that you didn't bring her back alive. Only that could have justified the Nightrender's summoning to them."

"Oh." If Rune hadn't already had a headache, this would have given him one.

"And finally, they are horrified that you told the Nightrender about the Red Dawn—at risk to all of us." Grace blew out a breath. "It is very hard to believe that you'd choose to remind her of that. We were blessed that she didn't remember on her own."

Rune slouched into his chair.

He'd bungled this one pretty hard.

"We don't have to tell you how disappointed we are, as parents," Opus said.

And yet, they were telling him anyway.

"We were against you summoning the Nightrender from the very beginning," Grace said. "We *told* you that it wasn't something we would ever consider."

Dayle had said he'd speak up for Rune at the meeting. Had the grand priest even opened his mouth?

Rune sighed. "We are on the precipice of a full-on Incursion. Something must be done." Telling them his worries had never worked before, though. Why did he think it would work this time?

"I know you have always been concerned about Incursions. I understand that you want to solve all the problems of the world, and that you feel greatly for those affected by malsites or living close to the Malstop." Opus placed a hand on Rune's shoulder. "The desire to do good in the world will make you a compassionate king."

Assuming he was allowed to become king, not unseated by the council in a coup. But Rune hazarded a smile. "I hope so."

"The challenge is knowing what you can actually accomplish and what issues must wait."

"Some things will wait only so long," Rune said cautiously. "If every generation of kings were to put aside the looming crisis of their time, surely it would be that much worse when it arrives."

Opus pressed his mouth into a line. "Of course. But malice has been threatening the world for thousands of years. It has *always* been an imminent threat, and yet when it spills over, we have *always* beaten it back."

Rune clenched his jaw. That was because they'd always summoned the Nightrender. Armies didn't have the power to do what she did. The king was giving credit to his predecessors for the battles she had fought, the lives she had saved, and the ground she had healed.

"Think of it as a cycle," the king went on. "A natural cycle of good and evil pushing against each other. Evil may be pushing now, but good will push back."

"Good and evil aren't some formless forces, Father." Rune kept his tone even. "Rancor are real creatures, eager to destroy us. As for good—we, humanity, must consciously choose to become that good. We must choose to push back. And I do choose that: I can't ignore this threat. I won't."

Opus rubbed his temples. "Do you think the Nightrender will return to Honor's Keep?"

"I have no idea." He wished she would, so that he could explain why he'd said those things—and tell her more about the Red Dawn. The truth was so much more complicated than a few words spoken in anger.

"If she does . . . and if she has removed some of our malsites . . . perhaps I will be able to get council approval for Dawnbreaker trials."

Rune's heart lifted. "Yes?"

"I'll try," Opus said. "The council understands that she will not be easily laid aside or returned to sleep; Dawnbreakers may be all that can placate her. But she must prove herself to us. She must *prove* she's come to work good in the world. Otherwise, we have every reason to fear her—especially now that she knows about the Red Dawn."

As far as the Crown Council knew before, the Nightrender had known about the Red Dawn this whole time. But there was no point in making that argument.

His best option was to be agreeable, if there was a chance that

Dawnbreaker trials might be held. "I'll visit the temple library and research the trials and battles the Dawnbreakers helped win. Surely the Crown Council will see the benefit in resurrecting this practice if they can understand—"

"Yes," Opus said. "We'll see. But go ahead. Research. At the very least, it will keep you out of trouble for a while."

Rune gave a deep sigh. "So what would the council like to see done with me?"

Grace pressed a hand to Rune's shoulder. "The council feels there are too many uncertainties right now. They're angry, and they want to see you punished, but considering the war, the the death of the princess, the Nightrender . . . No changes to your station will be made—for the time being."

So the decision was to not make a decision. Rune frowned.

"Rune," his father continued, "you should be aware that there are many councilors who still feel we should have elevated one of your sisters. You need to try harder to make these people your allies. Win them over. Flatter them. You do *not* want them as enemies. Do you understand? They have power of their own." The king paused a beat. "Your mother and I think—for now—that your best option is to stay in your rooms and *recover* some more. And, I suppose, visit the library. But certainly don't speak with anyone. Don't ride off anywhere. And please don't summon anything more. We'll run the kingdom. You focus on getting better."

Focus on not ruining anything else, they meant.

A few minutes later, the king and queen left Rune's rooms.

There was no chance of him sleeping now, not while he was thinking about how thoroughly he'd mishandled everything. Instead, he went onto his balcony and breathed in the cool summer night.

He'd have liked to blame Princess Johanne for all this. Everything had been going well until she disappeared and got caught in a malsite. But even in that, he found blame for himself. He'd allowed her to go off on her own. He hadn't insisted on sending guards after her, fool that he was. He was responsible for everything that had happened since.

Rune never thought he'd mourn an Embrian, but as he gazed into the glowing dome of the distant Malstop, he truly wished Princess Johanne were alive.

19.
HANNE

In the small, guarded room she'd been given for the night, Hanne slept poorly, her dreams full of malice and rancor. So when the queen herself arrived (after morning verses, which Hanne quickly learned were shouted from the streets so that everyone had to participate), Hanne was waiting, long since dressed in the beige uniform they'd provided.

With a small troop of personal guards before and after them—different guards from those who'd been in the throne room yesterday—Hanne and Abagail left the royal estate and stepped into the city, taking back streets. A queen and a future queen. Enemies. Although only Hanne knew it.

"The university isn't far," Abagail said as they walked. "That is where the work on this project is conducted. I've arranged a room for you on campus, and you'll be guarded at all hours."

Hanne had expected nothing less.

The queen went on: "I've spoken with the malicists and informed them that you will be joining their efforts."

That was surprising—or perhaps not, considering this was Ivasland. But the queen was speaking with these people directly? Face-to-face? Granted, the circle of people who knew about the mal-device was probably very small, but even so, Abagail apparently didn't realize that she was a *queen* not a messenger. Such things should be beneath her. There should be an intermediary. A master of malicists.

"I've told them nothing about you," Abagail said, "except that your name is Hildy Boone and that we have brought you in to help them finish the device. They may ask for more details regarding your education and how you came into this knowledge. Do not tell them anything. You're here to work, not to make friends."

Hanne was never here to make friends.

"I've written a dossier for you, with a believable backstory. Stick to it. Do not elaborate." Abagail pulled a folded sheet of paper from her pocket and gave it to Hanne.

The handwriting was small and neat, as though Abagail was used to conserving paper. It had names and towns, as well as a short list of educational interests and accomplishments. All of it implied she was from Ivasland.

"None of the people or places here have any relationship to any of the malicists. Your new workmates will not be able to challenge your history, unless you say something very stupid."

"What's a malicist?"

"Oh dear Vesa." Vesa was the Erudite, the patron Numen of Ivasland. Abagail looked as though she barely stopped herself from rolling her eyes. "A malicist is a scientist specializing in malice."

"I see." Hanne read the dossier again, then put it in her pocket. "Well, I had to make sure. Remember, I'm on your side."

Since she hadn't been sleeping much last night, she'd put a good deal of thought into how she might be able to use Ivasland's invention against them, or perhaps even have a similar machine constructed in Embria or Caberwill. She didn't *want* to break the Winterfast Accords, but she hadn't been the one to start this particular fire.

Abagail was nodding absently. "Yes, victory over our enemies."

Hanne followed the woman's gaze, at first finding nothing odd—until she noticed the stars in a few of the city's windows. They were made of angled lightrods, just the glass tubes without the metal casings. The sight truly seemed to shake Abagail.

Interesting.

First Athelney University was far more impressive than the royal estate, with tall brick buildings, plenty of light posts, and a cobbled path winding its way to a large fountain in a central courtyard. Not that the school was in *good* shape: dirt smothered every surface, doors hung crookedly, and the fountain held no water.

Yet, there had been efforts to repair it, and through classroom windows, Hanne caught sight of eager students and passionate instructors. This, Hanne understood, was also Vesa's grand temple. One of these buildings—Hanne couldn't tell which, not while they were walking so quickly—likely held the altars and other items of Numinous worship.

"The First Athelney University has seen better days," Queen Abagail admitted as they passed a plaque with lines from one of the verses, "but we give the school everything we can. Educating our youth is our best hope for the future."

"I find it fascinating that everyone in Ivasland is guaranteed an education, regardless of station. It's quite different where I'm from." In Embria, everyone knew that educating peasants was a waste of resources. (And possibly dangerous, should they learn words like *revolution* or *advocacy*.)

Of course, if the kingdom was educating at every level, then the students were learning exactly what the rulers wanted them to learn. Ivasland was good; everyone else was bad.

Hanne tucked that idea away for later.

"It is different." Abagail said it proudly, like she didn't realize her kingdom needed more farmers and fishers, not more archaeologists and architects. She motioned to a plaque as they walked past:

THE STRONGER AND MORE FOCUSED OUR MINDS,
THE BETTER IVASLAND WILL THRIVE.

And then another:

IVASLAND'S FUTURE IS MY FUTURE.

These phrases were among those Hanne had heard shouted from the streets this morning. It was all part of Ivasland's centuries-long effort to mold perfectly loyal citizens. Even Abagail, Hanne supposed, was a victim of this conditioning.

The knowledge didn't make Hanne hate her any less, however.

"Through hard work and necessity," Abagail said, "our students have developed technologies our ancestors only dreamed of."

"And do you think the kingdom is faring better than it was when you took the throne?" Hanne lifted an eyebrow. "Are the people better fed than they were ten years ago? Twenty years ago?"

Queen Abagail frowned. "In many ways, we are doing better. Our schools are well funded, and research has led to hardier crops. We've made infrastructural improvements to help our roads and buildings last longer, and our mines are safer than ever."

Having traveled through Ivasland, Hanne rather doubted any of these things were true—but she needed the queen to cooperate, so she bit her lip against further antagonizing.

The queen told her more about the university as they took the stairs to one of the tower laboratories, and that was where Hanne smelled it:

Rancor.

The scent was faint, but her eyes watered with desperate tears, and the back of her throat itched, and even her hands began to shake—

No, no, the beast wasn't here. It couldn't be, because she was doing exactly as it had ordered. *Exactly*.

Half a dozen guards blocked the way back down the stairs, but even they wouldn't prevent her from fleeing if necessary. If these Ivaslanders were keeping a rancor in the tower, she'd gather up all her obsidian and escape this wretched kingdom.

And promptly (probably) die.

She breathed in through her nose and out through her mouth, ordering her hummingbird heart to slow.

All she had to do was help them finish their mal-device. That was the only thing it had demanded of her. And if she could do this, she could do anything. She could take the crowns of Embria and Caberwill, and Ivasland, too, while she was at it; the southern kingdom clearly needed a much stronger leader, and she could deliver the improvements they were desperate to attain.

Just one step at a time. First, the mal-device.

"It does smell rather bad," the queen was saying. "That's why we moved this laboratory up here, where the wind can whisk away the stink. On still days, though . . ." She wrinkled her nose.

Abagail pushed open a door at the top of the tower.

"Your Majesty!" A trio of young men stopped what they were doing and bowed. No, they were two young men and one young woman; her hair was cropped short and she wore trousers like the boys, but she was much prettier than either of them. She looked at Hanne, appraisingly. Appreciatively?

Hanne smiled at her.

The girl dropped her face to hide her own smile.

"These are our malicists," Queen Abagail said. "Bear, Barley, and Mae. The rude one is Barley."

One of the boys—the scrawnier of the two, who wore glasses and had crow's feet around his eyes from squinting—frowned. Barley, presumably. "I think you mean Mae is the rude one."

The queen ignored him. "These are the best malicists in all Ivasland. They've been working on the project since its inception. They know everything there is to know about trapping and moving malice."

"Pleased to meet you," Hanne lied. "I'm Hildy Boone. I suppose you've been told I was coming."

"Just yesterday," Barley said. "But we don't need your help."

"We're glad to have you," said Mae, the girl still looking at Hanne in a way that left no doubt she saw through the embedded road grime and weeks of starvation. Even in this state, Hanne was the best-looking person in this room and everyone knew it.

"This is where we're developing the device." Queen Abagail motioned around the workroom, indicating all the cluttered tables and shelves packed with bits of metal and wire, alembics and books, bottles and tubes of strange substances, and many other unidentifiable objects. A large sheet of paper, crisscrossed with lines, rested on a table near the trio of researchers, weighed down with a handful of small cogs. A diagram.

"It doesn't look like much," Hanne said. "And everyone here is awfully young."

The queen's lip curled in annoyance. "I'm sure the machine will look more impressive when you finish it. As for the abundance of youth, well, Bear, Barley, and Mae are rising stars in their fields. We chose to employ students for this task rather than professors, due to the freshness of their thoughts and their openness to this work."

Something in that sentence made Mae visibly flinch.

How interesting.

"It's an honor to work with all of you," Hanne said finally.

Hopefully, with the rancor's knowledge branded into her mind, finishing the machine wouldn't take long. The faster she did this, the faster she could leave. Besides, it seemed entirely likely that her absence was causing problems for Embria and Caberwill. She wasn't certain how long she'd been missing in regular time, but even a few days could have dire consequences for the kingdoms and their alliance.

And if those brutish Caberwillines had harmed Nadine, Hanne would kill them all.

Finally, after a significant look Hanne's way, Abagail left the laboratory.

"All right," Hanne said when she was alone with the malicists. "Let's get started."

The machine wasn't large—only the size of a stack of books, plus the bulb protruding from the top. The metal plates that would hide the machine's innards were unscrewed and lying on the table, giving Hanne a good look at the tubes and wires that ran inside.

"We've had two main hurdles," Mae explained.

Hanne nodded absently, still looking over the machine while she wore her best judging face. She needed to learn about it without revealing that she had very little idea of what she was seeing. The rancor had told her *only* what the device required in order to be complete, but if Hanne wanted to bring the design to her own people, she needed to understand it. Certainly, she could try to steal the diagram, but in the hour she'd been in the lab, Bear and Barley watched her with suspicious eyes, and Mae . . . Mae just watched her.

Mae pointed to an opening covered by a fine metal mesh. "The biggest was drawing in malice from malsites without absorbing other matter as well. We tried several different filters, but eventually settled on a system that takes in everything and allows only non-malice to exit through the valve over here." She pointed to the other side of the machine. "This way, the bulb fills up, and everything that isn't malice is forced out by pressure."

"Yes, that seems logical." Hanne tried to remove the filter to get a look at it, but it was soldered into the machine. Chances of her being able to identify what it was made from were slim, anyway.

"Of course, that means we need a containment bulb that can withstand pure malice. It's so corrosive that it disintegrates every material we've tried." Bear motioned at a series of glass and metal bulbs on a shelf. Most were blackened and eaten away from the inside. "We even tried obsidian, but not surprisingly it weakened the malice. Without full potency, it's useless as a weapon."

Well, that made *perfect* sense. Why weaken a weapon against one's enemies? Hanne hadn't been giving Ivasland enough credit, she realized. They could be as ruthless as anyone.

"All that said, we've had measurable movement of malsite pellicles when we've placed a device just inside." Bear grinned widely.

"Just in the bipermeable pellicles, of course," Mae added.

"Unfortunately," said Bear, "the basic nature of unipermeable malsites prevents us from using those, unless we can somehow draw *all* of that site's malice into the machine. Otherwise, the machine can go in—"

"But it can't get out." Hanne bit the insides of her cheeks to keep her expression neutral. "Yes, that's how unipermeable malsites work."

"Fortunately," Mae said, "there's an ever-burning forest not too far away. We go there when we need to test."

Hanne pulled away from the machine, suppressing a shudder. "All right. Show me exactly how the machine is supposed to work. Every little piece."

The malicists glanced at one another, but Abagail must have been very persuasive because Mae, for one, got right to work showing Hanne the intricacies of the mal-device.

It was slow and difficult, as the malicists understood their machine and what they intended for it to do, and Hanne . . . Well, she had the rancor's instructions but no context, which meant the first day was spent teaching her the basic functions of the machine, then quizzing her about the function of each part. Hanne wasn't stupid, by any means, but her mind had been shaped for politics and manipulation. If she couldn't remember the difference between a capillary and capacitor, it was only because there had been gaps in her education.

But when she escaped this wretched kingdom, she intended to know everything about these vile machines and turn Ivasland's technology back on them.

Finally, the day came to a close, and the malicists—having accomplished nothing but teaching Hanne about the machine—began to clean their workspaces.

"We won't be forced to work through the night?" Hanne asked, surprised.

"No, it's too dangerous," Mae said. "We try to minimize the number of flames in the workroom because of the toxic and combustible substances we use. Even light globes are banned from this tower, unless everything is locked away in protective containers."

Hanne looked into one of the cupboards Barley was closing, just in time to see a bright red warning symbol on one of the jars.

"The globes don't actually cause problems," Mae whispered conspiratorially, "but early on a fire broke out and set us back two months, and we had to blame it on *something*. Now, they never make us work after dark."

"That's very clever," Hanne said, though when she ruled everything, she would make sure the people who worked for her never deceived her in such a way.

The four of them headed down the tower stairs, where guards joined them for the walk through the building and across the courtyard. Their assigned dormitory (where Hanne would also be sleeping for the remainder of her stay here) wasn't far.

"Do guards escort you every night?" Hanne asked Mae.

Mae spoke quietly. "Yes, every night. They're here to keep us safe."

"From what? No one knows what you're doing, do they?"

Mae's gaze darted across the courtyard. "They don't know exactly, but sometimes I think they can smell it."

Hanne followed to where Mae had glanced. There, in a window, she caught sight of another star made of lightrods. "I saw those this morning. What do they mean?"

"Nothing," Mae said quickly.

Well, that was suspicious. Those stars in windows were clearly *something*. It seemed like Hanne should find out what, exactly, was going on there.

The next morning, the news broke all across campus:

CROWN PRINCESS JOHANNE FORTUIN OF EMBRIA TRAPPED IN MALSITE

All five university newspapers had some variation of the headline, as well as the local Athelney papers and the national paper. Hanne had made the front page of every one of them.

"What a *tragedy*." Barley dumped an armful of newspapers onto one of the worktables. For his collection, he'd said, as they'd walked across the courtyard with their guards in tight formation around them.

"The most tragic thing I've ever heard," agreed Bear, sarcasm dripping from his tone. "Is it a surprise, though? They say she was never . . . right."

Hanne balled her fists. They were talking about *her*.

"Now that's not very nice." Mae went about the room, opening cupboards and retrieving tools and papers and mal-device components. "It is a tragedy that anyone was trapped in a malsite, although it's definitely better for us. Imagine if she actually had married the prince and their armies united. Doesn't bear thinking of."

"The alliance between Caberwill and Embria is in response to this machine." Hanne hooked her pack on a peg by the door; it had been lying on her bed last night, packed with necessities: a spare beige uniform, soap, and so on.

"So you sympathize with them?" Barley narrowed his eyes. "You think their alliance is right?"

"I think no kingdom has ever used malice as a weapon before. Not in thousands of years, anyway. Surely it isn't a surprise to you that the rest of Salvation would try to prevent the machine from being completed." Hanne walked to the window and gazed over the courtyard. It was light outside now, just after dawn, but the stars in the windows still shone brightly. "Surely everyone here has asked themselves whether the ends justify the means. I have."

The room was quiet for a moment.

Mae glanced down at her hands, her eyebrows knitting together. "Neither Caberwill nor Embria value human rights the way we do—decency, education, food for all. None of those monarchs have ever held themselves to the same standards Ivaslander kings and queens have for generations, before or *after* the Red Dawn. In war, there is no reward for doing what's right. I understand why King Baldric and Queen Abagail have decided that we must act before it's too late."

Bear nodded in agreement. "They hate us more than anything. They would join houses rather than let us thrive."

That wasn't right. Hadn't she just said it? The Fortuins and Highcrowns would join houses rather than allow Ivasland to *break the Winterfast Accords*. But she couldn't say that.

"I see." Hanne turned away from the window. "So you'd get your hands a little dirty in order to stop someone who's jumped whole-body into the filth?"

"Sometimes we must," said Mae.

Hanne would have liked to think about that more—wasn't that what *she* was doing, after all?—but if Abagail felt the sense of urgency to develop the machine was lessened because she believed Hanne was trapped . . .

That meant Hanne needed to finish this and get out of here as quickly as possible, before Abagail decided she wasn't desperate enough to need an Embrian to help finish the device before the allied kingdoms crushed her.

"Yes. Sometimes we must get our hands a little dirty," Hanne muttered. "That way, we can stop someone else who's covered in filth."

"Yes," said Bear. "That's exactly what we've been talking about."

"No," Hanne said. "I think that's how we contain malice."

"By throwing it into muck?" Barley scowled.

Hanne let out a grunt of frustration. "How do you build up a tolerance to poison?"

"Oh!" Mae's face lit up. "You ingest tiny amounts your body can fight off. You teach your body how to respond to it so that if you're ever given a lethal dose, you stand a chance at survival."

Bear was frowning at Hanne. "What a strange metaphor. You could have said something about throwing flour on a surface to keep dough from sticking, or spreading compost to fertilize fields, but you went for poison. Something is wrong with you."

Hanne's fingernails bit into her palms. *Not right. Something wrong.*

They could say whatever they wanted about her, but she was on the cusp of tearing this whole place to pieces. She just had to hand them the answers for the problems they could not solve. "Perhaps if there's a way to mix the bulb material and malice. That might fool malice into behaving as though the metal is a pellicle."

"You think you can fool malice?" Barley narrowed his eyes. "As though it's alive?"

Hanne waved that away. "I mean in the same way the same ends of magnets repel each other, or as malice itself tends to gather like quicksilver. It's just the property of the substance."

"You're right," Mae said. "Which means we just need to figure out what material to mix with malice."

"What materials have you tried to use so far?" The answer to their problems was titanium, but Hanne couldn't simply hand them the answer. She had to lead them to it.

The malicists went through each of the burned-out bulbs, describing the properties that seemed more- or less-useful against the malice.

"Titanium corroded the least." Mae held up the container, which still had the bright shine of metal in a few places even though most of the bulb was blackened. When she turned it, Hanne saw a hole that had burst open as though from pressure.

"Then it seems like titanium is our best bet," Hanne said. "How soon can we test?"

Soon, all three malicists were buried in their notebooks, pencils scratching as they made calculations quicker than Hanne could follow.

"We'll want to introduce the malice during the reduction process," Bear muttered, writing furiously.

"But we'll have to do it close to a malsite in order to have access to the malice. That will take time. . . ." Barley flipped through pages in his notebook. "We can use the ever-burning forest near Boone. If we take the proper precautions, we could use the ambient malice there to create the alloy."

"How much should we use?" Mae asked. "Too much and we risk another blowout." She motioned to the cabinets of destroyed bulbs.

"Hmm." Hanne pretended to think, as though she didn't know exactly what the rancor had told her in that crushed-carapace voice. "Start small, I would say. One part malice, one hundred parts metal?"

"Yes, yes." Barley wasn't sneering now, just writing numbers as quickly as he could. "I'll arrange for transportation to Boone and obsidian-tinted glasses."

Mae leaned closer to Hanne. "The glasses cost a fortune, but they'll protect our eyes from the malice fires."

"Ah," Hanne said softly. She didn't want to think about visiting malsites, with or without protection.

Barley was ignoring them. "We should be able to go in a few days, after we've got all the math on paper."

"This is it!" said Bear, excited now. "Once we can contain the malice, we can tell the queen the device is ready. Ivasland will crush its enemies, and we'll be heroes."

"Don't be foolish," said Mae with a laugh. "Scientists never get to be the heroes."

They worked throughout the day, the malicists making notes and calculations, while Hanne pretended to work. Instead, she inspected the plans for the device and took in the contents of the cupboards, especially the ones labeled COMBUSTIBLE.

It was afternoon when Mae slid into a chair next to Hanne; their feet bumped, but Mae didn't pull hers back. "I'm sorry I was a little short with you yesterday."

"About what?" Hanne tilted her head, as though she had no memory of the moment Mae had declined to talk about the stars in windows or the stiff silence that had sat between them the rest of the walk to the dormitory.

"I used to have these friends," Mae said softly. "The kind who'd say their only crime is caring too much about Ivasland—loving it too much, believing in our ideals too much. Do you follow me? Some would call us radicals. We had big ideas. We thought we knew what was best for Ivasland."

Hanne waited.

"There were five of us," Mae went on. "Originally, anyway. We called ourselves a five-pointed star, with Ivasland in the center. We saw ourselves as protectors of Ivasland's true values of equity and education. We didn't like that Ivasland sold so many light globes, water filters, and other things that *we* invented to Embria or Caberwill. We hated that we must rely on our neighbors for materials to build those products—and that they can charge us whatever they want for the materials! It isn't fair that we do all the work but they get all the benefit. So we wanted Ivasland to be more self-reliant, to strike better trade deals—ones that benefitted *us* more than they did *them*. And then, rumors came that the queen and king might be looking at studying malice. We were appalled, of course, but then I was tapped for the project, and, well, everything changed for me.

"I reasoned that studying malice was different from using it. Even when Bear, Barley, and I were given instructions to build the machine, I told myself that it was better *we* use a device like this, rather than Embria or Caberwill." She straightened. "We would use it responsibly. We would use it to remove malice to a different location, somewhere it couldn't hurt people anymore. Of course, then it turned into a weapon. But still, better for us to possess such a thing."

It was better for no such machine to exist at all, but Hanne didn't say that out loud. Instead, she whispered encouragingly, "Still, you hoped that if you stayed on the project, you might have some influence over its use? The king and queen may call it a weapon, but it could be more, too? A way to free Ivasland of its malice?"

The tightness in Mae's expression melted away. "Yes, exactly. And now we are so close to finishing it. I really feel you've provided the breakthrough we need."

Hanne lowered her eyes demurely. "I want you to know, I feel the same way about Ivasland. This is a place of knowledge and grand ideals. I'm conflicted about the machine being a weapon, but it's better for us to have something like this, rather than Embria or Caberwill getting to it first."

"It's the same as you said earlier," Mae said. "I'm getting my hands dirty for a reason."

"What do your star friends think?"

"I'm not allowed contact with them anymore, but sometimes I get notes under my door telling me to stop, asking why I've betrayed Ivasland. And when the stars were only in *their* windows, I believed they were sending a message to me. Me, personally. But now, with more stars showing up every day . . . I think the movement has grown beyond the five of us." There was a beat of silence. "Four of them, I mean."

Hanne touched Mae's hand. "It must be so hard."

"The hardest part is wondering if they're right."

Mae turned her hand over and laced their fingers together. Just for a moment.

"It's better to have someone moral working on this, like you. Surely they know that. Surely they trust you to put Ivasland's ideals and interests ahead of your own ambition."

Mae gave Hanne a curious little smile. "Everything I do is for Ivasland."

Then, from across the workroom, Bear called, "No more secret whispering. Mae, double-check my math here."

With a faint smile at Hanne, Mae got up and went to help.

Just as the day was closing, Abagail came into the workroom, a troop of guards at her back. "How is everything going up here?" the queen asked. "Is everyone getting along?"

"Better than that," Bear said. "We've had a breakthrough. Hildy was enormously helpful. In fact, we have a hypothesis to test as soon as we finish our equations."

The queen's gaze darted to Hanne, who feigned a smile. In truth, her heart rate was speeding, and sweat gathered under the beige uniform. It was unclear if the malicists wanted her to go to the malsite, too, or if Abagail would even allow it, but Hanne knew one thing for sure: she needed to escape before then, because she would never, ever set foot in a malsite again.

"Very good," Abagail said. "I'm pleased to hear that Hildy has been such a useful addition. You're all dismissed early to rest up. Barley, if you have a few minutes, I'd like to hear all the details about your work these last couple of days."

The spectacled malicist glanced at Hanne, eyes narrowed with suspicion. "Of course, Your Majesty."

Hanne hefted her bag. Then, when no one was looking, she grabbed a jar marked DANGER: COMBUSTIBLE before following the others out of the laboratory. There was no chance for her to overhear any part of the conversation between Barley and Abagail, but Hanne already had a terrible suspicion about what they were discussing.

Her.

It had to be her.

Abagail, for all her dubious practices in ruling, was not a stupid person. If Hanne had been in Abagail's place, she would have her suspicious prisoner killed as soon as the mal-device was ready—which was mere days away now. And with all the questions surrounding Hanne's sudden appearance and knowledge, it seemed equally possible there would be some torture before the killing. *Who sent you?* They would ask. *Who are you?*

Hanne had fulfilled her obligation to the rancor, giving the malicists everything they needed to complete the machine. Surely that was all that was required of her, right? It wouldn't come after her now?

The number of guards doubled as they reached the bottom of the tower stairs and headed through the hall, and Hanne made her choice.

If she stayed, she would die. She had to leave. Now.

"Mae," Hanne said as the group emerged from the building; the air was still and thick, like a held breath, while above, clouds hung low and dark, heavy with rain. Impossibly, there were more guards. "I need your help."

The other girl looked at her askance, running her fingers through the short strands of her hair so that it stood on end.

Hanne leaned in closer, keeping her words soft enough that only Mae could hear under a rumble of thunder. "I think I'm in danger."

Mae's inhale was sharp. "You're not exactly who you say you are, are you?"

Hanne considered, then shook her head. "I've done what was asked of me, and now I'm expendable."

The other girl glanced around at all the guards. There were *so* many more than there had been before. Mae's eyes grew wide and worried. "When do you think they'll move against you?"

Thunder rolled across the campus, rattling Hanne's bones. "I don't think I'll live out the night."

Mae glanced over her shoulder. "Bear and I could create a distraction—"

"No!" Hanne winced, then softened her voice. "I don't trust him."

That implied that Hanne trusted Mae, which she most certainly did not, but the malicist heard what she wanted. "This is so troubling," she murmured.

It was the king and queen's own fault, really. If they'd always been as good and pure as they liked to pretend, as good and pure as the five-pointed stars wanted them to be, there was no way Mae would believe any of this. But those monarchs had ghosts in their grips, and Mae knew it.

"I know," Hanne said. "I'm sorry to ask for your help. I know it puts you in an awkward position."

And again, as the cloud-shrouded sun fell behind the university buildings and fine droplets escaped the thunderheads, Hanne gazed up at the stars glowing in windows.

Mae followed Hanne's eyes up to the stars. "You're with them, aren't you?"

Hanne bit her lip, as though worried. It was always best to let people fill in the missing details on their own; they did a better job convincing themselves than she ever could.

"Do they know about the device?"

Hanne thought about the other day in the throne room, when the guards and secretary had been made to leave after she started talking about the mal-device. She thought about the next morning, when Abagail had looked at all the stars in windows—as though there were *more* than usual. "Yes," Hanne said. "The device isn't the secret you believed it to be."

A pained look crossed Mae's face.

"Can you help me?" Hanne touched Mae's arm. "I'm sorry that I can't tell you more right now, but if I ever see you again, I'll explain everything." She made a show of swallowing hard, of glancing downward at Mae's lips. "I do hope that I'll see you again."

A moment stretched between them. Then, quietly, Mae said, "All right. I'll help you. Just tell me what you need."

Right on time, because the dormitory was looming over them now. Hanne pulled out the jar she'd stolen from the laboratory and said, "Do you have a match?"

The softness vanished from Mae's expression, replaced by panic. "Dear Vesa. We're all going to die."

EXCERPT FROM NADINE HOLT'S DIARY, DECIPHERED FROM EMBRIAN MICRO-CODE

She's dead. Truly dead. I don't know what I'll do now.

I'll explain.

Yesterday, Lady Sabine and I visited Victoria Stareyes and Prudence Shadowhand, both who were on Lord Bearhaste's list. We discussed many things, including the war, our mutual loathing for Ivasland, and—of course—Princess Johanne. I wanted them to understand that she desires peace, above all, and would do anything to achieve it, even if that meant marrying a handsome prince. They laughed, but there was something odd about it. Prince Rune is not a unifying figure, it seems, but Hanne could be.

This morning, I had breakfast with Princesses Sanctuary and Unity Highcrown. The meeting was carefully monitored, of course, by half a dozen Caberwilline soldiers, but we had a nice little talk, mostly about supporting our relations—brothers, cousins—in their ascent to power. They were delightful girls, one quiet and one outgoing, and both with the serious nature of so many Caberwillines. Then, it was time for them to move on to sword training, so I returned to my rooms—Hanne's rooms—to take notes on the princesses' likes and dislikes, the goals and grievances, and anything else

Hanne might find useful. Just as I began, though, I heard a clatter from out my window.

Prince Rune and the Nightrender had returned.

Without Hanne.

I couldn't hear what they said, but the Nightrender flew away—right past my window. Shaken, I staggered back and sat by the fire until someone knocked on the door.

Everything is a blur, but I do remember a man called Rupert Flight—an earl on the Crown Council—asking if I believed in the alliance. There were other questions, some about my relation to the Fortuin side of the family, my duties as a lady-in-waiting, my closeness with Hanne. Then he asked if I would consider marrying Prince Rune in Hanne's stead, in order to preserve the alliance.

Earl Flight left after that, saying I had only a few days to respond, as they would wed Prince Rune and me the same day he was to wed Hanne, and someone *would need to make alterations to Hanne's gown. These Caberwilline nobles are so direct. I find myself looking for hidden meanings, but I believe he was earnest. He—and several others on the Crown Council—wish for me to marry Prince Rune, since Hanne cannot.*

It seems so drastic. And yet, perhaps Hanne would encourage it?

I have no idea what to think about this. I will visit with Hanne's other ladies; I will seek guidance from Lady Sabine. If I thought that any of my letters made it to Embria, I would even seek counsel from Queen Katarina, but they are out of reach.

Knowing that I will never see Hanne again—it's made it too hard to think clearly. I just don't know what to do anymore.

20.
HANNE

Hanne pushed the jar into Mae's hands. "Just . . . do something with it."

"Do you know what this is?" Mae's grip turned white around the jar as she tucked it against her stomach to keep the guards from spotting it.

"Of course not." Hanne glanced up at the dormitory. If they didn't act soon . . .

"It ignites on contact with water. On humid days, moisture in the air is enough to do it."

Both Hanne and Mae turned their eyes to the sky, where the clouds trembled under the weight of a coming storm. Ivasland storms were notorious, as torrential as they were rare.

Already, Hanne's clothes were dotted with raindrops. "Oh," Hanne murmured. "Well, I guess I'm in luck."

Mae's eyes went round as Hanne grabbed the jar back—then hurled it toward the dry fountain in the center of the courtyard.

"Run!" Mae screamed, at the same time as Hanne shouted, "Ivasland must honor the Winterfast Accords!"

A second later, an explosion rocked the courtyard.

Blinding white light burst out from where the jar had impacted, followed by a rush of scalding air—and then Hanne was on her back, all the breath pushed out of her lungs. Her ears rang from the slap of sound, and it seemed like the whole world was spinning above her. But no matter how much she hurt, she had to get up.

Slowly, Hanne rolled over and climbed to her feet as drizzle turned into rain, making the pale fire burn brighter. Maybe this hadn't been such a good idea after all, but it was done and there was no point in second-guessing herself now.

Hanne grabbed her bag and looped it over her body again. It felt heavier and the ground buckled under her, but still she managed to stagger away from the burning fountain.

She walked into someone—

A guard grabbed her arm—

Without thinking, she drove her elbow into his diaphragm and her knee into his groin. The move was sloppy—the ground wouldn't stay still and Hanne couldn't see straight yet—but the man doubled over and she pulled away.

The courtyard was in flames. That substance burned hotter as rain poured from the sky. Even the paving stones began to melt under the heat. People ran every which way, screaming, though Hanne had trouble hearing them over the ringing. Something about the mal-device? Something about stars and betraying Ivaslander values?

It didn't matter. Nothing mattered, except getting away.

Hanne grabbed hold of a doorframe, breathing the hot, wet air as she tried to focus. She'd created the perfect distraction, but now she was disoriented, hard-pressed to tell which way was which, and she couldn't risk going in the wrong direction. Every second was precious.

"Help!" The voice was weak. Hanne peered through the smoke and rain to see Mae not far away. Her legs were trapped under one of the fallen guards, and she couldn't seem to get enough leverage to roll him off.

The fire was struggling against the rain, but the substance Hanne had thrown was still spreading outward on the wet cobbles—moving toward Mae.

Hanne's fingers dug into the doorframe.

She needed to go. But Mae had helped her.

She had important things to do. But Mae might die.

Mae *would* die.

Did it matter? She was an Ivaslander, responsible for building the mal-device and getting Hanne into this mess to begin with.

Hanne should let her die. She should let them *all* die.

But as the ringing in her ears subsided and the ground beneath her stabilized, Hanne found herself running toward the malicist. There were still guards everywhere, most prone on the ground, some rushing to help citizens. Lots of people were running away from the fire, still screaming—many of them aflame.

"Help!" Mae cried again, just as Hanne reached her.

"Stay still. I'll get him off you." Hanne knelt and pushed the guard, rolling him slowly off Mae's legs. The man didn't react to being moved, and Hanne didn't check to see if he was even alive.

Mae scrambled back from the body. "You came for me!"

Hanne started to say no, she'd come to ensure Mae lived to finish the machine, but movement on the far side of the courtyard stopped her. Someone was emerging from the building that held the laboratory tower.

Abagail.

If the Ivaslander queen caught her now, this would all be for nothing.

"I have to go." Hanne lurched to her feet. "I have to get out of here before she finds me."

"I'll come with you."

Across the way, Abagail Althelney looked up and her eyes locked on Hanne's. Rage, hatred, and horror filled the queen's glare as she shouted at the guards with her and pointed straight at Hanne. "Arrest her!" The words weren't audible over the rush of fire and drone of rain, but Hanne read them well enough on the woman's lips.

Mae followed Hanne's gaze. "No, go. I'll buy you time."

Hanne had no choice but to trust the malicist now.

Improvising, Hanne gave a ragged yell and made a show of pushing Mae toward the growing fire. The other girl took the hint and threw herself dramatically to the ground; while everyone's focus was on Mae, Hanne seized the opportunity and *ran*.

She ducked and wove through the flames until she reached the rear of one of the university buildings. Peeking back into the courtyard, she saw the guards had swooped in to help Mae to her feet again. The malicist was safe—not that Hanne cared. Instead of caring, she hiked her bag higher on her shoulder and watched as Mae sobbed false tears in Abagail's arms.

This whole plan had been messy and ill-conceived, and if Hanne could have done it all over again—well, she'd have been smarter about it, certainly. But she'd been given limited options and no time to prepare.

Besides, Ivasland had done this to itself. She'd merely been a spark to the kindling Abagail and Baldric had laid out. Those stars had been in windows even before Hanne arrived.

Mae pulled back from the queen and pointed away from where Hanne had run. When the guards broke off to pursue Hanne, they ran in the wrong direction.

Hanne smiled, and then she bolted.

Sweat and rain had soaked Hanne by the time she finally reached the chicken coop and recovered her bundle of obsidian. Then she hurried on to the stables where she'd left the sad, nameless nag she'd taken on her way out of Caberwill.

Someone had combed him, fed him, and even slathered some kind of paste over his legs. Quickly, Hanne searched out his tack and saddled him.

Through the drenching rain and stink of smoke, Hanne hurried toward the outskirts of Athelney. But there was someone in her path, a cloaked figure standing in the dark, their hood pulled low.

Hanne stopped and slipped her dagger free of its sheath, but before she could decide whether to attack or try to ride past (and risk this person telling Abagail they'd seen her), the hood fell back to reveal Mae's face.

"I thought I would find you coming this way." Mae motioned for Hanne to follow her into an alley. "The queen sent her guards to go find you, and in all the confusion, I got lost on my way to the dormitory."

"There was a lot of smoke and fire," Hanne agreed as she drew her horse into the narrow alley. An overhang sheltered them from the worst of the rain, which drummed louder than ever.

Mae produced a small light globe and shook it, making it glow. Her clothes were torn, and smoke had smudged onto her face, but otherwise she seemed well.

"You came looking for me?" Hanne asked. "Why?"

"I just"—Mae shrugged a little—"wanted to say goodbye. Before you left."

Oh. Hanne tamped down a smile. "Nice of you to see me off."

"I don't suppose you'd tell me where you're going." It wasn't a question; Mae already knew the answer, so Hanne didn't bother voicing it.

"Be careful of Abagail," Hanne warned instead. "She's not what you think."

Mae didn't argue. She knew. Of course she knew. She had been directed to break the Winterfast Accords. "Who are you really?" Mae asked instead. "Are you even from Ivasland?"

Hanne bit her lip. It would be foolish to tell this malicist anything about who she actually was. In spite of Mae's reservations about the project, she still worked directly for the king and queen of Ivasland—the very people who wanted Hanne dead. This girl would fulfill her duty to her monarchs, as surely as Hanne had satisfied her agreement with the rancor. (Well, not so much an agreement as a ransom, which she'd had to pay herself.)

Before all of this, Hanne had always thought that people who allowed themselves to be compelled into service to those more powerful simply lacked the inner strength to say *no*. But now, she understood a little better. The rancor was capable of hurting her in new and terrifying ways if she resisted.

And Mae . . . She was in a similar position, Hanne thought. Not with a horrifying, laws-of-nature-defying monster from the Dark Shard, but close enough. Abagail and Baldric did have quite a bit of malice (and people willing to use it) at their disposal.

"Hildy?" A hesitant note entered Mae's voice. "Is that even your real name?"

"I can't tell you." In another world, it might have been romantic that Hanne was a secret princess from an enemy kingdom, here against her will and nearly killed for what she knew. But romance had never been part of Hanne's story.

Even so, she touched Mae's hand. Just to see. Gazing down at Mae's light-brown skin against her pale fingers, Hanne searched her heart for some sort of feeling. There was a small thrill at the contact, an attraction, and a willingness to do more than hold hands, should the opportunity arise. But no uncontrollable softness or warmth, like she felt with Nadine. (Not that she was interested in Nadine like *that*, but she knew what she felt for her cousin was love.) Feelings—or possible feelings—for anyone else were lined up against the strength of that bond, but they always fell short and were summarily disregarded.

"All right," Mae said. "Well, then, I suppose I should go. We both have things to do."

Kingdoms to conquer.

"Yes," Hanne agreed.

"I'm glad the mal-device is nearly finished," Mae said conversationally. "After we visit the ever-burning forest, I'll be able to—not rest, I suppose, but go back to work I enjoy."

Hanne almost found herself asking what work that was, but then she remembered that she was on her way to Caberwill after this, to get married and become queen of everything. What Mae liked doing in her free time was of no consequence.

"We have a lot of newspapers in Athelney," Mae went on. "Some have evening editions, as well as morning. On the way to the dormitory, I saw a new headline saying that the princess who was trapped in a malsite is no longer there. Supposedly, she's dead."

A chill marched up Hanne's spine. "Supposedly?"

Mae shrugged. "If she isn't, then certainly she's on her way to Caberwill now. Queen Abagail, of course, is surely relieved that we can finish ahead of schedule. I'd wager we have seven or eight days before a working prototype is ready."

Hanne could hardly breathe. Did Mae know? Could she have guessed?

"Well." Mae dug through her pocket and removed a folded piece of paper. "I hope to see you again sometime. I've written down my address, in case you ever want to visit me. Or write, at the very least."

Then, before Hanne even realized what was happening, Mae kissed her. Just a soft press of the lips, and then the other girl was gone—back into the rainy night, vanished from Hanne's view.

It had been rather nice.

Slowly, Hanne looked at the paper. Sure enough, there was an address written in hurried letters. On the other side of the paper: blueprints for the mal-device.

Hanne stared at it for a moment, unsure whether the malicist was trying to help her, warn her, or threaten her. Perhaps all three.

At any rate, she'd done what she'd come here to do—deliver the solution to the mal-device into her enemy's hands—and she'd accomplished a few extra things as well: widespread knowledge of said device, a resistance, and even a riot.

And now she had the plans for the device itself.

Hanne tucked the paper deep into her bag, where it wouldn't get wet, and then she mounted her horse and ran—not from Ivasland and her would-be murderers, but toward something:

Toward power.

Toward freedom.

Toward conquest.

21.
NIGHTRENDER

The prince had lied, Nightrender decided. He *must* have lied, because she would never kill people. She *protected* them.

Do you?

She wasn't capable of mass slaughter.

Aren't you?

Her very existence was dedicated to serving humanity. She was their weapon against the darkness.

Oh really.

Nightrender clutched her head, wishing she could rip out this dark, ugly voice, but there was no way to free herself from it.

She flew.

For days, she swept low over the countryside, scanning for yellow ribbons and listening for the soft tinkle of warning bells. Wherever she found them, she went in. Shredded the pellicle. Plunged her obsidian blade into the ground and called on the cleansing fire of the Numina. Time slips, gravitational anomalies, vacuum bubbles: all sent searing pain through her, making her gasp and choke back tears, but none were as difficult as the first, as that had been the only malsite defended by a rancor.

At least she finally understood the reason it hurt: she was a monster. The holy fire she called down was poison to her now, because she had turned against humanity.

Why, though? She must have had a reason.

Humans were messy creatures, constantly working to bring about their own demise. Perhaps she'd simply decided to help them along?

No. She wouldn't. Not ever.

Except you did.

Yes. She had. And now she was paying for it. This agony every time she cleansed a malsite could only be because of her actions four hundred years ago—it was proof enough that Prince Rune had told the truth.

She suffered now because she deserved it.

Today, a fresh ringing of bells pulled her attention down, away from the spiraling thoughts and relentless voice. She dived toward the ground, relieved to have something to do. Something to hurt.

You do like hurting things. It is your nature.

Nightrender landed on a hill with a heavy *thunk*, then stood and tucked her wings behind her. Beloved came free of its sheath as she looked upon an ever-burning forest.

The trees were dark and skeletal, while spirals of black smoke marred a perfect sapphire sky. It was a forbidding place, and if there weren't legends about ghosts haunting the innermost depths, there should be.

Still, people *could* pass through ever-burning forests, as long as they took the proper precautions. This one, with its relatively small fires, wouldn't normally have been a priority for her—there were so many other malsites that were larger and more dangerous—but she'd been careful to clear an equal number of malsites in every kingdom, and it was Ivasland's turn again. Besides, having a forest available for hunting and logging was probably a priority for the people of Boone, the nearby town.

With a long, fortifying breath, Nightrender started down the hill, past the bells and yellow ribbons fluttering in the wind. Exhaustion made her feet drag, but she pushed through it. Rest meant more brooding, more unwelcome thoughts, and she wanted to skip that.

Better to do something good, even if it felt horrible.

Banners of smoke twined around her as she entered the forest gloom, and the sun vanished behind the heavy haze above.

No life survived here. Ash fell thick on the ground; scorch marks scarred every blackened tree. Charred leaves and twigs crackled under her boots, one of the three sounds that permeated the quiet: her passage, the wind, and the fires.

The fires were unnatural. Inextinguishable. They burned on individual trees, on bushes, on the carcass of an unlucky deer, and the light they cast was twisted—toxic—and hurt her eyes. Humans were in even more danger: the firelight would blind them if they looked directly at it, and without proper treatment (a drop of Nightrender's blood in each eye) they'd find themselves dying of a mysterious fever only a few years later.

Malice fires never went out.

Not unless she put them out.

This forest didn't have many fires, but in the past, she'd cleared infernos that threatened the safety of people for leagues around. The people of the three kingdoms should count themselves lucky she hadn't abandoned them with one of *those* massive malsites.

You just left them with a thousand smaller ones. Much kinder of you.

"No, you have the measurements wrong—"

"I don't. You need to trust me—"

The sound of voices—human voices—drew Nightrender to a small, smoky clearing where a trio of masked and goggled people stood over a small table. They had some sort of burner set up, and a handful of other devices she couldn't fathom. A wagon and a small troop of soldiers stood nearby, wearing eye and face protection as well.

Nightrender emerged from the trees, scowling deeply. "Tell me what you're doing here."

"Science, obviously." A young woman looked up, and with wide, round eyes, dim behind the obsidian-tinted goggles, she took in the wings and sword.

Very quickly, she realized who she was talking to.

"Nightrender!" She dropped the flask she'd been holding and fell to her knees.

"Nightrender?" Both young men she'd been bickering with followed her gaze, and then the guards all turned. Next, everyone was genuflecting like their lives depended on it. The sour stench of their sweat grew under the constant stink of smoke and malice, and someone—one of the young men, perhaps—peed a little.

Why are they worried? They're not royalty.

Nightrender scowled; the voice clearly thought it was hilarious.

Figuring out what the group was doing here—and getting a better answer than *science*—would have been the smart move, but they were all so unbearably terrified and she couldn't stop thinking about what the Red Dawn must have looked like: blood, fire, bodies. . . .

"Get up," she said. "All of you need to leave immediately. I'm going to cleanse this malsite and you don't want to be caught in it."

The entire group scrambled, sweeping their belongings into crates and hauling everything to the wagon so quickly it was a wonder the glass instruments didn't break. Within minutes they were gone, riding through the forest as speedily as the smoke and trees and underbrush allowed.

She waited for a little while, listening to their retreat. The young woman and a young man chattered excitedly in that giddy way humans did when they'd survived something they shouldn't have, while the other young man—the one who'd peed—was crying. The guards shushed them, and soon the clatter of the wagon was out of hearing range.

Nightrender was alone again, except for the malevolent forces inside the malsite.

Whatever the scientists and their guards had been doing—it had probably been of no account. Ivaslanders were forever studying the world: marking it, gauging it, calculating it. Most likely, they were royal-employed scientists from Athelney. She put it out of her mind.

Now, she steeled herself against the impending pain.

You deserve it, murmured the voice. ***You're a murderer.***

She walked farther into the woods, stretching her senses to feel how deep the contamination ran. The last thing she needed was for the fires to fight back, like the plants in the first one had. No, when she struck, it had to be planned perfectly. Precise.

A sour stench, like rot, made her pause.

But no, it wasn't rot. It was something else. Something more dangerous.

She wrinkled her nose and followed the odor, readjusting her grip on her sword. Just because she hadn't run into a second rancor yet didn't mean there wasn't one here. Or hadn't been one here recently, rather, because the stench was not as potent as before. It was fading, drifting off in the wind and getting lost with the acrid reek of smoke and ash.

Silver glinted in the light of a nearby fire, drawing her closer.

Every muscle went tense, ready for attack. Every sense strained, waiting for danger.

Carefully, she picked her way around a fallen log and found herself before a trio of tall trees. Their roots, blanketed in ash, had long ago twisted together like a decorative knot. They arced above the silver object, winking on the ground.

Nightrender tilted her head, listening, and when nothing happened for several moments, she sheathed her sword. Whatever had made the stench was gone. Now it was just her and this . . . whatever this was.

She knelt and scooped ash away from the curve of silver.

It was a bowl, its inside stained with a rusty film of blood and coated with cinders.

This . . . was not good.

She kept digging deeper beneath the twisted roots, until her fingernails caught on fabric. She pulled it forth and found a canvas sack. Upending it, she discovered three small bundles wrapped in black silk.

The first held ash, different from the forest around her. Mindful not to touch, she bent to smell it. Human. The ash had been human, once.

The second scrap of silk carried small cream-colored particles: crushed pearls, if she had to guess.

The third concealed dried flower petals the familiar purple of nightshade.

With trembling hands, Nightrender tied off the bundles again and stuffed everything—even the bowl—into the sack.

You know what they're doing.

She did. Someone had summoned a rancor.

It didn't take much: a small collection of death, a bit of malice, and a dark intent. With the right words, anyone could call a rancor, and the Malstop wouldn't even be able to stop them. It was almost never done, for obvious reasons, but such a summoning spell *was* possible—and the gravest sin imaginable.

You must have had a good reason for killing them all. Was this it? Was this what the kings of old did to deserve their slaughter? Was this* their *rite?

"No," she whispered. "This is a new summoning." The scent was only days old, a week at most. The forest ash hadn't completely covered the bowl.

Is it? The voice gave a pleased little purr in the back of her head.

Burn everything. She'd responded to it. Acknowledged it. Now it would never leave her alone.

Nightrender tied the sack tight and clipped it to her belt. Then, without pause, she drew her sword and plunged the blade deep into the tree roots, calling the fire of the Numina into her.

An agony of ice fractured her head, but she was braced for it and she breathed through it, pushing herself to focus on what was important: cleansing the malsite.

Her first strike wasn't as sharp or precise as she'd intended, and the malice-soaked forest knew it. Fires flickered out—but recovered in seconds, burning brighter, higher. Hot orange flames reached toward the sky, releasing heavy black smoke that thickened and surged toward her. It wrapped around her like ropes, but shredded as she flared her wings.

This was going to get bad.

Above her, smoke and fire coiled together, twisting and bending until it shaped itself into a massive serpentine creature with wings and horns. Flames roared across its entire body, making her eyes sting and water. Within the beast's depths, vile green and black threads glimmered: malice forming bonds between substances that were not meant to combine.

The fiery dragon spread its wings wide, catching trees and brush alight as it moved through the forest. It towered over the canopy, illuminating the banks of black smoke—impossibly huge as its eyes settled on Nightrender below.

There was no warning: a jet of fire shot from the dragon's jaws.

Nightrender whipped her sword into guard position and braced herself just as the fire reached her. It rushed down, an inferno of red and gold and sickly pea-green, and split around the flat of her blade.

Nightrender drove her sword into the dragon's leg, shredding threads of malice even as fire licked around the obsidian. She twisted the blade and sliced across, and the leg drooped and spread into the ground, leaving only a flaming stump in its place.

But even as she watched, the leg began to grow back.

She growled low in her throat, searching the beast for another weakness, but any limb she removed would only regenerate. And it didn't have a heart or brain to pierce. . . .

Wait.

The malice dragon fired another blast of flame, forcing her to guard, but not before she'd caught sight of a dense knot of darkness in its chest, where the malice threads were thicker and stronger. It *did* have a heart—a dark heart made of smoke and malice—and if she could break those bonds, that would be the end of the dragon.

There will just be something else.

Nightrender bent her legs and arched her wings, ready to fly straight into the heart and cleave it in two, but the dragon didn't obey physics as she did. Without any kind of push-off, the beast lifted itself into the air and flew straight for the haze-veiled sun.

Nightrender followed. With a roar, she burst through the forest's cover of smoke and brandished her sword, gaining on the dragon with every beat of her wings.

But the dragon was fire and smoke and malice, and so, so swift. It whipped around to face her, spitting small blasts of flame. She dodged and spun away, falling a short distance before her wings flared and she pushed herself upward once again.

They circled each other, Nightrender cutting and the malice dragon spurting fire, skimming over treetops and tumbling through the air. She strained her wings, pushing herself harder until she finally had an opening: she came around in front of the dragon, inside its wings and talons, and she was staring straight into its wicked heart. Her eyes burned with heat from the fire, but she didn't blink. She didn't hesitate.

Half blinded by sparks of ice-white pain, Nightrender plunged her blade into the malice dragon's heart, severing the black and green threads with a short twist and jerk.

Numinous fire surged into the beast, burning away all the malice, and—without those magical fibers holding everything together—the fires of its body went out, the smoke thinning until there was nothing left. Just blue sky.

Nightrender blinked to clear her vision, gasping for clean air as she pumped her wings. They were heavy—her whole body was heavy—but the malsite still waited below.

She gathered her strength and flew back into the forest. There was less resistance than before—only a few fires straining toward her in a threatening manner—and within an hour, the burned trees were simply burned trees. Like a sore cleared of infection and allowed to scab over, the forest would heal.

Yet her work was not finished. (It was never finished.) People from the surrounding towns might have seen the dragon, and so she trudged from one place to another, asking the residents if they needed to be treated for fire-blindness.

They slammed their doors or ran away from her, some clutching the small jars of "obsidian" they wore around their necks. They feared her more than they feared the malsite they'd always known. She was the strange and unknowable—the monster.

She looked the part. With ash and sweat matting her hair, her armor ripped and hanging off her wiry body, burns and smoke streaking her face, she was not the version of Nightrender mortals preferred to see.

And so, without healing anyone who might have looked upon the dragon, she returned to the hill where she'd landed earlier. The forest was already more serene. No constant cover of smoke, no sinister fires hiding within.

Was she a monster? She had always thought herself above humans. A servant of sorts, yes, but still better. She had awareness that spanned ages, a sense of scale they couldn't comprehend. The Numina had created her to defeat darkness, and one day she would.

Or so she'd always believed.

For the hundredth time, she searched all her memories for any hint of the Red Dawn, any clue as to why she would have hurt humanity the way she had. But no matter how hard she looked, no matter how she tried to narrow it down, the hole remained.

And then another memory flashed out, a pinprick of pain in the back of her mind.

Nightrender bit her lip, struggling to recall what she had forgotten. But it was gone. Completely gone.

How was she supposed to keep going like this? She was losing everything, all her history, all her knowledge, all her experience. All of *her*. And clearly, it wasn't going to stop. The gaps were growing.

She couldn't fend off this Incursion without her whole self. She needed to do something about this. Soon. Otherwise, she would be little more than mortal herself.

Nightrender wiped tears off her face. (It was only because the malice fires hurt her eyes, and definitely not because she couldn't remember the melody to her favorite sonata.) Her body shook with exhaustion, but there would be no rest.

It was time to stop feeling sorry for herself.

22.
Rune

Rune had all but sequestered himself in the royal reading room at the Grand Temple library, returning to his own quarters only to wash and change clothes—and to sleep no more than biology absolutely required. The rancor, though dead, continued to haunt his nightmares.

It was much better to stay up late reading about the history of the Dawnbreakers—about how many heroes had died grisly deaths beyond the Malstop.

Grand Priest Larksong ambled into the room, pushing a cart of newly restored ancient tomes.

"Don't you have people to deliver those for you?" Rune barely looked up from his notes.

"Yes, of course, but it's nice to visit you up here. No one bothers me while I'm with the crown prince."

Rune snorted. "They don't want my recklessness rubbing off on them. You're the only one who doesn't mind the risk."

Outside the open door, John Taylor gave a faint *hmph*.

"Except for John, who is paid to take the risk," Rune said, then looked back at Dayle. "Thank you for the delivery. What I've read so far has been illuminating."

"I'm just glad these old manuscripts are getting some use." Dayle gently unloaded the books, stacking them with the others Rune hadn't yet read. "We're fortunate that the librarians and grand priests of old were able to save these after the Red Dawn. Now they are some of the most precious in my collection."

After the Red Dawn, books on the Nightrender and her champions had been purged all across Salvation, even from the greatest libraries. By royal decree, of course. From the new royals. The old royals were, obviously, dead.

"I found some ancient journals that may explain how to send the Nightrender back to Winterfast Tower," Dayle went on. "We'll know more after the restorers have finished repairing them."

Rune just nodded and made another note as to how Dawnbreaker training should work. Of course, it seemed unlikely there would be time for training before they were asked to help stop this Incursion (assuming the Nightrender ever returned, and assuming he could even raise the men), but one day, when he was king of Caberwill (assuming he lived long enough), he intended to restore the practice of Dawnbreaker trials. The next time she awakened, there would be an army waiting for her.

"I don't suppose you have any news from the council?" Rune asked as casually as he could.

"Oh, plenty of news, but none of it good." Dayle started to smile, but then a loud *thump* sounded on the reading room balcony.

Rune's heart lifted into his throat. Slowly, he unsheathed his sword, which had been lying on one end of the table. John's blade was out, too, as he came into the room.

The knob turned, but when the door swung open, *she* was on the other side. The Nightrender.

Her hair was tangled, and streaks of soot and blood and other . . . substances were smeared across her armor. She looked angry, but it didn't seem directed at him—this time.

Rune lowered his sword and let himself breathe again. "You're back."

"Nightrender." Dayle gave a respectful bow.

John didn't say anything, and he didn't lower his sword.

"What happened?" Rune laid his sword on the table and took a halting step toward her.

She clenched her jaw and, without speaking, dropped a sack onto the floor. Out spilled a smooth silver bowl and three pouches of black silk, and a stench that made the backs of Rune's eyes itch. Acrid like fire but ancient and rotting. Malice.

"You brought me a gift." Rune coughed into the crook of his arm. "That was very nice of you."

"It isn't a gift."

"I know. I was—" He shook his head, feeling foolish. They were, as far as he was aware, still having a fight. Joking wasn't acceptable yet. "Sit," he said, "if you like."

"All right." She stepped over the spilled-open sack and took in the sight of the reading room, all warm wooden furniture and globes of chemical light. There were plenty of places to sit, but most of the chairs were generously cushioned and richly upholstered, and she was covered with unspeakable substances. She was not human, but also not unaware that she would cause someone additional work if she sat on something absorbent.

Quickly, Rune pulled a wooden chair from the table. "Here."

"Please don't touch the books," Dayle said. "They've already been through so much."

The Nightrender shot him a narrow-eyed glare as she perched on the edge of the offered chair, arranging her wings just so. There was a stiffness to the way she held herself, as though compensating for a bone-deep weariness. "I know the value of these tomes as well as you do."

Dayle cringed. "Of course."

"John, it's all right." Rune looked at his guard. "You can put your sword away. She's not here to hurt me. Are you?" He glanced over his shoulder.

The Nightrender gave a faint shake of her head.

"As you command." John sheathed his sword, but he didn't look happy about it.

"I would like to speak with you alone, Prince Rune." The Nightrender scowled at John. "I promise I will not harm him."

Rune nodded to John, who frowned deeply, and then Dayle, who looked faintly offended.

"I'd very much like to know about these items," Dayle said. "Please."

"The prince may tell you later if he wishes. *I* do not wish to tell you."

"I'll tell you," Rune said to Dayle. "Now, please."

The guard and the grand priest went out into the hall, and the door swung shut behind them.

"Dayle will definitely listen at the door," Rune said as he went to the sideboard and poured a glass of water from the pitcher there. "Just so you know. He says he's too old for shame."

She heaved a sigh. "Mortals."

Rune brought the glass of water to the Nightrender. "I'm glad you've returned. I've been hoping you might give me a chance to apologize."

"That isn't why I came here." She removed her gauntlets, tucked them into her belt, and then accepted the water.

"Oh." Rune swallowed hard and tried a different approach. "Can I order something for you? Coffee? Food?"

"No." The word came out sharp, but then she exhaled slowly. "Yes, please. I don't remember the last time I ate."

He gazed down at her a moment, watching the careful way she sipped her water, and searched himself for the courage to say aloud how relieved he was to see her. He went to the door instead, and made a quick request of the two men lurking out there.

When he shut the door again, the Nightrender's glass was empty.

"More?" he asked.

She handed him the glass, which he refilled and gave back.

Suddenly unsure what to do with himself, Rune sat in the chair next to her, questions crowding his throat. He settled on the least offensive.

"What is all that?" He nodded toward the spilled-open sack, still lying in front of the balcony door.

"They are the materials one would need to summon a rancor."

A chill forced its way through Rune, and when he blinked, he saw its face not a breath from his. He could hear its terrible voice and smell the stink of nightmares. . . .

He shook himself. The rancor was *dead*. He'd watched her kill it.

"I found these things while cleansing an ever-burning forest."

So she had been clearing malsites. That was a good sign. But *this* . . .

"Who would summon a rancor?" The words felt wrong in his mouth, like sounds his tongue hadn't learned how to shape. "Why would anyone do that?"

The Nightrender shuddered. *Shuddered*. It was such a human response, something he hadn't expected from her. "There have always been cults that worship the rancor, Prince Rune. They are dark and secret things, not meant for eyes like yours."

Eyes like his? What did that mean? What kind of eyes did he have?

"But *why* would someone worship the rancor?" he pressed. "The Numina—"

She shook her head. "You know that answer. You said yourself that you don't believe the Numina care, because they do not act on your behalf. You may view them as apathetic, indifferent to the plights of modern mortals, but these cults see the Numina as *negligent*—as cruel as anything from the Dark Shard. And so, they have decided to worship the beings that *do* deign to venture to the laic plane."

"Rancor want to conquer our world. How could anyone think that's better than beings that don't interfere?"

The Nightrender placed her glass on the table. "You don't understand. This isn't simple worship. They seek to placate the rancor and obtain favors from them. Power, wealth, long life: the rancor promise to deliver all those things and more, and they have the ability to deliver them, if by twisted means. Even though these people know the rancor's end goals, they assume any cataclysmic event won't come to pass in their lifetime."

Leaving the problems *they* created for their children's children.

Someone always had to solve these long, slow-building problems, and it seemed unfair that it was never the ones who'd created them. Worse, there were people like his parents, or his grandparents before, who simply pretended such problems didn't exist—as though there wasn't a looming, long-announced calamity that threatened humanity's very continuance.

Rune looked away, still struggling to understand how *people* could allow such evil into the world—into their own lives. Summoning rancor? Making deals with them? It was unconscionable.

"People used to read," the Nightrender muttered. "There are dozens of books on the subject."

"People still read." Had she somehow not registered the fact that she'd found him in the *library*? In the *reading* room?

Her tone turned frosty. "Clearly there are gaps in your education, Prince Rune. You should know that people have been summoning rancor as long as there have been people and rancor. Everyone wants power, and some are willing to do *anything* to get it."

Ire rose in him as he motioned at the books stacked around the table. "I read everything I can find, Lady Nightrender. One might argue that books are my closest friends." His only friends, after his brother died, and considering the Nightrender had neatly declined his offer. "I spent my childhood reading everything that I could find about the Nightrender. About you. About the rancor and the Malstop. But most of the books about your awakenings, your wars, your deeds—they were burned after the Red Dawn. That's the only story anyone really knows anymore."

That had been more than he'd meant to admit, but she couldn't dismiss him for the ignorance his ancestors had forced upon him. Not when he'd done his best to learn everything there was to know about her and her world, in spite of it being a forbidden subject. For years, he would have done anything for even a crumb of extra information.

"Yes," she murmured, "let us talk about the Red Dawn."

Rune almost swallowed his tongue.

"I've—I've been wanting to apologize for my outburst," he began awkwardly.

Though she was clearly exhausted, her gaze was steady. Resolute. "It doesn't matter. I just need to know what happened. I need to know why I"—here, her voice cracked just the slightest bit—"slaughtered every member of every royal family in every kingdom. That is how you said it, I believe."

His chest felt like it might split open and spill his whole heart on the floor in front of her. Clearly she'd been torturing herself these last days—because of *his* words. Because of what *he'd* said to her in a fit of anger. He should have held his tongue. He should have been kinder. She was still a person, wasn't she? A person with feelings and fears, even if she didn't talk about them.

He softened his voice. "I wish I understood it. I wish I could tell you everything."

"Surely you can tell me *some*thing." Her expression was hard, but there was true pain in her eyes.

"I am sorry." His jaw felt too tight to make words. "At first, I assumed you remembered. When I realized you didn't—it seemed dangerous to tell you. No one wanted it to happen again, after all."

Her chest expanded with a long breath. "You took an enormous risk in summoning me."

Rune nodded. "I didn't want to distract you or burden you, or . . . trigger more death. I needed you to help me—to help us—and I thought if I told you about the Red Dawn, you'd change your mind. Or worse." Every word was like stripping off a layer of armor. "I tried to use you. Manipulate you. I withheld the truth. And for that I'm sorry."

The Nightrender unfolded herself from the chair, standing tall.

Rune rose, too, only a breath between them. He could feel the heat off her body, smell the sweat soaked into her armor.

Dark eyes searched his, reading the truth branded upon his soul: He was ashamed. Afraid. Alone.

"I want the truth from you," she whispered. "All of it."

He nodded.

"Never lie to me again. Not directly and not by omission. You are my summoner, my Dawnbreaker. I will not accept betrayal."

The words might have sounded like a threat to anyone else, but Rune was close enough to hear a soft undercurrent of sadness, a thread of deep anguish and longing. She was more than human, but she was not invulnerable to emotion; he should have seen that from the start.

He swallowed hard. "You have my word."

She nodded and returned to her chair, her movements worryingly stiff. "I am ready to hear it."

"Hear what?"

"The Red Dawn. You just said that you would tell me."

Oh, right. But *now*?

Instantly, Rune regretted that he'd spent no time at all since she'd left figuring out a better way to explain to her what she'd done.

He braced himself. "Everything I told you at first was accurate. The fall of Sunview, the great army you took into the Malice, and that you went back to sleep without clearing away the malsites. But the part between those last two events—that's what I skipped before."

It was difficult to watch her face as he spoke. She listened with the same intensity she did everything else, and Rune rather felt as though it wasn't just *what* he said that she was listening to but *how* he said it.

"The stories say simply that when you returned you went mad and slaughtered every royal in every kingdom. That is the Red Dawn: the blood of kings and queens staining the walls of Honor's Keep, Solspire, and the royal estate in Athelney. You were sent back to your tower, after. Forced, I assume. I have no idea how." Having seen her fight, it must have been a deadly task.

Slowly, the Nightrender's gaze swept across the books and journals. "I imagine you'll know soon enough."

Rune cringed but pushed forward with the story. "There was political chaos for a time, but eventually new families ascended to the thrones. Mine. Princess Johanne's. Books were burned, paintings destroyed. People wanted to forget about you, and the new rulers were happy to oblige. We're fortunate that any of the books here were saved."

"Tell me what they are about."

That was much easier. He tapped one he'd been reading earlier. "This is about Dawnbreaker trials and training. And those"—he motioned across the table—"talk about rancor and the hierarchies of the Dark Shard. There's even a note added into one that talks about a rancor king that was sum—"

"Show me that book."

Rune produced it and flipped to the marker he'd left. "It stood out because the note was added later, in the margin. You said rancor kings couldn't come here without being summoned. I remembered that. And then here was a story about it."

They both looked at the mess of summoning materials still on the floor.

The Nightrender returned her gaze to the book, reading. "No, Prince Rune. Such small things would not be enough to summon a rancor king. It would require a sacrifice, a rancor king's name, and *immense* power."

"What would happen if a rancor king were summoned?"

"Everything terrible that you can imagine, followed by things you cannot imagine."

Having recently expanded the number of terrible things he could imagine, this was unwelcome news. "For example?"

"For example, rancor kings cannot be killed."

Burn. Everything.

"Well, that's just *unfair*. If someone did summon a rancor king, how could you stop him?"

"I suppose I would have to incapacitate him, drag him to the Rupture, and force him through. Then we would all have to hope that no one ever summoned him again."

"But why couldn't you kill him?"

"It's the nature of what they are." The Nightrender's jaw clenched. "Rancor rule by conquest. To kill a king is to become the king."

Oh. And a Nightrender turned rancor king—that was not a horror the world would survive.

They both looked at the note again. It was old, in spider-crawling handwriting, and difficult to decipher. It read:

Winter solstice, burn prisoners, rancor king will come.

Then the date, four hundred years past.

"It doesn't say that they did it," Rune said tentatively.

"It doesn't say that they didn't." The Nightrender looked at him. "If there were ever a rancor king on this plane, we should all hope that I sent him back to the Dark Shard."

"But you don't remember. So if he was here . . . maybe you didn't."

Slowly, her expression grim, she shook her head. "I would prefer to tell you that I would not have left such important work undone, that nothing could have prevented me from hurling him back into the depths of the Dark Shard. But . . ."

"But there are still malsites," Rune finished.

She nodded. "I hate that I cannot remember."

"And I hate that we forced ourselves to forget." He touched the tome she'd been reading. "Priests of old risked their lives to save these books. Those who took charge wanted everything about you purged from our collective memory. And the survivor—she suffered the most."

"The survivor."

Rune's breath caught as he forced himself to look at the Nightrender, her wretched expression, the porcelain of her knuckles where she fisted her hands. "Yes, there was a survivor. Just one. A princess."

"Tell me of her."

"Some accounts say she was the one to summon you, but no one knows for sure. And no one knows why you spared her." He gave the Nightrender a moment to offer an explanation, but she remained quiet, jaw tensed, eyebrows knit. "What all the versions of the story do agree on, though, is that she was punished for surviving. For living. Possibly for summoning you. In every version, she was thrown into the dungeon, tortured, and eventually executed."

"For surviving." The Nightrender's voice caught.

Rune nodded.

"Tell me her name."

"I don't know. The stories never give her one. They call her the Spared Princess. I'm not even sure what kingdom she was from. I've heard she was from all three, by now."

Pain flashed across the Nightrender's face, so brief he might have imagined it.

"Perhaps it isn't true," he said. "Perhaps you weren't responsible for the Red Dawn."

She lifted her eyes. "Unless you are unsure of your own lineage, the Skyreaches are all dead."

He shook his head. "No, I mean, perhaps someone else did it and accused you. People kill people all the time."

"People do," she allowed.

"Or perhaps it was a rancor, and blaming you ensured we wouldn't summon you again. Perhaps a rancor king—if one was here—had something to do with it."

"No rancor would have spared the princess."

"And you would have?"

She stayed silent.

"Why?" He wanted to think she would have shown compassion to the one who'd summoned her, but there was no evidence that the Spared Princess was even the summoner. Just legend. But the Nightrender clearly didn't want to answer the question, so he went on. "If you did do it, there must have been a reason, right?"

More silence.

He kept his voice quiet. "There are people who believe that what happened four hundred years ago was divine judgment. They believe the previous monarchs were no longer worthy of ruling—or living."

She lifted an eyebrow.

"Listen, I don't know what happened then, but I can say with certainty that *you* care more for humanity than most humans. You've given your entire existence to stand between us and the unwavering evil of the Dark Shard. If you did what you're accused of, then there must have been a reason."

Her voice was soft, raspy. "I cannot imagine a good reason."

They sat for a moment before Rune pushed. "Why did you ask about the Spared Princess?"

The Nightrender pushed herself up and walked to the balcony door, wings like shadows behind her. She swept aside the curtains and gazed outside. "If it's true," she whispered, "and I committed those acts, then there is one person I would not have been able to harm."

"Why? Because she was your summoner?"

The Nightrender opened the door and stepped outside, leading him across the length of the balcony where they stood side by side, looking over the city and cliffs and fields below. "She could have been my soul shard, but I cannot remember her face, her name, or anything about her. She has been erased from my mind as cleanly as though she'd never existed."

"Soul shard." The words warmed through him, distantly familiar, as though he'd known about this before but had forgotten. "What does that mean?"

"When I was created, a piece of my soul was broken off. That shard of my soul was born into a human."

"With only part of a soul?" That seemed unfortunate.

She looked at him askance. "Water is poured from a pitcher into a cup; it is still water. Wind cuts a tuft off a cloud; it is still a cloud. My soul shard is a complete soul of its own, but also part of mine."

"And you wouldn't harm your own soul."

"Never."

He leaned his hip on the balustrade and searched her profile for answers. All he found was a deep sorrow etched across her features. "How did your soul shard end up in exactly that time and exactly that place? It can't be a coincidence that of all the times you've awakened, *that* was when your soul shard appeared."

The Nightrender offered a sad smile. "My soul shard is always here. Her, him, both, and neither. They are reincarnated into different people across time: as my soul is immortal, so is theirs."

"Oh." Rune's heart pounded. "And your feelings for this person . . ."

"They are my companion, my tie to mortals, my reason for fighting. I would protect this person no matter the cost." She pressed her fist to her heart. "We are bound together at the deepest, most intimate levels. My soul knows them, as they know me. And still, they are different people every time. I must learn them anew, but it is a joy to do it and to be reunited." As she spoke, her tone lightened; somewhere, underneath her grim sorrow, a warmer, happier person was revealed, more human than ever.

A knot of jealousy formed in Rune's stomach, although he tried to squash it. He shouldn't feel that way about some poor, long-dead princess, or anyone else who'd come before. They were gone, and if even just the memory of them brought the Nightrender any measure of relief, he should feel glad of it.

But she couldn't even *remember* the Spared Princess.

How many others had she forgotten?

This was a tragedy, he understood suddenly. To forget someone so important, to have no idea of their name, their face, of their experience together—it was the worst thing Rune could think of.

When his brother had died, he'd nearly drowned in the grief. But he still had memories.

The Nightrender, though—all she had was the understanding that she *should* want someone, but she had no idea who.

"It is not a romantic attachment, like the stories used to say. There were always books and plays about such things, but they were never accurate. And yet, my soul shard is the most important person to me, always, every awakening." The Nightrender gazed up at the sky, darker now with twilight. Moonlight limned her features, a faint silver glow against her sharp lines, making her even more ethereal than before. Did she do this on *purpose*? "You asked before if I have a name," she murmured, so softly he almost didn't hear. "I do. I've told only one person: the first incarnation of my soul shard. Every other incarnation, no matter how different from the previous, has remembered it."

"Oh."

He wished he'd never asked. He wanted to be this soul shard, but there was nowhere in his mind that held the answer of her name. Just nothing. Just a mystery, like a spot of blackness in the night sky where he thought there should be a star.

"Nightrender, I—"

Her posture stiffened as she looked back toward the door. "The food you ordered is coming. And someone else. They have news."

Rune's jaw tightened. He didn't want to leave this balcony, this safe, isolated pocket where the Nightrender told him secrets and his whole chest felt hot, swollen with unfamiliar emotion. In the space between now and someone entering the reading room, Rune imagined a hundred tiny moments that he would miss because of this news—whatever it was.

He imagined the Nightrender realizing that her face was filthy with smoke stains and other evidence of battle. . . . And he imagined her look of relief when he produced soap and water.

He imagined the way her nose and cheeks and chin would be covered in fluffy white suds. . . . And he imagined a stream of clean water rinsing away the lather to reveal clear, smooth skin.

And he imagined brushing a stray bubble off her jaw. Touching her in the gentle way he often wished someone would touch him.

Then his brain caught up with his heart; she'd as soon throw him off the edge of the balcony as allow him to touch her like that.

He imagined slapping himself.

He didn't know her name. He wasn't her soul shard. He wasn't anything to her, except the prince who'd secretly summoned her and repeatedly disappointed her.

"Do you have plans to pursue whoever summoned the rancor?" he asked, moving back toward the door. He was such a fool—one who hadn't realized until just now that there were no stories of the Nightrender taking romantic partners, and why was there any part of him that believed he might be the first?

"Whoever summoned it was already gone. I do not have time to investigate and seek out that individual. The Malstop weakens, Prince Rune. I must go through the Soul Gate soon. The Malstop will repair itself, but only if the pressure of evil inside eases. And"—her expression was hard—"now, I suppose I must search for a rancor king, if there is even a possibility that one was once called here."

He pushed open the door and went back inside the reading room. The squeak of the cart was just now reaching his ears. "I'm surprised you didn't ask Embria or Ivasland for help. They're bound to you in the same way we are."

"They are also angry with me in the same way you are." Her eyes softened, then dropped to the floor. "I have but one friend."

Rune's heart clenched, and an apology sat on the tip of his tongue. He'd been so cruel to her that day.

"He's a good friend to have," she added. "He's brave, and one day he'll be a fine king."

At least he was useful to her somehow. Except . . .

"I'm afraid my standing is . . . not good right now. I'm doing my best to restore the Dawnbreaker trials, but I can't promise you anything. Not yet." He motioned to the books strewn across the table. "Still, I'm trying. I plan to discuss it with my parents and the Crown Council as soon as tomorrow."

She looked up, her dark eyes alight with hope.

"Don't get too excited. They don't like me. This won't make them like me any more. But I can tell them about these rancor summoning items. Perhaps they might develop a sense of urgency. Do you know if it was the same rancor we fought in the time slip? Is that how it came into this world?"

"I cannot say. They smell alike, but many rancor have a similar odor."

Rune wrinkled his nose. "I see. What about where you discovered these things?" If they could find out *who* had summoned the rancor . . .

"No." The word came out sharp, like a dagger. "I will not say."

Ah. Because it was one of their enemies, and she wouldn't insert herself into the war. Petty mortals and all that.

"I'll figure out a way to persuade them, or die trying. You returning here will help my case. You've already done so much good. Perhaps you could come and tell them about all the malsites you've destroyed."

"I could speak to your council, or I could bury myself in an anthill. They are equally appealing options."

Rune laughed a little. "I've often felt the same way."

"We could skip the council altogether," the Nightrender suggested.

"And go straight to ants?"

She flashed a smile. "My army does not have to be Dawnbreakers. Any army would do, including the army Caberwill plans to send to Embria and Ivasland."

Such an action would leave Caberwill vulnerable to attack from both its neighbors. The king and queen would never agree. "There is no way. My parents wouldn't consider it."

"Perhaps they would feel differently if I told them what will happen to Caberwill when the Malstop fails and thousands of abominable rancor pour forth. Rancor have no capacity for mercy. It will be vile havoc. And if there truly is a rancor king on this plane, or on the edge of it, the outcome will be even worse."

Rune swallowed hard. "Worse?"

"Consider again the things you cannot imagine."

Rune's heart sank.

Voices sounded from the hall, muffled, and then a knock.

"Enter," Rune called.

A palace servant stepped inside, her eyes flitting to the Nightrender—tall and dark and still covered in death—and then to Rune. Behind her, the food cart was being pushed away.

"Your Highness," said the servant, "you're needed back in the castle."

"What's this about?" Rune asked. "Where is the Nightrender's food going?"

The servant flushed. "It's urgent. It's about Crown Princess Johanne. She's alive. And she's here."

23.
Hanne

"Tell us again how you escaped."

Hanne had been sitting in the Caberwilline king and queen's office for twenty minutes, practically suffocating with the heat of so many bodies packed in. There was Hanne, obviously, the monarchs, the monarchs' personal guards, and then the four guards who'd discovered Hanne when she'd tried to enter the Brink Tunnel—the passage that cut straight through the mountain to permit access to the southern part of Caberwill. The tunnel wasn't meant to be a secret, as it was important for transport, but she had to admit it was quite well guarded. When the patrols had spotted her (and discovered her dagger), they'd refused to leave her alone. They'd escorted her into Honor's Keep through the servants' entrance, and now she was trapped in this sweatbox of human stink.

"Your Highness?" Queen Grace spoke gently, but she was the kind of woman who used that gentleness as a weapon. It was honed to its sharpest, cutting so cleanly the victim didn't feel a thing until they were already bleeding. "Your escape?"

Hanne had told them already, but she supposed this was the sort of inquisition that required multiple tellings of a story. Forward, backward, from the middle out: they were trying to catch her in a lie.

"I told you, I can't be sure what happened. Yes, I was caught in the malsite. And yes, I saw Prince Rune and everyone coming to look for me. But then they left. I didn't see anyone again."

"And your escape?" the queen asked again.

"The malsite was a time slip. I had weeks to explore it, and after a while, I found a thin spot. I used my obsidian to dig at it, and when it was big enough, I crawled out." It sounded like a plausible story. As plausible as anything else. And it was simple, which was important, and grounded in the fact that the Malstop was known to have thin spots, so it stood to reason that malsites might, too.

King Opus looked up from his notes. "Rune went back to the malsite days ago. You were not there."

"I've been wandering the countryside for some time." That was somewhat true.

After escaping Athelney, Hanne had ridden her stolen horse until she came to the border, where she sold her nag to a man who smuggled her across. From there, she'd had to walk the king's road northeast to the Brink Tunnel, trading her things one by one for room and board, fresh clothes, and the occasional ride in the back of a wagon. It wasn't Crown Princess Johanne Fortuin's *typical* travel style, but she'd gotten where she wanted to go—and no one had identified her until she was ready.

The rancor, thank Tuluna, had not bothered her again. It was done with her, and she was free to complete the journey her patron Numen had set her feet upon months ago. (Although Hanne still hadn't heard a word from Tuluna since before she'd become trapped in the malsite. The silence was agony.)

Hanne rubbed her face, as though bone-weary. "I've never been to Caberwill, Your Majesty. I'm ashamed to admit that, in my disorientation, I became very lost." She looked it, too, still thin from her stay in the malsite. But she was clean, and though she wore a dress that was unacceptable by princess standards, it was quite serviceable for a person needing to go about unnoticed.

"Hmm." The king looked at his paper again, frowning. "Lost enough to make it to the other side of the mountains."

She'd come from the south. From Ivasland.

"There are a lot of passes through," Hanne said. "I hardly realized I'd crossed until, when I asked for directions to Brink, someone told me to go north."

Hanne hated playing the fool, the princess who couldn't find her way out of a wooden box, but people believed it.

"Very well," said the queen. "Let's move on. What about how you got into the malsite to begin with?"

This was trickier, and she risked revealing a lie with any answer she gave. And where there was one lie, there were often more. No matter what she said she was in trouble here, because if she revealed the truth—that she and Nadine had intended to meet the turncoat, Devon Bearhaste—then she was conspiring against the Highcrowns. If she maintained the story of simply taking an afternoon walk, then she had a chance . . . unless they'd forced Nadine to tell them the truth.

That was a dark thought, but the Highcrowns were surely not above torture. They were brutes.

Fortunately, they weren't very bright brutes.

"First, I need to know that my cousin is well. Nadine Holt. She's a sister to me, and I've been so worried—"

"Lady Nadine is staying in the east wing, along with the rest of the delegates from Embria." King Opus waved away Hanne's concern. "You'll see her soon enough."

Relief swelled up in Hanne's chest, and she didn't try to hide it. Let them see what Nadine meant to her; it made her story all the more plausible. Because her relief *was* for her cousin's good health, but also for herself; Nadine would never tell anyone what they'd really been up to, so long as she was unharmed.

Unless *they* were lying.

Which they probably were.

Ugh.

"I need to see her before I can go on." Hanne gripped the water glass they'd given her. "I need to see her with my own eyes."

The monarchs glanced at each other, and the queen shook her head ever so slightly.

Dread closed Hanne's throat. If they wouldn't let her see Nadine, then something was definitely wrong.

"We must ask a few more questions," said the king. "We all thought you were dead, and it's very important to get the facts straight."

"I've told you everything." A faint whine entered her tone, and she tamped it down. She was going to be a *queen*. Queens did not whine.

"You haven't." That voice came from the door to the office. A moment later, Prince Rune strode in, somewhat disheveled but just as handsome as before.

"Hello, son." Opus didn't bother to hide his frown. Interesting.

Rune turned toward Hanne. "I'm relieved you're here, Princess Johanne. And I'd like to hear the full tale of your escape, as well as how you came to be trapped in the malsite in the first place, but for now I'm just relieved that all tensions with Embria can ease. I hope you will consider writing a letter to your parents and informing them of your safe arrival in Brink."

Alliances were such fragile things.

"I will, of course, write to my parents at the earliest opportunity. We wouldn't want to start a war with this, would we?" She laughed a little, but no one else did.

Rune shot his parents a significant look, and then said, "We are all very thankful that you're alive, my lady."

The room was quiet, and finally Hanne pulled herself to her feet. The guards tensed, but she'd already been relieved of her dagger. "Your Highness," she began, her voice soft and gentle. "My prince . . ."

A look of discomfort crossed Rune's eyes, but he banished it quickly. Or disguised it.

Perhaps claiming him had been too much. Their relationship had been cordial but distant, and she'd been trapped in the malsite for so long she'd nearly forgotten where they'd been before all this began.

She could use this, though.

"Forgive me," she said quietly. "The malsite was a time slip. I survived by myself for weeks, while only days passed for you. I had a lot of time alone. To think."

He nodded. His parents watched. The guards went back to pretending they were invisible. Caberwillines were so easy to manipulate.

"I came to"—she forced a catch in her voice—"appreciate how kind you'd been to me before. When you had your men send supplies into the malsite—even though you had no way to know I was still alive—I understood that you have a selfless and generous spirit. I'm embarrassed to say how often I thought of you, and how many, ah, conversations I imagined."

His eyes widened.

"If you're still willing, I'd like to continue with our original plans. There's no point in wasting any more time or risking our alliance again. I'd like to get married as soon as possible." She waited a beat and repeated, "If you're still willing."

Rune hesitated.

Hesitated.

Then, almost imperceptibly, his eyes darted toward his parents, and at last, he nodded. "Yes," he said. "I am. The alliance between Caberwill and Embria is of utmost importance."

"Yes, of course it is. But in addition to that, I've grown very fond of you—or, at least, the idea of you—and I'd very much like to learn if there's any truth to what I imagined."

"Oh." A note of surprise entered his voice, and for a long heartbeat, Hanne wondered if she'd overacted in her role. But then he smiled and said, "I, too, look forward to knowing you better. We have long lives ahead of us, once this matter with the Winterfast Accords is settled, and it would be best for both of us to make our time as pleasant and productive as possible."

The king gave a small nod of approval, and that was that. The wedding would be held on the original date—tomorrow, she realized, once someone pulled out a calendar.

"We will continue to investigate Lord Bearhaste's death, as well as everything else related to this unfortunate episode. Thank all the Numina you have returned to us unharmed." Grace stood and came around her desk to embrace Hanne. Her voice dropped to a whisper, for only Hanne to hear. "We wish you happiness. Just remember, I am still the queen of Caberwill. If you have secrets, I will learn them all."

Hanne unleashed her best smile, the kind that dazzled people from half a league away, and let Queen Grace's words roll right over her. Grace might be the queen of Caberwill for now, but soon she would be dead. Then Hanne would be the queen of Caberwill, and eventually the queen of all three kingdoms. The queen of everything.

She smiled even brighter, imagining that kind of peace.

"You can't smile your way through this alliance."

"Your Majesty, I'm getting married to your eldest son tomorrow. I have every reason to smile."

Grace flinched, clearly trying to decide if the jab about her *eldest son* was intentional. (It was.) Hanne offered a small curtsy and moved toward the door.

"By your leave, Your Majesties," she said, "I need to see my cousin now and prepare for the wedding." Without waiting, Hanne strode out the door, soldiers following closely.

Soon she would see Nadine. Soon she would be able to let down her guard while her cousin watched over her.

But in the hall, someone stood in her way.

It took Hanne a moment to put everything together—the great black wings, the light-slashed new moon on her chest, and the immense, nightmarish sword peeking over her shoulder—but finally Hanne understood what she was looking at.

The Nightrender.

"I heard you'd come here," Hanne said, keeping her tone light.

People all over Caberwill had been talking about the Nightrender, but none of their descriptions did her justice. She was tall—too tall—and sharp faced, with soot covering every part of her body. Black hair hung limp with dried sweat, charred at the ends and knotted beyond salvation. She was not pretty, Hanne decided, and it was far too easy to imagine what her parents would think if this creature walked into their throne room looking like some sort of carrion bird.

The Nightrender stared down at her for a moment. "I'm pleased you're not dead."

"How nice."

"We're all happy Princess Johanne is alive." Rune came up and stood between them, looking suddenly uncomfortable.

The Nightrender hardly acknowledged him. "But there was no weak spot in the malsite."

Anger coiled in Hanne's stomach. How dare this creature speak to her in such a way? How had she even heard Hanne's story?

"It doesn't matter what you say," Hanne said icily, "because one thing will always be true: I would never have been trapped if not for you."

"Princess Johanne—" Rune snapped his mouth closed when she shot a look at him.

"You." All the rage and terror of the last few weeks rose to the surface, clogging any sensible part of her that knew enough to fear the Red Dawn. Although now, after what she'd endured, she feared only one thing: the Dark Shard, and the threat of *that* was over. She had done what she needed to survive. "You should have cleared the malsites hundreds of years ago. You should have kept us safe from the rancor. And you should have protected us from the worst darkness our world has ever seen. But you failed. Not just with apathy or boredom, but with malice all of your own. You turned on the people you promised to protect and slaughtered hundreds. You are the monster."

Stark, horrified silence rolled through the hallway. The monarchs had emerged from their office, followed by guards, and now they were all just waiting to see how the Nightrender would react.

She continued staring down at Hanne, her face completely without expression and her hands motionless at her sides. Then, softly, with no inflection whatsoever, she said, "How unfortunate I didn't meet you before agreeing to rescue you."

"You. Didn't. Rescue. Me." Hanne sidestepped and went on her way—toward the east wing where her cousin was being held.

They had a wedding to prepare for.

24.
Nightrender

"So." Nightrender looked at Prince Rune, who watched the empty space where Princess Johanne had just stood. "This is the princess you were so eager to rescue."

"She's usually better behaved than that." He smiled stiffly, like he didn't quite believe the words himself, and then glanced at his parents. "Well, Mother. Father. As my fiancée is no longer dead, I'll be getting married tomorrow. And the war is, of course, canceled."

Nightrender hid a smile. This bold prince was a nice sight.

"No, we won't be going to war with Embria, Elmali be praised." The queen touched her heart as she said the name of Caberwill's patron Numen. "Assuming, of course, you make it through the wedding."

"Of course I will." Prince Rune frowned. "I've done everything in my power to make this happen. I don't know how she managed to survive a malsite, but I'm grateful. The alliance is back on. We can focus on the things that matter most." The prince cast a meaningful look from his father to Nightrender and back.

"Ah, like your Dawnbreaker trials." King Opus nodded slowly. "Perhaps the Crown Council will support you, once you're married. Even Charity won't be able to easily dissent."

Prince Rune lowered his voice. "Perhaps you should stop appointing Duchess Wintersoft to the Crown Council, if you're so often at odds."

"You know we can't," Queen Grace muttered. "She has too much support."

The king turned his attention to Nightrender. "So there has been more than one triumphant return today. I'm glad you've decided to come back."

That was likely untrue, but Nightrender would work with what she had. "I've come to request—"

Prince Rune touched her arm. "Let me," he said softly, just for he "Tomorrow."

He would have more power after tomorrow, with his position secured by marriage.

Nightrender nodded and turned back to the king. "I've come to request clean clothes while my armor mends itself." Even now, she could feel the numinous fabric growing, stitching itself back together. It wasn't *uncomfortable* to wear her armor while it mended, but it did tickle sometimes.

"Of course," said the king. "I will have something sent to your quarters immediately."

"Thank you."

"Well, son," the king said to Prince Rune, "I suppose you have a wedding to organize yourself for. You should see to it."

The king and queen returned to their office. Prince Rune sighed and started down the hall.

"Tomorrow seems very quick for a wedding," Nightrender observed.

"It's not. It was the original date." Prince Rune rubbed his temples. "The chefs will need to work overnight to get the food prepared, and none of the parties or balls scheduled for this week happened, but the guests are here, the Grand Temple has been decorated, and the bride is not actually dead. That's as much as anyone can really ask for."

"I am glad for you." Nightrender pressed her lips into a line and veered toward the tower that held her quarters. Perhaps, in addition to clean clothes, she could have a bath. Perhaps that food cart was waiting for her. . . .

Prince Rune turned toward the tower with her. "I'm sorry about what she said to you. I was in the malsite only briefly, while she was trapped in there for days. Longer, for her. That kind of trauma would make anyone snappish."

"There's no need to apologize." Nightrender tightened her wings as she started up the stairs, keeping her voice low so it wouldn't carry to every corner of Honor's Keep. "She was correct about my failures, this awakening and the last."

Especially if a rancor king truly was involved somehow. If she hadn't sent him back to the Dark Shard before.

The dream flashed back into her mind, a castle in the Malice, twin

thrones in the center of a huge chamber. Why build a castle if not for a king?

Fingers brushed her arm, tightened, and she halted. Prince Rune stepped around and squeezed onto the stair with her. In the dimness of the stairwell, his eyes were warm and brown, and his gaze was soft as he looked at her. "Princess Johanne was cruel to you. It's all right to admit that."

"I have been cruel, too." She just couldn't *remember* it, and she hated this absence in her mind, this gaping nothing where memories ought to be. With every passing moment, pieces of her past broke off into oblivion, leaving her less than she'd ever been before.

"We don't know that it was really you—"

"It was," she said. "There is no need to assign the blame to someone else. I accept what I've done and I will live with that burden for all of eternity."

"*Have* you accepted it?" He stood close—so close she could hear his heart pounding—and his hand still rested on her arm, though he didn't seem to realize it.

She pulled away, leaving his hand stranded midair. "I don't want to discuss it, Prince Rune. This isn't the time. Besides, you have a wedding to prepare for."

His hands dropped to his sides, a look of naked dread crossing his face.

"You don't like her," Nightrender said.

"There are things I like about her. She's clever, resourceful, and determined. Those are admirable qualities." His gaze drifted downward, toward the glow of the stairwell archway. "Most royal matches are for politics, not love, and I never expected to be an exception."

Hollow sadness bubbled in Nightrender's chest, but she forced it back down. There was no reason for her to dislike this match.

Even if he *was* her soul shard—

You know he is. The voice slithered in the back of her mind.

Yes, she knew he was. There was no other reason she would have reacted so strongly when he'd been in danger, and no other explanation for her utter relief when he'd survived. He was part of her.

He just didn't know it.

But what did it matter if he married anyone? She'd been telling the truth earlier, about it not being a romantic attachment. So why did she care?

"You don't have to marry her." Nightrender clasped her hands behind her back.

"I don't have a choice."

"Of course you do."

His tone turned earnest. "No. Not if I want to do what's best for Caberwill. The kingdom can't take much more of this war. It needs to end, once and for all. Isn't it better if we can end it in an alliance, rather than in bloodshed?"

"You know I want the fighting to stop," she said. "Only then will we all be free of the Malice."

Prince Rune offered a hopeful smile. "Yes."

"Of course, you intend to make war with Ivasland."

"They assassinated my brother. They broke the Winterfast Accords. They will not be reasoned with."

"So it will be a slaughter. Caberwill and Embria against Ivasland."

"That is the way alliances work." He closed his eyes, as though he knew what needed to be done but couldn't say the words out loud.

"Your alliance could march with me into the Malice instead. We could push back the rancor once again, strengthen the Malstop, and give your union with Embria a true opportunity to work."

"Doesn't it *matter* to you that Ivasland is breaching the Winterfast Accords?" he asked.

"Of course. But the Incursion is already upon you. It should be prioritized. And there are penalties outlined in the Winterfast Accords for a kingdom that violates it. Travel restrictions. Tariffs."

Prince Rune pressed his mouth into a line. "I have always tried to protect my kingdom," he murmured. "I failed with my brother. I almost failed with Princess Johanne. I will not fail again."

"There are many ways to protect your kingdom, Dawnbreaker."

His eyes lifted to hers. "I don't command the army."

Nightrender waited.

Prince Rune gave a long sigh. "Very well. I will try. Tomorrow evening, after the wedding, I'll ask my parents to redirect the Caberwilline army to the Malstop and end this Incursion. Perhaps Embria will agree, as well."

A strange stirring filled Nightrender's chest. Hope? "Thank you," she said quietly. "I hesitate to admit this, but I fear what will happen if I must go alone. I fear that I will fail. I fear that Salvation will be like the rest of the world, nothing but darkness."

"Oh, Nightrender." His heart was pounding louder than his whisper.

She pressed on. "And still, my memories are vanishing, more and more every moment."

"We should figure out how to restore them, or at least save what you have left," Prince Rune said. "Perhaps Dayle has something in the temple library—"

"I am the weapon," Nightrender said. "First, I must fight. If we succeed in driving back the darkness, then I will gladly accept your assistance for myself."

"You don't have to be so selfless."

"Yes, I do."

Neither of them had moved for several minutes, and the stairwell was growing stuffy with their breath and the unpleasant stench that clung to her clothes and hair and skin. Even so, she wanted to remain in this moment, just the two of them standing close together.

Nightrender broke away from him and started up the stairs again. She glanced over her shoulder. "You know Princess Johanne lied."

A deep unease rolled off the prince in waves as he started to follow her again. "About what?"

"There was no weak spot in the malsite. She didn't escape the way she claims to have escaped."

"But she did escape somehow." Prince Rune's words echoed off the stone walls as they climbed. "And it doesn't change what I need to do."

"Be careful. That is all I ask."

"Why don't you trust her?" Prince Rune asked. "Because she lied? I lied to you, too, remember?"

That was true, and she would not forget it. "Trust my instincts, Prince Rune. I've seen many liars with many motivations. Both you and she hid something, talked around the truth, dissembled—but she means harm. I know it."

"All right. I will be careful." He met her eyes. "Come to the wedding."

"I'll take the anthill."

"Nightrender." He said it with feigned exasperation.

"I'd rather go into the Malice alone."

"I need you."

"You do not." She opened the door to her room and stepped inside. It was cleaner than before, the floor scrubbed and the walls covered in beautiful tapestries. There was a bed now—canopied and overflowing with pillows—and a large wardrobe and chest. "You do not need me, Prince Rune. Not for this. Humanity has only ever needed me for one thing: killing rancor. That is what I intend to do."

"What about your soul shard?" He seemed to trip over the words. "Haven't they needed you for more than killing rancor?"

Her heart ached with all the faces and names missing from her memory, stolen away like the treasures they were, and for a moment, she would have given anything—the whole burning world—to have them back. But then she returned to herself, her single purpose for existing, and looked at the young man in front of her.

"No," she said softly, although she wasn't sure that was completely true. "My soul shard is the most cherished *reason* I kill rancor: to protect them. That is why they need me. That is why the world needs me."

"Are you sure?" he pressed. "Have you ever asked your soul shard?"

"Such things should not matter to you. Not unless you believe you're my soul shard."

He sucked in a breath and was quiet for a moment. "I want to be," he whispered hoarsely.

The vulnerability in those words pierced her, leaving her no choice.

Prince Rune was an emotional creature, and she couldn't tell what he would do if he believed they were something . . . more. She must stop this. He must be married. The alliance between Caberwill and Embria wasn't perfect, and the two of them massacring Ivasland would be terrible—but there was time to prevent that slaughter, especially if their combined armies marched into the Malice instead.

That's a lot of* ifs**, the voice whispered. **If *things don't go exactly as you plan, then aren't you choosing sides in the war?

It was not anything like that, Nightrender reasoned. She was choosing the side of *less* war. And to accomplish less war, Prince Rune must never think that he was her soul shard. In fact, if he was, he *should already know*, because he would remember her name. But never had she been in the terrible position of losing memories faster than she could make them. What if the same dark magic stealing pieces of her had also stolen her name from her soul shard's mind?

What if he'd been robbed, too?

It didn't matter. She needed that army. She would spare him the uncertainty.

"Speak my name. If you are my soul shard, you will speak my name."

Medella. It would be so easy to whisper it, to mouth the shape of her name and help him along. She couldn't help but wish he would say it.

But as the moment lingered on, a light dimmed behind Prince Rune's eyes: hope dying out. "I'm sorry."

Keeping her expression stone, Nightrender nodded. She'd hurt him, but this pain would pass. "There's no reason to be sorry."

Prince Rune looked away, blinking rapidly. "I suppose I just wanted to be special to someone."

To her? Nightrender's throat felt tight, but she swallowed that unfamiliar sadness and said simply, "I will attend your wedding, Prince Rune." She would celebrate the hope of peace that he felt it promised. "But after that, I expect you to petition your parents for the armies. I need your help."

He gazed at her, eyes still glossy. "I'll ask them," he said. "I'll ask them to send Caberwilline men through the Soul Gate with you. The Malstop will heal, and then you and I will find a way to restore your memory."

More than anything, she wanted to believe him.

25.
Hanne

Hanne would never admit it later, but as Nadine opened the door to their suite, she cried. That was, her eyes hurt, her vision went misty, and her breath came in short little clips.

"H-Hanne?" Nadine *had* been crying—not just starting now but for days. Her eyes were red and puffy, and her face was as pale as white ash. She was thin, as though she hadn't been able to eat.

"Nadine." Hanne took her cousin's hands and squeezed. It just felt so *good* to see Nadine again, like a piece of her heart had locked back into place. "Nadine, it's all right. I'm here."

An instant later, Nadine swept Hanne inside the suite—abandoning the Caberwilline guards outside—where they fell onto the sofa, and the entire awful story poured out of Hanne in choked-off sobs and confusing detail. The chase, the captivity, the rancor and its terrible threats.

"I did it," Hanne whispered, because she was finally safe with the only person who'd ever truly cared for her. She could no longer contain the horror of what had happened. "I went to Athelney and helped those animals finish their machine."

Nadine petted Hanne's hair, which was stiff and tangled from the journey here. "You did what you needed in order to survive," Nadine murmured. "You made the only choice possible."

That didn't seem totally correct. Nadine wouldn't have given in to the rancor's demands. She would have sacrificed herself rather than give Ivasland everything they needed to destroy the other kingdoms.

But Nadine wasn't the crown princess. She wasn't Tuluna's chosen. (Hanne was beginning to worry she wasn't Tuluna's chosen anymore, but she stuffed that feeling down as deep as it would go.) No, Nadine was a good person. But she also wasn't utterly necessary to the plan for peace. Victory could come with or without Nadine . . . but not without Hanne.

Then again, Nadine was necessary to Hanne (and by extension the world), because Hanne worried she wouldn't care what happened to the world without her cousin in it.

"It's going to come back to me," Hanne said quietly. "Abagail Athelney will not hesitate to use the machine against Embria and Caberwill alike."

"In that case, we'll have to come up with a way to defend against it. You said you were able to take the plans for the mal-device?"

"In my underwear." She could feel the paper against her ribs, even now.

"Good." Nadine squeezed her hand. "Ivasland thinks they've won this war, but we will find a way to stop them. Now that the machine is finished, they'll grow lazy, overconfident."

That didn't sound like the Ivasland Hanne had seen, but Nadine had a point. Abagail was experiencing a false victory, while Hanne was playing a longer game.

"I scarcely understand the blueprints," she admitted. "We'll need to find someone who knows how to read them—and who can set about creating countermeasures. Increased security around likely targets, exploiting weaknesses in the machine's design—those sorts of things."

"I have a few people in mind." Nadine flashed a little smile. "I never stopped working on your behalf. None of us did. We've all been working tirelessly."

Hanne believed her. Nadine was the most loyal person she knew. "Good. Meanwhile, the Highcrowns have asked me to write to my parents, to let them know I'm here in Honor's Keep."

Nadine nodded. "That will be good. None of our messages to Solspire have made it through, I believe. Earl Flight—he's the information chancellor, the spy master, I believe—has had everything intercepted. The aviary is off-limits to us, and our own messengers have been prevented from carrying anything to Embria by horse. As far as I know, your parents are unaware that you were ever missing."

Of course they'd been unaware. They were happy to let Hanne risk her life to further Embria's goals, but couldn't even come here to see their only daughter married. Hanne's silence over the last several days might make them wonder if she was safe, and it was possible they'd sent troops to the border in anticipation of a double-cross attack, but that was all.

"When I write to my parents, I will encode a message describing the machine and what it does. Perhaps we can copy the plans themselves to send by less obvious means, too, to ensure Embria is as prepared as Caberwill for what's coming." Hanne sighed. There was so much to do, and they hadn't even gotten to tomorrow's wedding yet. "Oh, have you made any progress on turning anyone from Devon Bearhaste's list? I'm afraid I lost it when the rancor chased me, but—"

"I found it." Nadine smiled and pushed herself up from the couch. She crossed the parlor to a small writing desk, where she pulled a familiar sheet of paper from the drawer. It was dirty and torn, but still legible. "I discovered it when we were searching for you, and I grabbed it before anyone else could see what it was. We've all divided up the work, your other ladies and I, and we've made several good contacts. Lady Sabine has begun building her network. Everything is moving along just as we'd planned. Aside from the malsite, that is. But you're here now, and that's what matters."

"Good." Hanne found a dark smile as she stood, too. "Well, I'm getting married tomorrow, so I hope you didn't sell my dress for pocket money."

"I only thought about it," Nadine said with a wink. It was obvious she was emotionally exhausted but trying to hide it.

Hanne wished she could give her cousin time to recover, but events had made marrying Rune and securing an heir *quickly* vitally important. Plus, that Nightrender was here, presumably to do more than lurk about in hallways. She knew Hanne hadn't told the truth about anything.

But the Nightrender was Rune's problem to handle—for now. Hanne had bigger things to worry about.

Tomorrow, she would be one step closer to victory, and peace, for all of Salvation.

"All right." Nadine tucked the list of names back into the drawer. "Let's start with a bath and clothes."

"Then food."

"Of course. I'll order something right away. Would you like me to invite anyone? It would be good for other Embrians to see you."

Hanne sighed. She'd much rather a quiet night with her best friend, maybe doing something fun like plotting regicide, but Nadine was correct. She was always looking after Hanne's public image. "Yes, we'll have a small gathering. My other ladies, and Sabine, of course, and anyone from Lord Bearhaste's list you think worthwhile. They need to see my resilience—my tenacity."

"And they will." Nadine smiled broadly.

By Embrian standards, the dinner was a small, informal affair, with invitations rushed out and food prepared while Hanne bathed and dressed, her maids and ladies ensuring that she was as well-groomed as possible, given the circumstances.

Now, clad in teal brocade, hair twisted into a casual knot, and her throat, wrists, and fingers shining with obsidian, Hanne was sitting at the head of the table in the suite's dining area. It was a small space, not fit for even a dozen people, so the guest list was kept to a minimum. There were only two Caberwillines in attendance, those Nadine had expressed an interest in: Victoria Stareyes and Prudence Shadowhand.

"It's so good to meet you," Hanne said warmly, mimicking the way Nadine would have spoken the words. "My cousin has told me what good friends you've been to her during my absence."

"It's the least we could have done." Prudence was seven or eight years Hanne's senior, married to an earl twice her age. A political match, one that was mutually beneficial. Sabine—who knew everything about everyone, even in Honor's Keep—had reported that the earl was low on funds, and Prudence's family, though not nobility, was quite wealthy, thanks to the mines they controlled. In exchange for a regular income, the earl provided Prudence with a title and no marital expectations (beyond an heir; heirs were always required). "It's very difficult to arrive somewhere entirely new. When I first came to court, I felt like such an outsider."

Because she had been.

Still, Hanne couldn't fault a young lady for doing whatever was needed to raise her station. Ambition was such an admirable quality.

"Indeed. I am so grateful for your companionship these last days, Prudence." Nadine's murmur was gentle and kind. "Prudence, Victoria, I'd like to introduce you to the princess's other ladies-in-waiting. This is Lea Wiswell, Cecelia Hawkins, and Maris Evans." She motioned to each of them in turn. "And I believe you've met Lady Sabine Hardwick, who isn't a lady-in-waiting but one of Her Highness's most loyal advisers and mentors."

Lady Sabine offered a polite nod as she pulled her knitted shawl back up her narrow shoulders. "How pleasant to see you again." Her sharp eyes stayed on them as the staff served the first course, the typical soup designed to increase hunger so the main courses could be more fully enjoyed.

Weary and surrounded by thick stone walls and old sconces—now repurposed to house light globes, rather than candles—Hanne had never appreciated this taste of home quite so much as she did now. The sharp ginger and delicate herbs warmed their way through her.

"What a journey you must have had," Victoria said. She was the younger of the two, a future countess from the Stormbreak Province, and only recently arrived at court. Rumor, Nadine had told Hanne, was that Victoria's parents had hoped she would catch Prince Rune's eye and elevate her (and therefore her whole family) to a higher status. As if Rune would ever be permitted to court a mere (future) countess. "Honestly, I can't imagine how you endured, though if anyone could have, of course it was you. Lady Nadine has regaled us with stories of your cleverness and ingenuity."

Clumsy but well intentioned. Poor Victoria would be laughed out of Embrian court, where words were art, weapons, and disguises all at once. Victoria, a simple country lady, had no training. But she could be useful; Hanne (or more likely Lea, who had time for such things) could teach her how to speak and how to read the finer points of language.

"That is so kind of you to say." Hanne took a sip of her wine, one of the bottles brought over from Embria, originally meant to be served at her engagement ball. None of those parties had happened, apparently. Well, how could they, without the guest of honor and the assumed war on the horizon? "But let's not speak of my"—she made a show of biting her lip, looking uncertain—"ordeal. I want to know about life in Honor's Keep. It's very different from Solspire, from what I have seen."

"It's smaller," Maris provided. She turned to Victoria and Prudence. "In Solspire, Her Highness had an entire floor of the palace for her, all of us ladies, and the rest of her staff. There were days we walked leagues without ever leaving Her Highness's apartments." Maris glanced around the crowded dining space. "This has been an adjustment. I hardly feel able to breathe, surrounded by all this stone."

Lea and Cecelia nodded their agreement, while Lady Sabine—the oldest woman in attendance—simply lifted an eyebrow over the rim of her wineglass. "Honor's Keep has a stately quality to it, I think. The rulers of Caberwill have lived here for a hundred generations. Solspire is so new, by comparison."

"That's true," Lady Lea allowed. "But I still like it better."

Hanne quietly cleared her throat. "Though the differences between Solspire and Honor's Keep are vast, it's hardly fair to compare the two. Solspire was built for my family, when my ancestors took power after the Aska line failed." Was killed, she meant, but she preferred everyone to view their deaths as their failure to hold the throne. She addressed Victoria and Prudence now. "The old palace was dismantled and Solspire was constructed in its place, to celebrate the Fortuin family and our rise to the throne. Every generation has added something to it, and its splendor is unrivaled. Honor's Keep, however, represents stability, a continuity between dynasties. It was built to be defensible, and so it is."

Across the table, Victoria and Prudence both softened—just enough to let her know that her words had worked.

"But we're getting off topic," Hanne went on. "I want to know about life here. Festivals, banquets, formal balls—how many do you typically attend each week, and whose parties should we be sure to never ignore?"

Prudence and Victoria glanced at each other, looking uncomfortable as the second course was served: roasted duck and a rainbow of vegetables, all drizzled with a light sauce. Silverware and wineglasses were exchanged, and then the servants swept away, off to ready the third course.

"Well?" Hanne leaned forward. "Don't keep me in anticipation. I brought one hundred dresses from Embria—enough for a season, perhaps? I only hope they won't be out of fashion here."

"I'm afraid we don't have events quite so often," Prudence said softly. "Caberwilline monarchs have long viewed them as an expendable extravagance."

Hanne was well aware that there were few balls and banquets in Caberwill, of course. Everyone knew it. The number of events planned ahead of the wedding had been a difficult concession for Rune (and his parents) to make. "Ah," she said softly, lowering her eyes a fraction. "I suppose Caberwillines believe social gatherings to be frivolous, a waste of time and funds."

Neither Victoria nor Prudence said anything.

"In Caberwill, I suppose most of the ruling is done through the Crown Council or petitions to the king directly." Hanne cut and speared a slice of duck from her plate. "In Embria, ballrooms are where the kingdom's course is decided. We form alliances during a dance, raise or lower taxes over dessert, and hold trials in shadowed corners. Once, I witnessed an entire trade war between two rival families begin and end on a three-day party aboard the *Fortuin Jewel*—my mother's floating palace. I know it must seem a strange way of doing things, but we Embrians prefer to mitigate the unpleasantness of ruling.

"I see." Prudence took a bite of her meal, then gasped, her eyes widening. She washed it down with a sip of wine. "It's so spicy."

Hanne smiled around another bite of her own as Lea told the Caberwilline women about Embrian cuisine and the plethora of flavors enjoyed on the western side of the continent.

Then, the conversation turned toward the alliance—and Rune summoning the Nightrender.

"I thought it was incredibly brave." Lea pressed a hand to her chest and sighed. "He must feel so strongly for you, Your Highness, that he was willing to risk a second Red Dawn."

The thought soured Hanne's stomach, but she maintained her pleasant expression. "He possesses great courage," she agreed. "I know exactly how important this alliance is to my soon-to-be husband, because it is equally important to me. Had he been the one imprisoned in a malsite, I would have done everything in my power to free him."

"How brave," Maris said.

"Romantic," Lea agreed.

"It's all no less than what the alliance deserves," Cecelia finished.

"I found Prince Rune's defense of his actions quite compelling." Prudence took a tiny bite of her duck, her mouth pinching as she lifted her wineglass and gulped. "The way he stood up to his parents in front of everyone—it was unlike him. I've never seen him dissent quite so passionately before."

Hanne tilted his head. "How does he typically disagree with his parents?"

Prudence gave a tight smile. "Often, he will simply protest and urge them to listen to the people more, and his parents remind him that there are nuances to ruling that he cannot yet understand. He gives the appearance of ceding to them, but I suspect he holds it all against them. All of that is in private, of course."

"Ah, but you have found out." Hanne's gaze flickered to Lady Sabine, who was also eyeing Prudence with interest.

"I have my ways," Prudence allowed. "And, as you have certainly noticed by now, His Highness is not known for being subtle."

That was true. Still, Prudence, with her *way*, could prove useful. Sabine, who was still giving the young woman an appraising look, seemed to agree.

"Oh yes. Subtlety is not one of his strengths," Victoria said. "I assume we've all heard about his fight with the Nightrender in the middle ward, the day after he and she went to the malsite?"

Hanne lifted an eyebrow. "They fought?"

"Well, they argued." Lea pressed her napkin to the corners of her mouth. "His Highness sided with his father, while the Nightrender insisted the Highcrowns provide her with an army of Dawnbreakers to take into the Malice."

"He accused her of forgetting things," Prudence added. "He said she'd forgotten about the Red Dawn. And then she flew off, angry as could be."

"She flew right by that window." Nadine nodded toward the parlor. "I could have reached out and plucked a feather."

"More likely you would have lost a finger," Cecelia said. "I heard those feathers are sharp. They certainly looked it, didn't they? When we saw her in the throne room."

Maris gave a serious nod. "I would have sewn your finger back on, Nadine, if you had lost it to the Nightrender."

"How sweet." Nadine flashed a smile. "Fortunately, I was so startled that I didn't even think about it in the moment."

"What, exactly, did Rune side with his father on?" Hanne asked.

Quiet fell across the table. Then, Prudence said, "Presumably, the king had been considering whether to strike Embria before your parents found out that you were missing, Your Highness. And though Prince Rune's first instinct was to do anything to get you back— Well, when it seemed you must be dead—"

"He agreed with his father." Hanne nodded slowly. It made sense, in a Caberwilline sort of way. Hanne probably would have done the same, had their positions been reversed, although she wouldn't have begun with a military strike. No, it would have been a move so swift that Caberwill wouldn't even notice until it was too late. "Well. It's a good thing I arrived when I did."

"Indeed," Victoria said. "Your very presence here has prevented an unnecessary war."

All of Hanne's ladies hurried to agree.

As the conversation circled back to the Nightrender, how frightened everyone had been at her arrival, and the likelihood of another Incursion, Hanne contented herself to observe her four ladies, her spymistress, and the two women who would build on her authority here. And with each course that arrived, every bite of Embrian cuisine, Hanne grew more certain: she was on the correct path once more. All the things that had happened in Ivasland—she could move past them, fix them, and overcome them.

Soon, the world would see Hanne for who she truly was: a queen made for conquest.

Yes. Tuluna's whisper sounded in the back of Hanne's mind—wonderful and welcome after weeks of silence. ***A queen. My queen. The world's queen.***

26.
Nightrender

The wedding was just a wedding. Nightrender had been to dozens before—there was always a place set above where she could watch (or doze off) without anyone bothering her for favors—and she found them a little boring, to be honest.

Humans and their happiness. You should put an end to it all right here.

This wedding, however, was a little more interesting than the others, as Embrians occupied half of the Caberwilline temple. The nobles important enough to be here sat on the western side, dressed in bright colors that showed off their obsidian jewelry. They were a strange field of wildflowers in this large and somber chamber, surrounded as they were by carved stone, ancient tapestries, and shrines to the major Numina the Caberwillines worshipped. Elmali's was the largest and most prominent, but a shrine to Tuluna—the patron Numen of Embria—had been hastily erected and placed beside it.

On the eastern side, the Caberwillines sat in their neutral colors—grays, the occasional cream or tan if someone felt extravagant—and eyed the Embrians as though they gave off toxic fumes. King and Queen Highcrown sat at the front of the room, with two young girls at their sides. If they noticed the tension behind them, they didn't show it.

And then there was Prince Rune. He stood by the mahogany doors, his gaze locked on the floor in front of him, his expression like granite.

Nightrender started to look away, to give him some privacy while he considered his long future as a married man, but just then, the prince glanced up to find her watching. Their eyes locked, making her breath catch and a deep sense of longing stir in her stomach.

He started to smile, but a swish of fabric in the hall caught his attention. He looked away, that almost-smile replaced by a mask of royal poise.

A sliver of gold appeared first, shimmering just over the floor like the edges of a dragon's hoard, followed by Princess Johanne herself, immaculate in layer after layer of silk like she'd been wrapped in summer sunshine. She was beautiful, golden hair swept up into artful disarray beneath her black crown; a pair of curled locks hung around her face to soften her.

But there was nothing soft about this princess. Nightrender had seen that yesterday, and now, with that obsidian crown atop her head, there was no question about what kind of image she wanted to project. Hard, ambitious, and exquisite: she would permit no rivals.

Nightrender sucked in a sharp breath. She knew that crown—the Black Reign, humans had named it millennia ago—because it was one of the Relics created by the Numina to help protect Salvation. She hadn't seen it in centuries.

In ancient times, warrior kings and queens defending the people had worn the crown into the Malice, to protect them from rancor. It was a powerful ward against such creatures—and here was Princess Johanne, wearing it as a political prop.

And though the jagged spikes of obsidian must have been heavy, the princess kept her head high, her neck long and graceful, showing no discomfort as she took Prince Rune's hand.

Sparks of an ugly, slithering emotion coiled through Nightrender's heart, but she tried to stuff it down where she didn't have to look at it.

Are you jealous?

She was not. She had no reason to be jealous.

Do you have feelings for the prince?

She had no feelings for him beyond the intense protectiveness she felt for her soul shard in any incarnation (she still believed it was him, evidence or not). It wasn't possible. The Numina hadn't made her that way.

But you're broken, aren't you?

She was, perhaps. She had no idea what was stealing her memories or if there was even an end to this. But that didn't mean she was *jealous*.

Movement continued in the hall below, in spite of her roiling emotions. Everyone had risen to face the doors where Prince Rune and Princess Johanne stood, her hand resting delicately in the crook of his arm.

Embrian weddings had music here, as well as flowers and lengths of bright silk thrown over the couple as they walked by, but the Caberwilline version was far more subdued. The pair went alone and in silence, to symbolize the long journey of a marriage during which they must rely solely on each other, or something along those lines. Nightrender wasn't completely sure.

She closed her eyes and thought about killing rancor, distracted only by the sound of the grand priest at the fore of the temple. His voice lifted over the congregation.

"Tradition tells us of the Numina's immense love for us here on the laic plane," said Grand Priest Larksong, "and the sacrifices they made to ensure our existence. Both the Known and the Unknown are our great benefactors."

Nightrender knew the story of creation; the human version was flat-out falsehood, which stemmed from their limited understanding of the universe. (She tried *not* to think about how her understanding was growing more limited with every passing moment.) But they told the story again and again, because it made them feel better to believe they'd been crafted by divine hands.

It wasn't even a little bit true.

"As the Numina love us, we, too, have been granted the ability to love. It is, often, surprising and unexpected, but our love is what binds us together."

Prince Rune and Princess Johanne were halfway up the aisle now, striking in their black and gold. Both sides of the wedding guests admired them openly, and they did make a handsome couple.

You want to be with your soul shard. Are you going to let this happen?

Violence shot through her mind, an image of her ripping apart this entire temple to stop the wedding: blood dripping down the walls, mangled bodies strewn across the floor, and her placing Black Reign—the obsidian crown—atop Prince Rune's head.

Sickness turned in her stomach, and desperately she gulped from the glass of water that had been provided, but that didn't settle the nausea.

She was capable of that, yes—she'd been made for destruction—but never had she so vividly imagined that level of brutality against humans.

Except for the time you actually* performed *that level of brutality.

New images flooded her mind, tinged with a ruddy haze, too quick to fully understand: gilt hallways stained red with blood, brightly dressed people fleeing down them as she marched forward with her sword drawn, her wings flared so wide they dragged against the walls to prevent anyone from escape.

Then it was gone. Nevertheless, she knew what that moment was: the Red Dawn, her attack on Solspire.

She was going to be sick.

The horror of her actions rushed back to her, no longer tempered with denial.

She had seen it. She had *felt* it.

No, that wasn't right. She had seen and felt the first one, too, but the prince and princess were down on the main floor, enduring a long speech Nightrender had been too distracted to notice. She needed to focus on the present, on the smell of the temple, the droning of the service. There was no blood dripping down the walls, no bodies. . . .

She closed her eyes and exhaled slowly, trying to calm her racing heart, but the moment she did, something else prickled in the back of her mind, like darkness blooming in the distance.

It was unsettling.

She stood, but then sat again. Her movement had startled people, and the prince shot her a look that begged her to stay put.

And she *had* promised to attend, so even as the speeches went on—they all sounded the same to Nightrender: boring—she waited, drained her water, and struggled out from under the weight of guilt those foreign images had placed in her mind.

Just as Nightrender began to wonder if the temple was some kind of time slip, or if weddings *themselves* brought on that dark magic, shouts from the hall grew until they filled into the center aisle.

A pair of men stood there, both breathing heavily and drenched in sweat. Everyone—even the prince and princess—turned to look at them as one gasped out, "There's been an attack."

Prince Rune started to break away from Princess Johanne, as though to interview the messengers right then, but a soft cough from one of his parents reminded him of his place. He stayed, and Nightrender leaped down off her balcony.

Guests cringed away from her as she landed, and someone even had the nerve to start crying. But Nightrender didn't murder anyone on her way to the messenger, who was trembling both from exhaustion and terror.

"Tell me if it was malice," she said, loud enough to be heard over the now frenzied whispers echoing off the stone walls. As all eyes fell on her, she was glad she'd washed herself and her armor so that she wouldn't embarrass Prince Rune.

"Do you think she'll fight Ivasland with us?" someone murmured from the Caberwilline side.

"She's just as likely to kill us all," someone else replied.

One of the messengers had fallen to his knees, breathing heavily as he tried not to faint, while the other held himself up through sheer force of will. Their shock was severe; whatever had happened, it was bad.

"Tell me if it was malice," she repeated, more gently this time.

"It was—It was some kind of machine. It exploded and now there's malice everywhere. The messages said people are dying in broad daylight, and—"

"Tell me where." Her tone was dark, like the howl of wind before a storm.

To the man's credit, he still didn't collapse, even though he clearly wanted nothing more. "Just outside the village of Small Mountain. It's a farming town that supplies food for half of Brink. Do you know it?"

Nightrender didn't bother to answer. She left the temple without looking back.

27.
Rune

The rest of the wedding moved quickly, all the speeches and songs shadowed by renewed urgency. It was so hard to believe that something so terrible had happened—malice spilling across an innocent town—but it must be true. No one would lie about that.

Plus, he'd seen the Nightrender rise as though she'd sensed something happening, only to sit down again at his urging. He should have let her go. If he'd known, he would have, because that must have been the moment the machine detonated, killing people.

His people.

The horror of it turned in his stomach as he recalled his own brief encounter with a malsite. He, at least, had known what he was getting into. He, at least, had the protection of the Nightrender.

The people of Small Mountain had nothing. Just the most nightmarish death anyone could imagine.

Princess Johanne cleared her throat, drawing his attention down to her once again. She smiled brilliantly, utterly glorious in her obsidian crown and shimmering golden gown. Someone must have stayed up late taking in the seams, because the princess had definitely lost weight. Even her face, once full and soft, now had twin hollows under her cheekbones.

She did not deserve what had happened to her any more than the people of Small Mountain did. He hoped he would have the chance to tell her that later.

Although . . . the Nightrender had said Princess Johanne lied about her escape.

Well, perhaps he'd be able to get the truth.

In short order, Rune and Princess Johanne were pronounced married, with only a ceremonial kiss remaining. When she gave a small nod, he bent and they sealed the alliance—not just on paper, but with the rest of their lives.

A stark, unsatisfied sadness formed in him, building up to a lump in his throat. He smiled around it, because the smile was expected in spite of the fact that he'd just married someone he'd grown up believing was his enemy.

Princess Johanne was no longer Rune's enemy, but his wife.

His *wife*.

He needed to work with her—one day trust her—for the sake of both their kingdoms.

"Are you ready?" she murmured.

When he offered his arm, she placed her obsidian-jeweled hand there, and as one, they turned to face the crowd of both Caberwillines and Embrians.

Everyone stood, applauding so loudly the temple threatened to shake apart. Even the guards broke protocol to cheer. An alliance. Between two kingdoms. It was the first of its kind—and with no time to spare, as the messengers' arrival and the Nightrender's dramatic exit were fresh in everyone's memory.

This was where the breaking of the Winterfast Accords had led them.

Even with the thunder of approval rolling through the temple, even with the clever and fierce and beautiful wife at his side, that unsatisfied sadness rose up in Rune again. He wished he could follow the Nightrender—help somehow, like before—but this was not the time. Not only was the Nightrender the only one who could save Small Mountain, but Rune had just gotten *married*. It would never be the time again.

And there was no point in wishing things could be different.

Less than an hour later, Rune joined his parents in their office. He'd promised the Nightrender he would ask them for the army, once the wedding was finished, and he meant to keep that promise.

"Speak, but be quick." Opus sat at his desk, and Grace sat at hers. The office was a fine room of dark-lacquered walls, narrow lancet windows, and waiting heaps of papers and reports.

Rune sat in a chair between the two desks, feeling small in spite of the fact that he was a married man now, his future slightly more secure than it had been an hour ago. "I know this isn't what you want to hear right now—"

Opus sighed.

Perhaps he should have come up with a better opening than saying he knew they didn't want to hear what he had to say. That was a terrible way to get people to agree with him.

"We will talk about this until you do something about it." Rune made his voice hard. "The Incursion won't wait."

"What do you propose?" Grace asked. "Our options are limited, especially after this attack on Small Mountain. I know we said we'd discuss Dawnbreaker trials, but we simply can't spare the soldiers. Ivasland has already moved. Now everyone else will know they've broken the Winterfast Accords. We *must* respond."

Rune swallowed hard. "Are we certain that it was Ivasland? It's well before schedule." The autumn equinox—the suspected date for everything to be completed—was still over a month away.

"It must be them," agreed Opus. "If, indeed, a machine is the source of the calamity in Small Mountain, I intend to learn the truth of that. Sometimes the common people are confused or exaggerate or— Well, you've heard the sorts of things that they say. They cannot always be trusted."

"Fortunately," said Grace, "the Crown Council is assembling to address this crisis. And then, of course, we'll have another meeting that will include the Embrian dignitaries."

"This is the wedding day I always dreamed of," Rune muttered. "Meeting after meeting."

"Your sarcasm is inappropriate," Opus said. "However, if Abagail and Baldric *are* responsible for this attack, then the alliance is even more important, and the conflict even more urgent. If we find that Ivasland is responsible for the destruction of an innocent Caberwilline farming town—particularly Brink's breadbasket—then we will march on Athelney with the might of two armies. We will lay waste to their cities and universities."

This was the worst time to say it, but he'd promised the Nightrender. "Instead of going to war against Ivasland, you should send both armies into the Malice to stop the Incursion."

Silence.

His parents stared at him as though they were waiting for him to reveal he was being sarcastic yet again, even more inappropriately.

Rune plowed forward. "The situation is worse than you know. The Nightrender killed the rancor that Lady Nadine and Princess Johanne encountered, but there are almost certainly more."

"What do you mean?" Grace asked.

"I mean the Nightrender didn't return to Honor's Keep because she missed me." Rune rose from his seat and opened an expansive, relief-fronted cupboard. The sack the Nightrender had brought last night was here, where he'd asked John to put it this morning. As he carried it to his father's desk, a sharp, ozone stink washed over the room. "She came to bring me this."

"Dare I ask what's in here? More melted rancor parts?" Opus wrinkled his nose as he pulled the tie. The bowl and satchels spilled out, and the king lifted his eyes to Rune's. "What is this?"

"Items one would need to summon a rancor." Rune took his seat again. "I don't know where she found this—she refused to say—but it is more than possible that there is *at least* a second rancor out there."

"A second." Grace glanced at Opus. "This is not proof of a second rancor, only that someone attempted to summon one—or give the appearance of summoning one. Regardless, we have no reason to believe this wasn't the one killed days ago—in which case, the threat has been dealt with."

That was possible, Rune supposed.

Opus pressed his palms to his desk and pushed himself up, looming over the sack. "This is a desperate attempt to change our minds. But we have not chosen the situation we find ourselves in, and neither can we alter it. Ivasland is the threat we must address."

Rune stood, too, his back straight and hands at his sides. "I know Ivasland is breaching the Winterfast Accords, but I can assure you that this danger is just as real. She's warned me repeatedly that the Malstop is failing, and we now have a rancor and rancor-summoner. If we don't give the Nightrender our armies right this instant, thousands of people could die."

"They are dying right now," Opus declared. "In Small Mountain."

Rune flinched from the sting of those words. "They are, but the threat of an Incursion is even more serious than you fully understand."

"What do you mean?" Grace frowned.

Rune's heart pounded. He didn't want to say it, because it wasn't his secret, but he'd already said things he shouldn't, and if it would persuade his parents . . . "You already know that the Nightrender has lost some of her memories."

"Yes," Grace said. "She does not remember the Red Dawn."

He just hoped the Nightrender would forgive him for telling his parents her secret. "What I didn't tell you before is that she is *still* losing memories. We cannot afford to wait."

His parents looked at each other, some unspoken communication passing between them. In the back of his mind, Rune wondered if he'd ever develop that connection with Princess Johanne. Even if they never grew to love each other—as his parents had—he hoped they might at least understand each other.

"What do you mean 'she is still losing memories'?" Opus asked after a moment.

"Just what it sounds like." Rune rubbed his temples, imagining how terrifying it must be to lose pieces of one's past every moment. "She is forgetting things, and what happens if she forgets how to protect us? If we don't end this Incursion immediately, then we may not have another chance. That will be the end of Salvation, and unless you've sent off ships to explore other continents—"

"There are none," Opus said, deadly serious. "That's madness. There's nothing else out there."

"Just malice," Rune agreed. "Just entire continents bathed in darkness."

That was what he'd always been taught, anyway—why the final refugees of mankind had come to Salvation thousands of years ago. This was the last habitable place in the whole world. It was the last foothold for humanity. They could not lose it.

"So where will we go if we allow malice to overtake Salvation?" Rune asked.

Grace's gaze dropped to her desk. "Have you spoken to anyone else about this? Any of the Crown Council? Grand Priest Larksong?"

Rune hated questions like that; in books and plays, a murder usually occurred immediately after ensuring no one else knew the information. (His parents weren't going to kill him, of course, but they had plenty of ways to silence him.)

"I have spoken with the Nightrender." He remained standing. "I explained that I'm not the king of Caberwill—I am unable to command the army—but that I would ask for it on her behalf. Here is my offer: send our men through the Soul Gate with her, and I will no longer be her Dawnbreaker. I will stay here and do my duties. As crown prince."

Opus sighed. "My son—"

"Call it a wedding gift," Rune said. "Call it a gift for your grandchildren."

Call it anything you need, Rune thought. *Just don't make me disappoint her again.*

A knock sounded on the door, and the king's secretary, Echo, looked inside. "The Crown Council has gathered. They're waiting for you."

"Tell them we'll be there in a moment," Opus said. When Echo ducked back out, Opus let his eyes fall on the sack of rancor-summoning materials. His voice was unusually quiet when he spoke again. "If I do this, the consequences will be dire. We may violate the treaty with Embria if we do not pursue war with Ivasland. They may refuse to field their men. They may demand an annulment."

Rune held his breath.

"But I'll consider it, and I'll let you know first thing tomorrow morning."

Well, it wasn't a yes, but it was more than Rune had ever gotten from his father. Perhaps this would work out after all.

EXCERPT FROM NADINE HOLT'S DIARY,
DECIPHERED FROM EMBRIAN MICRO-CODE

Something amazing has happened.

Last night I was kneeling at my fire, praying to Tuluna for guidance. Earl Flight's question had been circling in my head for days—should I marry

Prince Rune?—and I had but minutes before an answer was required of me. Then I heard a commotion in the hall, a knock at my door—and there was Hanne. Filthy, skinny, but alive.

I'm afraid the next several moments are lost in a haze of joy. The next thing I remember, we were sitting on the sofa and she was telling me everything that had happened since we saw the rancor. Her captivity, the beast's demands, and her time in Ivasland. It all sounds so harrowing, but she's here now. She's here and that's what matters.

When she was finished, we talked about our plans, all the meetings with names from Lord Bearhaste's list. I wanted her to know that I hadn't lost faith—that I'd believed she would return, even when others believed she was forever lost to the malsite, and after she was presumed dead . . .
I intended to move forward with our plans as long as possible.

I did, somewhat hesitantly, tell her about Earl Flight's question. She said that she would have wanted me to do it—to fulfill her obligation to Embria and Tuluna, if she could not.

But now, as of this morning, she is married to Crown Prince Rune Highcrown.

I could not be happier.

28.
Nightrender

Nightrender was too late to help Small Mountain.

The attack had been swift. Deadly. Not only because of the machine with its malice pouring forth, but because Ivaslander soldiers had come as well, taking tactical advantage of the chaos. They'd cut through the unprotected town as swiftly as a hot blade through butter, burning crops, breaking windows, and looting shops, loading their prizes onto wagons—but they'd underestimated how quickly malice could spread. Now they were all dead. Their swollen, split-open bodies littered the streets, motionless beside their bloodstained swords and plunder.

The town was ghostly silent and cloaked in a heavy miasma. Nightrender followed twisting threads of malice to an inn, which was crumbling to dust before her eyes, then to a petrified general store—filled with petrified people, their stone faces frozen in terror. The cord of dark threads led her to a bakery next, the building turning into gelatin, and beyond that, a stable.

She didn't look to see what had become of the horses. Even she had her limits.

This was how Ivasland had broken the Winterfast Accords. This attack must have been the first field test of the mal-device—to see if it really worked for war, how quickly, what kind of damage its transported malice would do. That such a successful test had also laid waste to a harvest that should have been stored away for winter . . . Nightrender supposed that was an added benefit.

Even now, she could hear the distant flap of wings as courier doves flew to Athelney, bearing the news. Perhaps the recipient would be unhappy to realize that none of their soldiers had survived—but they would simply adjust their tactics for the next target.

Nightrender considered going after the birds and seizing the scraps of paper secured around their legs, but they would scatter as soon as they noticed her, and she'd spend too much time chasing them. There wasn't any hiding this, anyway.

Look at what they did in your absence. The voice coiled around her thoughts, squeezing tighter. ***Look at what you've permitted them to do, going to sleep before finishing your work. They are this evil only because you allow it.***

Nightrender shuddered, telling herself it couldn't be true, but terrified that it was.

You could rule them, suggested the voice. **Force *them to behave.***

"No." She was not made for ruling, but for serving. Protecting.

Protect them from themselves. You are too lenient with them; decide you will not be any longer, and punish them for their poor behavior. It is the only way children learn.

"Tell me what you are," she whispered.

You know what I am.

She didn't, and she regretted asking.

Conversing only encouraged it. She should have maintained her silence and dealt with . . . whatever this was . . . when the Incursion was over.

The crash of a house collapsing drew her back to the present. Moving toward the dust plume, she scanned the streets for any signs of life, but the malice had been thorough. Everyone for leagues out was dead.

All dead.

All. Dead.

And why isn't this darkness coming after you? Are you dead, too?

Somewhere deep inside her, a rush of horror sparked and wouldn't go out. But she had a job to do. She drew her sword and plunged it into the earth.

Prismatic agony exploded through her head, growing with every second. She bit the insides of her cheeks and *endured*, pushing the fire of the Numina out and into all the twisting and tangled filaments of evil that had extended into building foundations and walls, and wells, and bodies.

She burned until the malice was dust, and then even the dust disappeared.

Her sight began to clear. She staggered forward, breathing around the residual anguish of her own power, and struggled to summon the strength to do this again and again.

Cleansing malsites was like cauterizing a wound: violent, excruciatingly painful, but utterly necessary; no part of the infection could remain.

She walked on, toward the field where the device had been activated. It was from there the malice spun outward, its tendrils searching for life to destroy. The crops that grew on this particular field—once fat and healthy potatoes just a month or two from harvest—were yellow and limp, and they smelled like rotten death. Hundreds of people would go hungry because of this loss.

And all around the farm, dozens of workers lay dead, their corpses already bloated, wriggling with flies. They probably hadn't even realized what was happening. Worms moved through the earth, come to feast.

Finally, she found what remained of the device itself. It was a small metal box, an intake vent on one side, a cracked bulb on top. Perhaps the bulb was the boiler and reservoir of malice, the vessel it was drawn into; perhaps it had cracked from the *pressure* of that malice, releasing it out into the world.

Was that all it took?

This was the way humans had weaponized the very evil she'd spent millennia fighting to keep them safe from.

It was appalling. Horrifying. Disgusting that people could do *this* to others. But she was not shocked. She wished she could have been.

What a mess they've left you this time. If only you would teach them not to behave so poorly.

Nightrender gazed down at the machine a moment more, gathering the courage to endure this again. She needed to purge the traces of malice clinging to the shattered glass. Then she could rest. . . .

No, there was no rest. Not from the fight, and not from the pain the fight now caused. But she had to talk herself into suffering that blinding, head-splitting agony again and again, didn't she? So she'd take it one step at a time.

First, she would destroy the machine and the last of the Small Mountain malice.

Nightrender adjusted her grip on Beloved and drove the blade deep into the earth, concentrating her numinous fire into the pool of malice that had spilled beneath the machine. The pain was frigid and sharp, but she could hear the holy fire pop and fizzle, bursting like stars against the darkness. It lit the ground with flashes of electric white.

The purifying power was beautiful.

And it was agony.

Nightrender's vision tunneled and dimmed as she pushed the numinous fire deeper, twisting the blade this way and that until every shred of darkness was vanquished for as far as she could reach.

The field went quiet, her ragged breathing the only sound. A soft wind kicked up and traced across the ravaged town, carrying the wretched odor of malice.

Surrounded by utter devastation, she gazed down at the machine. It was useless now that it had fulfilled its purpose, although perhaps someone would be along to retrieve it. She should dispose of it.

She flicked the dirt and dead plant matter from her sword, sheathed it, and knelt on the blood-soaked ground, glaring at the device.

So small. So unassuming. Yet it had the power to devastate kingdoms.

Humans cannot help but escalate their aggressions, justifying their treachery as necessary. Important. The end results wash clean the stain of their actions.

Yes. There was truth to that, but people were more complicated than the voice seemed to understand. Their actions were almost never all good or all bad. Still, she could not bury the machine in Embria or in Caberwill, lest it be found and studied. She would have to find something else to do with it.

Heart weighed down with obligation, she produced a canvas sack. She was ready to gather up the device, but that was when she felt it. Before, it had been masked by the chaos and rot, but now she caught the sweeter energy that fluttered through the machine's making. It was familiar. Startling. It was all deceit and unknown intent concealed beneath smiles and gowns and pretty words.

As the sun started to fall into the west, a knot formed in her stomach. She closed her eyes, unsure what she should do. Prince Rune deserved to know, didn't he? Or would telling him mean taking a side in this war?

She scooped the device into her bag and pulled the drawstrings tight. First, she would burn the poisoned husk of this town—no one should see it like this—and then she would decide what she should do, if anything, about Princess Johanne of Embria.

29.
Rune

The rest of the day passed in a blur of endless meetings. The malice machine. Speculation about how Ivasland had finished it so far ahead of schedule. Questions as to whether the Nightrender would fight on their side, since *they* hadn't broken the Winterfast Accords.

"Doubtful," Rune said, "but you'll have to ask her."

"We don't need the Nightrender's help," Princess Johanne declared from the seat next to him. She still wore her wedding gown—and her obsidian crown. No one could look away from her. "We are strong enough to defeat our enemies on our own."

Several Caberwilline councilors nodded along with the Embrian nobles, and Rune had to give it to her: she was a born leader. People would follow her out of love or fear, whichever she demanded.

He had considered telling everyone about the rancor-summoning materials, but as the Nightrender hadn't said *where* she found them, that meant he couldn't be sure it didn't belong to someone at this table. So he kept his mouth shut. His parents didn't say anything about it, either.

Finally, the sun went down and everyone fell quiet from exhaustion. Then, Rune and his bride were dismissed to go make an heir.

His quarters had been transformed.

First, bright vases of flowers were everywhere in the parlor, and several of his books had been removed from their shelves to make room for small portraits of the Fortuin family: King Markus and Queen Katarina, as well as several aunts and uncles and cousins. (Interesting, since the princess had never spoken of them in any way that could be described as loving or familial. And it didn't escape his notice that Princess Johanne had chosen the most unflattering portraits.)

As for where his books had gone, Rune could only guess.

But the worst was what had replaced his dining table. There stood a small stone fountain, a carved crown in the center, decorated with precious gems. An array of light globes reflected off the water and the jewels, making him squint. Did it have to be *so* bright?

"Do you like it?" Princess Johanne dipped her fingers into the basin. "I had it brought from home."

Well, he hadn't thought a monstrosity like that had been sitting anywhere in Honor's Keep. It was garish. "Where will we eat?" he asked instead. "Since we no longer have a table."

"In the dining room with everyone else!" She flashed a hard smile, as if he were the town fool. "Would you like to see my room?"

Rune was somewhat terrified to see what had become of the previously neutral and inoffensive space, a plain chamber he had always used for quiet reading, but he followed her in. Her bedroom was much like his in that it had all the normal bedroom furniture, as well as a balcony door and a door that led into his room . . . but that was where the similarities ended.

The curtains, bed canopy, and sheets were bright strawberry silk, and the floor was covered in a thick, luxuriant teal rug. A trio of wardrobes—all painted to match the bed canopy—stood guard along one wall. A large painting of Princess Johanne hung over the fireplace; in it, she wore the obsidian crown, along with a rich mint-green gown that dipped low in the front, and an elaborate pendant of obsidian, sapphire, and emerald. She was stunning.

She was stunning in real life. The painter had made no "improvements" to the princess, because there were none to be made.

Just now, she was placing the obsidian crown on her vanity. She glanced over at him, then up at the painting. "Would you like me to wear that gown for you?"

"Now?" He almost choked on the word.

"If you'd like. You are my husband, and I want to please you." A coy smile turned up the corners of her mouth. She pulled a pin from her hair, letting the golden curls tumble down her back. With just a few steps, she closed the distance between them.

"I—" Rune tugged at his collar; the room was too warm, and he was having difficulty breathing. "You don't have to," he said at last. "You look wonderful as you are."

"That's sweet." When she was gazing up at him as she did now, it was difficult to remember any of his reservations about her. And then, when she traced her fingers down his arm and stepped directly in front of him, his attention was captured completely.

"Your Highness," he murmured.

"Hanne." She stepped closer until the hem of her gown brushed across the toes of his boots. "Please call me Hanne. I prefer it."

"Hanne," he repeated, a little hoarsely.

Again, those lips tilted into a smile, and she reached up to touch his cheek. "Do you think we should . . ." Her gaze dropped to his mouth.

Until a few minutes ago, Rune had been dreading this. He'd thought it would be an impossible topic to approach, especially given her recent hardships, but here she was, her fingertips trailing down the side of his neck, her breath shallow—from anticipation?

"It is expected of us," he finally managed to say, wishing more than anything he knew what to do with his hands. Touch her? Take her waist and draw her closer? She hadn't invited him. But she was touching him, so did that count?

"Do you *want* to?"

Well, his body certainly wanted to, but he didn't love her—or even like her, most of the time—and the idea of taking her to bed made a strange pit grow in his stomach. It seemed unfair.

And then there was the Nightrender. There was nothing between them—*nothing*—and he was *married* to Hanne, so why the guilt?

"Rune?" Hanne's fingertips had drifted down the side of his ribs. "Our kingdoms are counting on us."

"You're right." And abruptly, it didn't matter if he wanted to or not. (Even though he mostly did.) This was their duty. The alliance. Their kingdoms. Indeed, all of Salvation required an heir. "Yes. Let's do it."

"So romantic," Hanne murmured. "Perhaps let me be in charge."

As soon as it was over, Hanne was up and moving around the room, pulling on clothes, talking about her cousin. Rune couldn't believe she had the energy.

He watched as she ran a comb through her hair. Even in the dim lamplight, the gold glowed brightly against the dress she'd put on—violet with a silver mesh of reeled silk layered atop the bodice. "I'm going to visit Nadine."

"You are?" Rune sat up. "But it's our wedding night."

Hanne lowered her comb and looked at him. "Yes, and now I want to see my cousin. It's been a difficult day."

"Difficult because of . . ." He motioned around the bed. He'd thought it had gone rather well.

Hanne frowned and grabbed a jeweled clip from her nightstand. "Rune, beloved, I shouldn't have to remind you that people died today."

Oh. Right. He was being insensitive. Of course Hanne had strong feelings about raw malice set loose in the world. Less than a day married and he was already failing her. "We could talk about it," Rune suggested. "If you want."

She finished binding her hair into a low bun. "No, we talked enough at the meeting earlier. I want to be with my cousin now. She's really more like my sister. You understand."

"I see. Then I'll walk you there." Rune started to get up and get dressed, but his wife held up a hand.

"I'll go on with a guard, and you should go to bed. I'm sure you have a lot to do in the morning."

That was true. Troops were being readied, scouts were searching other towns for more devices that might detonate within Caberwill's borders, and regardless, Rune needed to corner his father and make another case for the Soul Gate.

Opus *had* said he would reach a decision by morning.

Yes, it would be best if Rune went right to sleep—and not obsess about the unfairness of being married to someone he didn't care for when he was daydreaming about someone he could never have.

Hanne shoved a pile of clothes—his clothes—into his arms. "Why don't you sleep in your own bed, darling? It will be more restful."

He was still in Hanne's bed, he realized. "Sorry. Yes. I'll go." He hugged his clothes to his chest as they walked into the parlor.

"Good. I'll be visiting Nadine until late, so don't wait up for me." Then she kissed him and whispered by his ear, "Unless you want to."

Then she swept from the room, leaving Rune to stare after her as the door swung shut.

Confused and guilty and more than a little tired of being ordered about by everyone, Rune sat on the edge of the ugly fountain and sighed. If this was marriage, he much preferred unrequited longing.

30.
Hanne

Nadine poured a cup of black tea and offered it to Hanne. "So the council had no real information concerning the Small Mountain attack?"

"Nothing. All the talk was conjecture. It was one worthless meeting after another." Hanne accepted the cup and sipped. The tea was hot and burned the roof of her mouth, but she hardly felt it. She'd been through so much worse.

"Nothing from my sources either." Lady Sabine dropped her knitting bag to the floor beside her chair, taking the tea Nadine offered. "I dislike waiting for information. There are *proper* channels in Embria. But everything in Caberwill is so far from everything else, and these awful mountains make travel so difficult. And the height! I can barely keep my breath here."

"I'm told we will all acclimate to Brink's elevation." Nadine sat with her own tea, gazing out the window for a moment. "I can't stop thinking about it. Small Mountain is such a tragedy, Caberwillines or not. Can you imagine?"

Hanne could imagine.

Something suspiciously similar to guilt needled, but she pushed it down where it couldn't bother her anymore—just like her mother had taught her.

She didn't want to talk about Small Mountain. Those farms. Those people. They'd been attacked because she'd given Ivasland the key to the containment material, but it wasn't as though she'd had a choice. Anyway, Mae and the other malicists would have perfected the device eventually. It would have been nice if the riot she'd accidentally started had delayed them—but she supposed rulers who wanted to destroy the world wouldn't be stopped by one small act of rebellion.

"I'm sure we'll know more in the morning." Lady Sabine sipped her tea. "But it is safe to assume that the town is lost. Otherwise, the Nightrender would have returned to report good tidings to the prince."

"Their relationship is strange." Nadine frowned. "Why does she like him so much?"

"Because he's very obedient." Hanne sighed. And since he *was*, perhaps she needed to talk with him about the way he carried on with that thing.

The summoning, his bravery at the malsite—all for Hanne, everyone said. But could she really be sure? Even when Rune had rushed to see Hanne upon her return, the Nightrender had been there. They'd clearly come *together*.

Rune was Hanne's husband now. If anyone was going to pull Rune's strings, it should be her.

"You know, you're right," Hanne said. "Their relationship *is* strange. I'm going to have to do something about it. But that's for another time."

"Indeed," Lady Sabine said. "We have more pressing problems right now. King Opus is considering sending his army into the Malice."

Hanne looked sharply at the old woman. She had been Hanne's parents' spymistress before their current spymaster had replaced her, and now she was Hanne's. "Explain."

Sabine blew steam off her cup. "Caberwill may be large, Your Highness, but nothing in Honor's Keep escapes me. Nothing. In the last hour, two of the grand general's runners have been seen with maps of the Soul Gate and the Malice itself. Opus has also been in midnight meetings with his closest advisers, and someone was sent to take inventory of the obsidian-tipped weapons in the armory."

"But there is no Incursion," Nadine protested. "Beyond a single rancor, that is, and it is dead."

"When did this enter the king's mind?" Hanne asked.

"Opus and Rune had a meeting directly after the wedding," Sabine continued. "And they have another scheduled for the morning."

So this was Rune's fault. Of course it was.

"I won't allow it. We must make our move against Ivasland," Hanne murmured. "Before any more machines are deployed."

"The unrest Abagail and Baldric are enjoying is very fortunate for us," Sabine said. "I plan to keep a careful watch over the five-pointed stars—as much as possible."

"Good." Hanne drained her tea and handed the cup to Nadine, who placed it on the table. "I will speak with the king."

"Now?"

Hanne stood. "Now. He must know that he cannot send the *Embrian* army into the Malice without my approval." It was actually her parents' approval that such a change would require, but they would never even hear the request unless Hanne made it. And she would not, because she intended to burn Ivasland to the ground.

Nadine stood, too. "Should I come with you? Or Lady Sabine?"

"No, I'll go alone. You don't have to worry about me."

"Someone should."

Neither of them named all the people who neglected to worry about the crown princess of Embria. The list would have been too long. Better would have been to list the people who did:

1. Nadine

Oh, certainly Hanne's parents wanted her alive and cared for, but in the way they liked their crowns polished and their hunting hounds fed: she was another useful possession and they expected only peak performance from her. No emotion. No vulnerability. No *weakness*. They'd seared away the parts of Hanne they didn't like, shaping her into a weapon even they wouldn't be able to control much longer.

Hanne would be queen of everything.

After a quick, reassuring smile for Nadine, she turned to Lady Sabine, who—to be completely fair—also cared for and worried about Hanne, but in a more means-to-an-end kind of way, rather than true, loving devotion. Hanne said, "Keep me apprised of the situation in Ivasland. And find out what you can regarding the Nightrender. Why can't she remember the Red Dawn? How close *are* she and Rune? I want to know everything about her."

"As you wish," Lady Sabine said.

Nadine pulled open a drawer and produced a bundle of cloth. "Now, I hope you won't need it, but since they seized your dagger yesterday, I took the liberty of getting it back."

Yet again, Nadine had helped Hanne beyond expectations.

Hanne smiled. This was how life worked best: the two of them against everyone else.

With a smile on her face and a dagger in her boot (and a pair of Caberwilline guardsmen trailing behind her), Hanne walked to the office where the king had interrogated her the day before. She flashed the two sentries standing before the door her prettiest grin. "Good evening, soldiers."

One nodded at her. "Your Highness."

"The king isn't to be disturbed," said the other.

"I'm afraid I must insist," she said sweetly. "It's regarding our alliance."

As she was speaking, and as the guards all exchanged uncertain looks, danger suddenly prickled the hairs on the back of Hanne's neck. Something was wrong. Something—

Hanne ducked and rolled out of the way in one motion, her body reacting before her mind even understood why. But instinct had saved her: a small bolt zipped past where her head had been and struck a sentry in the chest. His blood sprayed as he fell, and that was it: he was dead.

Without pausing to look for the attacker or to see what the other men would do, Hanne lunged for the office door and threw herself inside. The door shut with a *bang* as she scanned the room for new threats.

But the office was empty, save for the king.

"Princess Johanne!" He lurched to his feet, scattering papers. "What is this—" He stopped when the door flew open again, revealing a second guard slumping against the frame. A pool of blood was expanding through the hall. *All* the men were dead.

Now, she caught sight of the assailant: an older man wearing a beige shirt and trousers, calf-high boots, and worn leather gloves. He was in the process of exchanging his small crossbow for a pair of daggers when Hanne locked eyes with him, and she knew exactly what he was.

An Ivaslander assassin.

But was he after her or King Opus? The first bolt had been aimed at her, but he'd been hidden outside the king's office. Regardless of the truth, she needed to make this work in her favor.

"Your Majesty, you're under attack!" Hanne shouted.

If Opus was distracted by an assault on his life, then he wasn't paying attention to her.

The king cursed and drew a knife from the underside of his desk, while Hanne moved out of view of the assassin, pressing herself against a bookcase. Unless there was a secret exit to this room, the Ivaslander had them cornered and he knew it.

"You." Opus crouched behind his desk, his knife gleaming. "What is the meaning of this, Embrian snake? What have you done?"

Clearly Hanne had miscalculated. His hatred for Embrians was such that he would never ignore her, even in the face of a more obvious threat.

"Nothing!" She hadn't yet drawn her dagger from her boot, but she felt certain the moment she bent to arm herself, he would fling his own knife into her heart. "I came here to speak about our alliance!"

A scowl flashed across the king's face, but another crash came from the hall; a man was shouting for reinforcements.

"Who is that man out there, girl?"

"I think you know." Hanne glanced over her shoulder just in time to see another guard die in the hall.

"Hurry!" cried a guard from out of view. "To the king!"

"An attack on Small Mountain this morning, and now an assassin? I don't know how you managed to work this evil, but I know it was you." Opus rounded the desk and rushed at her. "After my guards subdue that man, you will be questioned. You lied about the malsite. *How did you escape?*"

Metal clanged on metal as more men arrived to defend Opus. There was, unfortunately, no one to defend Hanne. No one but herself.

Burn it. This was not going according to plan. Still, Tuluna the Tenacious would provide an opportunity; all Hanne had to do was take it.

"I did not cause this. I want to *destroy* Ivasland. This man is clearly here to divide us." She weighed her options. None were good. "Your Majesty." She wrapped her arms around herself and tried to look frightened, as though anything mortal could frighten her anymore. "We need to find a way out of here. Is there another exit?"

"My men will deal with this," Opus said sharply.

Hanne clasped her hands together, then made herself jump when something crashed in the hall. A curse, a thump, a gurgle: someone had just died, and it was not the assassin; none of the guards were moving into the office to make sure the king was unharmed.

King Opus's men were not dealing with this very well, from what Hanne could see.

She curled her shoulders in as though she were just a meek thing. "Your Majesty, please! Isn't there something you can do?"

He glanced toward the door, where the fighting was only escalating. Many men lay dead on the floor, their bodies punctured or slashed open. This Ivaslander was a true master of the art.

"Your Majesty?" She kept her voice small.

And then King Opus fully turned and faced the noise of the hall, the struggle of his men. It was just enough to show her his back.

She drew her dagger from her boot. At least now she wasn't defenseless, but as the fighting spilled into the office—two guards and the assassin closing in on the king—she wished for a weapon a little more substantial. She threw herself behind the desk for protection, hitting the floor hard enough to bruise.

The room was all chaos for a moment, furniture overturned, papers in the air. Another man died with the clatter of steel, and then the Ivaslander turned his murderous glare not on the king, but on Hanne.

"There you are." His voice was soft and raspy, like the scrape of scales on stone. "Abagail sends her regards."

Hanne repressed a shudder. The huge wooden block of the desk was between her and everyone else—the assassin, the king, the lone remaining guard—and her choices were almost none.

"He means to kill me!" she shrieked. "Your Majesty, I could be with child now! He's trying to kill my baby!"

But the king had already raised his knife and thundered toward the man.

Though King Opus was a giant, he moved quickly as he drove his blade toward the assassin's throat. The Ivaslander blocked and pivoted, throwing the sole remaining guard in front of Opus, and the two went crashing to the ground with angry and confused shouts.

Then the assassin turned his eyes to Hanne, daggers dripping with the blood of all the men he'd just killed.

The king hauled himself up and grabbed at the remaining guard. "Go," he said, pushing the other man toward the door. "Reinforcements. *Now!*"

King Opus could have saved himself, but ultimately he was a man who believed he would do better than anyone else in any given task—including saving the life of Princess Johanne, the living link of Caberwill's alliance with Embria.

Everything happened very quickly after that.

The assassin raised a dagger to throw at Hanne.

The king lunged at the assassin, his knife gleaming.

Hanne dove out of the way just in time; the assassin's dagger flew through the air, missing her by a breath.

Then, in the same movement, the assassin drove his remaining dagger deep into the king. The blade went into the chest and under the ribs, where it twisted—and the king's fate was sealed.

Hanne, however, was not idle during this exchange of blades and blood: she hurled her own dagger straight into the assassin's throat.

The assassin was dead before he hit the floor. And that was it. The king. The Ivaslander. Tons of guards—

Oh burn it, the *guard*. Hanne pulled the assassin's dagger from the wall behind her and ran into the hall.

"Sir!" she screamed, concealing the dagger in the folds of her dress. "Come back!"

The guard was at the other end of the hall, not quite to an intersection. He stopped and looked at her.

"The king has killed the assassin, but His Majesty is injured! He says he needs your help."

"Of course!" The guard ran back as fast as he could, not noticing that Hanne wasn't as frightened by all the bodies as she should have been; no, his focus was clearly on getting to the king in time to save his life. "Go find Stella Asheater, the grand physician," said the man as he reached the office again. His dark eyes were wide, his unshaven face sweaty. "And—and tell her to bring sheets."

Hanne nodded, but as the guard turned, she drew the stolen dagger and thrust it into his kidney, twisting the blade to make sure he died immediately. She'd have liked to give him a death without pain—she wasn't a monster, after all, and he was only trying to protect his king—but she imagined being stabbed in a vital organ hurt quite a lot.

"Sorry." She held onto the dagger as the man dropped. "I just couldn't allow you to tell anyone I was here."

Hanne stared at the mess of bodies.

This was all so unfortunate. She'd come to talk, and instead there'd been a massacre.

On the bright side—because Nadine would encourage Hanne to look on the bright side—Opus wouldn't be sending any armies into the Malice. No. The entire kingdom of Caberwill would be galvanized against Ivasland.

But first she needed to rearrange things.

Quickly, she moved the bodies and the weapons into positions that would indicate *all* the guards had been the assassin's victims, and that the king and the assassin had killed each other. With everyone in place, she yanked her own dagger from the Ivaslander's ruined throat. It was time to leave before the watch changed, or anyone happened by and saw the river of blood.

Miraculously, she made it to the east wing unseen. When she heard guards patrolling, she ducked behind a column and waited until they'd moved past. Then, she slipped into Nadine's quarters.

Lady Sabine was gone, and Nadine was sitting on the sofa, reading a sheaf of papers. She rose instantly. "Hanne, what happened? You're covered in blood!"

"I should be. I just killed two men." Hanne frowned at the floor, heart and mind racing now that she was out of danger. "And I had to take off my shoes so there wouldn't be tracks."

"What?" Nadine helped her replace the blood-covered dress with a plum-colored dressing gown, then pulled her to the sofa. "Tell me what happened. Are you all right?"

"Ivasland is trying to kill me." Hanne looked at her cousin and told her everything.

"The assassin killed the king," Nadine murmured.

"And I killed the assassin—but made it seem like the king did."

"All of Caberwill will be furious. There's no chance of the army going into the Malice now." Nadine took Hanne's hand, hardly seeming to notice the blood transferring to her own fingers. "But what about the other thing? Have you thought about that yet?"

"What other thing?"

"The king is dead. That means Rune is king. And you are queen."

31.
NIGHTRENDER

Nightrender had been carving out a firebreak all through the evening.

She had to ensure the razing of Small Mountain did not spread flames beyond the boundaries she set. Hauling away deadwood and other brush was heavy work; without Dawnbreakers, she had to do everything herself. But tonight, she preferred that. The work distracted her from the decision she didn't want to make: what to do with the information she'd acquired.

This was why she hadn't wanted to get involved with a prince. This situation exactly.

Well, not *exactly*, perhaps. She hadn't anticipated her prince getting married to a princess who'd been involved in the construction of a mal-device. But the *sort* of situation forced her to choose between remaining an impartial fourth party to the war—or becoming an involved fourth party.

Royalty made everything more complicated. But Prince Rune *was* her only friend, and he was married to the woman who'd caused this.

Is he your only friend because you are a monster now? murmured the voice. ***You can't even purify malice without blinding pain. Do you think the Numina have sensed the darkness in you? Do they know what you did four hundred years ago? Perhaps they are trying to burn you away, too.***

Nightrender gritted her teeth and continued working, but she couldn't argue with the voice's logic. It merely put words to her fears.

Was she a monster?

It was midnight by the time she went from building to building, dousing them in kindlewater. She poured it everywhere, but especially on the place where the mal-device had been, letting the liquid soak deep into the earth.

That was where she started the fire.

With only a flick of her fingers—and a shock of bone-deep pain—she sent a spark of numinous fire into the puddle of kindlewater.

Blue flames burst from the ground, and Nightrender took off into the sky, her wings fanning the fire as it burned along the row of rotten potato plants within minutes.

It was the only way to thoroughly rid the world of what had happened here.

Nightrender flew higher as heat rolled upward, and black smoke boiled the air. The inferno spread across the field and raced toward the town, a cleansing light that devoured everything in its path.

Satisfied the fire would reach every malice-touched part of the town, Nightrender landed and walked along the firebreak where she could monitor the blaze without inhaling smoke. (Not that inhaling smoke harmed her, but even immortal champions preferred clean air.)

Unfortunately, now that this sad task was complete, she had nothing to occupy her mind. The fire wouldn't burn forever, especially with the kindlewater making the flames hotter. It would soon run out of fuel, and then she would be forced to make a decision about whether to tell Prince Rune that Princess Johanne had assisted with the mal-device.

How much would that really count as her taking sides in the war? Did it make a difference that *malice* was being used? She fought malice. Surely this was her business.

But . . . did that mean that she needed to stand against any kingdom—or person—who used malice against others?

This was a line she had never anticipated needing to toe. How could she protect people like this?

You know what I think?

She ignored the voice, continuing along the firebreak. The flames had engulfed the town now, burning hot and bright against midnight, and clouds of ash obscured the moon and dimmed the stars. She tried to think about all the ways the sky had shifted in her time—the brilliant red glint of a dying star, the way old constellations slowly drifted into unrecognizable shapes—but the voice was persistent.

I think humans are the real monsters. Not you.

She clenched her jaw and continued along her path. Considering all the things humans had done to one another over thousands of years, it was hard to argue for the goodness of humanity. The invention of the mal-device was only the most recent example, and perhaps the next logical step, in their endless quest to destroy themselves.

Yes, it said. ***Look what they've done to themselves. Is that not monstrous?***

It was, wasn't it? But—

"I killed all the royal families in the Red Dawn. That was monstrous."

The voice chuckled darkly. ***You aren't an unreasonable person.***

"I'm not a person," she whispered. "I'm Nightrender."

You've spent lifetimes protecting them. Serving them. Going out of your way to ensure they live another generation. You have devoted everything to humans.

That was true.

Ask yourself what happened. Ask yourself why you would take such drastic action.

"I cannot possibly know that." She was already regretting the decision to respond to the voice. It was not her friend. Not her confidant. No, she needed to find out what it really was and remove it, same as a human might remove a gangrenous limb.

After she led her army of not-Dawnbreakers into the Malice.

They must have done something terrible, it pressed. Something to make you very angry.

Prince Rune and Grand Priest Larksong believed her actions had been divine justice.

She wanted to ask if the voice knew anything, or if its plan was just to annoy her to death, but she was very firmly *not* speaking to it now. Instead, she focused on the roar of the fire, punctuated by the shriek and crash of collapsing buildings. She had to decide quickly.

Tell Prince Rune.

Or don't, and let things unfold as they may.

He was her soul shard. She couldn't deny it anymore. He might not remember her name, and to protect his gentle heart she would never tell him what he was, but that didn't change the existence of their bond. Keeping this development from him would be a betrayal of her own soul.

So what mattered more?

The night began to die, and so did the fire.

Decide, she thought to herself. *Decide now*.

Sudden darkness blossomed in the back of her mind.

It was the same buzzing feeling from earlier—*yesterday* now—when the mal-device had gone off. So that must mean . . .

Nightrender gazed northwest, where the feeling had come from, and frowned.

Another mal-device had detonated.

32.
RUNE

A crash awakened him.

A bang.

And light flared beyond his eyelids.

"He's all right, Your Majesty. Just sleeping."

Rune groaned and tried to sit up, struggling to figure out what was happening. After Hanne had left last night, he'd stood on his balcony, watching the Malstop glow darkly against the night sky. He'd been thinking about what happened in Hanne's room, then the Nightrender and his guilt, then what happened in Hanne's room, then the inevitable collapse of the Malstop unless they sent an army or two through the Soul Gate . . . and then again what happened in Hanne's room.

Finally, he'd gone to bed, confused and agitated. He'd dreamed of violence and rancor, with malice flooding across the fields and towns of Caberwill. In his dreams, the Nightrender had fought until the darkness overwhelmed her, leaving him absolutely certain that she would die if she went into the Malice without him.

And now there were people standing over him, shouting, dragging him upright.

"Am I being kidnapped?" He blinked around furiously.

"Your Highness, there's news." John held one of Rune's shoulders, steadying him.

"John." Rune rubbed his eyes. "What are you—"

"Rune." Queen Grace's voice came from the parlor. "Get dressed. We must speak."

So he wasn't being kidnapped after all. Probably for the best.

"What time is it?" Rune dropped out of bed and closed the door, just enough so that he could get dressed without his mother watching.

"Not yet dawn." John was already pulling items out of the wardrobe. "This should do."

"Since when does my guard dress me?" Rune traded his nightshirt for a doublet.

"Since there's no time to wait for anyone else." John threw more clothes at him.

"Why? What's going on?"

John shook his head. "I shouldn't. Your mother will want to be the one to tell you."

A knot of anxiety tightened in Rune's chest as he finished dressing, then trudged into the parlor, where Queen Grace, Dayle Larksong, Charity Wintersoft, and Rupert Flight all waited—along with a half dozen armed guards.

For a moment, when Rune came in, everyone was quiet. There was only the splash of water from that garish fountain, which still dominated the place where he *should* be sitting down to eat breakfast in a few hours. All these people barely fit around the jewel-topped crown and pool of loud, burbling water.

"What's happened?" His voice was rough, but he managed to keep it steady. What had he done wrong this time? "Mother?"

She just motioned for him to approach, and when he did, he noticed the tear tracks glinting on her cheeks.

She was crying.

The last time he'd seen her cry, they'd been attending his brother's funeral.

"My son." Grace's voice was thick with emotion. "Last night, an Ivaslander assassin crept through the halls of Honor's Keep and murdered several men-at-arms—and your father."

Midnight flared across Rune's vision, and suddenly he couldn't breathe.

"Ivasland." The word came hollow, and suddenly the world was spinning out of control around him. "Ivasland killed Father."

First his brother, and now his father. They had no morals, no honor, no sense that *perhaps* it was unwise to go around killing monarchs. *Perhaps* it would rain down fire on their cities. *Perhaps* Abagail and Baldric did not understand proportional responses.

Roaring filled Rune's mind. Was he still standing up? He couldn't tell. He closed his eyes.

"Rune," his mother said. "Rune, can you hear me?"

"Your Highness?" That was John.

"Shall we call for the grand physician?" Charity asked. "I believe he is swooning."

"No!" Rupert's voice was sharp. "No physicians. He's just in shock."

Because what if someone should see Stella Asheater rushing through the halls to help him? Rune would look weaker than he already did.

Finally, Rune opened his eyes to find that he'd made it to the floor. John released his shoulders and stepped back as soon as Rune was capable of holding himself up again. "I'm—" Not all right. Never all right. His feelings about his father had always been so complicated, especially after his brother had died, but none of that mattered anymore. His father should be alive.

He would be alive.

If not for Ivasland.

Ivasland was a thief. His family. Peace. Baldric and Abagail had stolen so much.

"Rune," said Grace, but if there was a question or a statement in there, she never gave it voice.

They stared at each other for a moment, Rune and his mother, and he didn't know what to do. She was grieving, and if he'd been a better son, he would have consoled her. And if she'd been a better mother, she would have consoled him. But neither were what they should have been to the other, so they just waited, like one of them would give in.

Footfalls sounded in the hall. Hanne and Lady Nadine appeared in the doorway, with more guards behind them.

"I've just heard the news." Hanne pushed into the room. She looked beautiful already, dressed in a sapphire-studded gown, her hair pinned into a hasty bun, her lips painted a deep red as she pressed them into a frown. How did she look perfect *already*? It wasn't even sunrise. "This is terrible. First Small Mountain—"

In all this chaos, Rune had forgotten about Small Mountain.

"—and now this. We must retaliate."

"We will." Rune clenched his jaw. "We will retaliate."

"What of the assassin?" Hanne looked at Grace. "Is he in custody?"

"He's dead." Grace didn't look at Hanne. "Opus killed the Ivaslander assassin. It was his final act."

"Good. The king was a very brave man. An assassin deserves no mercy."

"I would have liked to question him," Rupert muttered. "What did he hope to accomplish?"

Hanne touched Rune's shoulder, her caress gentle as she traced down his arm and slipped her fingers with his.

"I don't know," Rune murmured. "Find out if you can, but it doesn't matter. Ivasland will suffer for what they've done to Caberwill."

Hanne nodded. "Embria will see to it."

"*I* will see to it." A quickening *thump-thump* crashed through Rune's head.

"You are the king now," Rupert said. "You have that right."

King.

Rune was king.

Because his father was dead.

That was why Rupert and Charity and Dayle were packed into his rooms. That was why guards were everywhere. That was why they'd come bursting into his quarters in the predawn, to make sure he was alive.

Because he was king now.

King Rune Highcrown.

It didn't feel real—not yet—but Rune knew what he had to do. From the moment he'd become heir, his father had been preparing him for his death. "We'll hold a funeral and coronation today."

"I will have everything arranged at once, sire," Dayle said.

"Thank you. The funeral should be fit for a king, but the coronation can be quick, for now. We'll have a larger ceremony after."

"After what, Your Majesty?" Rupert asked.

"After we win this war." Rune set his shoulders. "Send orders immediately. I will lead our troops to the Ivasland border and lay waste to everything I find. I swear to you, nothing will remain. Not a school. Not a temple. Not a throne. Nothing but vengeance."

33.
NIGHTRENDER

Just after dawn, Nightrender reached the second detonation site. She'd followed the tug of new dread and anguish halfway across Salvation, around the thinning Malstop, and here she found a small Embrian town, prestigious enough to have its own militia, which was currently engaged in moving people away from the entrance to a mine.

The mineshaft must be where the device was located.

As Nightrender flew over the town, her shadow stretching over the crowd assembled in the central square, people stared up at her, some crying out in fear or relief; several clutched tiny bottles around their necks, as though the glass-diluted obsidian could protect them from her. As though they *needed* protection from her.

They shouldn't worry, murmured the voice. ***You only slaughter naughty royals.***

She pushed the voice aside and flew over a path packed with miners on makeshift stretchers and militia soldiers erecting barriers to prevent people from coming any closer. Some of the evacuating miners tried to rest, slouching beneath the scattered conifers or leaning on mounds of barren rock, but soldiers always hurried them onward.

The entrance to the mine was clear, save a small squad of militiamen waiting for her. When she landed, they knelt and offered a salute. It was all so professional that she almost couldn't tell how afraid they were—of her, or the malice released within the mine.

"Nightrender." The oldest man stood. "We're glad you're here."

Are they?

"I'm Lieutenant Farr. Thank you for coming to Silver Sun. I wish it were under better circumstances. I assume you know that we've been attacked."

She nodded, eyeing the small silver pins on their jackets, which indicated their ranks and where they served; these were small circles with rays spreading outward. She supposed they could be suns.

"We've evacuated the mine to the best of our ability, but it's too dangerous to search for survivors while there's still malice down there."

"Tell me what happened." It wasn't much of a mystery: the entrance to the mine had grown sharp silver teeth, which dripped with rust-colored blood. The area stank of death and vomit.

"Last night, a man posing as a miner walked in." Farr didn't quite look at the opening, like he was picturing everything, thinking about just how this town got into such a terrible mess, but couldn't actually bear to look at the place where it happened.

It *was* difficult to look at.

"He didn't stay in long—not even an entire shift—which was suspicious to the guard. Not to mention no one knew him. Then some real miners came out and said there was some kind of machine down there, but by then it was too late. The tunnel system started to . . ." He turned back to Nightrender, apparently deciding that she was easier to look at than the mine entrance. "You'll see, I suppose."

She would see. She was always the one to see the things deemed too terrible for humans to look upon, the things they could not bear.

"Bring as much kindlewater as you have," she said. "And firewood, if anyone can spare it."

Farr's eyebrows rose, and the other soldiers looked at one another uneasily.

"Unless the miners want to work around what's left of those trapped inside."

"Can't we—" One of the younger soldiers tried to look at her and flinched. "Can't we bury them?"

She cocked her head. "If anything remains after the burning, you are welcome to take it. But I do not think you'll want to go in there, even after I've cleared out the malice."

He backed away, looking nauseated.

"As for the miners who escaped but were in the mine when the device detonated, make sure they're quarantined. I will ensure they carry no malice inside them." No corruption could be permitted to linger.

She turned and strode into the mine, not waiting for the soldiers to agree to her demands. They would comply. They were too afraid not to.

When she was only a few paces into the mine, the mouth slammed shut behind her with a loud crash and rumble of stone, plunging the cave into darkness. When the tunnel went quiet again, she could just hear the soldiers outside calling for her, asking if she was all right. She didn't feel like yelling, so she ignored them.

There was no light in this part of the cave, now that the entrance was blocked; even her eyes couldn't detect the faintest trace.

But she was Nightrender. She was never without light.

Pale fire glowed around her hands, granting just enough illumination for her to see through the pitch black. It hurt, of course, but it was a dull headache, a bruise, and she could manage for the time being.

There, along the walls, she noted more jagged teeth of silver—ingrown and illogical—all wet with blood. The tunnel ahead constricted and eased, constricted and eased, in long, rippling motions—as though it were swallowing.

There was no way to get to the device except down this passage.

Malice sank deeper into the rock, curling around veins of precious metal and seeping into the underground aquifer. It was insidious, and she would have called it *clever* if it had a consciousness, but as it was she had to settle for *adaptable*.

If she didn't hurry, the malice would infect the entire town.

She went about cleansing this developing malsite the same way she had the other: plunging her sword into the wall or floor, burning away veins of malice, and spreading holy fire in between fine grains of earth and shifting plates. The pain struck, as she knew it would, and it slowed her work, but she didn't let it stop her. The magic-infused obsidian of Beloved drove into the rock without so much as chipping. What use was a Nightrender thwarted by mere stone?

As the ripples through the throat of the mine tightened, she sheathed her sword and braced herself, holding the tunnel open through strength alone. When the swallowing movement passed, she found her hands covered in sticky red bits of pulverized human.

So many workers had been crushed just within sight of escape. They were plastered against the walls, dripping down the curves and chisel marks, mashed beyond recognition.

Did Princess Johanne know that a mal-device had been delivered to her home kingdom?

Would she care?

Probably not. The voice seemed to echo as the tunnel opened into a larger chamber, crisscrossed by wooden walkways and ramps, abandoned carts parked throughout. ***Why would she care? Perhaps she likes malice. You should kill her.***

Nightrender paused at the top of the first ramp, one hand bracing her on a rocky section of the wall, and breathed around the voice's dark temptation.

The mal-device wasn't far—perhaps halfway down the cavern—and all she had to do was burn away malice and take the device somewhere people would never find it. Perhaps the bottom of the ocean, although she didn't trust what was down there to behave any better than the humans.

What *was* down there? The memory flashed out before she could grasp it.

Frustration clawed at her, but she had to let it go. There was work to do.

Below, the cavern was relatively still, but a long grinding noise came from deep within the darkness; it *was* moving with malice, but not like the tunnel had been. Perhaps she'd reached the stomach.

"Hello?" A man's cry came from far below, across the great chasm. "Is someone up there?"

Nightrender's heart leaped. A person. "I'm here." She forced her voice to be calm and level. "I've come to help you. Tell me if you can walk."

A faint sob echoed through the cavern. "Thank Malvir and Luho." The Numina of Hope and of Mines. "Thank you. Thank you."

Carefully, Nightrender started down the ramp, following the black stains of malice closer to the device.

"Who—Who are you?" asked the man below.

Telling him the truth was a bad idea, given how scared people were now. And the precarious state he was in. "Someone who wants to help."

"Good." His voice was softer again. "Good. I don't think I can walk. My legs are hurt. Something's on them."

"I'll get you."

The man coughed, loud and wet. "Hurry. It's not safe down here. There's something moving."

"It's only the walls." That probably wasn't as comforting as she'd meant it to be. "You'll be fine. Tell me about yourself."

It would keep him distracted from the horror around him.

"Well, I'm a miner. I have a family—a wife and a daughter."

"Tell me their names. And yours."

"I'm Michael. And they're Beth and Little Beth. My wife is a weaver. . . ."

He kept talking, and Nightrender kept working.

Down she went, cutting apart lines of malice where she found them, making bright, frosty light scatter through the space. It wasn't long before a new movement sounded below. Not the man. Something else. Something bigger.

"Something's happening!" Panic cut through the man's voice "Help me!"

Light erupted from Nightrender's hands, illuminating the entire cavern, and she peered far below to where Michael lay on a ramp, pinned down by a broken beam across his legs. Dirt and debris coated his skin, and underneath all that, he was very, very pale. Blood loss, perhaps. And fear. But he was alone down there—no sign of anything lurching toward him.

"What's that light?" The words grunted out of him as he turned his head and raised an arm to shield his eyes.

She let the light ease, plunging the depths of the mine back into darkness. "There's nothing. You're fine." If the mine hadn't eaten him yet, it likely wouldn't start now.

"I'm fine." He sounded distant now, less afraid.

Strange that he'd composed himself so quickly, but it was better than listening to him scream at shadows until she finished her work above.

Piece by piece, she drove her sword into pockets of malice and moved deeper into the chamber until finally she reached the mal-device.

Such a small thing, causing all of this.

"What are you doing?" Michael sounded closer now, somehow, even though she hadn't reached him. But perhaps it was just his voice echoing off the shifting walls. "Are you coming to help me?"

"I will." Right after she destroyed the source of malice in here. She gazed down at the mal-device; it was identical to the first in every way, including the prickling energy of Princess Johanne.

"When?" Irritation sharpened the miner's tone.

"A moment." She positioned her sword just above the machine, gathering her strength to drive back the darkness.

"Talk to me." Now his voice came from a different direction—slightly off to the left. Not even the shifting walls of the cavern could account for that. "I want to know where you are." Again, he'd moved.

She knew the truth.

She turned the sword and swung just as Michael's face appeared in the darkness. Filthy. Furious. Dead.

With holy fire crackling down the blade, Beloved sliced open his chest and tarry blood spilled out, drenching the mal-device.

With an ear-splitting shriek, it—because the dead miner was a revenant now, no longer a man—rushed at her, grabbed for her. Ragged fingernails scraped at her armor, but revenants were weak and she was ready. Her blade arced around and sliced into its legs.

Mind-shattering pain blinded her for a moment, making her stagger backward and grip Beloved even tighter, but there was no time to reorient herself. The revenant had dropped to the ramp, but not because she'd hurt it—only because its broken and bleeding legs would no longer hold it up. It reached for her, grasping with a horrible strength, but she was faster. She thrust her blade into its neck, burning it from the inside out with numinous fire.

Nightrender gasped, biting her tongue to keep from crying out, but it hurt *so much*. Her vision flared red, then grayed. A buzzing filled her ears.

Have you considered giving up? Even the voice seemed farther away. ***You don't have to do any of this anymore.***

She wouldn't quit. She wouldn't. Not even if her power was trying to sear away her own darkness. "Perhaps I deserve this," she whispered, drawing her blade from the charred revenant.

The creature fell backward off the ramp and into the cavern below.

When it hit the bottom, stillness spread throughout the mine. She stared down, sadness swelling in her chest. He'd died while talking to her about his family, and she hadn't noticed. She'd been too busy fighting off her own pain as she'd cleansed the malice.

And now she had to finish.

But a low groan sounded, and then another. Dread filled her as she lit the space.

Revenants—a dozen of them—shuffled and limped up the ramps, lugging rocks and pickaxes and planks of rotting wood.

A faint, exhausted whimper found its way out of Nightrender's throat. Every part of her body ached, and the support beams and rock walls wavered in her vision slightly. She was in no shape to fight these revenants, but what choice did she have?

The dead creatures closed in on her.

Arms shaking with strain, she lifted her sword and summoned her power.

34.
HANNE

Death brought everyone together.

"How do you think Rune arranged the funeral so quickly?" Nadine mused as she and Hanne made their way across the outer ward. Captain Oliver and the other Embrian guards followed in their wake, far enough back that they couldn't overhear.

"He didn't. This is Dayle Larksong's work. As the grand priest, he plans a funeral for every monarch. You never know when you'll need one." Hanne tried not to fuss with the bodice of her dress; even though her seamstress had taken it in this morning, it still didn't fit right. "You have to admire Rune's flexibility, though. Yesterday, a wedding. Today, a funeral. He's really very good at attending events."

Nadine flashed a secret smile. "I believe that is the first compliment you've ever paid him."

"That isn't true. I've also said he's very obedient."

"Hanne."

"Believe what you will." Hanne tapped her chin as they caught sight of mourners. "Cousin, I believe we overdressed. Funerals here are much less extravagant than at home." In Embria, royal funerals involved parades, day-long speeches, and elaborate balls celebrating the life of the deceased monarch. Some funerals even included competitions, if the late ruler had been particularly fond of a certain sport. But in Caberwill, they simply marched the casket through the town in a most somber procession, then held a public service in the Grand Temple. Burial in the castle crypt was private.

They turned a corner, and the immense gates of the castle wall loomed before them. Golden sunlight spilled over the parapets, making Hanne blink. She could just see Dowager Queen Grace, Princesses Sanctuary and Unity, and Rune; they stood together, waiting for the casket to be brought out so they could ride ahead. Hanne was expected to join her husband.

"I hate funerals," she murmured.

Nadine shot her a look, silently reminding her that if Hanne had her way, there would be several funerals, and she would be expected to attend them all.

"Oh, I know." She strode toward the waiting royalty. "But perhaps now that I am queen, I will write a royal proclamation banning funerals."

"What will we do with the bodies after the war?" Nadine asked, playing along.

"By the time I sign that proclamation, the wars will be over. I will have conquered everything. We will have peace."

"Of course," Nadine said. "And no one will ever die of illness or old age."

"We'll see. Even queens have only so much power."

A dark memory suddenly welled up in the back of her mind—hot slices over her face, dark pressure on her chest, and eerie green light pouring through her whole body—but Hanne pushed it back. Buried it. Smothered it. If she could have destroyed that memory and held a funeral for it, she would have. She would have made the exception.

Worriedly, Nadine touched Hanne's arm, but by then they'd reached the Highcrowns.

Hanne greeted the Caberwilline royalty and, doing her best to appear sad but strong, took her place beside Rune. Members of the Crown Council, various nobles from both the Caberwill and Embria sides, and other important figures would all meet her today, some for the very first time. She needed to give them a lasting impression of compassion, confidence, and competence. Nadine had planted those seeds while Hanne had been "dead," and now it was time to . . . water them. Or dump compost over them.

Hanne wasn't a farmer. She didn't know *exactly* the next step in the metaphor, but she did know she had to win these people over. She needed all of Caberwill ready to unite behind her.

Nadine stood with the other ladies-in-waiting behind Hanne, and all of Hanne's Embrian guards were behind them. Quickly, Nadine reached forward and gave Hanne's arm a gentle squeeze. It would come across as sweet and supportive, and, most important, like Hanne had friends who believed in her.

And, while they weren't friends—barely acquaintances—Hanne scanned the Caberwilline faces until she spotted Prudence Shadowhand and Victoria Stareyes; the two stood a short distance apart, the former with her husband—a well-dressed (for a Caberwilline) earl—and the latter with a group of other young noblewomen, many who had the appearance of eager outsiders. When Hanne and Victoria exchanged brief nods, the nobles surrounding her flashed curious, impressed looks.

Satisfied she'd raised at least one of her new allies in the esteem of her peers, Hanne turned toward the grand priest, who was beginning a prayer to Elmali, the patron Numen of Caberwill. "Glory to the Stalwart, the Steadfast, the mountain on which we stand . . ."

Sunshine warmed Hanne's skin and voices hummed around her, some in prayer, some in remembrance of the dead king. It was a pleasant day, and aside from needing to attend the funeral for a man Hanne hated, everything was finally going to plan. Life—post-malsite, post-rancor, and post-Ivasland—was looking up.

Then, everyone else was looking up as well.

Their gazes were fixed westward as gasps fluttered along the procession of nobles, officials, and merchants. They'd all stopped moving, no longer interested in greeting the Highcrowns or extending their condolences.

Dread coiled in Hanne's gut as she, Rune, and the others turned and followed all the eyes.

"What's wrong with it?" Princess Sanctuary asked.

"I think it's broken," Princess Unity answered.

And finally, Dayle Larksong: "Dear Known and Unknown alike. We should have listened. She warned us, and we didn't listen."

They were talking about the Malstop.

Normally, it was a distant wall of shimmering white-blue, a vast and unknowable darkness behind the sheen of ancient magic. Though translucent, no one could mistake the barrier for anything other than *solid*. . . .

Until now.

The Malstop was stretched impossibly thin, like a bubble about to burst. Gossamer veins of silver scuttled across the sheerest areas, where deep, bloody red showed through. It was as though the magic were trying to compensate, but it wouldn't be enough. Even leagues away from the Malstop, the sharp odor of ozone reached Hanne.

Darkness drenched her mind, ruddy skies and glasslike shards filled with monsters. It was all she could do not to bend over and vomit right there, as terror reached through her chest and gripped her heart with blazing fingers.

"Hanne?" Nadine had stepped forward, and now her hand rested on Hanne's shoulder.

Hanne was trembling, her mind overcome with memories of the malsite and the Dark Shard. The hollowed-out hunger, the starless black sky, the agony of constant terror: these things would haunt her forever. And they were about to be unleashed on Salvation.

"I will conquer fear," Hanne whispered to herself. "I will conquer everything."

Nadine squeezed her shoulder. "I know. I believe in you."

As everyone continued staring at the failing Malstop, Hanne closed her eyes and prayed to Tuluna. *Tell me this is part of your plan. Tell me I will create peace for all three kingdoms.*

You will make a peace the world has never before seen, Tuluna answered. ***Finish the wars and make peace. An Incursion cannot hurt you.***

A deep sense of comfort enveloped Hanne. An Incursion could not hurt her. Tuluna would protect her. All she had to do was follow their instructions.

Hanne stepped forward, gazing down the lines of nobles and merchants and everyone else who'd come to see their king laid to rest.

"Do not be afraid." She made her voice strong, powerful. "Be concerned, be vigilant, but do not be afraid, because fear is what the Malice wants. That the Malstop is weakening *is* worrying, but it can be fixed. It has been fixed in the past, and so it will be once more."

Tell them you will do it.

Hanne drew in a sharp breath. *I will fix the Malstop?* She whispered in her mind. *How?*

Trust me.

She did. She trusted Tuluna more than anything in the whole world. So she said, "I vow, here, before all of you, that *I* will find a way to fix the Malstop. On the Embria-Caberwill alliance, on my marriage to Rune Highcrown, and on the memory of dear King Opus the Third: I will ensure safety for all Salvation."

There was no applause, but a few people at a time, the mourners began to nod, some holding their fists to their chests, others gazing at her with a terrible hope in their eyes. They already wanted so much from her, and she would give and give to them—more than they deserved—because she was Tuluna's chosen, and it was her destiny to deliver peace.

35.
NIGHTRENDER

Nightrender gasped awake.

Slowly, the ringing in her ears faded. Shadow spots narrowed into pinpricks until at last she could see again. Her breath came in faint rattles, sharp with the taste of bile and blood, but the dark pressure of malice was gone. She'd done it. She'd cleansed the mine.

And then . . . And then she'd passed out from the pain.

With aching stiffness, she sat up and looked around. The bodies on the ramp and floor were unmoving. Dead. *Truly* dead.

The world had never forgotten to remind her how atrocious malice and the rancor were, but sometimes the obscenity of it all became so acute that even she could hardly stand to look. But she did look. She could not look away. The truth of the Dark Shard's attacks on the laic plane were so wretched that someone needed to bear witness, and no one else alive was built to do it.

Only her. Always her.

She trudged back to the surface, pausing only to wipe away some of the tarry blood that stuck to her skin. There was nothing to do for the stuff that had soaked into her armor; the numinous fabric would expel it over time, as the cuts and tears mended themselves.

The walls of the tunnel had stopped moving. They weren't quite wide enough for carts anymore, but there was plenty of space for her to walk without having to squeeze. When she came in sight of the exit, sunlight poured in. The opening was strange, still twisted like a screaming mouth, but the teeth were gone, at least.

Lieutenant Farr and the rest of his men waited outside, barrels and jugs of kindlewater sitting along the path, as well as carts of firewood—everything she'd requested.

"Nightrender." Farr saluted, turning a faint shade of green as he noted the gore splattered across her entire body. "What—"

"You don't want to know." It was the sort of thing humans said when they secretly couldn't wait to tell everyone, but she meant it. He didn't want to know. He'd never again sleep peacefully if he did.

He clenched his jaw and glanced at his men, and then nodded. "All right. Were there any survivors?"

"No." Not in any sense of the word. "I am sorry."

Farr gazed at her a moment. "We all have family who worked down there."

She thought of Michael, of Beth and Little Beth, and how they would never see him again. She imagined their faces when they heard the news, how their expressions would probably look like these men's: crumpled, devastated, utterly lost. That humans could feel so fiercely for one another was comforting, but it made their willingness to kill all the more baffling.

"Set a guard by the entrance. Do not let anyone into the mine until I've finished."

"Is it still ea—"

"No." She hated interrupting, but she didn't want him to say aloud that the mine had been *eating* people. "Just don't go down there. I will take care of it."

The lieutenant's mask slipped, and it was clear he understood that something unspeakable awaited the curious. "Very well."

Then, alone, she carried barrels of kindlewater and piles of firewood into the mine, staging everything so that it would burn hot and purifying. The soldiers kept offering to help, their training too strong to resist, but she refused; seeing what had happened to their countrymen would only enrage them further against Ivasland.

When all the wood was placed and the whole cavern was drenched in kindlewater, she set the fire and emerged from the mine just as smoke started to trickle from the mouth.

The soldiers were waiting for her. "We've quarantined all those who escaped, as well as everyone they've come into contact with, as you requested."

"Then I will inspect them for traces of malice. To be certain." Even with her memories vanishing, she knew the power of fear and suspicion. She needed to pronounce everyone clean to prevent the survivors from being shunned for the rest of their lives. "As for the device, a similar machine went off in Caberwill. It was accompanied by a score of soldiers."

The men glanced at one another. "The only soldier here was the one who planted it," said Farr. "We captured him during the evacuation."

"Tell me where he is."

"I'll take you to him. The gallows is nearly set up."

"Gallows."

"Yes, we plan to execute him."

Humans killing humans. What a shock.

She pushed the voice away. "He should be arrested and taken to Solcast for questioning and judgment."

Farr shook his head. "Magistrate Stephens claims he has authority over this matter, and he's calling for execution. So are the townspeople. You saw what happened in there. People want justice."

Justice. Nothing here was *justice*.

Aren't you tired of it?

Farr ordered his men to take up guard positions outside the mine, then motioned her along. "I'll take you to the quarantine."

She fell into step with Farr, wondering if she should take a moment to clean the worst of the carnage off herself. Most people didn't respond well to anyone covered in the blood of friends and enemies alike. And considering the stories that had been told about Nightrender these last four hundred years . . .

"Thank you for coming to our aid," said Farr. "I don't know what would have happened if you hadn't arrived when you did."

"The entire town of Silver Sun would have been swallowed whole, trapped inside the depths of the mine, without sunlight, without breathable air, and without hope of escape. There would have been no survivors." She looked at him askance. "The town of Small Mountain in Caberwill is gone because of an identical device. I could not reach it in time."

He paled and didn't say anything the rest of the walk into town.

People crowded the square, everyone yelling and pushing around the gallows where the Ivaslander stood, a noose already around his neck. The black-masked executioner stood at the lever.

As Nightrender approached the platform, quiet rippled outward and people retreated, making a path for her and the lieutenant. Well, for her. The lieutenant followed in her wake.

"I can take you to the quarantine—"

"I want to see this." She walked to the front of the crowd, pretending like she didn't notice the space people made around her, as though they were terrified to get too close. Or perhaps it was just the smell.

An official climbed the stairs to the platform, keeping the executioner between him and the Ivaslander. Magistrate Stephens, if the clothes were anything to go by: he wore a fine linen shirt dyed deep green, and half a dozen silver pins glittered on the collar. He was completely at odds with the prisoner, a small man who wore the drab clothes of an Embrian miner and a hard, determined expression.

"This man stands accused of delivering a machine that unleashed malice!" Magistrate Stephens glared over the gathering of miners and townspeople. "Thankfully, I have been informed that the malice is gone, cleansed by the Nightrender, who came to our aid."

People in the crowd looked at her from the corners of their eyes. They looked at her sword. At the blood staining her armor.

"But today was not without loss. Many were not able to escape the mine in time, and their deaths are unendurable." He narrowed his eyes at Nightrender, like she should have been able to save those killed before her arrival. She wished it had been possible. "Thank Nalradis and Dinlis"—the Numina of Justice and Vengeance—"we were able to apprehend the man responsible for this crime against Silver Sun. The required seven witnesses have already given their accounts. This man is guilty, and he will be punished."

A rush of eagerness spread throughout the square, responding to blood with more blood.

Magistrate Stephens turned to the Ivaslander. "State your name for our records, followed by your last words."

The prisoner lifted his eyes. "And if I refuse?"

"You will die either way."

The man started to nod, but stopped when the noose cinched around his throat. "My name doesn't matter. You've already made your decision about me. But I want to tell you a story before I die."

The square went eerily quiet.

"The device I planted in your mine is the result of years of labor. Three young scientists worked day and night to design and build a machine capable of sending malice from our kingdom into yours."

Three young scientists.

Abruptly, Nightrender recalled the trio in the ever-burning forest near Boone, accompanied by a handful of guards. When she'd demanded to know what they were doing, they'd said *science*. What if they'd been the same people? What if she'd witnessed them working on the device, and she could have stopped it?

How do you live with yourself? The voice gave a deep chuckle.

"Why would you tell us this?" Magistrate Stephens asked.

"Because this isn't a story about the scientists," the prisoner said. "This is a story about the Embrian who came to help."

From the humans, gasps rose all around. Shock. Disbelief. Anger. A few people started to mutter, but they were quickly shushed because the prisoner was about to speak again.

"I didn't see her myself, but they say she was beautiful, with long golden hair and a silver tongue. She made the queen and the scientists trust her—until she incited a riot to escape. But she left the scientists with the answers to their problems, and the mal-device was finished not just on time but *ahead* of schedule." A wicked smile curled the edges of the prisoner's mouth, in spite of his impending execution. "Some say she looked a lot like your princess Johanne—the same princess who just married our mutual enemy in Caberwill."

Angry shouts rose up around the square.

"He's a liar!" someone screamed.

"Shove him into the depths of the mine!" yelled another.

"No Embrian would ever believe such blatant fabrications!" Magistrate Stephens lifted a hand, waiting for the din to die down. "Our fair princess would not assist Ivasland. Haven't you heard? We are allied against you."

"Are you?" asked the prisoner. "Your deceitful nature always reveals itself. I would pity Caberwill—if they were worth pity."

"Liar!" Someone in the crowd threw a rock, but Lieutenant Farr—vanishing from Nightrender's side—quickly put a stop to more hostility before it escalated into something unmanageable. *Lots* of people were clutching stones, she noticed. They'd come here eager for violence, with Dinlis's name on their lips.

Nightrender walked toward the stairs, and everyone pushed backward to make space. Some tossed insults, but no one threw a rock at *her*. By the time she reached the platform and looked out over the crowd, the square was silent, save the breath of wind and the faraway crackling of the thinning Malstop. It looked terrible—almost exhausted. The hour was later than she'd realized.

And this execution—violence itself—did not help. The malice fed on depravity in the laic plane, after all.

She had to say something to calm them down. She had to make them see reason.

Nightrender steadied her voice. "This man is telling the truth. I have seen two of these devices now and they"—no one would believe her—"feel like Princess Johanne. She was involved."

A low rumbling resumed in the crowd, and the prisoner's eyes settled on her as he tilted his head, heedless of the rope around it.

She held his gaze for a heartbeat, then turned back to the magistrate and restless crowd.

"I encourage you to send this man to Solcast to meet with your king and queen. He should tell them what he knows and be given a chance to argue for his life. Seek clarity before you respond to death with more death. There has been enough today."

"We *should* go to Solcast," a woman shouted. "And find out why Princess Johanne is helping our enemies!"

"It doesn't matter *why*," a man called. "If she's helping them, that's enough for me."

"We've been betrayed!" cried a third person. "The Nightrender says so!"

"I'm going to tell my cousin in Center View!"

"Tell everyone! They deserve to know!"

"How many towns will the Fortuin family destroy?"

"Kill the Ivaslander!"

The townspeople roared with confusion and anger, and then the rocks *did* fly. Stones pelted the Ivaslander, hitting his face and his body.

"Stop!" Nightrender shouted, but no one listened. Furious people pressed against the platform, pulling at the man's clothes, crowding into the magistrate, and grasping for the lever the executioner stood over. "Stop this!"

It was too late. A handful of people heaved the lever—dropping the trapdoor beneath the Ivaslander. He fell a short distance, then he kicked until he finished dying.

She could not save the man from this fate, nor prevent the others from killing him. Even interfering, even speaking up, had changed nothing. She was so *tired* of all this violence.

They think they're so much better than the rancor, whispered the voice. ***They are just the same.***

"Shut *up*." She clutched her head.

But as the mob intensified, and people screamed for Fortuin blood, Nightrender was not so sure the voice was wrong. She'd spent millennia protecting people from rancor, but they couldn't be bothered to meet her halfway and protect one another from their baser impulses. Instead, they found new and inventive ways to destroy one another. They thrived on it.

Malice thrived on it, too.

Humans were destroying themselves. And Salvation.

Now that the Ivaslander was dead, his body swinging on the rope as people continued to throw rocks at him, the mood was shifting. More and more cried out for Fortuin blood, and those with means announced they would ride to Solcast tonight. They didn't want answers; they wanted revolution.

Nightrender stood there, staring out at the mob of angry townspeople, disappointment growing thicker every second. The magistrate had left the platform, having declared he would demand the royal family answer for this, and even Lieutenant Farr was nowhere to be seen. The mob was moving, everyone piling supplies into carts and gathering up every sharp object they could find, and soon they began to leave Silver Sun.

Then it was just Nightrender, the body, and the few who weren't able to march on Solcast.

Regret settled in her stomach. She shouldn't have spoken. She shouldn't have confirmed that Princess Johanne had been involved. She'd broken her own code.

The town square was quiet now, littered with papers and footprints and stones, so there was no one to complain as Nightrender cut the prisoner down from the noose and lay out his body. There was no one to see as she set him and the gallows on fire; it was possible that he'd been contaminated by malice during his exposure.

By the time the fire went out, night had fallen and there was nothing left but ash.

"Nightrender?" It was the young soldier from this morning—the one who'd asked if they'd be able to bury the bodies from the mine. He was still here?

"The fire in the mine has burned out," she said.

"Yes," he replied, even though she hadn't technically asked a question.

"Tell me where Farr is."

"He's gone with the others to Solcast."

That was disappointing. She'd hoped he would be a voice of reason.

"Are you all right?" the soldier asked.

"I . . ." She wasn't sure what she'd been about to say, but it didn't matter. On the eastern horizon, the sky changed.

For as long as anyone could remember, the view from Silver Sun had looked the same, comforting in its way. But now, for the first time in four hundred years, the Malstop flickered out and in.

Out and in.

The Malstop was failing.

EXCERPT FROM NADINE HOLT'S DIARY, DECIPHERED FROM EMBRIAN MICRO-CODE

The coronation was beautiful.

It was a small ceremony, but we have been assured another—far more grand—celebration is in the future, just on the other side of this war. For now, it was an intimate, elegant ceremony, consisting of the Crown Council, the queen mother, and Princesses Sanctuary and Unity—as well as a select few from the Embrian side, thanks to the alliance.

I do think it was the first time in centuries that a (future) monarch of one kingdom has attended the coronation of another. How very historical. How fitting that it was Hanne who would bridge this chasm.

While Rune did look particularly handsome today—dressed in his best black brocade, his hair neatly combed, and obsidian flashing in the light every time he moved—Hanne, of course, outshone him. She outshone everyone. She wore brilliant sapphire, with sky and aqua accents, and a golden trim that one could not help but link back to that perfect wedding gown she wore only yesterday. And, of course, she wore the black crown. (Speaking of the crown, I could not help but notice the way the Nightrender reacted when she saw it, as Hanne walked into the temple. I don't know what, exactly, the reaction was, but the fact that she had a reaction at all is probably significant.)

At any rate, Rune knelt before the grand priest. The priest said a few words—something about honor, duty, and strength—which Rune repeated, and then the priest placed King Opus's crown onto Rune's head. Then everyone clapped, and Rune was officially king.

I did note that Duchess Wintersoft did not look as pleased about the continuity of the monarchy as others did. Indeed, I think she even leaned toward Princess Sanctuary and whispered something in the shape of, "This should be you." The princess, to her credit, frowned at that. Charity should have been subtler. Nevertheless, she's clearly identified herself as an adversary not only to Rune—but to Hanne as well. Sabine and I will have to keep an eye on her.

It is a shame that King Opus was killed so quickly after the wedding—before we were ready—and we will have to work hard to ensure Hanne's name is unsullied by assumptions. Indeed, she even attempted to delay being named queen consort—for the sake of appearances—but Rune insisted. The kingdom needed them united in title, as well as everything else.

And so, our conquest of Salvation is well underway.

36.
HANNE

"There you are," Rune said, coming out to stand beside her.

Hanne had been staring at the Malstop for almost an hour now. The putrid stench of malice filled the air, but the barrier in the center of Salvation hadn't blinked out again—not since earlier, when she'd been changing clothes and caught the flicker from the corner of her eye.

Forget the Malstop, Tuluna murmured. ***You have peace to forge.***

Hanne wanted to forget it—wanted to follow her Numen's instructions—but even now, with the Malstop shimmering whole in the distance, she couldn't fight the shudder that worked through her. The reek of malice. The horror of the Dark Shard.

Haven't I promised that no harm will come to you? An Incursion cannot hurt you.

"I know it's difficult to look away." Rune rested his hands on the balustrade before them.

"Not so hard when my new husband is right here." Hanne flashed a smile at him, but Rune's gaze was now focused on the Malstop, as though his attention alone held it together. "Let's go inside. Tomorrow will be your first full day as king, and you'll be leading armies off to war. You should be rested."

Rune frowned. "I should take the armies into the Malice with the Nightrender."

"Has she even returned?" Hanne glanced over her shoulder, as if the Nightrender might be standing behind them right now. But they were alone.

"Not yet." Rune's eyes were hard. "Do those towers look different to you?"

Hanne followed the direction of his glare. There, around the Malstop, were long-abandoned guard towers. They were bent a little more than they had been earlier. Almost as though they'd tried to run away from the nightmare they'd watched over for thousands of years.

"I think they're the same." Hanne rubbed her thumb over the scratch she'd taken from the onyx cat, shortly before she'd become trapped in the malsite. It was a scar now, a soft ridge. "Of course," she went on, "I've only been here a few days. I don't know what the towers usually look like. Do *you* think they look different?"

"Perhaps." Rune's scowl deepened.

Hanne touched his arm. "Let's go inside," she suggested again. "Now that you are king, there is some urgency in ensuring an heir is on the way."

That made his expression lighten. "Hanne." He turned to face her. "I wanted to thank you."

"For what?"

"For helping me today." Gently, he touched her forearm, then let his hand fall back to his side. "We did well together, I think."

"We did." Hanne smiled to herself. It had been a long day, beginning with the *total and complete shock* of finding out that King Opus had been murdered in the night. Followed by the funeral, followed by the brief coronation.

It had been a quick ceremony, given all the matters that now required a king's attention. Council meetings. Troop movements. War.

Hanne was looking forward to the grander coronation, the second one, which would occur after Rune returned from putting Ivasland in its place. Then there would be feasts and dances, parties that lasted all night.

She had stayed with Rune throughout the day, a helpful and dutiful wife. She was careful not to overstep, because overstepping would alarm the councilors and others she needed on her side. But she was hardly a meek or silent presence. She offered thoughtful encouragement and advice every half hour or so—just often enough that people thought her wise and considerate.

"I worry about you leading the armies into battle," Hanne said. "In Embria, kings never join the army. What if an arrow should strike you? We don't yet have a child."

Rune just gazed at her. "In Caberwill, a king who refuses to accompany his army is not king for long. But I assure you I will be well protected. John will be with me every moment, as well as the rest of my new guards. I'll be as safe as anyone can be, I promise."

"I just worry," Hanne said softly, in the way she'd learned he liked. "I couldn't bear to lose you."

He gave her one of those looks, the kind that said he was never sure if she meant it when she said things like that. And, well, she didn't, but she did need him. For now.

They went inside just in time to hear a knock on the main door.

"I'll return in a moment." Rune stepped out, leaving Hanne to finger comb her hair and check her reflection in the mirror. Her reminders of needing an heir had been serious. The death of King Opus had come sooner than she'd planned, and while she wasn't sad to lose him, she needed to fully establish her power here in Caberwill.

Without a Highcrown child, she would have no legitimacy here if Rune perished. It was that simple.

Everything would fall into place, as long as she followed Tuluna's instructions.

"Are you sure?" Rune's voice came from the other side of the door.

Someone responded—a man—but his voice was too low to carry.

Worry set in Hanne's stomach. If anyone had even a hint that Hanne had witnessed Opus's death . . .

The door opened and shut, and Rune came back inside. His face was haunted, and he barely looked at her as he said, "We have information regarding the mal-device."

She sat on the edge of the fountain. "Small Mountain?"

"It's gone," Rune said. "Completely gone. Reports say it was burned to the ground. No sign of the Nightrender."

"And the people?" Hanne asked, infusing as much compassion into her voice as possible, because Rune worried about his people. Caberwillines were soft like this, worrying about the common folk like they were beloved pets. They didn't understand what Embrians did: peasants needed to be ruled, and ruled strongly.

Hanne would cure him of this—eventually.

"There's no one left." Rune sat beside her, placing his hand on top of hers in a manner meant to be comforting. He faced her. "Silver Sun, thank all the Known and Unknown Numina, is still standing, but it, too, sustained heavy losses. Dozens of miners were killed before the evacuation began."

Silver Sun. But that was—

"That's in Embria. It's nowhere near Small Mountain." Alarm rose in her voice, no matter how she tried to tamp it down.

He nodded. "I'm sorry, Hanne. There was a second mal-device. There may be more we don't yet know about."

Deep, hot anger boiled inside her.

Queen Abagail had done this. She'd sent that assassin after Hanne, nearly ruining everything, *and* she'd destroyed one of Embria's most useful towns. This was the sort of slight that could not be overlooked.

"Ivasland has so much to answer for," she murmured. Then, a burst of inspiration pushed her to her feet. "Bring her to me, Rune. Bring Abagail to Caberwill so that I may be the one to rid our world of her treachery."

"Rid the—"

"She had your father and brother murdered. She's sent her malice machines to our kingdoms. She deserves to die."

Rune's words came slowly. "And you'd do it yourself?" He looked up at her, a strange distance in his eyes. Hmm. This Rune was not the guileless creature she'd married. "Do you think you could?"

Burn it. This wasn't going how she'd planned. No, he should have been tripping over himself to do anything she asked. Something was definitely wrong here. She didn't have the upper hand in this conversation, and now she hardly knew how to proceed.

"Conscious of what torment she has caused both of us," Hanne said carefully, "I think I could do anything. It would mean keeping our kingdoms safe from her, her assassins, and the builders of that burning mal-device. Ivasland has inflicted so much pain."

He nodded thoughtfully. "All right."

Good.

Right?

He was still nodding, though not in reply to her anymore, but in response to whatever he was thinking. A decision. "You should know," he said, "that I've heard yet more troubling news. So troubling I could not bring myself to believe it."

"What is it?" She had the distinct feeling she wasn't going to like whatever he told her, but information was the most valuable resource of all. (Aside from obsidian.) It could be wielded as a weapon or a shield, and there was no such thing as having too much.

"I've been told," he said cautiously, "that someone helped Ivasland complete the mal-device."

Oh.

Double and triple burn everything.

This. This was the heart of the news he'd just received from the hall—the alarm and disbelief. This was why he had the nerve to ask if she would kill Abagail herself.

"A flock of doves arrived from Embria," Rune went on. "A mob from Silver Sun is on its way to Solcast as we speak. They want answers."

They wanted blood. That was how mobs worked.

But he hadn't said he knew of her involvement yet, so Hanne reached for a look of innocence. "Who would help finish the device? Another Ivaslander, I'm sure, but I don't see why you're telling me—"

"The reports accuse you."

Hanne gasped and stepped backward, hands flying to her chest. "Rune. Husband. That is a lie. Even if I'd wanted to help our enemies—the kingdom we allied against—when would I have done such a thing? I've been with you since the moment you stepped into Embria."

"Except when you were in the malsite."

"Yes." She allowed a note of panic into her words. "And then I was *trapped*. In a *malsite*. I nearly died. You know this."

"I do." He looked at her, a worry line forming between his eyebrows. "But I cannot ignore this information."

"They lied, Rune. They lied to you, whoever told you that I had anything to do with the mal-device. I have never seen one. I don't know anything about them. I would not aid our enemies, and I would not harm Embria."

The prince frowned, not in anger but in disappointment, and slowly, he stood and walked to the far side of the room, gazing out the window.

Burn it. He didn't believe her.

He saw her only as a deceiver, which—to be honest—she was, but he wasn't supposed to know that. Not until it was too late. And if he didn't trust her, then she was no longer in control of their relationship.

Hanne *hated* whoever had told him. Burn that miserable informant. And *burn* the malicists and Abagail and everyone else in Ivasland. Burn that whole burning kingdom.

She would punish whoever had done this to her, revealing her secret before she was ready. They would all pay. But first, she had to restore her relationship with her husband, if that was even possible. If he trusted this informant more than he trusted her, what could she do? How could she regain his trust?

Unless.

Unless she confessed the rest of it. The why. The circumstances.

But telling him all that would be revealing her weaknesses, her fears, and everything she had been so careful to hide. She had few options, though, and Rune—predictable Caberwilline that he was—would respond to this. He would want to protect her.

She closed her eyes. "I didn't have a choice."

Rune looked over his shoulder.

She allowed the fear to tremble through her words. "I knew I would die in the malsite. If not from thirst and hunger, then from old age. Time moved differently there, and I had no hope of getting out. None. But then, it came to me."

The prince didn't speak, but he was listening to every word. Evaluating. Deciding whether to believe her ever again.

She had to keep going, had to tell the truth.

"The rancor." She pulled her arms around her, shivering with the memory. "It told me to go to Ivasland and finish their device. It told me how. And it told me that if I didn't follow its orders, it would destroy me." That vision of the Dark Shard rose up in her mind, yawning through her like a nightmare that would never fade.

"So you did it." Rune's words sounded hollow. Faraway.

"I did it." She sounded hollow, too, like her voice suddenly wasn't her own. "I went to Ivasland and gave their malicists the last piece of their puzzle, and then I escaped, because I knew Abagail and Baldric intended to have me killed."

"You should have come here first," Rune said. "Before going to Ivasland."

She stared at him.

"We could have figured out what to do together. I'd summoned the Nightrender already; she could have helped you, too."

Hanne very much doubted that.

"I wanted to come here," she said. "I knew you would help me." That was a lie. She'd only wanted to return to Nadine. But Rune would like it.

"Why didn't you?"

"I tried. I meant to follow the Brink Way all the way here, but then I saw it. Smelled it." She shuddered. "The rancor."

A faint shiver worked through him, too.

"I knew that it would come after me if I didn't obey its directions immediately. I knew it would kill me." Worse than that, even, but she couldn't bear to reveal quite so much to Rune, no matter how much sympathy it would win her. "But it's over. There's no point in debating what I should have done when I can't go back to change it. I did the only thing I believed would save my life so that I could live long enough to come here, marry you, and crush Ivasland. Then, perhaps, the war would end for good. I did it for the chance of peace."

Silence stretched between them, broken only by water splashing in the fountain and the moaning of wind outside. Rune wasn't much of a mystery—not usually—as he tended to do what was best for his country, but this time, she wasn't certain how he would respond. She'd made herself need him, in his eyes, but they had always been enemies. Even now, they were on opposite sides; he just didn't know it.

Something was different about Rune, though. He was weighed down with grief and anger and a thousand other things. He was king now.

But after a moment, Rune strode toward her, his expression fierce and determined. "Tell me what happened to you in Ivasland. Tell me what they did to you."

She did. She told him about the meeting with Abagail and Baldric, the way they'd hidden the mal-device even from their own people, and the way she had feared for her life every moment. "If they'd known my identity," Hanne said tremulously, "I'd be dead. They would have killed me right away."

Rune nodded, still brooding.

"But I managed to steal the plans to the device," Hanne added. "It won't prevent them from building more malice machines, but perhaps the plans will be useful. Perhaps knowing how the machines are built and operated can help us mitigate another attack. I would have shared the plans with you earlier, but . . . I was so afraid."

"Perhaps they will be of use." Still, he wore that expression of exhaustion and disappointment. But no longer anger. She was getting through to him.

"Abagail and Baldric would have killed me," Hanne reminded him. "They nearly did, but I escaped just in time."

"And then they came to destroy our alliance."

"Yes," Hanne murmured. "They tried to stop our wedding by sending their mal-device to Small Mountain. They mean to starve us over winter. And destroy centers of production, like Silver Sun."

Muscles in Rune's jaw flexed, and she could see the decision settling in him.

"We will crush them, Hanne. For what they did to you. To me. To both our kingdoms. I will bring their monarchs before you and together we will end this war. This alliance means more than anything else."

A smile curled up the corners of Hanne's lips. Maybe honesty wasn't so bad after all, when used wisely.

37.
Rune

Midnight.

Rune had been trying to fall asleep for hours already, but it wasn't happening. He'd get partway there, his mind going fuzzy and thoughts spinning wherever they wanted, but then they'd land on reality: he was king, they were at war, and he was woefully unprepared. Without fail, his heart would skip and he'd jerk out of bed, and only after a long drink of wine did the anxious feeling leave.

Of course, then he worried he'd be hungover in the morning. When he had to lead his army to war. His father would have been disgusted. And when Rune thought about *that*, the sleepless hours just grew longer.

By midnight, he'd repeated the process three times and was finally falling asleep. Then—*crash*—something bashed against the balcony door.

He leaped out of bed and reached for his sword, but he quickly became entangled in his sheets.

It didn't matter. The Nightrender strode in, a dark shape with her wings held wide, a revolting odor pouring off her. She glared down at him, finding him only half dressed and sprawled across the floor.

"Get up." She yanked the sheets off him and flung them away, then paused, her head cocked as she listened. "She is in the other room."

"Hanne? Yes." Rune picked himself up and shook a small light globe, granting himself just enough illumination to see that the Nightrender was once again covered in vile substances. "Dear Known Numina. What happened to you?"

"Keep your voice down." She glanced at the door that led to Hanne's room, a storm flashing behind her dark eyes. "It is of vital importance that I speak with you, but she cannot overhear."

Rune rubbed his face and tried to hide the way he shifted to breathing through his mouth. The Nightrender smelled like death. "All right. Should we go to your room? You can"—he wished he hadn't drunk quite so much wine—"scrape off the massacre you're wearing."

He'd meant to tell a joke there, but his head buzzed with alcohol and it didn't sound funny when he said it out loud.

The Nightrender clearly didn't appreciate his attempt. "I set three fires, beheaded over a dozen revenants, and cleansed the malice from two towns. Surely you don't expect me to be dressed for a royal ball."

"Mal-devices! Right." That was a little loud. In the next room, Hanne groaned, and if he didn't want to wake her, he needed to get out of here as quickly—and quietly—as possible. "Go," he said, waving the Nightrender to the balcony again. "I'll meet you in your room in five minutes."

She narrowed her eyes. "Don't be late. Time is short."

"I'll be there," he promised.

Then she was gone, out the window and into the air.

It took more than five minutes for him to pull himself together and put on real clothes, but finally he got out the door and into the parlor, where Hanne waited by the fountain. She'd lit one of the globes, so light sparkled across the water and gemstones, casting her in a gentle glow.

"Where are you going?" She smoothed down her nightgown, giving him a glimpse of the shape of her body.

"Taking a walk. That's all." He didn't move from his bedroom door, because he had the strangest sensation that if he walked past her, he'd get caught in her gravity and find himself unable to leave. Anyway, *should* he leave? She was his wife, and he was sneaking off to see another woman.

But the Nightrender wasn't interested in him like that, so it didn't matter. Did it?

It mattered because seeing her mattered to *him*.

Rune would go to her, his heart filled with longing, while his wife—the woman he was supposed to be spending time with—sat here alone, wondering where he'd gone.

The Nightrender needed to tell him something, though. And he was her summoner—her Dawnbreaker, at least in name.

"Can't sleep?" Hanne said almost gently.

He shook his head; his voice couldn't be trusted.

"All right." Hanne ran her fingers through her curls, and again he thought he should stay.

Before he lost his nerve, he slipped past his bride and went into the hall. John Taylor was on duty, waiting just outside the door, and the guard fell into step behind Rune without being directed; the entire castle was on alert after the assassination the previous night.

On one hand, Rune was glad he (probably) wouldn't be assassinated in his own home, thanks to John's presence (although Opus always had had several guards with him . . .). On the other hand, it was difficult to sneak off to see the Nightrender if he wasn't alone.

"I need you not to ask questions," Rune said.

"It isn't my place."

"And you won't comment about this," Rune went on. "To anyone else, I mean."

"Of course not." Irritation stung the guard's voice.

Finally, they reached the base of the Nightrender's tower. "Wait here," Rune said.

The guard's jaw hardened against whatever protest he might have voiced, but he nodded. Rune wound his way up the stairs and opened the unlocked door.

The Nightrender had already cleaned up and washed her armor, so she smelled considerably better. And thank goodness, because he didn't have the stomach to bear it again. Now, she stood in front of a newly polished mirror, wearing a focused frown as she jerked a comb through her long, tangled hair.

Rune shut the door, and her gaze flicked up to meet his in the mirror.

She threw the comb down. "I thought you would be here sooner."

"Sorry," he said. "I was delayed."

She just glared at him. "I have something important to tell you."

His shoulders sagged as he glanced around her room. It was nicer than before, but not nice enough. There was a table with two wooden chairs; a washbasin and a tub, both filled by tap; and light globes in sconces along the walls. She deserved more.

When he was king—wait, he was king *now*. Fine, then. He would ensure the Nightrender had quarters to rival a queen's. He'd make it a royal decree.

"Sit." Her tone softened. "Tell me why you are sad and drunk."

"I'm not drunk." He pulled out a chair and misjudged the speed, hitting himself in the shin. "Maybe a little," he conceded, sitting carefully. "Wait, this is my table."

The Nightrender crossed her arms.

"My table. From my rooms. Now there's a horrible fountain—"

"It is my table now," the Nightrender said. "And you were saying something of actual importance."

Oh, right.

"I'm afraid there have been new developments since you left." Since the wedding, but he didn't want to mention that part. Even slightly—just slightly!—inebriated, he knew he didn't want to remind the Nightrender that he was now a married man. Not that it would have mattered, anyway. Ever, apparently. But still. "My father is dead. Assassinated last night."

The Nightrender sat across from him, her wings neatly tucked away and her expression unreadable. "Tell me how you feel about that."

Was his relationship with his father so obviously bad that she knew better than to say anything more? Because it wasn't just Rune's loss; it was much broader, with far-reaching ripples the world might never truly understand but through the lens of history. "The death of a monarch is always dangerous for a kingdom's health," Rune said cautiously. "And my father was a strong king."

She nodded, as though she heard what he didn't say. "You will be a strong king, too."

His heart stumbled over itself. Did she really believe that? "I hope so. We'll see if I'm given a chance to prove myself." At her lifted eyebrow, he continued: "I was never the first choice to succeed my father."

"But you *are* king now," the Nightrender said, "with the support of your mother, at least some of the council, and the royal family of Embria."

That was true.

Rune swallowed a lump in his throat, wishing again he hadn't drunk quite so much. "Do you want me to finish combing your hair?"

The Nightrender stared at him.

"It's only half done." He motioned around his head, suddenly aware that his own hair was wild from tossing and turning.

Her fingertips wove through the ragged edges of her hair, but then she forced her hand down. "We have more urgent matters."

Rune wished *he* could put his fingers through her hair.

And immediately, he tried to unmake that wish because he was a married man, and he'd just *lied* to his wife about where he was going, and if he was going to run his fingers through anyone's hair, it should be *Hanne's*. Guilt gnawed at him, relentless. The thought made him feel like a monster.

"Now that you are king," the Nightrender said, "you no longer need to ask permission to send your army somewhere."

"That's not completely true. There's still the Crown Council, and Embria, and my mother holds a lot of influence—"

The Nightrender stood, wings like a dark cloak behind her. "You could send your army through the Soul Gate. You could do it now."

"I want to. I do. But I cannot ignore the assassination of a king—of my *father*. You know how dangerous that would be. What kind of ruler would I be if I didn't respond to this attack on Caberwill?" He heard his father's voice in those words. King Opus had always been talking about strength and making difficult decisions.

"One who prioritizes human survival above the scrabbling of mortals. One who understands that his parents and grandparents and great-grandparents left him with tremendous obstacles, but that those obstacles are not insurmountable. You can be the one to take action and save your descendants."

Rune clenched his jaw and growled out, "My father was just murdered. I must respond. Caberwilline kings do not show weakness." He rubbed his temples. "If I don't take immediate action, it won't be long before I'm overthrown. By my own council. By my own mother. By one of my own sisters—and a councilor who wishes to be regent. There are too many people who don't want me on my throne, and I promise you, they are even less likely to help you."

"You would let the world fall to darkness for your own ambitions."

"No!" Rune surged to his feet, making the chair scrape backward. "I'll *stop* the darkness, but burn it, Ivasland is hammering us. People are *dying*." With a hot lump rising in his throat, Rune threw open the gallery doors, but the night air was humid and heavy, providing no relief. "You need to wait while the alliance stops them from reducing two-thirds of this world to ruin. We can't go into the Malice with more malice exploding at our backs, ripping the kingdoms apart."

"There is no time to wait." The Nightrender followed behind him, silent save the rustling of feathers.

"You don't have to answer to councils or queens or hordes of furious subjects. You don't have to provide revenge for the assassination of a king, his men, and everything that burning mal-device did in Small Mountain."

"Your quest for self-worth makes you selfish." Her words were sharp and brittle with the truth. "I had hoped you were better than this. I believed you would help me, not push me aside anytime you saw opportunity to raise your station."

"My station? We're talking about mal-devices and *chaos*. I don't owe you anything!" The words tumbled out of him, unstoppable now. "I'm not your soul shard and my feelings don't matter. I know how bad the Malstop is—I can see it! But don't you understand? This isn't about me. This is about Caberwill. I can send my men into the Malice, but *Embria won't follow*, and Ivasland will rip apart the realm while we're in there dying for you. Let me settle with Ivasland, let me convince Embria to commit their men to this, and I can give you a combined army at full strength. If. You. Wait."

She stepped back, hurt. But then, slowly, she drew a long breath and lowered her wings. When she spoke again, her voice was soft. Strange. "The Malstop is flickering."

"Yes." His heart wrenched. "How bad is it? I mean, how bad is it *really*?"

"Dozens of rancor could have been set free when it was at its weakest. Certainly, there will be many new malsites forming." The Nightrender drew a shuddering breath, and for the first time since they'd met, Rune saw true vulnerability in her. Gone was the distant, aloof creature who'd come to Brink, swearing to destroy the rancor and cleanse the world of darkness. No, here was a young woman who feared for the future, terrified in the way he himself was terrified.

No, *more* terrified than he was. And if *she* was that afraid . . .

"Rune—King Rune, I mean." She closed her eyes and turned her face skyward. "I cannot do this alone. There is but one of me, and I am not what I once was. My memories flash out like stars, and I do not know how to recover them. Without all my experience, I am a lesser creature, and I am almost out of time. I cannot defend humanity if everything that made me mighty is gone."

"You are more than your memories," he tried, but it was no use.

"Perhaps before, but it's even worse than you know. Now—now everything *hurts*. Cleansing malsites, killing rancor, using my power: it all hurts."

His words were mere wisps. "What do you mean?"

"It used to feel good. Righteous. Restorative. It used to make me stronger. Now I suffer the reflection of every strike against evil, like the holy fire is trying to purify me, too."

"Are you sure?"

"I would not lie about this." She closed her eyes. "I *must* venture into the Malice. Tonight, before my memories fail me. Already, I've lost my making, countless awakenings, and . . . things I'm not even aware are missing. They're *gone*. And should I need to face a rancor *king*—my own power may destroy me. Without the support of you and your men, I'm not certain this Incursion can be stopped. I'm not certain that I can win."

He was touching her before he realized. It was brief, butterfly soft, but his fingertips traced her cheekbone down to her jaw. The caress was electric, just as powerful as he'd dared imagine. And when she listed toward his touch, a word balanced on the tip of his tongue—

—but the moment he opened his mouth to speak, it was gone. Like a language he used to know but had long forgotten. His hand dropped to his side, fingertips alive with the memory of her skin.

"I need your help," she whispered. "It isn't too late to save your world."

But it would be soon. The Malstop had opened. He'd seen the chaos just one rancor could create. Two? Twenty? A hundred? That many could rip the world up from its roots, especially if a king commanded them. A king she could not kill. A king no one could kill, without the risk of becoming him.

Rune *wanted* to say yes. He wished he could. Surely he hadn't imagined their connection. Every time she came to Caberwill, it was to see him. To ask him for help. If he could give her what she needed, shouldn't he? Even if it cost everything else?

It would be so easy to say yes.

But . . . "You said you had something important to tell me."

The emotion vanished from her face, replaced by the guarded expression she usually wore. "I'm no longer certain I want to tell you."

"Because you think it will affect my decision?" he asked. "I haven't changed my mind. I cannot field you the men. Not yet."

The Nightrender stepped away from him, wings arched. "Two malice machines detonated yesterday: the first outside Small Mountain and the second in the Silver Sun mine."

He curled his hand into a ball, like he could trap the texture of her skin. "I've heard the reports. Ivasland has so much to answer for."

"On both machines, I noticed an energy—one I had not expected. I hoped I might have been mistaken, but the Ivaslander who carried the device into the Silver Sun mine confirmed her involvement. Princess Johanne herself helped break the Winterfast Accords."

Rune sighed. "I know."

"You know."

"I do have spies in Embria." Rune again felt the shock of that news, the chill that had run through him as Rupert Flight related the events in Silver Sun. "I've confronted Hanne about it. She confessed to everything."

"Her actions endanger all of Salvation. The Incursion will be worse because of what she did. I thought you might care."

"I *do* care, but you don't know what happened to her. That rancor trapped her in the malsite. It *forced* her to go to Ivasland and help with the mal-device. She feared for her life."

"*You* would have died before allowing a rancor to dictate your actions."

"Even if that were true, not everyone would act that way. Learn something about mortals, Nightrender."

She stepped back. "And when the Malice extends across all of Salvation?" Her wings lifted, dark feathers framing her pale face. The light-slashed moon on her armor gleamed as she stalked toward him. "I will say it again: There is only one way to end this Incursion. Send your armies with me through the Soul Gate. Accompany me as I banish the rancor king back to the Dark Shard. I've said I cannot do it on my own. Your selfishness—your *pride*—will be the end of everything."

"This is not about my pride. My hand has been forced. Can't you understand that?"

"Your fighting only feeds malice." She was an eclipse, blacking out everything else as she leveled her inhuman glare on him. "Even justice and revenge are nothing against the magnitude of what rises within the Malice. Time is short, King Rune, and if you refuse to do what is right—what is *necessary*—you will be the king of ashes and ruins, of devastation and disappointment. You will be the king who could have stopped the rancor, but turned away when given the opportunity. You will be just like every other unworthy king before you."

The words cut, but Rune had been trained to fight back. "It isn't my duty to stop the rancor. It's yours, and you're the one who will fail because you can't do it without me—without my army of *mortals*. What a burning champion you are. You can't even remember how to be yourself."

She went still. So, so still, like a statue perfectly carved. Exquisite in every way, except for the damage he'd caused.

He fumbled for an apology, but it was too late. "Nightrender, I shouldn't have—"

"Goodbye, Rune." Tendons on her neck cast black shadows as she looked up and west, and her wings rose high. "We will not meet again."

Before he could figure out how to take back his foolish words, she was gone. In the air. Flying toward the spiral of stars. A faint wind stirred in her wake, the only thing remaining of her. And then the air, too, went still. He was alone.

38.
NIGHTRENDER

There was but one way through the Malstop: the Soul Gate. It was an ancient and immense entryway, built directly into the side of a mountain, bracketed by twin towers housing temples to the Known Numina and the Unknown (to mortals) Numina. The Soul Gate was one of the few truly neutral grounds on Salvation. No kingdoms ruled this place. No humans lived here.

Nightrender soared above the foothills, heading straight for the two pale and twisting towers, rising beyond the dawn-dappled clouds.

It was beautiful, if one didn't know what waited beyond the white-blue glow of the Malstop.

Nightrender landed before the gate. It was massive, with multiple parts. First, an iron portcullis, then the great rim of the Malstop; beyond that, a tunnel carved its way straight through the mountain, with another portcullis at its other end.

The gates, the tunnel—they let out into the red wasteland of the Malice.

Nightrender approached, a small, dark figure against the bright barrier. Her boots scuffed the shell-pale paving stones as she approached the gate, but before she reached it, the maintainers emerged from their towers. They were vaguely human shaped and possessed the translucent quality of ghosts—and, like ghosts, they glided toward her with the unhurried pace of immortal beings.

"Hello, old friends." Nightrender lifted her hands, palms up, and bowed her head. They were not old friends, not exactly. She didn't even know their names—or what they were. They'd guarded the Malstop as long as there had been a Malstop, and aside from herself, they were the only constant between awakenings. Sometimes, to feel less alone, she thought of them as friends.

"Nightrender. You've come at last." Known spoke with a soft tenor, hollow and strange, and they looked at her with ice-blue eyes.

"It flickered," Unknown said. "We could not prevent it."

Both maintainers shuddered, their forms rippling with the movement.

"I know." Nightrender closed the distance between them. "I saw it."

"We will not let it falter again," said Known.

That wasn't a promise either of them could make, but she appreciated the effort. "The time has come for me to journey into the Malice."

"We cannot guarantee your safety, nor the safety of your followers."

"I understand." Nightrender glanced behind her, where her Dawnbreaker army should be standing at the ready.

"But where are your followers?" Unknown asked softly.

Nightrender's throat went tight, and she could hardly speak the words. "I have no followers." Prince—*King* Rune had forsaken her. He had broken all his oaths as Dawnbreaker, soul shard, summoner, and friend.

She was trying not to think of him anymore.

"Very well." The maintainers led her to the Soul Gate's lock and lever. Along the gate's stone frame, dozens of markings blazed to life, burning the same electric blue as the Malstop, as numinous fire. The words were in a pre-Shattering tongue, a dead language, but she still understood them.

AFTER THE SHATTERING: WAR.
BEFORE THE MENDING: PEACE.

A loud clanking sounded, chains on pulleys moving deep inside the earth. The portcullis hauled itself open, and Nightrender passed through, the maintainers at her sides.

They stood before the Malstop, a low hum vibrating through them. Behind Nightrender's eyes, a cold dagger started to slice.

"These are worrying times," said Known. "And you do not look well."

"And yet I must go forward." Alone. She would accomplish little without her Dawnbreakers.

The maintainers nodded, both of them, and ran their hands along the barrier. If touching the field hurt them, they wouldn't tell her.

Finally, they found the seam—or created one, she was never sure—and peeled back the substance of the Malstop. Normally, it would be wide enough to accommodate her entire army, ten at a time, but as she was the only one going through, the maintainers opened the Malstop wide enough just for her. The low noise of the magic shifted, given almost a hollow quality, raising just a fraction in pitch.

"Thank you."

"Do not thank us. Put an end to the evil inside." It was what they said every time, but now, it seemed more ominous, colored with a dire warning of what would happen if she failed.

"Hold back the night. I will do my part." Then she stepped through the Malstop.

It sealed behind her, making hairs on the back of her neck stand on edge. The deep thrum settled back into its normal frequency. In the tunnel, the air was sour with the stink of malice: she took a few deep, acclimating breaths and glared down at the far side of the Soul Gate.

She drew her sword. Beloved, Defender of Souls.

The tunnel was empty, of course. Rancor had learned long ago that there was little point in forcing open their side of the gate to wait for her; certainly, there had been times they'd made it *difficult* for her to push through the tunnel, but she'd always bested them. (Although suddenly she couldn't remember how.)

Sword in hand, she moved toward the far gate, gaining speed with every step, until she was running, and her wings were giving her lift, and finally she was flying. By the time she reached the opposite side of the mountain, the portcullis was grinding open, and she careened up and up and up, into the chill and angry sky, dusky red and shot with lightning.

The Malice stretched before her, wild and ever-changing, but she set her course for the castle she'd seen in her dream. She knew where it was. She could feel it.

That was where she would find answers.

This was the Malice on the eyes: A landscape made of despair and horror. Gray and brown, streaked with the bright scarlet of fresh blood, a dull, rusty glow filling the sky like death in all directions. There were slight ripples in the topography here and there—sludgy rivers, skeletal plants that might generously be called trees. The heart of the Malice sat inside a giant crater, and there rose the castle, some obscene blend of stone and blood and human bone, but it was too far to see any details, even for her.

This was the Malice on the ears: A long, low hum from the barrier, so deep and pervasive it made even rancor want to claw open their heads. The sound was less punishing the closer one moved to the center of the land—the Malstop was a sphere, after all—but even so, it was impossible to ignore. Usually there were howls and screams and polyphonic roars—the violence of rancor attacking rancor—but so far, the flight had been horrifyingly quiet.

This was the Malice on the mind: Pure, unadulterated madness; hopelessness; and moments so long people died of thirst and hunger within them. There was nothing comforting here.

This was the Malice on the body: Eventually, it killed everyone. Even Nightrender knew that she was dying. One day, the poison of this place would overtake her, but until her ancient enemies claimed their victory, she would fight. Moving forward step by step, wingbeat by wingbeat.

Alone, at least, she could fly. Alone, she didn't have to worry about the lives being lost or the men regretting their choice to follow her. She didn't have to consider the loved ones they would leave behind. Even if their bodies made it back, there would always be a piece of them missing, lost to the Malice.

Alone, she needed to worry about only herself.

And the whole world, if she failed.

She would not fail. Could not. But right now, she was afraid. That castle should not be there. Her memories should not be vanishing. She should not have slaughtered the royal families four hundred years ago.

About halfway to the castle, she became aware of a horrific roar from below—it was like an entire forest of trees crashing over at once, but it went on and on, growing louder with every wingbeat.

Rancor. Hundreds of rancor screamed at her from a flat stretch of land, clustered into tight formations. Into ranks. Like an army.

Red-hot alarm shot through her. They weren't just standing there, waiting for her to pass over; no, they'd been sent to meet her Dawnbreakers on the field.

Her army would have been slaughtered in moments.

Rune would have been slaughtered if he'd come.

A command rang out below and bows lifted.

Bows?

Since when did rancor use weapons? They *were* the weapons.

She pushed her wings harder, rising into the upper reaches of the red sky until the tips of her feathers grazed the Malstop. But the bows were enchanted with old and arcane magic; a hundred arrows flew straight for her, gaining speed as they rose.

As the barrage reached her, Nightrender tucked in her wings and rolled out of the way, dropping around the arrows. They caught in the bright energy of the Malstop for only a second before plummeting harmlessly to the ground below.

But she hadn't been fast enough: two arrows grazed her, making her shoulder and leg sting with hot pain.

She could ignore it.

Heavy wingbeats—not her own—suddenly reached her. They came in too fast, *something* slamming into her with shocking speed. Black and gray wings—boney and membraned like a bat's—filled her vision for a half second before the rancor grabbed her shoulders and looked at her face-to-face. It was vile, all teeth and mushroom flesh. Its claws cut into her armor, piercing her skin.

A winged rancor. If she'd ever seen one before, the memory had been stolen away, leaving her with no knowledge of how to fight them.

You used to be so strong. You used to fight so well.

With a furious cry, she curled and kicked, shoving it away as she swung her sword to slash. But the creature was fast. It flew at her again, swiping her with those long claws. Fire ripped across her face and chest.

Another winged rancor had arrived, this one smaller but no less deadly. It rushed her, screaming so loudly her ears rang. She ducked its blow, but searing pain erupted in her spine and a shock of numbness worked through her wings. The first rancor had struck her undefended back.

Nightrender's wings hung loose, useless. She fell through the air, plunging toward the distant ground—and the army of rancor waiting.

Their clawed hands reached for her, grasping, as the roar of their blood-lust crescendoed.

Both winged rancor shot after her, slamming themselves into her again and again, knocking her around the sky like a toy. But new, furious strength filled her, firing into her numbed wings. She clutched her sword—

And then she was flying again, gaining height. She raised Beloved and plunged it into the nearest pursuing rancor, pouring numinous light into the strike. That familiar icy pain shocked through her, but there was no time to feel it: the first rancor burned away, sizzling into glowing embers and ash, but the other unhinged its jaw to reveal twin tongues as it lunged for her.

She swung her sword around, black glass glittering, but she wasn't fast enough. Above her, a third rancor appeared. It screamed at her, slashing, dripping its acid saliva, and wounded her again—this time cutting deep into her left wing.

Nightrender shrieked, dropping again, more quickly than before. The pair of rancor clawed at her as she fell, and spasms of pain made her sword swings wild, but she didn't stop.

Then, her body slammed into the ground, thrusting her shoulder out of place. She rolled, rocks jamming into her spine and wings and stomach.

At last, she went still.

She didn't move for a moment. Groaning, disoriented, she wasn't sure that she could. But slowly, every muscle straining, she pulled in her arms and pushed up to sit. There was a haze in her vision, growing thicker. Had there been poison on those arrows? What kind of poison affected *her*? But through the ringing in her ears, through the veil of venom across her eyes, she realized where she was.

Dark shapes surrounded her. A constant dull roar of oppressive noise. Rancor. She'd fallen straight into the monstrous army.

Nightrender struggled to her feet, but her left knee gave out and she started to sink back to the ground—then pulled herself up again. Her sword hung in her hand, almost too heavy to lift. But she would not die without fighting back.

For a moment, she hated Rune—hated all the humans of all the kingdoms—for ignoring her warnings, for letting her come here alone, for doing this to her again and again. For a moment, she didn't have to wonder why she'd tried to put an end to it four hundred years ago.

I will show you everything. I will show you the truth.

Then, the rancor descended on her, tearing at her armor, ripping at her flesh, and yanking at her hair.

This was it. She had waited too long. Tried too hard to persuade the humans to help. Wanted too badly for them to forgive her—to love her.

It was too late. She would not win this fight. The Malstop would fail. The three kingdoms would fall. And humanity would vanish entirely.

39.
Hanne

After a (fake) tearful goodbye, Rune was gone, off to conquer a kingdom for her.

It seemed like everyone had turned out to watch the new king ride to war. After a short speech from the queen mother, and a short speech from Rune, and a few short speeches from the more experienced generals, Hanne was feeling relieved that Caberwillines weren't known for being loquacious. Didn't the war have a schedule to keep? Hanne did.

Back inside Honor's Keep, she walked beside Dowager Queen Grace, as was her right. With King Opus dead and Rune riding out, it was up to Hanne to rule the kingdom—along with that annoying council—and Grace to assist, as she was more experienced.

To effectively take over, however, Hanne needed to get ahead of any rumors about her involvement with the mal-device. She'd spent all the boring speeches thinking about what to tell Grace, and finally she decided that simple was better: one of her enemies in Embria was smearing her good name.

"Your Majesty, I'd like to speak with you. Privately, if possible." Hanne lowered her voice. "It is urgent."

Grace looked at her askance. "Of course. Let's go to my off—" The last word choked off.

How surprising. Hanne hadn't thought Grace and Opus really cared for each other. Perhaps this was an act, but even if it was, Hanne needed to appear sensitive to it. She put her hand on Grace's arm and guided her to the queen's sunroom (Hanne's now, technically), with a troop of bodyguards behind them. Hanne's neck was starting to hurt from the strain of wearing her crown (she'd wanted to make an impression during the speeches, and she had; no one else wore a solid obsidian crown), but she wasn't about to send it back to her quarters. Not when she needed to command the dowager queen's attention.

When they reached the sunroom, Grace told the guards to wait in the hall, then ordered the servants to bring refreshments.

The door shut.

But they were not alone.

At first, it was just that prey-like awareness Hanne had honed in the malsite, a sense of alarm she couldn't ignore. The stink gave it away: decay, ozone, and the metallic tang of blood. A rancor was here.

I am not afraid, she thought. *Tuluna protects me. An Incursion cannot hurt me.*

She pressed any quaver out of her voice as she glared around at the couches and tables and potted plants. "What do you want?"

"Johanne, are you well?" Grace frowned at her. "I know it can be difficult to see a husband off to war, but you knew this was going to happen. If you need a physician—"

"Quiet." Hanne wished she'd brought her dagger, but there hadn't been a place for it in this gown or these shoes. Still, her crown sat heavy on her head. The obsidian rings and necklace and brooch warmed her skin. "I'm not talking to you."

"Then—" A rancor appeared on the far side of the room, near the sideboard, and Grace bit off her question. Her hands flew to the pendant at her throat. "Great Numina."

The rancor hissed, baring its barbed teeth. Just the sight of the creature nearly threw Hanne back into the malsite, back into that vision of the Dark Shard. This was not the same rancor—it was taller and wider, with different patterns of mottling across its body—which meant she was indeed unlucky enough to meet two of these monsters in her life.

But she was not the same Hanne as before. She was powerful now. Ready. And she was not helpless. She would never be helpless again.

"What do you want?" This time, the question came out stronger. Fiercer.

Queen Grace released a slow, shuddering breath. "I should have listened to her," she whispered to herself. "I shouldn't have told her to leave."

"Daghath Mal is pleased with you."

As before, listening to the rancor was terrible. Its voice was like glass shattering, like eyeballs squishing. Warmth spilled around Hanne's ears, but she didn't touch them to check for blood. That would show weakness.

Still, she couldn't help but ask: "Who—"

The rancor grinned. "Daghath Mal, the King from Beneath. He watches your every move, and he applauds your"—the teeth gleamed wickedly—"tenacity."

Hanne sucked in a breath, but that was all. No weakness. She wasn't afraid.

Hummingbird wings beat inside her chest, faster and faster.

"You," continued the rancor, "fulfilled your purpose in Ivasland."

Hanne glanced at Grace from the corner of her eye, but she couldn't tell if the queen understood the rancor. The woman just stood there with her hands covering her bloody ears, her whole body quaking. But it wouldn't be long until she became accustomed to the noise, and if she even *started* to understand what the rancor was suggesting—that Hanne had done the bidding of evil—then Hanne would have no choice but to kill her.

Yes, Rune had understood why Hanne had gone to Ivasland, but Rune was desperate to make this work, and painfully honorable even when he shouldn't be. But in Grace, Hanne saw an older and less-clever version of herself. She recognized ruthlessness when she saw it. Grace could ruin everything.

"Leave." Hanne dared a step toward the rancor, but its foul stench was almost overwhelming. Couldn't the guards outside smell it? Hear it? "Or do you mean to kill us?"

The queen strangled a sound in the back of her throat. First her son. Then her husband. And now her.

Hanne had no intention of either of them dying (today, anyway), but she had to admit that it seemed entirely possible the rancor sought to slaughter everyone in Honor's Keep, one by one. Starting at the top.

"If I wanted you dead, you'd be dead. No, I bring you new orders." The rancor slipped toward her, closer until she could feel the heat of its body, taste the stench of its breath. "Know that refusal means death."

Her eyes cut to Grace, but the queen didn't seem to register the words yet. She looked wretched, though: blood streamed from her ears, between her fingers, and down her hands and wrists.

"What do you want?" Hanne asked it.

"You view yourself as a conqueror," it said. "A peacemaker."

Hanne nodded.

"Can you understand it?" A note of panic entered Grace's voice. "I think it's trying to speak."

"You must prove it." The rancor crept closer, its teeth clicking. "Put an end to her suffering. Kill the queen and become the queen."

Hanne looked at Grace: the way the queen's hands trembled, the shadows deepening beneath her eyes. This woman had sent armies into Embria for all Hanne's life. She *should* die. But Grace would die on Hanne's time, when it fit into her plan, when a second royal death so soon after her arrival didn't look wildly suspicious.

"No."

"No?" The queen's voice rose to a hysterical pitch, believing Hanne's reply was for her, for the question of whether Hanne could understand the beast.

"No?" The rancor hissed. "You would defy your king?"

"I bow to no king," said Hanne. "Especially not yours."

"Dear Elmali. You *can* understand it. It *is* speaking." Grace turned on Hanne. "Are you one of them? Are you a rancor in disguise?"

"Then you are no conqueror," the rancor sneered. "You won't take what is yours."

That wasn't true. Hanne was the most ambitious person she knew.

But how could a queen's death be *this* necessary to a rancor?

She almost didn't see it move. It simply seemed to shift out of existence. Then it lunged for Grace—claws out, teeth bared.

Queen Grace hardly had a chance to scream, but scream she did, and the guards in the hall tried to throw open the door—but it was stuck, held fast by some dark power.

In spite of herself, Hanne screamed, too, but she wasn't going to run. She would never run from these monsters again. Instead, she wrenched the obsidian crown off her head—ripping out strands of hair with it—and thrust the points into the beast.

It was all so fast.

The rancor was tearing out Grace's throat, blood spraying like a breaking wave. Guards pounded on the door, calling for their queen, yelling to be let in. And Hanne was striking again and again, driving the jagged spikes of obsidian deep into the mushroom flesh. There was a pop, and then the creature howled in agony as shards of volcanic glass broke off into its body.

It fought back—of course it did—but Hanne had fury on her side, and fear, and a thousand other feelings she'd always been taught to hide. She was driven. Possessed. She would not be cowed into serving rancor ever again.

The pounding on the doors continued even after the rancor had stopped struggling.

Hanne gripped an obsidian tine that had come off the crown, and she began to saw. Slice by bloody slice, her hands and arms stinging, she removed the rancor's head.

Only then did the guards manage to get inside. They immediately looked to Grace, whose body was so broken that even Hanne could not stand to see it, and one of them retched. Hanne didn't blame him one bit.

She stood, gore dripping down her forearms and fists, gripping the broken pieces of her obsidian crown. The stench of carnage made her want to gag, but she swallowed back the taste of bile until she could speak. "A rancor has killed the dowager queen. I have killed the rancor. But this one creature's death is not enough retribution for what has happened here."

"How—How did it get here?" a guard captain asked. "The Malstop . . ."

Still coated with rancor blood, Hanne's skin was burning, blazing hot. She needed to wash it off, to neutralize the acid, but first, she needed to seize control of the situation.

"The Malstop has been thinning," Hanne said. "And last night it flickered. Who knows how many rancor were released or how many new malsites were created?"

Guards and gathering nobles crowded the door, pressing their hands or handkerchiefs against their faces. "The dowager queen," they breathed. "She's been slain."

"Soon," said Hanne, "we will conquer Ivasland. We will make them suffer for the assassination of King Opus. We will make them suffer for *everything* they have done."

No one cheered, but a few of the stricken nobility nodded their agreement.

Hanne didn't need their enthusiasm, only their obedience. "When we have conquered Ivasland, we will march on the Malice." This Daghath Mal—this *rancor king*—would learn that no one controlled Queen Johanne Fortuin.

"But the Nightrender—"

"The Nightrender has done nothing for us." Hanne clenched her jaw, gripping the broken crown in tight fists. "Remember the Red Dawn. Remember the malsites, like the one I escaped. We cannot count on her to perform her duties. No, we must take our fate into our own hands. I have vowed to fix the Malstop, and I will, but we cannot stop there. Begin training more soldiers at once. Forge obsidian-tipped weapons. Under my rule, a united Salvation will march on the Malice and destroy everything inside it. We will end the Incursions once and for all."

40.
Nightrender

She did not die.

Not right away, at least, although with the pain searing through her body, she wondered if death might be preferable.

What did death look like for someone such as her? She must have known at some point, but she could not remember anymore. She couldn't guess whether something good waited for her, or whether that was even possible, with all she'd done and left undone.

She'd been sent to protect humanity, and now—after thousands of years—she'd failed. She'd as good as killed them herself.

Perhaps death, for her, was this: memories and thoughts and feelings fading away until there was nothing left.

Perhaps she had been dying since the moment Rune summoned her.

Minutes—or hours—later Nightrender opened her eyes.

She was in a cavernous space, octagonal in shape. Bone chandeliers hung from the high ceiling, studded with blood rubies that gave the room a red cast, but little real illumination. Eyes glowed in the darkness, and it seemed as if the entirety of the rancor army had come here, such was their number.

For a moment, she imagined the empty wasteland from here to the Soul Gate, left undefended. Nothing stood in the way of a human army now. An army could siege the rancor castle.

Not that anyone was likely to do that. Rune had made himself clear.

Nightrender clawed at her heart, but there was no way to rip out her feelings. Now, the best she could hope for was forgetting.

The rancor filling the room were unnaturally quiet. They watched her, restlessly, like dogs hoping their master would release them to eat the scraps of the prey they had hunted and deposited at his feet.

Their master.

It hurt too much to turn her head yet, but even so, she could see that the center of the room, where twin thrones stood, remained bathed in dusky shadow. A pale figure sat there, immense and motionless . . . and then hot pain fogged her vision.

"You've been unconscious a long time. I've been watching your injuries close and your armor mend itself. It's fascinating. Do you think you'd die if you were torn apart? Or would the shredded pieces of your body eventually work their way back to one another?" The voice paused, thoughtfully. "I suppose that's not something you'd want to test."

Nightrender knew that voice.

Currently, it originated from the occupied throne, but it had been in her mind since she had awakened in her tower. It had taunted her, guided her, tested her.

"No." Her voice sounded so weak, so groggy and desperate. She wasn't even sure she could lift her sword, let alone swing it. The rancor had done everything short of tearing her into a thousand pieces. Her armor had done its best, but even the numinous fabric could only take so much before it split apart. "You can't be."

"You sound like a child." The creature unfolded itself, stood, and came to her. It was larger than the other winged rancor, and it was a glossy, alabaster white, the blinding flesh red-veined with rancorous sigils—although the moment she recognized them, the memories of how to read them vanished. "You disgrace yourself by rejecting what you know to be true."

Revulsion pulsed through her. "You shouldn't be here. Rancor kings can't leave the Dark Shard."

"I arrived here centuries ago," he said, his gentle tone at odds with the venom in his glare. "Then you came to stop me from—well, from doing what rancor kings do. Conquest, you know. We had a wonderful discussion, and then you left. But I found you fascinating, Nightrender. Do you remember me?"

Of course she didn't. She'd never seen him before. At least—her blood chilled—that she could remember.

The rancor king sighed, as though put out.

"I am Daghath Mal, King from Beneath, Guardian of the Rupture, and Conqueror of All." Then, he bent over her and grinned, his mouth too wide, his teeth too many. "What a shame they've done this to you." He reached for her, dragging his clawlike nails down her face in an agonizing caress. Blood dripped down her cheek. "Humans are animals, aren't they?"

He was too close. She wanted to pull away. But she couldn't, not lying on the floor, and not with her body in such a broken state. "No matter their faults," she whispered, "they are better creatures than you."

"Perhaps you only insist because you cannot remember how they betrayed you." Daghath Mal grabbed her head—one clawed hand on either side—and leaned in close. Foul breath overwhelmed her for a moment—

And then everything shifted. She was here, but in a different time.

> The castle wasn't yet complete, but its foundation had been laid and some of the scaffolding erected. It was as stark as ruins. The Rupture—visible in the center of the castle—was a bleeding sore on the world, oozing black slime and a deep-red light. A person could die just from looking into it.
>
> All around her, Dawnbreakers fought rancor, while she battled Daghath Mal himself. She had been shocked to find him here, having somehow dragged his way through the Rupture, but more immediate was the need to send him back.
>
> Her sword cleaved the air as he shifted in and out of reality—

A red haze surrounded this vision, and though the memory was shown through her eyes, it wasn't *her* memory. It was *his*. This was his memory of seeing her memory.

How? And did he have *more* of her memories?

> She was standing over the rancor king's body, her sword point digging into his throat. The Dawnbreakers had fled—she'd ordered them to go, the battle all but finished. Only a few beasts remained in this cradle of darkness, watching Nightrender best their king.
>
> "You won't kill me," Daghath Mal breathed. "I know you won't."

No. She wouldn't. They both knew she would not risk becoming him—if that was even possible. But she didn't need to kill him, only injure him enough to throw him back into the Rupture, back to the Dark Shard. His prone body was mere handspans from the portal between planes. All she had to do was push him in.

"Wait," Daghath Mal said. "Your humans. Do you know what they did?"

The bead of black blood pooled wider on his throat, but Nightrender waited. She could drive the sword deeper at any moment, then fling his body into the red depths of darkness. She was strong in this memory, and battling evil only made her more powerful.

"They broke their treaty. The Winterfast Accords."

That was impossible. Humans knew better than that.

"Tell me why you think this," she said. "Tell me what proof you have."

"I am the proof," Daghath Mal said. "I am here, after all. You know as well as I that kings are unable to cross worlds unless we are called by name."

A shudder ran through her. It was true, but no one should have known his name. The names of every rancor king had been wiped from creation before her making.

"Tell me how," she demanded.

"It takes a great deal of work to summon a rancor king," Daghath Mal said. "A great deal of *power*. Not just anyone can do it, or I'd have been here eons ago. But three royal families, with their many scholars, their great treasuries, their hoarded Relics . . . they might accomplish such a task. If they performed the ritual at the same time, in the same way."

"They would never." A burst of numinous fire raced down the length of her sword, pouring agony into the rancor king's body.

"Do you think humans are so innocent?" He cried out

as another bolt of light shot into him. "One by one, unbeknownst to the others, all three royal families sought my help to destroy their rivals. They called me here. They begged me. They claimed they wanted peace—*their* peace—so I promised to help." He grinned up at her, blood coating his rows of teeth. "They came to *me* for aid, because you refused to be anything but a neutral observer. And so, they broke the treaty. They used the darkest malice against one another."

Nightrender's blade dug deeper into the rancor king's throat, and white-blue power sparked again down the obsidian. "I don't believe you."

But a piece of her did. They had been behaving strangely. Guiltily. Even her soul shard had been hiding something. Nightrender closed her eyes and remembered Loreena's face, the weight in the princess's eyes. There had been something strange there—a burden of conscience?

No. The horrible thing was that Nightrender *did* believe Daghath Mal.

The Incursion. Mortals had started it themselves. But they could not control the kind of chaos they'd invited into the laic plane. It would have overwhelmed them, and the force of evil they'd summoned would have shaken the earth even beyond the Malstop, weakening the fabric of the world to the point of disaster.

So they'd summoned her to save them from their own foolishness. Their own betrayal of the Winterfast Accords.

Daghath Mal grinned, all his teeth showing. "I see you accept this truth."

Rage boiled through her. Not only had the royal families broken the Winterfast Accords, they'd summoned a *king*. And she could not kill him. Not without becoming him.

With that kind of power, she could shatter the world to its roots. Nothing would survive her, Nightrender turned into a rancor king.

How *dare* they do this to her. How *dare* they lie to her? Manipulate her? Use her?

Red flared through her vision, as another spike of power surged through her sword. And Daghath Mal—he was grinning. Grinning at her.

"You feel it, don't you? This anger? This hate?"

She did. It was unlike anything she had ever experienced before, and every pulse of numinous energy between them sent bolts of ice through her head. But she couldn't stop it; the anger was overwhelming.

A dark thread spun between them, growing heavy with wrath as it buried itself deep into Nightrender's soul.

"Such behavior should not go unpunished," he said.

For the first time, Nightrender agreed with him.

The memory faded until Nightrender was again in the *now*, with Daghath Mal's clawed grip tight on her face, the bone castle finished and soaring above her, and the silent audience of rancor watching from the perimeter. The Rupture wasn't visible from the throne room, but she could sense it nearby.

Daghath Mal's claws dug deeper into her cheeks. "Do you remember me now?" he asked.

The dark thread, the uncontrollable fury, the sinister voice in her head: it was all him. She had been infected by his anger, unable to restrain herself. He was the reason for the Red Dawn.

And now he showed her something that she had forgotten.

How had he come to possess her memories?

She gave a short gasp as understanding unfurled in her mind. "You are the monster stealing my memories."

"No, I am not." He laughed a little; it sounded like mountains crumbling, crushing entire cities beneath the rubble. "I am the monster that will *restore* your memories."

41.
Hanne

Nadine threw open the door just as Hanne arrived.

"You're safe!" Relief flooded through Hanne, so raw and powerful. She almost couldn't stand it.

"Yes, of course, but you—" Nadine pressed her mouth into a line as she took in Hanne's appearance.

Her hands were sliced open from the obsidian crown, and the acidic rancor blood had eaten through patches of her clothes and skin, but nothing—not even her own agony—could keep Hanne from her cousin. There could have been another rancor, after all. It could have come after Nadine; if this rancor king knew so much about her, it would know that Nadine was the only person Hanne truly cared for.

Hanne's fists trembled around the broken crown. If anything had hurt Nadine, she would have burned the world to the ground.

"Blessed Tuluna! Hanne, we have to get you to a physician." Nadine couldn't quite keep the horror out of her voice.

"It's fine," Hanne said. "I just need to wash off."

"You need stitches." Worry creased Nadine's brow.

They left the gore-covered crown in the parlor, grabbed clean clothes, and then hurried to the grand physician herself, where Hanne was washed and treated and wrapped in bandages. When the grand physician stepped out of the room so that Hanne could rest, Hanne told Nadine everything that had happened.

Nadine's eyebrows pushed together. "What even *is* a rancor king?"

Hanne lowered her gaze to her hands, the snowy bandages hiding all the blood she'd spilled. "It's what it sounds like."

"And it—he?—cares that Queen Grace is dead. Why?"

That was more puzzling. "Well, I intended to get to it eventually, when it was most beneficial. Perhaps the rancor king means to foil my plans. Her death must put me at a disadvantage."

They were quiet for a moment, thinking.

"Queen Grace would have been a strong ally while Rune is in Ivasland," Nadine offered. "If you'd succeeded in winning her over, she might have protected you from your enemies here. Charity, certainly, and perhaps the rest of the Crown Council. If the King from Beneath was the true author of your mission to Ivasland, perhaps it is *you* he wishes to harm. Or perhaps he was testing how far he can bend you to his will."

Hanne nodded slowly. "Yes, I think he must be. But I don't take orders from rancor. I *destroy* rancor."

Even as she said the words, it was hard to believe she'd actually *done* it. She'd killed a rancor with her own two hands. And if she must, she would do it again.

Grand Physician Asheater stepped into Hanne's sickroom again and handed Nadine an envelope. "I have personally fetched these from my stores. You'll find several labeled herb packets inside. For tea. Some for pain, some for wakefulness. The queen may find she has trouble sleeping."

The grand physician frowned, as if she, too, anticipated having trouble sleeping. She would likely be inspecting the body. Bodies, that was, because there were two: the former queen and the rancor.

"Thank you, Grand Physician." Nadine tucked the envelope under her arm. "How often should she have her bandages replaced?"

"Every morning, please, or anytime the pain changes or becomes unbearable. I'm concerned about the wounds festering."

Beneath the heavy bandages, Hanne flexed her hands experimentally. A spiderweb of stabbing shot up to her elbows, but that didn't bother her; she could withstand a little pain.

What worried her was the thought of rancor blood mixing with hers, and what unknown ailments that might cause. But Tuluna was on her side, and surely their holy presence would burn away any pollution.

She would also, she resolved, double the amount of obsidian she wore. It couldn't hurt.

A few minutes later, they were alone once more. "I know you should probably stay in Rune's apartments, as is befitting of your station," Nadine said, "but I'd feel much better if you stayed in my suite, where I can tend to you. You've endured so much, and now you can't use your hands. You should be close to the people who care about you."

"It's a shame his chambers are so small," Hanne murmured. "Only a few rooms. Who thought that was enough space for a prince and his wife and both their households?"

"I believe your presence there was meant to be temporary," Nadine said. "Just long enough for you to get pregnant. Then you would have moved into your own suite with all of us to care for you."

"I see." Hanne, who'd had bigger problems on her mind, hadn't actually paid all that much attention to how often she would be moved around. It seemed like a huge inconvenience, though, and something of an insult. She was the new queen, after all. "Perhaps," she said slowly, "I should simply move into the queen's chambers, as the former occupant is no longer with us."

Nadine sounded hesitant. "As of a few hours ago."

"The royal chambers should never go empty. Surely Caberwillines believe it to be bad luck, don't they?"

"I'm not sure. . . ."

"They're a superstitious lot. And besides, I *am* the queen now, and it's increasingly clear that I need my ladies with me—at all times. There's space enough in the queen's chambers, I should think. If I'm going to be moved about the castle again, I would like to move into the last location I will ever live—at least until I return to Solspire." She paused, considering. "And while we are at it, we should have Rune moved into the king's chambers. It would be good to do that while he's away. He won't be disturbed."

"I think he'll be very disturbed. His father—"

"Isn't using those rooms anymore."

"You might not want to phrase it that way to anyone else," Nadine advised.

"Well, no. But you understand." Hanne had never needed to mince words around Nadine, but she appreciated the occasional reminder when it came to other people and how they may view her statements. "It wouldn't do for me to live in the queen's chambers while Rune keeps his former rooms. I would look arrogant. No, it must be done at once. He will overcome the discomfort. He knows the price the crown carries."

Nadine was quiet for a moment. "All right. I'll order your belongings to the queen's chambers and Rune's to the king's. It may take some persuasion, so don't expect it to happen overnight."

As long as it happened.

"While we are discussing the future," Nadine said cautiously, "I wondered if I might make a request."

"Of course." Hanne felt for Nadine's hand. "Of what nature?"

"I want a new title. An additional title, that is. I'd like to be your royal adviser, so that others are not so free to dismiss my opinions."

This made sense and was easily granted. In Embria, Nadine had constantly been ignored by the royal side of the family. Of course she wanted more security now, right at the moment they had been given the opportunity to create a new world together. "It will be a scandal, even for Caberwillines. A lady-in-waiting who's also an official adviser? I like it."

"They may be so distracted by all the death that they won't even notice for a while. But I do have my first official advice for you."

"Yes?"

"Write to Rune before someone else does. Tell him what happened—but only what you want him to know. After all, you were there. And you're his wife. Your opinion counts more than anyone's. Shape his view to your benefit."

That was all a very good assessment. Hanne smiled. "All right, adviser. What's more intimate? My own letterhead? Or the crown stationery, to show I've fully integrated?"

"Use yours," Nadine murmured. "No one else has access to it. There will be no question of the letter's authenticity."

Very soon, a portable desk was brought in, along with pens, ink, and the specified paper. Hanne began to write. It was slow work, thanks to the wrappings and pain, but it would only seem genuine if she did it herself.

My dearest Rune,

I write with the heaviest of hearts, knowing that this letter will reach you as you march toward war, when your mind should be on your men, when you already carry too many burdens on your shoulders. But I feel I must be the one to inform you of the fate that has befallen your mother.

I am deeply sorry to tell you that your mother has been killed, only hours after your departure.

She was a strong woman, a brave woman, and a true and dedicated mother. Though I knew her only a short time, I admired her. In my eyes, she embodied every quality of a bold and wise queen. Clearly, Elmali the Stalwart favored her.

You must wonder what could steal such a person from the world, I know. I will tell you, but please be warned this is a difficult account to write, and it will be difficult to read. There is no easy way to tell you, no way to make it less terrible. Please, forgive the bluntness of my report, as I myself am still struggling to accept what has happened.

This morning, as your mother and I were discussing how much we will miss your presence, how brave you are to go, a rancor appeared in the sunroom. Somehow, it had barred the door, preventing our guards from coming to our aid.

Boldly, as only a mother of Grace's stature could, she put herself between the beast and me. With this final act, she gave me the second I needed to take the obsidian crown from my head and fight back. I was able to kill the rancor, though not before it took her.

My greatest regret in this world will always be that I could not do more to save her.

This must come as an enormous shock, I know. I believe I am in shock, as well. But you—you've lost so much in your life already—and now, both parents as well. It is so unfair, so cruel.

I must conclude that our enemies are afraid of us, of what our alliance means, of what we could accomplish together. They would not go to these lengths if they did not fear the combined might of the Stalwart and the Tenacious. Therefore, they launch these vile attacks, hoping to drag us down with grief, hoping to prevent us from doing what is right and righteous.

But they will not succeed. I will never give up the fight for peace across all of Salvation, and I will never cede the fight against malice. I know that you feel the same. Perhaps that isn't much comfort now, with the pain so fresh. Would that I could hold you now and lend you whatever strength I have left.

Given these attacks on your family, you must be concerned about your sisters. Please, know that I will care for them as though they were my own. I have already ordered extra guards to them and armed all of the castle watch with obsidian. I will personally ensure their safety and see to their well-being. After all, they, too, have suffered these great losses. And when you are able, please write to them. They will need you, especially.

Lastly, for now, I will oversee arrangements for your mother. She deserves something grand, something befitting of her legacy, but I would not hold such a memorial of her life without you present. When you come home from the war, we will have a proper service, bestowing upon her the highest Caberwilline honors.

My husband, I am, as before, deeply sorry that all these struggles are part of our story. We knew it would not be easy, but neither of us could have predicted these incredible burdens.

Yet I know we will overcome them. For Salvation.

All my love,
Hanne

By the time she finished writing, her hand was throbbing and her vision swam. Fortunately, Nadine had already made the grand physician's pain tea, and while Hanne waited for the ink to dry, she drained the entire cup.

"There," Hanne said. "Not an exact account, but the account he needs to hear. There will be no other versions."

"And you signed with love."

Hanne placed her teacup back in its saucer. "It's a nice touch, don't you think? Rune is sensitive. He needs someone to love him, especially now." She didn't have to mean it. She would never *love* Rune Highcrown. But she could pretend.

"I think he will appreciate it." When the ink was set, Nadine folded the papers and sealed them with Hanne's royal crest. "I'll see to it that this reaches him soon." Her mouth twisted with thought. "There are still Sanctuary and Unity."

"What?"

"The princesses. Rune's sisters. You just wrote a whole paragraph about taking care of them."

"Oh. I'd forgotten their ridiculous names. Caberwilline parents are cruel."

"I couldn't agree more."

"Well, I'm not going to kill them. Certainly not anytime soon. They're only children, and I'm not a monster." *Not like my parents.* But she didn't say that out loud. She would never, not even to Nadine. The darkness in the woods, the fire, the pain—those were secrets she would never tell. "Perhaps they could be sent to a faraway temple," Hanne mused, shaking off the memories. "Or we could betroth them to Embrian lords. They could be useful to us, if we teach them what we want them to know."

"They would still have a claim to the throne."

"I am willing to consider betrothals and relocations. Nothing else. Not now." She bit her lip. "If they do become a problem and less-deadly solutions don't work, I will figure it out."

Nadine moved to kneel beside Hanne, carefully touching the bandages. "I know this has been difficult, and it's not anything like you'd planned. But look where we are. You are queen. Peace is within reach. It's just on the other side of these two final wars that we *can* win under your leadership. Take this world. Forge it into what you want it to be."

Hanne's gaze fell on the broken obsidian crown, which a servant had brought in at Hanne's request. Even after it had been wiped clean, a film of gore still marred the perfect blackness. She would not soon forget how it felt to saw apart her enemy. "I am a forging fire," she murmured.

"Yes," Nadine said kindly. "You are."

No. The voice came from deep inside Hanne's mind. Tuluna the Tenacious. ***I am the fire that forged you. I am an inferno. You are my sword.***

Hanne closed her eyes. *Of course,* she prayed. *I am nothing without you.*

Very good. Tuluna's voice turned gentle. ***And now, my beautiful princess, pay attention. I have a task for you.***

42.
Nightrender

Nightrender swallowed the taste of blood and bile that rose in her throat. "You would restore my memories."

Daghath Mal sat back. "I would."

For a moment, Nightrender allowed herself to imagine all her memories flooding back, filling the blackening sky of her mind. They would be fuzzy, perhaps, like the one he'd shown her, but she didn't need crystal clarity—only knowledge. History.

The temptation wormed into her heart. Soul shards. Battles. A melody she used to hum. She could again possess a deep understanding of rancor and Numina and humanity. Her own life, as real and accessible as it had once been.

But just as quickly as the desire rose, it died.

"You have no such power." She pushed herself up until she was sitting, finally registering that the scabbard on her back was empty; no weapon weighed it down. Beloved was gone. "And even if you did, no promise of yours could be trusted."

Daghath Mal drew back, as though offended. "Lady Nightrender, I keep all my promises."

"Four hundred years ago, you swore to help the royal families destroy their rivals."

"And I did. They're dead, aren't they?"

A chill swept through her. That was true. They were dead.

Because she'd killed them.

"You intended for that to happen," Nightrender murmured. "You told me about the broken treaty, anticipating my anger. You must have pushed. Exaggerated. Made everything seem worse so that I would go there and—and—"

Daghath Mal cocked his head. "They summoned me to destroy one another. How could I make that sound *worse* than it is?" He laughed a little. "Perhaps I encouraged you, yes. I didn't want you to throw me back to the Dark Shard, so I told you a story. A *true* story. You took my anger into yourself and flew off, boiling over with rage. You were glorious, Nightrender. I only wish I could have seen your wrath made manifest through my own eyes."

Divine judgment. That was what Rune and Grand Priest Larksong believed of the Red Dawn. What would they think if they knew all of it had been orchestrated by Daghath Mal?

"You've put false images into my head before," she said. "The wedding."

"I never claimed *that* was real. Merely a suggestion. I thought you might like it."

Nightrender bared her teeth at him. She had to get up. She had to kill him.

No. She couldn't *kill* him. But she could find the Rupture and throw him back to the Dark Shard. He'd be trapped once more—unless some foolish mortal summoned him again. But she might buy humanity another few millennia.

Or not, Daghath Mal whispered in her mind. ***They keep breaking the Winterfast Accords.***

With a painful lurch, Nightrender forced herself to her feet, ignoring the screaming anguish inside her body. Wet blood covered the stone floor where she'd been lying, but her wounds had closed and she could once again feel her wings. The right one moved, but the left—no.

"Let me tell you why your memories are vanishing." Daghath Mal took a step toward her, his own wings spread wide until he was the only thing that she could see. "After the Red Dawn, when the royals were dead and their blood ran off you in rivers, your eyes cleared. You realized what you had done. And then"—his mouth turned into a sneer—"you begged forgiveness. You made yourself *low* before the mortals. But they did not forgive you."

Nightrender tightened her fists.

"Instead, they captured you. Bound you. In fact, you *let* them. They performed a dark ritual to strip your memory of the Red Dawn, but humans have limited experience with magic and they cut too deep. After, they took you back to your tower, where you went back to sleep. And then they abandoned you, telling only the tale of *your* mistake.

"The sleep preserved your memories, as it does your body, but the instant you awakened, the degradation began. Soon, you will be little more than human yourself, at least in mind. You may have your powers, but without the knowledge of using them . . ."

She had wanted answers; now she wished for ignorance.

"They did this to you. They betrayed you in every possible way."

Anger built up in the pit of her soul. She had thought it impossible to grow even more disillusioned and disappointed with humans. But no. They had taken their war to the peak of obscenity. They'd *maimed* her. They'd made her think all this was her fault.

"They did this," she whispered. "They took my memories. They are the ones killing me."

Daghath Mal still filled her view, overwhelming. "They are not worthy of you. Why do you remain a servant to those who will never appreciate your power?"

Why indeed? Because she'd been built for this? Because she had no choice?

"You do have a choice. For thousands of years, you've allowed yourself to be the weapon, but I want you to be the warrior."

"Tell me how," Nightrender hissed. The rage was boiling up again, the same uncontrollable anger she'd felt four hundred years ago. How dare mortals violate her mind? How dare they obliterate everything she was?

"Just decide," he murmured. "Just decide that you don't want to save them from themselves. They refuse to give you the one thing you truly want."

"An end."

"You have told them that their wars only feed malice, yet still they continue to fight." Daghath Mal shook his head. "And they expect you to rescue them every time the scales tip away from them."

"It isn't fair." Everything inside her was white hot. She could hardly breathe around the conflagration of anger.

"I am angry, too," said the rancor king. "I have been betrayed, too."

The dark thread burned between them as Nightrender looked up and met his terrible eyes. "Mortals." The word sat sour on her tongue.

"Yes. Eons ago, when the world shattered, I was cast down. Changed. Into this." Daghath Mal stretched his arms and wings wide, his whole body on display, unguarded. "They made me what you see."

If Daghath Mal had been part of the Shattering, then he was even older than she. "Tell me how they changed you."

Deep laughter rumbled out of him. "It no longer matters. I am a king, the most powerful in the Dark Shard. Humanity is the architect of its own unhappiness. But I will put an end to that. I will give them what they do not deserve: peace."

As if she hadn't been begging for peace for thousands of years. "There is no way—"

"Yes, there is." Daghath Mal lowered his wings and stepped aside, revealing the twin thrones that stood in the center of the chamber. They were immense, made of metal and bone. One held a long, cloth-shrouded object balanced on the arms.

Beloved, Defender of Souls.

She knew its shape, the scent of it. Her fingers ached to grasp the hilt, but she did not reach for it. Not yet. "You took my sword."

"I couldn't have you attacking me. Not before I'd had a chance to make my offer." Daghath Mal slid the tattered fabric off Beloved, careful not to touch any part of the obsidian. "We could rule this world together, Nightrender."

Her eyes cut to him.

"You could be my partner. My queen." Daghath Mal moved around her, pale and flickering, skipping in and out of phase. "This second throne was built for you. After our first meeting, I finally understood that we should not be enemies. We are the same, you and I. Mortals fear our power, and they constantly demand we use it—for them."

"Your queen," Nightrender echoed. "You would make me your equal."

"You already are." He appeared before her again, and one clawed finger scraped up her throat and toward her chin. "What an inconceivable terror you could be, if you chose. A waking nightmare upon humanity."

She could be. She could hurt people the way that they had hurt her. She could make everyone pay for what their ancestors had done. She could rid this whole burning world of mortals.

Except one.

Her soul shard.

Nightrender took a step backward, away from Daghath Mal and the twin thrones. A red fog was fading from her thoughts. Had she truly been considering—

Nightrender, Daghath Mal whispered in the back of her mind. ***You know now what they did to you. But I would restore the memories they stole. Be my queen. Stand with me.***

"I was made to defend the people of Salvation." She didn't sound as resolute as she'd intended, though.

"For how long?" he asked. "Forever?"

"If I must." She leveled her stare on him. "You should not be in my mind."

You opened this door, Nightrender. Four hundred years ago, you had me at the end of your sword, burning through my insides with your power. And we shared something intimate: profound hatred. It was only an instant, but through that, our connection was established.

It was clear then: why he could whisper into her thoughts, why using her power caused pain, why she'd even felt tempted by the idea of taking the throne beside him. She had built a link between them, a product of the energy surging through her sword as he fed her growing anger. And now, that same power attacked the dark place he occupied within her, the terrible rot of his influence.

"I don't want anything from you." Nightrender forced the words out one by one.

"You want your past," he said.

That was true, but she could not—would not—bargain away her freedom. He would withhold memories in exchange for services, select only the knowledge he wanted her to have. She had no interest in more double-edged promises.

"I may not remember everything," she rasped, "but I know I'm not a monster. Siding with you would make me one."

A growl escaped Daghath Mal's throat. "You are making a mistake."

No. Nightrender had sworn to defend the people of Salvation, and she would not forsake that promise. Even now. Even knowing what they had done to her.

She was better than their betrayal.

Before she could doubt herself, Nightrender dove for her sword.

Her muscles screamed as she lifted Beloved into the air and swept it straight for the beast's throat. Lightning shot through the throne room, a brilliant flash of white-blue that lasted just long enough for Nightrender to see the hundreds of rancor lining the open space, their claws still dripping with her blood, their serrated teeth black with shreds of her hair.

Then the room went dim again, her sword completed its arc, and the rancor king was nowhere to be seen. Slowly, warily, she turned a circle, fingers clenched around the hilt.

Don't fight this, he whispered into her mind.

There: a shudder in the air, an eerie body slipping in and out of existence. She charged at him, heavy wings dragging behind her, but he was gone before she got there, shifted to yet another space.

Become my queen.

"No." She pushed everything into that word, raising her sword to guard. This was it. Her last stand. She would throw him into the Rupture or die trying. Even if she did succeed, the rest of his army would descend on her, showing no mercy. But at least she would have righted this wrong. "I will not join you. Not now. Not ever."

"Very well." He sounded resigned. Sad, even.

A rancorous howl split the air and the hundreds were on her in an instant, clawing and ripping, grasping at her wings even as the black-glass feathers sliced through their flesh. Rancor pushed in tight, all trying to get a taste of her, leaving no room for her to fight.

Numinous light burst out, driving back the beasts as freezing pain splintered through her. She leaped for the nearest throne, forcing her good wing to rise and give her lift.

Standing on its back, barely keeping her balance as she swung her obsidian blade, she didn't stop fighting. Brilliant, cleansing fire spread through the mob, stunning some, destroying others.

She swung, sliced, and screamed as claws raked down her legs. A heartbeat later, that rancor burned away in holy fire. She sent three others after it, quickly losing count as the beasts kept coming and she kept fighting.

Her muscles strained. Her head throbbed. Her body began to fail her as the horde pushed and thrashed, climbing over one another to reach her.

They were legion. She was one. But she would not quit, no matter how much it hurt.

If this was her final fight, she would give it everything she had left.

43.
Rune

"Our scouts have spotted someone in the woods, sire."

"A messenger?" Rune asked. After hours of hard marching, the army had stopped for the night. Tents rose along with the full moon and the scent of cooking meat. Rune's stomach had rumbled as he and Tide Emberwish strode from tent to tent, speaking briefly to soldiers and support alike. It was good for morale, the grand general had told him earlier, for the king—especially a new king—to make personal connections with his men.

"Could be, Your Majesty." The runner took a sip from his canteen and wiped sweat off his brow. "He was coming from the northeast, near the tunnel exit. Perhaps from Brink."

A knot of dread tightened Rune's chest as he glanced toward the mountain, which loomed high against the starry sky. They'd been gone only a day. They were barely away from the city. What kind of news was so urgent? Bad news, that's what. He was quickly losing faith in any other kind.

"Have the messenger searched thoroughly," Tide said. "And find out if there's anyone who can vouch for him."

"Yes, Grand General. Your Majesty." The runner bowed, capped his water, and then set off again.

Rune and Tide resumed walking through the camp, all Rune's personal guards—John and the new ones—following behind them.

"We'll eat well for a few nights," the grand general said, nodding toward Rune's grumbling stomach. "But once those supplies run out, it's hardtack and whatever we hunt on the way there. There's a store set aside for you, of course. Kings don't eat like common soldiers."

"I don't need anything special." Rune gazed across the camp as full dark settled. There were thousands of people here, not just soldiers, but cooks and cleaners and smiths and fletchers. All these people were following him into war. Because he was king.

"You may change your mind when you've had nothing but stale biscuits for a week straight."

Rune agreed, but didn't admit it out loud. He'd been riding with the grand general all day, discussing tactics and contingencies, and while he was grateful to benefit from a lifetime of experience, he didn't want Tide to think he needed to be coddled.

"That's quite a sight!" The voice came from one of the cooks.

Rune followed the man's gaze to the Malstop, which glowed white-blue over the trees and hills. It was a reminder of the death that waited inside. It looked sick, the barrier. Thin. Stretched and rotting away from the inside.

"Did you see it flicker the other day?" asked another cook.

"I did. Makes you wonder if aught got out."

Rune clenched his jaw as he and Tide walked past. That flicker had merely been the first. And whether the next was a week or a month away—it didn't matter. The Incursion was upon them.

Just like he'd been telling his parents since they'd nearly lost Hanne to the malsite.

"Don't let camp talk get to you," Tide said. "Incursion or no Incursion, we have a human war to fight first. Don't let anything distract you. You're the leader now, and your focus needs to be sharp. True."

Rune pulled his gaze away from the Malstop, but he couldn't help wondering if the Nightrender was in there yet. Was she all right? He hated not knowing. He shouldn't have spoken to her as he had, with such anger and defensiveness. He'd said things he couldn't take back. Again.

"I've sent a dove off to the Embrian grand general, confirming their readiness," Tide was saying now. "We'll flank the Ivasland home army from both sides. They're camped just across their borders and . . ."

This was all information Rune knew, but Tide clearly thought he needed to hear it again. Rune's mind turned back to the runner, and the messenger from Brink. How soon could he have that message?

"What do you think, Your Majesty?" Tide asked.

Rune didn't have time to respond because a sudden wave of sickness crashed over him, and despair rose up and up and up, filling his throat. His heart clenched, and something in his soul twisted in anguish.

"Sire!" John lunged for him. "What's happening?"

But then a rush of hot, sulfuric-stinking wind raced across the camp.

Trees bowed in horrified supplication, while tents shuddered violently and coughed out scores of soldiers. Shouts rang out in every direction.

"Are we being attacked?"

"Is it Ivasland?"

"Has Embria betrayed us?"

Alarm bells pealed through the night, but it was too late. The stench of malice was thick in the air, and Rune knew what had happened: it wasn't a messenger from Brink, but an Ivasland saboteur.

And he'd brought a mal-device.

Rune straightened, wrenching away from John. "Run!" he yelled at all the men around him. "Run as fast as you can!"

"Get the king to safety!" Tide shouted. "Carry him over your shoulder if you must!"

"Sire, let's go!" John grabbed Rune's arm and dragged him into the center of all his guards. "Now, sire!"

Rune's heart was thunder as the guards formed a wedge around him, and he lost sight of everything except sweat-soaked uniforms and flashes of firelight between the men's bodies. Quickly, they pushed away—to where, Rune couldn't see. All around him, horses whinnied, hounds bayed, and people screamed as they headed away from the expanding field of malice. The stench of it was overwhelming.

"To the king!" someone shouted beyond Rune's line of sight.

"Capture the Ivaslander!"

If anyone was following any sort of orders, Rune couldn't tell. His guards kept a tight formation, half carrying him through the growing chaos. He strained to look around, to see what foul effects the malice was causing, but there was no sign of the air changing to poison, or gravity readjusting.

Whatever it was, though, the army of Caberwill was no match. Only the Nightrender could save them from this horror, and she was out of reach.

Rune fought a surge of anger. This wasn't her fault. It was Abagail and Baldric who'd done this. They'd struck a powerful blow against the Caberwill-Embria alliance. They hadn't even needed to send their army. Just the burning machine.

It always came back to that machine.

As Rune blindly moved along with his guards, he had a flash of what it must have been like in Small Mountain or the mine in Silver Sun. The fear. The panic. The rage for everyone who'd caused this.

Hanne. By her own admission, she'd given Ivasland everything they'd needed to finish the device early.

And now it was fracturing his army.

"Up, sire!" one of the guards shouted over the roar of malice and people fleeing. A quivering horse was pulled into their ranks and Rune mounted, stepping into cupped hands, as the saddle and stirrups had been removed only half an hour ago.

"Get clear of the malice and regroup by that ridge." John climbed astride behind Rune. "And if anyone sees the grand general, by the Known and Unknown, protect him!"

Several of Rune's new guards yelled their agreement, and then John kicked the horse. They shot away, riding as fast as they dared go in the uncertain, dust-diffused glow of campfires and moonlight. Everything was ghostly and gray, but from this height Rune finally had a chance to see what the malice was doing to his army.

Great globes of it—each the size of a cart—rolled across the campsite, leaving trails of oil-slick, shimmering residue behind. Just the sight was revolting, enough to turn the stomach. But inside, beyond the rainbow sheen of malice, Rune saw other places. Farms, with people working the fields. A dressmaker's shop, with a seamstress taking measurements. And a craggy mountaintop, with no one present at all.

Everywhere Rune looked, there were different scenes hidden inside the malice spheres. They rolled through the campsite like heavy bubbles, hard to see in the flickering light.

Just then, a person hit one. A soldier. A new recruit, by his insignia. And when he touched the malice sphere, which held the image of a snowy forest, he vanished.

Rune sucked in a breath.

"Burn everything," John muttered behind Rune. "What is it doing to them? Is it trapping them? Miniature malsites?"

"I think—" Rune swallowed the taste of acid in the back of his throat. "I think I see him in there." Indeed, inside the sphere, Rune could just make out a shivering figure, the deep brown of his uniform already coated with snow. It wouldn't be long before he died of exposure.

The horse continued to surge forward, dodging now-uncontrolled campfires, which reached toward them with orange and scarlet fingers. They skittered around other spheres, which showed all manner of places. A bakery. A cellar. A canyon stretching far below.

"Can you see the ridge?" John cried.

Rune blinked dust and smoke from his eyes, but the ridge where he and the other guards were to meet was nowhere in sight. He could see only people fleeing the malice spheres, bolting away from the flames that seemed to grow hands and stretch after them.

"I don't! The smoke—" Rune coughed. He cleared grit from his eyes again.

And then he saw it:

A sphere containing a ruddy-cast room, a sea of rancor, and a familiar winged girl.

Nightrender.

His heart pounded as he took in her state. She was standing atop an enormous throne, swinging her sword with all her might. Her left wing was broken. Her face was a mask of blood. Her armor was shredded, soaked with viscous gore and sweat. A writhing mass of rancor pressed around her, climbing over one another to get at her. She was fighting so hard, but how could she defend against all this?

She couldn't.

They would kill her.

"No." The plea slipped from him before he realized. "No!" He reached for the Nightrender's sphere, as though he could pull her out. The horse, feeling the shift of Rune's weight, turned with him, stumbling through the muck and dirt.

"What are you doing?" John shouted in Rune's ear. "What—" Then he seemed to see what Rune was looking at—*who* Rune was looking at. "She's not real! It's an illusion. We have to go!"

A fist closed around Rune's heart as he stared into the sphere.

It was real. He knew it like he knew air, like he knew the sun and moon, and it didn't matter that he wasn't her soul shard because he'd *felt* something just then, something that had come from the connection they shared.

She'd gone through the Soul Gate—alone—even though they'd both known she was in no state. The last thing she'd said to him was that they wouldn't see each other again.

But there she was, just through that globule of malice. She twisted and cleaved a wide arc at the beasts around her, but her body shook with the effort. Ulsisi—the Numen of Pain and Sorrow—but she was *so* injured. And she'd said—she'd said that fighting hurt her. Using her numinous powers *hurt*.

"She needs help!" Rune started to struggle, ready to dismount and run to her.

John held him fast. "She's not real!"

"She is, John. I know she is."

"I'm sorry, sire. I can't let you—"

"You don't have to let me." Rune threw himself off the horse and rolled as he hit the ground. And then he ran.

"To me!" he called, just in case anyone could hear him over the din. "Follow me!"

Hoofbeats sounded behind him. John—perhaps others—were in pursuit. "To the king!" John yelled.

With all his strength, Rune ran toward the malice sphere and splashed into it. Cold blackness enveloped him, the bottom of a frozen lake, but he had to believe. Malice bent the laws of reality, making the impossible real. If it could speed time or reverse gravity, then surely it could take him to the Nightrender's side right now.

He'd forsaken his oath before, but the truth was this: Rune Highcrown was the Nightrender's Dawnbreaker. He would do anything to save her.

44.
HANNE

"Do you understand your orders?" Hanne gazed down the table at her ladies, meeting their eyes one at a time. She'd called them here to Nadine's suite for a late dinner, and as soon as their plates and silverware were set aside, she'd told them what she needed—what *Tuluna* needed.

Because it was what Salvation needed.

"Yes, Your Majesty," they all said.

Lady Sabine sipped her wine, then said, "I will have Captain Oliver select his fastest riders, his most discreet soldiers. But it will take some time to get to Athelney and back, particularly if the fighting reaches the capital."

"The materials should be easy enough to procure," Cecelia said. "Between both Embria and Caberwill, we have access to all the mines and smithies we'll require. I'll put in the orders first thing in the morning."

"The titanium will be the most difficult to obtain," Maris said, "but I have someone in mind."

"And the guard towers?" Hanne leaned forward. "We need access to all twenty-four of them. There is no plan without the towers."

"I believe we can manage," Lea said. "Those in Ivasland may be difficult, but they will be distracted by the Embrian and Caberwilline armies flanking them. They will be in no position to wonder what a few men are doing at the towers—if they even see them. Only the best will be chosen for this mission."

"Good." Hanne turned to Nadine. "You've been quiet. What are you thinking?"

Nadine glanced at the obsidian crown, which earlier had been scrubbed clean of rancor blood and gore. Now it sat on a pedestal, the broken tine in the center. "I admit," Nadine said slowly, "I have some concerns."

Permit no dispute.

"What concerns?" Hanne wished Nadine had brought this up earlier, in private rather than in front of the other ladies-in-waiting and Sabine. They knew, of course, that none of them would ever replace Nadine as Hanne's favorite, but it wasn't like Nadine to offer them ammunition. She must have been thinking on this for a while.

"I can't help but wonder how this will affect the Malstop," Nadine said. "It's already so thin. Surely this will put the entire structure at risk."

Do not allow her doubts to infect the others.

Hanne's heart pounded. She needed Nadine to believe in her—to believe in this plan. It had surprised her, too, when Tuluna had first given her their instructions, but then she'd begun to see how it could succeed. It was painful, but necessary.

"The entire structure of the Malstop is already at risk." Hanne forced patience into her tone. "The pressure is building from inside. It needs to be let out. But it needs to happen in a controlled, intentional way, so we will choose when it happens. We will be prepared to protect Salvation."

"The army of Caberwill is commanded by King Rune," Sabine said, "and Her Majesty commands the king. He will take Ivasland for her, and with that, he will take their army, their weapons, and their machines. Soon, the armies of all three kingdoms will be Hanne's to direct."

"It will be like lancing a wound," Hanne said. "Though it will hurt, it will speed the healing process."

"At Opus's funeral, you said you would fix the Malstop. This is your plan?" Doubt still shone in Nadine's eyes.

"None of us want to do this," Hanne said. "But Salvation must be saved."

"I know," Nadine said. "And you have never led us astray before. You have my support."

Hanne's shoulders relaxed, now that Nadine was with her. "This will work," Hanne said. She trusted Tuluna in the same way Nadine trusted her. "It will fix the Malstop."

Frantic knocking sounded on the door, and Nadine hurried up to answer it.

A messenger stepped inside, breathing heavily. "Your Majesty! There's been an attack!"

"Another? Where?" Hanne rose. "Speak! Is it another assassin?"

The young man edged backward in proper fearful reverence. "A mal-device detonated in the king's camp."

A shiver worked through Hanne. "What did it do?"

"We have only one report so far, but apparently it made"—he frowned—"portals. Hundreds of soldiers have been transported to different locations. One even appeared in Honor's Keep. In the kitchens. That's how we know about this calamity."

Rage filled Hanne's stomach. Abagail Athelney continued to torment her. "Then the army is gone? Transported to the moon, for all we know?"

"We aren't certain, Your Majesty. It will take some time to regroup."

Hanne's mind whirled with the new information—the threats and the possibilities. Just on the other side of the mountain, there were dozens of portals that led all over Salvation. It was dangerous . . . but, perhaps, it could be made into an opportunity. Obviously *some* of these portals were stable. The man in the kitchens had come to no harm.

"First," Hanne said, "post men in the kitchens. The last thing we need right now is an Ivaslander making war on our dinner. And I want a complete list of where the other portals lead. Any one of them could be strategically useful."

"There's more, Your Majesty." The messenger hesitated. "The man said King Rune—"

"What about King Rune?"

"He was caught in one of the portals. No one knows where he is." Then, the messenger backed out the door as fast as he could without actually running.

Hanne exchanged a dark look with Nadine. Her position here was not secure; as far as she knew, she was not pregnant. She needed Rune still. If he died without giving her a child, she could lose everything.

"Where could he be?"

45.
NIGHTRENDER

Light erupted, slicing open the red gloom of Daghath Mal's castle.

Rancor peeled away from the sliver of white illumination, and Nightrender stole the opportunity to attack. Every arc of her obsidian blade sent frost stabbing through her head. Every burst of numinous power made agony blacken her vision. But she couldn't stop. She had been created for this, and she would do it until she was no longer able.

You are losing this fight.

Of that, she was very aware.

Yet every rancor she killed bought humanity another hour, another day.

What is the point? They will use that time to keep hurting one another, and I will keep rattling the bars of this cage. What will you do when I am free?

Nightrender could not think beyond this moment, lest the weight crush her.

But now that shard of bright light was a beacon, drawing her eyes. From her vantage point atop the thrones, she could see straight into the breach. It was a window to somewhere far away, where flames licked the nighttime sky and panicked soldiers ran and shouted. But that wasn't what kept her attention. No. It was the figure running toward the window—running *through*.

Rune Highcrown.

He burst into the throne room with a shout and a swift swing of his sword. A rancor fell, and he immediately moved onto the next.

She'd seen him fight before, just briefly at the malsite, and even then it had been clear that he was skilled. But that had been nothing like this. Something had changed in him. Now he fought with a dancer's grace, confident from years of practice, every line of his body an artist's stroke as he cut and blocked and stabbed and turned.

It seemed impossible that he had crossed the continent in a single stride, and yet, here he was. Fighting for her.

But his presence meant he could die.

"Rune!" Her voice was lost under the clangor of violence, the screeches and grunts of rancor, the scraping of talons on the bone floor.

Though he could not have heard her, he looked up. His eyes met hers.

Then: a word she'd thought was lost forever.

A name. *Her* name.

She didn't hear it—not out loud—but saw it form on his lips.

"Medella." The shock of it made him gasp, as though her name were lightning he'd caught in his hands.

He remembered.

He remembered her name.

Her soul shard knew her at last.

The connection between them locked into place—like a gold thread that spun from her heart to his, a light, a strength.

He said her name again, this time with a disbelieving little laugh, and—

Freedom.

The dark tether that had bound her to Daghath Mal frayed and snapped apart. In her mind, in the place where he used to whisper, there was only quiet. A haze lifted from her eyes, and a hum vanished from her ears. She hadn't even realized they had been there, but now that this terrible magic had broken away, she felt clean for the first time in four hundred years.

Nightrender swung Beloved, beheading a rancor in a single stroke.

And there was no pain.

None at all.

Euphoria surged through her. Fire strengthened her muscles and sharpened her wings. Every cut, every hit—Nightrender's might swelled within her as she fought, cleaving through rancor that were only now learning what it meant to battle the Sword of the Numina, the Hero Eternal.

Rune pushed forward, moving away from the portal just in time for another man to arrive, this one on horseback. It was John, his guard. Two, three, ten more soldiers surged through the portal, weapons swinging. Rancor screamed under the sudden onslaught. These men were but mortals, but in the Malice, with this many rancor pressed so close together, every swing of the blade struck home.

Numinous light flashed. Rancor blood misted in the air, sizzling where it hit skin and armor. Her burns faded within moments; she hardly felt them beneath the fire of her own righteous fury; on the men, though, they smoked.

Rancor bodies piled up around her. Power sang through her sword, her true strength finally unleashed. She cut and she stabbed, lashing out with her good wing, feathers slicing into rancor flesh. But now the bulk of the rancor were pressing toward Rune and his guards, the easier targets.

If only she could fly, she would race through the room and defend him and the others. But her left wing still hung at a wretched angle, refusing to move.

She must take the slower, deadlier way.

Nightrender leaped off the thrones and pressed forward, her sword flashing. It felt so *good* to fight, to destroy evil. She had almost grown used to the pain, but now that she was free she understood how much it had held her back.

Waves of holy fire raced across the room at her command, burning through her enemies. There were rancor—and then there weren't.

"What has happened?" Daghath Mal's voice came from everywhere at once. "What did you do?"

Nightrender smiled grimly as she thrust her sword into the back of a rancor's skull. She was free of him, free of his whispers and influence.

Rune was near now. Nightrender could feel him, a magnetic pull on her very soul. His men formed a ring around him, but already two were dead, with another clutching a wound in his side. A quick glance at the breach told her no others were coming through, so this was all the help she was going to get.

She needed them alive; she needed them to pull Rune back through the breach and to the dubious safety of Salvation. Then, she would finish here. For the first time, victory seemed possible.

She might succeed.

The rhythm of battle wore on, as familiar as the sun rising and falling. She killed, and she did so quickly, efficiently, blood making the floor slick and sticky. Her good wing flared, cutting rancor to ribbons; Beloved flashed, severing skin and muscle and bone. Her armor stitched itself together, quickly now, as it drew upon her power.

Ahead, however, Rune and his men were flagging. Three more had died.

They were outnumbered. No matter how valiantly they fought, she would not be able to reach them in time. For every rancor that fell, another pressed into its place.

She needed to change tactics.

"Enough!" Nightrender called. "Daghath Mal, I would speak with you!"

At first, nothing happened. Rancor battled on, and another guard fell—unable to withstand the claws and teeth. But then the horde withdrew, hunching low as they glared hungrily at her, Rune, and John—the lone survivors.

Great alabaster wings beat the air as Daghath Mal landed directly before Nightrender.

She glared up at him. "You may surrender now."

Daghath Mal chuckled, fanning his wings. "Ah, you thought because your power is restored that you might win."

Nightrender glanced at Rune. His eyes were narrowed, hard. Black blood dripped off his sword—what was left of it. Acid had already eaten away the sharp edge. John, too, was hampered by his blood-burned weapons.

Neither could endure more.

"But there is no winning," Daghath Mal said. "Not for you."

"Every moment I prevent your release is a victory to me." Nightrender flicked a glob of blood off her sword. "You may believe superior numbers are all that matter, but know this: I will kill every rancor in the Malice; I will tear down this castle bone by bone; and I will drag your maimed and bleeding body to the Rupture, where I will hurl you back into the Dark Shard. It may take me days. Weeks, even. Years. But I will overcome you."

"Your soul shard would die."

"No. He and his guard will return to Salvation through the breach."

Daghath Mal made a thoughtful noise deep in his throat, then motioned at a rancor. It threw itself at the portal—and bounced back.

"It's one way," the rancor king said, coldly amused. "None of us shall escape through it."

Not even Rune. The thought speared Nightrender, but she had to be strong. Resolute. "If my soul shard is to perish, he will be reincarnated."

"But you are losing memories," Daghath Mal growled softly. "What if you don't remember what a soul shard is next time?"

Nightrender flexed her fingers around Beloved's hilt, readjusting her grip. "Regardless, I must destroy you."

Daghath Mal considered her, his thoughts unreadable on his monstrous face. "Then we are at an impasse. Should we give in to our instincts, we will both lose what matters to us. You, the boy. Me, my kingdom. However, perhaps we can come to an agreement."

Rune stepped forward. "I would die before making an agreement with you. Nightrender knows this." His heart was pounding; she could hear it even over the low whining of the rancor, the scraping of their claws, the hissing of their sweat as it hit the floor. But it was brave of him. He had always been brave.

"You are her soul shard," Daghath Mal said. "Even if she could sacrifice you for her own victory, do you know what your death would do to her?" The rancor king tilted his head. "You have suffered the loss of many loved ones, have you not? For example, your mother—"

"My mother is alive." But Rune's voice trembled.

"Is she?" Daghath Mal gave a low chuckle. "This morning, there was a rancor attack within the walls of Honor's Keep. It butchered the grieving dowager queen. It was so unexpected. No one could have stopped it."

Rune glanced at Nightrender. She didn't know what had become of Queen Grace—but she knew that Daghath Mal, slippery though he was, rarely lied.

Rune's expression fell. A strangled sob choked out of him.

"The way you hurt now," Daghath Mal said quietly, "is but a fraction of how Nightrender would feel if you died. I know how she thinks, how she feels. I've had hundreds of years to study her mind and memories—all of them—and I have seen the devastation wrought by the death of a single soul shard."

Nightrender's fist curled. "My grief is no greater than anyone else's, and it is not a weapon."

"Imagine," Daghath Mal murmured to Rune, "the pain your death would cause her. I am imagining it."

Daghath Mal flickered. Before Nightrender could move, Rune's sword was gone from his hands. Daghath Mal pulled it from him, flung it, and neatly beheaded John; he was dead before he hit the ground.

"No!" Rune bellowed, but Daghath Mal materialized behind him, one clawed, yellowed hand around Rune's throat.

Nightrender went absolutely still.

"How should we do this?" The rancor king's whisper echoed throughout the space. "Slowly? Quickly?" The tip of a claw dragged across Rune's skin.

"Don't." The word slipped out before she could stop it. She swallowed the sour taste of fear. "Please don't."

A dreadful grin spread across Daghath Mal's face. "Then hear my offer."

Silence smothered the chamber, leaving only the sound of Rune's ragged breathing.

"Tell me," Nightrender said at last.

"No," Rune protested. "Whatever he offers, don't take it."

A long rumble pushed through the onlooking rancor. Hundreds remained, watching from over the corpses of their fallen brethren. They writhed against one another; one pressed too close to her, and she shifted her good wing and sliced open the beast with a snap of feathers.

Daghath Mal's gaze tracked the newly bisected rancor as it dropped in pieces to the ground. He looked annoyed. "I want Rune," he began. "I won't kill him. I simply . . . want him here. In the Malice. You may have him back when I leave this place."

"That is preposterous." Her feathers bristled.

"In return," Daghath Mal said, "you will leave the Malice without killing another rancor."

Rune would stay and she would go.

No, that was unacceptable. She could not possibly leave her soul shard here, unprotected but for Daghath Mal's word. Anything might happen to him.

"You seem reluctant. Allow me to explain how hostage-taking works: neither of us would kill the things we wish to kill." Daghath Mal smiled at her, both rows of teeth showing.

"I *know* how it works," Nightrender said. "I do *not* know why you would propose this—or why you would abide by any rules."

"It's simple. For eons, I made glorious battle in the Dark Shard. I fought my way to the Rupture and claimed it as my kingdom. Yet Salvation eluded me. My fury grew every time my forces were thwarted—by you. You, Nightrender. You slaughtered my armies, always *just* preventing my godhood. But no matter, because I will wrench the Rupture wider. I have allies on the laic plane now. And I still have something of an army. Sadly, significantly less than I did an hour ago. But enough."

"You assume that I would give you a chance to rebuild your forces in exchange for Rune's life." Nightrender shook her head. "Perhaps you do not know me as well as you believe."

Daghath Mal pressed that hooked claw into Rune's throat. The skin dimpled, then broke. Blood trickled. Rune's expression twisted with shock, then pain.

"I know you will," Daghath Mal said. "You cannot stand to see him hurt. You could allow anyone else to die—but not your soul shard."

It was so hard to take her eyes off Rune—the fear on his face, the blood pooling in the hollow of his throat—but Nightrender forced herself to focus on the rancor king.

"Agree to this ceasefire. Should I kill Rune Highcrown, you would know." Daghath Mal's tone remained polite, conversational. "And then, I would fully expect you to return and annihilate my entire army."

"Should *you* kill him," Nightrender said. "You've said nothing of your followers."

Daghath Mal grinned. "Very well. Should I, or any other rancor kill—"

"Or injure."

"*Permanently maim* Rune Highcrown, shall we compromise, the agreement would be void." The rancor king's claws pressed against Rune's throat. "Do you agree?"

"I will speak to Rune first," Nightrender said. "As the decision significantly involves him."

Daghath Mal shoved Rune forward.

Rune staggered toward her. She caught him, turning him away from his dead guards, and opened her good wing to provide an illusion of privacy. "Tell me how badly you're hurt," she said.

"I'm fine."

"You are not."

"Yes," he insisted. "I am."

She didn't argue. Humans had a long tradition of telling one another they were fine when they were clearly not, and that tradition seemed to bring them a significant amount of comfort.

Rune exhaled, his gaze falling to the bodies scattered on the floor. "All these men followed me here. John followed me, even though he knew what would happen. They died for this. For me."

"They died so you could live."

"And will I?" Rune asked. "Will you take his armistice?"

"You would be his hostage." Nightrender swallowed hard. "But you would be alive."

Rune touched his heart, perhaps gauging his own grief and weighing it against hers. "I think you should finish this. He is weakened."

"But not weak enough." Nightrender searched his face. "If we take his offer, he would gain time, yes. But we would, too. And we need that time—we need an army. We need Dawnbreakers. And I—I need you alive."

Emotion flashed through Rune's eyes. "Will I remain here forever?"

"No. The next battle in this war will come. He will press against the Malstop harder than ever. Then I will be forced to return, to fight, and you will be released."

"Or killed."

Nightrender stepped close to Rune—so close that humans would call it intimate—and slipped a feather into his hand. It was ragged, bloodied, and razor sharp. "You are my soul shard. I would see you free."

"Your soul shard," he whispered, the feather vanishing into his armor.

"When you didn't know before . . . I thought I was sparing your feelings."

"I felt it. I always felt it, even before you awakened." He gazed at her, his expression torn between wonder and grief and terror. "All right. If you think this is the best course, I will remain. I will believe that you can find a way to stop him."

"Very well." She touched his face, gently committing the lines and curves and texture of his skin to her memory—what was left of her memory, anyway. "Be warned: malice is a force of corruption. The longer you stay here, the more it will seep into you—change you. You must fight it. You must be strong. Every moment is a battle you must win."

Rune gave a sharp, indrawn breath. "How long before it overtakes me?"

"You will last until the instant you stop fighting. Remember, some battles are fought solely for the sake of resisting."

That was the thing about darkness: it never wavered, it never tired, and it never stopped pressing itself against the light.

"I won't forget." Rune closed his eyes and breathed. He was terrified. She could hear the *thrum* of his racing heartbeat, the rasp of his shallow breaths, but he was being courageous. For her. To protect her. To protect Salvation.

They were still standing so close together, with her fingertips resting on his jaw. And when he met her eyes once more, his emotions pulsed through the golden thread that spun between them—fear and sorrow and longing. Her own heart beat with the same surge of feeling.

A breath later, his lips were touching hers. First with a question. Then with a faint, conflicted sigh.

Nightrender shivered and echoed his movements.

Their kiss was slow, cautious, questing. It was a contradiction of sensations. It made her feel like something long-caged was finally being released—and like pieces of her were squeezing too tightly with want. Though she had seen humans kiss a thousand times before, she had never understood the appeal. But now that it was happening to her, she was beginning to grasp the power.

It was more than the warmth of his mouth against hers, the motion of his jaw under her fingers, or the nearness of their bodies—nothing but breath between them. It was an acknowledgment of emotion and attraction. It was a promise.

And it was a goodbye.

Rune stepped back, watching her face while his own twisted with guilt.

Nightrender's hand fell to her side. They had both forgotten, it seemed, that he had already made a promise to someone else.

"Thank you," she whispered, "for this memory." She would carry it with her, a bright star in her darkening sky. One day, it would burn out, too, but until then, she would treasure it.

Rune nodded stiffly. "You should go. Find Hanne and get her help. She is on our side."

Nightrender simply nodded and lowered her good wing, finding the rancor had already moved away, making a path.

Daghath Mal had known what they would decide.

She shot Rune another look.

"Go," he said. "I trust you."

And so she went.

She left the throne room, the castle.

She made her way toward the towers of Known and Unknown, every step feeling like betrayal. How could she leave him to the torments of the Malice? But there was no other way to protect him, none that she could see.

How quickly her victory had become surrender.

As she walked, pains from all her injuries set in: the broken bones in her left wing, her still-bleeding wounds. Her eyes started to flutter closed. Her toes dragged, but step after step, she forced herself on.

When sections of the Soul Gate rumbled open, when the Malstop buzzed and split around her, Nightrender staggered through.

Outside the Malice, she dropped to the ground and lifted her face to the clear sky, the spiral of stars far away, and the dawn, which glowed just below the mountains, limning them in molten gold.

"You're back," said Known.

"What has happened?" asked Unknown.

Nightrender's eyes ached with tears. "The Malstop is under attack, my soul shard is in peril, and a rancor king has come to Salvation. I have borrowed time with Rune's life, but I do not know what to do."

The maintainers looked at each other, and then Known rested their palms on the crown of Nightrender's head, while Unknown placed their hands over Nightrender's heart.

"Close your eyes."

When she did, numinous light blazed brighter than dawn, enveloping them all.

And where a swath of dark nothingness had fallen across her memory, a new star flared to life.

Acknowledgments

Publishing a book is a team effort. Many thanks to:

My agent Lauren MacLeod, one of my favorite people in the whole universe, who championed Nightrender, Hanne, and Rune from the start.

My editor Mora Couch, who understood and shared my vision for this book. I'll be forever grateful for the time, care, and attention given to making *Nightrender* the best book it could be.

The incredible team at Holiday House, including Sara DiSalvo, Aleah Gornbein, Terry Borzumato-Greenberg, Miriam Miller, Erin Mathis, Kerry Martin, Amy Toth, Chris Russo, Nicole Gureli, Lisa Lee, Judy Varon, and Della Farrell. I could not be more thankful for such a dedicated team.

The amazing cover artist, Yonson. I mean, wow.

Additionally, I'm so grateful to have amazing friends and colleagues who supported me throughout the writing and production of this book, including Martina Boone, who immediately saw the potential in my fragment of an idea and dropped everything to talk about it late into the night.

Eternal appreciation to Cynthia Hand, Valerie Cole, Erin Bowman, and C.J. Redwine, who were there for this book every step of the way, with brainstorming sessions, feedback, and emotional support.

Thanks to Leah Cypess, Kat Zhang, Francina Simone, Fran Wilde, Erin Summerill, Alexa Yupangco, Cade Roach, Adrienne Bowling, Elisabeth Jewell, Kelly McWilliams, Aminah Mae Safi, and Wren Hardwick for encouragement and/or reading, and generally being awesome humans across the board.

Extra special thanks to Pintip Dunn, Kathleen Peacock, Brigid Kemmerer, Erin Bowman, Mary Hinton, Kathryn Purdie, Tricia Levenseller, Lisa Maxwell, Nicki Pau Preto, Kendare Blake, and Lelia Nebeker for their kind words about this book, some before it was even finished.

My ears would like to thank Caitlin and Sidney Powell of Neoni, whose music I listened to a *lot* while working on this book.

I'm so grateful for the camaraderie of the Zoo Slack group and the #FantasyOnFriday girl gang.

Love to my supportive family.

Where would any author be without librarians, booksellers, and educators? Thank you all. And super special thanks to my bookseller friends at One More Page Books in Arlington, VA.

And, as always, thank *you*, the person reading this book.